IF A DRAGON CRIES

THE LEGEND OF HOOPER'S DRAGONS - BOOK ONE

GARY DARBY

GARY DARBY'S BOOKS

1

In the churning fires of Hades where boiling pits shine as if some monstrous demon stared out with scarlet eyes, there are but evil devils and wicked dragons that inhabit that noisome world.

The roaring flames spew out wispy clouds of stench that swirl and curl, but there is one foul smell that overcomes all — the putrid reek of dragons.

Devils and demons are cruel beyond what the mind can imagine, but even they cannot match the callous malice of dragons. Long ago did Hades's demons rip out their hearts and fling them into the scalding cauldrons, but dragons — dragons are born without a heart.

Instead of a warm, beating heart, dragons have a jagged piece of ice that leaves them cold and empty, without feeling, without a soul. Their place is to murder, to destroy, and leave all behind in ruin. Families left with no homes, crops burned to cinders, wives left without husbands, husbands having to bury wives, children forced to place their beloved father, mother into the cold, dark soil.

A child left behind without even that.

I hate dragons.

I always have.

I always will.

As the greatest dragon slayer in the whole Northern Kingdom, I yearn for my next dragon kill. I delight in watching the green life-fluid flow from their torn bodies to soak the ground and most of all, I thrill in hearing their death rattle as they take their last breath and watch their eyes glaze over in death's final slumber.

Usually, I exterminate them one at a time, but now I've been ambushed by four of the loathsome creatures. I could try and escape their death snare, but my hatred pushes me forward, no matter the enormous challenge I face.

If these fiery, skulking beasts, with their cat's eyes fixed on me with ravenous stares and their scales gleaming in the morning light wish to challenge Hooper, the mightiest drachen slayer of all time — then so be it.

The four slink and slither to each side, no doubt getting set to unleash their dreaded dragon fire. Two sapphires, or blues as they're sometimes called, with their scales and eyes mirroring the clear sky hunker down in the swaying grass as if readying to either pounce or take to the air.

Some say that sapphires are swifter than even the wind. If they do sky, I admit, fighting two on the ground and two in the air will challenge my skills to their very limit.

A violet drake, or purple, as it's more commonly called, lowers its four-horned head and slinks off to my left. Its talons, as sharp as any fine blade, dig deep into the knee-high saw grass. Its gambit is obvious, trying to get behind me where it can bring its powerful tail into play and impale me with its two long, sharp tail spikes. The color of royalty, it is devious and sly, and I'll have to keep a particularly sharp eye on him.

I counter with nimble and quick feet, keeping the purple beast to my front. His growl is low, rumbling deep in his throat. His violet-colored eyes, twice the size of a golden ducat, flick back and forth, seeking another route to gain an advantage. He paws at the ground, his talons ripping up great chunks of dirt and grass.

I smile in self-satisfaction. The violet is frustrated. That's good. A frustrated dragon is a confused dragon and therefore easier to slay.

Then there's the scarlet or red dragon. The most powerful of all dragons and the one that I really have to watch. Reds are the warriors of the dragon realm. Crimson scales harder than iron, fangs sharp enough to split a tree trunk in half with one bite, tail spines that can gut a man wide open in one swipe, and dragon fire so hot that with one burst a whole forest goes up in flames.

Slaying a red dragon by yourself is oft the stuff of legends but to kill a red, two sapphires, and a violet all on your own makes you the legend.

The red narrows its evil eyes and bares its fangs, a sure sign that it hungers for my flesh. I swing my finely-honed sword from side to side, keeping it and my dragon scale shield between me and the brute. The other three hiss and weave their heads from left to right, getting ready to pounce. I have to watch their every move, for dragons, as everyone knows, are not only merciless and evil but scheming and cunning as well.

Four against one. Heavy odds, but I've never backed down from a fight, nor have I ever lost. I again heft my gleaming and superbly crafted sword, swing my shield around to face the ferocious beasts and advance on the craven creatures.

Suddenly, I realize that the beasts have lured me into a trap. I'm hemmed in on all sides. A cliff at my back, dragons to my front. Surely, this will be a fight to the death — theirs or mine.

I set my face in a hard, determined look, knowing the battle will be fierce and long, but I will not give up nor give in until these four despised beasts lie at my feet, either dead or groveling in submission for me to spare their cowardly lives.

Only, their pleas for mercy will fall on deaf ears. For me, the only good dragon is a dead dragon; preferably with my sword or lance delivering the death stroke.

I settle my helmet on my head, draw back my sword, its sharp point glistening in the sunlight, and prepare to charge. I —

"Hooper!"

I cringe and duck my head at the sharp yell. My sudden movement causes the wooden bucket on my head to abruptly fall to the ground with a clunk. I lower my manure rake and shovel to slowly turn to find three faces staring at me.

Standing in the paddock's open gateway is none other than Dragon Master Boren Dracon. His face is hard, his eyes like ice. In fact, if his face were a block of ice, his scowl would be such that it would cause his face to crack in a dozen places. No, make that two dozen places.

Next to him, is Malo, the Barn Master. If Master Boren's face is icy cold, then Malo's expression resembles the coals in a searing hot fire. His face is as red as any crimson dragon, and I can't help but see that he twitches his skillfully sharpened Proga lance against his leg, a clear sign of what may be my fate later on after Master Boren has left.

Standing nearby is Helmar Stoudtman, novice to Master Boren. His expression is a mixture of amusement and resignation. A look I know all too well.

"Hooper," Malo growls, "just what are you doing?"

I bite down on my lip and glance at the four sprogs, or baby dragons, that sit at my feet. They've plopped down on their hindquarters, wiggling their tails in the dirt and staring up at me expectantly.

Their pollywog faces hold a silly grin, their tongues hang out at one side, and they dance around on their tiny front talons as if eager to continue their part in my charade. From the lively gleam in their eyes, I can tell that they found my little game most entertaining.

"Uh," I stammer and motion to the four, "I was just getting the sprogs used to us dragon workers." I duck my head toward Master Boren, "As the Dragon Master ordered."

Without a word but with his stare even icier, Master Boren adjusts his woolen tunic. Clearly visible on the front, encircled by dark scarlet and azure colors are the images of a crimson and sapphire dragon with riders holding aloft sword and bow, the insignia of the House of Lorell.

I, of course, bear no seal on my plain tunic as befitting my rank within my adopted House. In an icy tone, Master Boren says to Malo,

"You come with me while I check on the golden." He gestures to Helmar while saying, "Take care of this mess here and then check on Wind Rush, make sure she's ready for auction."

Taking Malo with him, Master Boren strides away to the barn to inspect the pride of Lord Lorell's dragon herd, Golden Wind, the only Golden Dragon in the whole world, or so it's believed.

With a sigh loud enough to be mistaken for a dragon's growl, Helmar steps inside the paddock. It's then that I notice that he's carrying his longbow and arrow quiver over his shoulder, which usually means only one thing, a stag hunt with Cara Dracon, the beautiful and only daughter of Master Boren.

He sets his bow and quiver to one side and kneels to scratch under the chins of the four sprogs who practically fall all over each other trying to get his attention. Hoping to divert his attention away from my earlier antics, I say, "Going to hunt for venison later, Master Novice? Perhaps with Mistress Cara?"

"If I can get done with my work soon enough," he mutters, "and don't have to stop and answer fool questions."

I lower my eyes and take a step back. He doesn't say it, but Helmar's meaning is entirely clear. Stay out of my way, Hooper, I've no time for the likes of you or your shenanigans. As he reaches down to the sprogs, I can't help but feel the tiniest twinge of envy. What would it be like to go hunting and be alone, even for an hour, with the lovely and winsome Cara Dracon?

For me, nothing short of paradise.

Helmar scratches the four dragon sprogs under their chins. His fingernails scrape tough skin that will soon start to harden into scales and cover their entire bodies except for under and over their wings and a small spot on the very top of their skulls.

The Death Mark, some call it.

Many people believe that dragon scales make the beasts impervious to arrows, lances, swords and the like. But that's not true. Even without hitting the Death Mark, a well-placed metal-sheathed arrow to a dragon's eye, or under the wings, or if you're really good or lucky, between the scale plates of a very young dragon will kill the beast. The same with sword or lance.

Difficult to do, yes, but thank goodness, not impossible.

The four sprogs snuggle close to Helmar and lift their muzzles higher, each jostling for position to get his attention. "And how are Wind Glow, Wind Strider, Wind Sparkle, and Regal Wind doing?" he asks.

Not letting Helmar see, I frown and shake my head at the names that Master Boren bestowed on each of the new babies.

The crimson, or red dragon, is Wind Glow. One sapphire Master Boren called Wind Strider because she's already fast on her feet, a promising sign that she'll be very swift in the air. The other sapphire is Wind Sparkle because she has a greenish-blue line down her back that glitters in the sunlight, and the purple he called Regal Wind.

Me, I have other names for them; He Who Walks in Poo, She Who Squats in Poo, She Who Runs in Poo, and He Who Wiggles in Poo. I think my titles are much more suited to their temperament and current activities than the Dragon Master's names, though I wouldn't dare say that out loud, of course.

"They're fine," I dully answer. "They eat — they sleep — they poop, and then they do the same thing. Over and over."

Helmar grunts in answer. "You can't expect them to do much else, they're just wee ones, you know."

Just then, there is a rush of dragon wings and over the birthing barn's steep roof flashes a sapphire dragon followed by a crimson. They make a sharp arc in the air and begin to settle to the ground just beyond the paddocks. In the sapphire's neck saddle sits a rider whose jerkin bears the symbol of a castle with crossed lances, while the crimson's rider is outfitted in the gleaming light armor of the king's Dragon Knight Legion.

Helmar stands, takes one look, and orders, "Go find Master Boren, now! He's in the barn checking on the golden. Tell him there's a king's courier along with a Dragon Knight in the paddock field."

I suppose I hesitated too long at the sight of the two for Helmar roughly pushes me and snaps, "Move!"

I stumble away and at my best hobbling gait go through the birthing barn's side door. Once inside, I quickly trundle down the broad way that splits the barn down the middle until I reach the last giant stall. Inside, Master Boren and Malo stand near the pride of Lord Lorell's domain, Golden Wind, the golden dragon.

The beast turns her head toward me, but she's neither agitated nor interested in my appearance as she's seen me often enough in her enclosure, mucking it out and changing her water to know who I am. To her, like everyone else, I'm just Hooper, Lord and Master of the Manure Pile.

I hurry over to Master Boren and duck my head while saying, "Master Boren, pardon the interruption, but Helmar sent me to tell you that a king's courier and a Dragon Knight just landed in the paddock field."

Obviously irritated at first by my intrusion, Master Boren's glance changes to one of concern, and he hastens out of the stall without a word. Malo lets Master Boren push ahead before he slows and as he passes by, pushes his face close to mine. "Playing games when you're supposed to be working are we? Well, we'll see how much you enjoy the little game I have in store for you later on!"

I bite down on my lip, knowing what's to come — one more red and raised Proga scar to match my others. Malo rushes off, leaving me to pull the heavy gate shut and snap the bolt to lock the gateway. I sort of sneak my way through the paddock ways to where the others have gathered as I've never seen a knight up close, and this might be my only chance to see one of the King's Own.

I slip into the paddock where I had been working as Master Boren has the group gathered in earnest conversation just past the pen. I tread softly over to where I had left the implements of my lofty calling, manure rake, shovel, and wheelbarrow.

Under Helmar's watchful eye, the sprogs have been patiently waiting for my return and as soon as they see me, come running in that stumbling, off-balance and decidedly ungraceful manner of theirs. Naturally, Regal Wind trips over his own feet, crashes into Wind Glow, and both go down in the dust. The sprog's attempts at running remind me of a cross between a duck and a newborn foal who hasn't quite found his legs yet.

I pick up my rake, trying to look as inconspicuous as possible. Master Boren and the others are so intent on their conversation that none of them pay me any attention. I push the sprogs off to one side and go back to work though I do manage to position myself close enough that what I hear almost causes me to drop both rake and shovel.

"Anders," Master Boren demands of the courier, "are you absolutely sure of this?"

"Aye," the young man replies, "and the king has sent messengers out to all the Great Houses. I just came from Lord Lorell's Manor House."

"Wilders!" Master Boren spits the word out as if he's bitten into a sour plum. "And this has been confirmed? There's no doubt?"

The tall and slender knight, his helmet crested with red plumage indicating that he's a legion officer, steps forward. "I'm afraid so, Master Boren. I received the same information just before His Majesty's courier arrived."

"Wilder scum!" Master Boren all but growls. His face is dark, angry but I can also hear a note of anxiety in his voice. And well it should. We all should be anxious if the barbaric, bloodthirsty Wilders have indeed spilled out of the far hinterlands to raid and pillage.

"I thought the Drachen Wars all but put an end to the Wilders?" Helmar questions.

The captain shrugs. "We destroyed most of their lairs, but evidently they've grown strong enough over the last twenty seasons to again start raiding again — in strength."

He pauses long enough to take a deep breath and let his face harden. "Strong enough apparently to destroy the House of Dornmuir."

"What?" Master Boren sputters. "What are you saying?"

"The House of Dornmuir is no more, Dragon Master," the knight gruffly replies. "His Lordship and Lady Dornmuir are dead and most of their holdings burned to the ground. Three days ago."

I all but drop my rake. A Great House destroyed by the loathsome, fierce Wilder dragon riders whose raids out of the nether lands leave nothing but death and destruction in their wake.

"That's barely a hundred leagues away, Master Boren," Helmar rumbles, "less than two days by a dragon skyride."

I turn and stare toward the nearby forested hills and beyond to the higher knolls. The spruce tree's dull olive coloring is brightened by the birchen tree's light-green spring leaves. Somewhere far beyond there, a Great House lies burning, perhaps even the villages that often are part of the holdings. And with them, the villagers and the dragon workers lie dead, Wilder arrows buried in their bodies or burned to death by Wilder dragon fire.

To me, there's only one thing more cruel than Wilders.

And that's the three emerald dragons whose fierce, heartless dragon breath destroyed my world and left me scarred and torn.

2

Out of the corner of my eye, I watch as Master Boren turns his head and eyes as if to study the lush, spring-green meadows and beyond them, the thick forest filled with black spruce with an occasional white birchen trunk breaking the dark line. His expression is one of grave apprehension, a look that I've never seen before on him though from this moment on, we should all be wearing the same expression.

From what I know, Wilders take few prisoners and those that do fall captive soon come to envy those who died in the initial terrifying onslaught.

"Even now," Master Boren mutters low, thrusting his jaw toward the dark woodlands, "we may have eyes and ears watching our every move, waiting to ravage Draconstead as they did Dornmuir."

"I don't think so," the knight captain replies. He points toward the set of low hills, and I peer in the same direction. Several crimson dragons, their scales catching the early morning sun as if each were a glowing ember, sail low over the dark-green forest.

"You've pulled your patrols in closer," Helmar states.

"Yes," the captain answers. "Though it's been several days since the attack on Dornmuir, I don't think the Wilders are anywhere close to us. If they were, my knights would have spotted them long before and sounded the alarm."

I squint to get a better look as except for the legionnaire standing next to Master Boren, I've never seen a knight skying on a red before. A pinpoint of light seems to be astride each dragon. It's sunlight bouncing off the knight's armor. They're too far away for me to see their lances or dragon heart bows they carry or their faces, for that matter, but it's somewhat comforting to have them so close.

"For the time being," the captain goes on, "it's the best I can do. However, as soon as we get our additional complement of knights, we'll be able to stretch the patrols out farther."

"Give us an extra layer of protection and warning for Golden Wind," Master Boren states.

"Yes," the knight replies, "but just so we're clear, my knight company is stretched very thin. If the Wilders do attack Draconstead, I'm afraid we won't be able to give you much time to spirit her away."

I frown at his remarks, another company of knights, in addition to the hundred drog guards we already have? Seems to me it's a lot of fuss over just one dragon. Yes, yes, I know she's a golden dragon, the only one in the Northern Kingdom, or the whole world for that matter, and supposedly only the third born in all of history. Still, it only matters if you actually believe all that hokum about how's she's a mystical, magical dragon.

Which I decidedly do not. Not for one instant.

Dragons aren't magical, they're vile, callous, dumb beasts without feelings, and it's fate's utterly cruel joke that the one Drach in all the land who passionately hates dragons, me, has the miserable misfortune to live on a dragon farm. That means that practically every waking moment of my miserable life I'm around the foul beasts.

Why, that even goes for my sleeping moments, because I sleep in the birthing barn with dragon sows who are either preparing to give birth or just recently added a sprog to Lord Lorell's already large dragon herd.

"Is it still the king's plan to move Golden Wind to Wynsur Castle?" Master Boren asks.

"Yes," the knight captain quickly answers. "Another reason for the additional company."

My ears perk up at that. They're planning to move the golden away from Draconstead? I like the sound of that. That's one less dragon that I have to feed, water, clean up after, and well, one less dragon, period. That bit of news is every bit as good as the news about the Wilders is bad. Still, one less dragon in my world is a good thing, a very good thing.

"How soon?" Helmar questions.

"Unfortunately," the captain begins slowly, "the Wilders' foray pulled the company we were expecting to join us off in the chase after the raiders. Addleton is the closest legion garrison, but it'll be at least two, maybe three days before we can expect their company to join us."

"That long, huh?" Boren mutters with a grimace. "Two or three days that we'll have to fend for ourselves."

"What about the drogs?" Helmar questions. "Will we see more than the hundred we have now?"

The captain shakes his head. "I've received no word that more are on their way. Even if the king had sent out another hundred at the first news of the Wilder attack, it would still be close to a fortnight before they arrived."

Master Boren and Helmar exchange quick, disappointed glances before Master Boren says, "And no doubt our closest neighbors will be unwilling to give up any of their drogs, either."

"Can't really blame them, Master Boren," Helmar replies. "They've no doubt heard of the Wilder raid."

"What if," Master Boren mutters low, "we took it upon ourselves to sky Golden Wind to Wynsur with your knight company and what dragon workers we have here that can wield a bow or sword?"

The captain shakes his head. "I'm sorry, Dragon Master, but that won't work. For one thing, we don't know where the Wilders went, they could be between Wynsur and us. More to the point, from the reports, even if we could arm every dragon worker you have, even combined with my riders, we simply don't have enough of a force to fight our way through."

I can clearly see the exasperation on Master Boren's face, but before he can speak, the knight clears his throat and motions to the courier. "There's one other thing, Dragon Master."

"Prince Aster," the courier begins, "will be meeting with Lord Lorell at his summer Manor House to discuss moving the golden dragon. You, your son, your novice, and the captain here, are to meet them the day after tomorrow at mid-day."

"That soon?" Master Boren snaps.

"Yes," the courier replies, "the king is quite anxious about the golden's safety, and it's my understanding that he's tasked Prince Aster with ensuring that all goes well with the move."

Master Boren runs a hand over his thick, graying beard, his agitation evident. He lets out a long breath and says, "Well, one does not disregard a royal command. Still, it gives us little time to organize here before we have to leave."

To the legion captain, he orders, "Bring the drogs in closer, have them work the woodland edges and the meadows but leave the stead buildings to my dragon workers."

He swings around to Helmar. "Arm every worker who can carry one with a sword. Those with some skill with the bow gets one of those as well, along with a full quiver. What we lack here in swords or bows, I'll send up from the town's armory. Set up outer patrols around the buildings. For now, cut back on all stead duties — nothing is more important than guarding Golden Wind. Understand?"

"Understood, Master Boren," Helmar answers.

He lays a hand on Helmar's shoulder. "You take care of matters here at the stead proper, I'll swing by the meadows and inform the Meadow Master on my way into town. Once I get to Draconton, I'll speak with the mayor, see if we can't organize some sort of village guard alongside our lone Low Sheriff. And, of course, I'll let my son know of the meeting."

He starts to turn but then says to Helmar, "Tomorrow eve, join me at Dracon Haus. You'll sup there and spend the night. We'll leave at first light on the following morn."

"Yes, Dragon Master," Helmar answers.

"Unless the meeting takes overly long," Master Boren goes on, "it's my intention to be back as soon as possible. Malo, once Helmar and I leave for the manor you'll be in charge here until our return."

"Yes, Dragon Master," Malo acknowledges, his palms pressed together.

Master Boren turns to the captain and the courier. "Anything else from you two?"

"No," the knight captain answers. "I'll be returning to my troop and will see you at the manor."

With that, the two trot over to their dragons and moments later are skyborne. "Malo," Master Boren orders, "increase the golden's feed, I want her well fed for the long journey to Wynsur."

"Of course," Malo swiftly replies, "anything else?"

"No, not until we know the prince's and Lord Lorell's plans."

With that, he spins away, taking Malo with him. Helmar starts to turn but notices me on the other side of the fence. He comes through the gate, eyes narrowed as he approaches. "Listening in, Hooper?"

"Uh, just finishing this paddock, Master Novice."

"Hmm." He steps closer until his face is so near that I can see the individual hairs of his short beard. "Well, what you heard, you keep to yourself. I don't want any crazy rumors getting started. Master Boren and I will inform the other workers, not you, understand?"

"But, of course," I quickly answer, ducking my head low. Helmar turns and just as Master Boren had, studies the dark forest that surrounds Draconstead and which with its dense thickets could easily hide a small army. "Master Novice, may I ask, do you actually think the Wilders would rampage here?"

His answer is a quick, disdainful snort. "Hooper, don't be stupid. We have the only golden in the world. If you were the Wilder clan chieftain and you thought you had a chance to capture such a prize, wouldn't you at least try?"

He lets out a long sigh and turns toward the rising sun. "The question is, why would you call attention to yourself, such as attacking House Dornmuir, instead of striking here first?"

He scratches at his stubbly beard. "That doesn't seem to make sense."

He abruptly jerks himself upright as if he suddenly realizes his surroundings. "Why am I wasting time talking to you? Get back to work and remember — not a word of this to anyone, or you'll answer to me."

"Yes, Master Novice," I quickly reply. "I've never handled a longbow but will I be given a sword too, like the other men?"

Helmar's curt laugh is biting, and he sizes me up as if I were a side cut of three-day-old meat. "If you were a man like the others, Hooper, and could even hold, much less wield a sword, then yes, but no such word applies to you, so there's your answer."

With that, he tromps off, leaving me to watch his broad back and straight, tall form before I glance down at my scarred hand and arm. My face clouds up a bit, and I mutter, "I never realized that it took two hands and arms to swing a sword."

I open and shut the fingers of my good hand and glare at my own little dragon crowd. "I still have one working arm. If I can rake and shovel dragon manure, I can hold a sword, don't you think?"

They, of course, don't answer as dragons, being dumb brutes, can't speak. Instead, they just waggle their tails a bit and let that pollywog grin crack their ugly faces. "Oh," I grouse, "what do you know, anyway."

Just before the sun-high meal, I deliver my constant companions to their respective mothers and hurry to the meal house. As usual, I'm shoved to the very end of the line so that by the time I get to the two cooks, fat Marly, and skinny Larl, what's left for me is the butt end of a loaf of rye bread, a thin carrot, and a fist-sized hunk of goat's cheese.

At that, I consider myself lucky, most days even the cheese is gone by the time I get to the serving table. Of course, I don't stay and eat with the other workers. If I tried, they'd just toss me out on my ear anyway, so I save them the time and me the lumps and make my way back to my little corner of the world in the birthing barn.

At the pile of musty straw and old hay that's my bed, I reach into a particular spot and my fingers soon find soft fur. A small body wiggles under my touch before two black eyes framed by gray circles and a wet, cold nose poke themselves out of the straw.

I break off a piece of cheese and hold it out. "Here you go, Scamp," I murmur. Two paws shoot out of the hay and clamp themselves around the goat curd. I smile, watching Scamper devour the cheese.

Scamper is my one and only friend. He's an orphan. Like me. I found him three seasons back. He was a cold, wet pup hiding and shivering underneath a dripping bog berry bush. Next to him was his mother's body. From what I could tell, a spear had run her through, most likely from a drog — a brute that's a cross between a goblin and a troll and which many Great Houses, such as ours, sometimes use as guards against wild dragons, wolves, and other beasts of the forests.

Somehow, she got away from the drog and with Scamper in her jaws managed to escape. She saved her kit but paid the ultimate price. If she hadn't, the drogs would have gotten the two of them, and I wouldn't have Scamper, and he wouldn't have me. My life would be even more miserable than it already is — if that's possible.

I run my hand over his soft fur again, and he practically purrs. Don't get the idea that Scamper is a cat. He's not, nor is he a dog, he's a . . . Well, he's just Scamper.

Four squatty legs hold up a stubby, rounded body with gray and brown on top and with soft, cream-colored fur on his belly. His two large ears can swivel frontwards and backward, and his short button nose is always sniffing around for food. Tiny, sharp teeth that seem to be set in a perpetual grin, and two eyes that are deeper and darker than the blackest of nights — put them all together and that's Scamper.

Han, the previous Barn Master, said I could keep Scamper as long as he didn't cause trouble and didn't disturb the dragons. It went without saying that also meant that he stayed away from our band of guard drogs. If not, they would kill him and toss him in their eating pots, just for fun.

But Scamper is a quick learner. He knows not to show himself when the drogs come through the paddocks and the barn areas. And at night, he hunts where they don't. When it comes to the dragons, well, they actually seem to like having him around.

I break off a piece of carrot for him, and when's he's finished, he paws at my tunic and shoves his little face so close that we're almost nose to nose. *Mrrrr?* he asks.

I give him a quick scratch under his chin. "Sorry, Scamp, that's it. Maybe we'll do better at last meal."

With that, he dives back under the straw until he's all covered and I trundle down the broad way that marks the barn's middle. The birthing barn is exactly that. It's where the female dragons of Dracon-stead come to give birth to their sprogs. Yes, dragons are perfectly capable of giving birth in the wild, but Lord Lorell pampers his dragons.

Right now, we have eight birthers; two reds, five sapphires, and the golden dragon, though we have enough room for twice that many. Four have already given birth recently, and four are still waiting, including the golden. I have to admit that I'm grateful that there are only eight dragon sows now. When the barn becomes completely full, I'm so busy that I rarely get more than two or three hours of sleep at night.

Sometimes, none.

At the barn's far end, I stop before the giant-sized stall and wait. As usual, the supposedly magical Golden Wind is lying down on all fours, but her head is up, and she watches me as I come up to her enclosure. "What are you looking at?" I mutter darkly under my breath as I stand in front of the stall's large gate.

I stare at the golden. Her golden cat's eyes meet mine, and I think to myself, dragon mothers sometimes die while trying to birth their young; what if our golden and the rest of the birthers died while attempting to give birth?

Now, that would be magical.

She finally unlimbers herself and at a leisurely pace plods over. I stick my head through the railing, and she takes in a deep whiff.

Then she snorts loudly, blowing my short, brown hair every which way. I back out while she turns and lumbers away. Even though I've been in her pen dozens and dozens of times, I have to go through this ritual each time so that her nibs can assure herself that it's just me, Hooper, the Manure King.

Brushing my tangled hair back down with my fingers, I mumble, "Good thing you don't have the sniffles, or I'd be wiping dragon snot out of my hair."

As I enter her stall, I admit, I have to stop and gaze at her for a moment or two. You see, dragon farms such as ours raise red, or scarlet dragons, blue or sapphire dragons, and purple or violet dragons.

Green or emerald dragons, oranges, and yellows are found only in the wild, and sea-blue, or turquoise dragons reside in the ocean. No one raises wild dragons, for as Master Boren is fond of saying, "They are born free, and they will die free."

But a golden dragon, that's something altogether different. Our golden, Golden Wind, is not only the only one in the kingdom, she is the most prized and valuable of all dragons, supposedly worth more than all the dragons in the world.

She is also the most feared beast of all.

You see, according to legend, when a golden dragon is born, it portends a great disaster that will befall the land. However, the lore also says that the golden will birth a very special dragon who will save us from whatever calamity descends on the world.

The first golden, as folklore goes, was Star Wind. It's said that she gave birth to the sapphire Storm Rider, the swiftest dragon of all. Storm Rider carried Palto the Healer from village to village when the Great Plague swept across the world. Thousands died, but Palto saved many, many more than that thanks to the swiftness of Storm Rider.

The second golden, Noble Wind, came at the time of the First Great Wilder Rampage when hordes of Wilders spilled out of the Land Forbidden and raged across the realms. It's said that Noble Wind gave birth to the mighty red dragon, Crimson Fury. He carried

Lord Braveson in the final, victorious battle that felled the vicious Wilder warlord Malonda Kur.

And now, we have Golden Wind and she is the reason that we have a whole company of the king's knights patrolling the forests that surround Draconstead. Plus, we have almost a hundred drogs that stand guard both day and night in and around the meadows and forests that surround Draconstead proper.

All to protect this one dragon. Naturally, on her long flight to the royal stables at Wynsur Castle the king's knights will accompany her, and most of the drogs will make the overland journey, leaving us with a handful of drogs and ourselves to protect Draconstead.

Of course, that stuff about the golden being extraordinary and birthing a unique baby dragon is all nonsense, and I believe it about as much as I think dragons are mystical and magical as Master Boren believes.

The sooner they rid Draconstead of this creature and take her to Wynsur the better, and it is none too soon for me. If I had the chance, I'd go just as far in the opposite direction, away from all dragons and away from the Drachen Mensch, or as we're sometimes called, the Dragon People. True, I'm a Drach, but in name only. I want nothing to do with dragons and that makes me a pariah among my own people.

I learned very early in life to be careful of what I say about dragons and how I act toward the beasts, so no one really knows how I feel. And that's the way I intend to keep it until I can make my escape.

And yes, I do mean to flee from this hellhole and take Scamper and myself someplace where there are no dragons and no Wilders to bring horror and anguish that rips at soul and mind.

My only fear is, does such a place actually exist?

3

I jerk upright and throw my coarse, thin blanket to one side. My heart thuds in my chest, my eyes fly open, and I thrust my hands out as if to ward off some rampaging monster. My heart pounds so loud it's as if I can hear dragon wings beating in the air above me. Just as they did on that awful night of hellfire.

The nightmare doesn't come as often as it once did but when it comes, the memory is like dragon fire, burning, searing, and filling me with an anguish that sometimes takes hours before it finally cools down to the point that I can think about anything else again.

I take a deep breath and bury my head in my hands. The early morning is cool, on the brink of actually being cold, but still, I wipe clammy dampness off my face.

A tiny silver sphere of sweat forms on the end of my nose and hangs there for an instant before it drops to the straw. My mouth works, but no words come out, only a guttural groan of pain and loss.

The rustling of dragon scales in a nearby birthing stall causes me to raise my head and the pain in my eyes is replaced by pure hatred. I stare at the dragon, Glittering Wind, a sapphire who stirs restlessly in her giant enclosure before she settles back down on all fours and goes to sleep.

Hate fills my eyes, my mind, my soul as I stare at the foul beast.

I can't ever forget. I won't ever forget. I only have one nightmare, but it will stay with me forever.

I hear a faint fluttering high above me. The whiteback morning doves that live in the barn's rafters are waking, which means that dawn is not far off. However, my day begins well before daybreak. Malo will be making his rounds soon, and I'll be the first he wakes.

I retrieve my threadbare blanket that I tossed onto the barn's loose chaff and lie back onto my musty straw bed. I know I have little time left before Malo appears, but sleep is a precious commodity, and I'll take whatever moments I can get. My bristly blanket used to cover all of me when I was younger, but I've grown some, and now it only reaches down to my knees.

But if I curl up just so, I can huddle most of my body under the thin covering. And now that we dragon workers are back to Draconstead's high meadows, with its early spring cool, sometimes cold nights, I also keep my goat's hair tunic on at night, with the hood up to cover my head. And I leave my pants and socks, holes and all, on at night, too. Together, they're just enough to ward off the cold. Most nights.

I close my eyes, but my effort to drop off to sleep is wasted. I hear Malo's footsteps shuffling through the loose stubble just in time to roll out of bed before he plants his boot in my backside. He holds his lantern high, and I can see not only the leer on his thin, craggy face but the short, finely pointed Proga lance he always carries.

"That's good," Malo cackles, the lantern's light casting his yellow and broken teeth in garish relief. "You're getting faster." He shoves the lance menacingly close and smirks. "Better a boot and another bruise than this again, eh?"

My hand goes instinctively to my side, to the fresh wound that still bleeds just a bit and at times feels like someone has put a hot coal to my flesh. The bleeding will eventually stop, but the pain stays for several days.

Malo may be getting old, but he can still move pretty fast, especially with his Proga lance. I'll take his boot over the searing lance any day. I overheard one of the other dragon workers say that getting bit by the lance was akin to lying naked, "on a fire ant nest for a day." I wouldn't know. I've never sat or lain on top of fire ants, but I've had the lance put to me more than once, and if given the choice, I might try the ants next time.

As for my bruises, yes, I have a goodly collection of black and blue marks. If there were a contest among the other workers who had the most, I'd win easily. Course when you're a puny runt, and you look like me, scarred arm, leg, and face, what else is there to expect? Still, though my bruises are plentiful, I'll take them over the Proga.

"Get the cook's wood and water," Malo orders, "then start with the yearlings' paddocks, Wind Fury's first. The trainers will be working with him first thing this morning."

He turns and points to the closest empty stall. "Have that cleaned out by noon. The master may be bringing another sapphire birther to the barn this afternoon."

I give a quick nod in acknowledgment and reach for my boots. I have to work at getting my feet into them as the thigh boots are too small for me, but I can't have new ones till next spring. I'm hoping that one of the other workers will throw away his old pair. Since they're all older than I, naturally their boots are larger. Still, I'd rather have oversized boots that I can stuff straw into and fill the space to prevent blisters than to have to bend my toes in an awkward, painful fashion all day long.

I've thought about cutting the toe ends out of my boots or going barefoot, but neither is something you do when you work around dragons with their sharp talons and their never-ending supply of dung.

Seeing that I have my boots on, Malo moves away, taking his light with him. I don't rate a lantern, nor even a candle, but in the little hole I call home, I know every part by heart, even in complete darkness. Besides, there's nothing I need to find, everything I own is on my body, except for my blanket, which I quickly tuck in my little secret hiding spot.

I reach into the straw just above where I lay my head and touch a warm, furry body. For an instant, Scamper rouses, and I say, "In early today, huh?" Lots of times, he spends the whole night hunting and usually doesn't return until past dawn.

I slide my hand down to his tummy. Nice and full. That explains why he's back so soon. He probably tried, but can't put another worm, stickle bug, or maybe a nest of termites in that cavern he calls a stomach. "I've got to go to work, Scamp, but I'll try to sneak something out of the meal house for you. You go back to sleep."

I can feel him wiggle in delight under my hand before he quickly quiets down and falls asleep. I scuttle out the barn's side door, my tunic hood still up, and hurry up the path that runs past the meal house to the woodpile. The early morning dew on the grass wets my pants below my knees, and I can see my breath in the air. Even by early-morn starlight, it's not hard to find the wood as the woodcutter's been busy and the smell of newly cut timber wafts heavily on the light breeze.

I stop at the woodpile that rises to my chest and stare at the darkness that shrouds Dielong Forest. I can make out the closest stand of birchen trees, their white trunks standing in stark contrast to the gloom of the spruce-filled forest behind them.

Somewhere deep in this same forest was my family's cottage and I stand staring for just a moment thinking how apt the name is for Dielong Forest, especially when it's dragons that do the killing. My breath is a short plume in the cool air, and my eyes turn hard as I rub my good hand over my scarred arm. I wonder to myself, what would have been better — to suffer a long death or to live like this?

I don't have an answer, so I load myself up with split wood to the point that my knees almost buckle. But if I don't completely fill the wood bin for Marly and Larl, there'll be no dawn meal for me, or maybe even a middle meal, either. I labor back down the path, staggering under the wood's weight. I quietly fill the box that sits next to the kitchen's back door, careful not to wake the two cooks.

They'll be up soon enough, but if I wake them before Malo does, well, I can forget about any meals for the day, and maybe even tomorrow. I hurry over to the stone-rimmed well. Four full, heavy buckets of water later, I'm done with my meal house chores just as a faint glow spreads across the horizon.

Later, with the early morning sun peeking just over the horizon, I'm in the paddocks. I've had my first meal, more bread, cheese, and a piece of turnip. Before I went to the stalls, I dashed into the barn, split the cheese with Scamper and then picked up my dung rake, shovel, and wooden wheelbarrow before heading outside.

To my chagrin, Malo has me take the four two-week-old sprogs with me again. Most likely, for the next month or so, I'll have these smelly beasts with me most everywhere I go during the day. They're too young to go to the trainers just yet, so I get to shepherd them around while going about my chores.

Their mothers understand what I'm doing; still, when I approach their birthing stalls, I have to endure several moments of their sniffing, to make sure it's just me, Hooper. Once I have all four sprogs rounded up, I put them in the barrow and head for the paddocks. They think it's great fun to ride, but I only do it because otherwise, it's too hard trying to get them out of the barn.

Have you ever tried to herd cats? Same thing with baby dragons, only worse. Cats mill around a bit but definitely will stay out of harm's way. Not these four. If I don't keep a sharp eye on them, they'll head in four opposite directions including into Wind Boomer's stall where one misstep from the big crimson dragon and we'd have a squashed, dead sprog. Not to mention that if that happened, I might end up with no head.

Lord Lorell takes raising his dragons very seriously, and his dragon workers had better, too — or else.

Once inside Wind Fury's pen and after closing the gate, I dump the sprogs to one side. To me, a newborn sprog's head looks like their mama sat on it. Sort of flat and with four little nubbins marking where their horns will grow. Between squashed head and its back end is a fat toadlike body that ends in a snippet of a tail that reminds me of a writhing worm caught on a fishing hook.

From head to tail end, each of these sprogs would match up against a good-sized watermelon in size. They'll grow to be a hundred times bigger than what they are now, of course. They grow so fast that it won't be long before I won't be able to pick any of them up.

And they smell.

Think of a rotten egg the size of a melon. Ugly, stinking, and something only a dragon mother could love.

They don't smell all that much better when they're adults, either.

I can't wait until they're a little older, and then the dragon trainers get to be their constant companions. I hate being around dragons as it is, but the birthing season is the worst.

I get busy as Wind Fury, a red dragon from last spring's sprog crop, has been busy, and my barrow is almost full of muck before I pause, lean against my rake and glance toward the rising sun, a deep reddish orange against the dark-blue sky.

I once saw something called a tangerine, down in Draconton's market. A fruit it was and supposedly, it had come from far south of here but its color was the same as this morning's sun.

High overhead, the sunlight paints a few remaining wisps of clouds the color of a chestnut horse. The clouds themselves look like a horse's tail and streak the blue before rushing away toward the east.

I can't help but think that if I were anywhere else but here, it would be a beautiful morning.

But I am here in this dragon hell-hole and as I take my eyes off the sky, a dirt clod comes sailing past my head and before I can duck, another thick chunk of sod catches my ear. The sting is enough to make me whirl angrily, but it's the laughing faces that bite even more.

"Hey, sausage boy! Or, should we say 'quack, quack, mama duck, get your head out of the muck' and back to your job."

Hakon and Arnie, the two novice blacksmiths, lean over the dragon paddock's top railing and grin, or rather, sneer at me.

"Eaten any sausages lately?" Arnie snickers. "Roasted over an open fire maybe?"

Both boys snort and jab each other with their elbows. Dragons may be at the top of my hate list, but I admit, Hakon and Arnie come in a close second. "Why don't you two go nail a couple of head rivets in those skulls of yours," I retort.

Hakon and Arnie look at each other in puzzlement. "Did the walking sausage," Hakon sputters, "just try and make a joke?"

"It was a joke, right?" Arnie says ominously, his eyes hard and cold.

"Of course," I quickly reply. "Everyone knows your heads are too thick to drive a skull rivet through."

The two glance at each other, unsure if I was poking fun at them or not. Hakon runs a hand through his stringy red hair and points a finger toward the stockade's far end. "Hey pooper scooper," he chortles in his reedy voice, "you missed a big pile over there."

He leans farther over the rail, his eyes narrow and threatening. "And I better not be stepping in any of it while I'm working either if you know what's good for you."

I turn to see what he's pointing at, a slurry mound large enough to fill one whole wheelbarrow, just left by the crimson who casually plods away, oblivious to the extra work he's just given me. I screw my mouth to one side and what little bravado I had toward Hakon and Arnie slips away. "I'll take care of it," I mutter.

"You better," Arnie says and then juts his square chin out at my four little companions that huddle at my feet. "And make sure you clean up after your little ducks too, or you'll get what you got last time." He pumps his fist in front of his ruddy, pimpled face to drive the point home. Laughing, the two jump down off the railing and tromp off.

Not all of my lumps and bruises come from Malo, you know.

I pull the sleeve of my forest-green tunic farther down over my burned, disfigured arm. I know what the scars on my arm and face look like. As if someone had left a sausage on the fire pit coals too long. Hooper the Sausage Boy, some call me.

One of my many titles thanks to the cruelty of dragons.

I hear the paddock gate opening and turn to find Helmar entering the enclosure. I wipe at the grit on my face while he eyes me as he sets his bow and quiver to one side. He adjusts his scabbard that holds a sword's dark hilt and grunts with a small upturn of his lips. "What happened, did you stumble and plant your face in the dirt?

You want to be careful, you might find yourself in something else next time."

"Yes sir," I quietly answer. "I'll try to be more careful." The smile in his eyes tells me that he saw everything, but I know from experience to keep my mouth shut. When you're Hooper, the lowest of the low, you have no voice, and you're barely visible to anyone else, except when they need someone to do the really filthy work.

I glance over to where Hakon and Arnie are striding away. They're both the same age as I, sixteen summers going on seventeen, but there the similarities end. They're tall and well-muscled whereas my skinny and halting body would make a scraggly scarecrow look good. They're in training to become Master Dragon Blacksmiths whereas all I'm in training for is to become the Master of the Dung Heap.

Just then, the crimson comes shuffling over. Helmar reaches up to scratch him between his eyes, something dragons love. "How's Wind Fury doing?" he practically croons to the young scarlet.

He gestures to the red's side scales. "Help me check his loop rivets, Hooper, let's make sure they're not coming loose."

He takes one side, and I take the other. When farm dragons are about two months old, and their scales harden enough, the blacksmiths place small body rivets in front of and behind where the wings join the body. Then, they run lightweight chains through the rivets and bind the wings to the body to keep the dragon from flying off.

Sometimes, if the dragon is headstrong and wants to climb up and over its stall's high fence, the trainers will use heavier chains through the rivets and fasten them to a sturdy wooden post set deep in the paddock's center. The chains are long and loose enough that the dragon can roam freely in its pen, but not long enough for the animal to climb to the fence's top rail.

For a red, this youngster is quite docile, so I don't have to be too wary of his sharp fangs as I get near his head. Even so, a nip from a dragon twice the size of a grown horse and you might find yourself missing fingers or an ear.

As I finish and move around his snout to speak to Helmar, the red gives me a head-butt. For a dragon, the blow was actually gentle, but still, it almost knocks me over so I slap him hard on his muzzle, right between his soft nostrils. He gets a hurt look to which Helmar says in a reproving tongue, "Hooper, he's only playing with you, no need to clip him on the nose."

I turn and give Helmar a respectful bow. "Master Novice, if you would like to frolic with this beastie, then do so, but I don't play with dragons."

He runs a soothing hand between the dragon's eyes. "I wish I could, but I'm too busy today, some other time perhaps."

Watching him practically croon to the scarlet drake, I can't help but ask, "Helmar, why do you like dragons so much?"

He practically sneers at my question. "Dragons are wealth and power, Hooper. And for me, a chance to become a Dragon Master of a Great House, like Master Boren. And that means a fine home, good food, even a servant or two."

He checks the wing chain's last few links before muttering, "And for me the only way up the ladder."

I understand his answer. Like me, Helmar is a "cast-off," someone who wasn't born under the House of Lorell's coat of arms. His father, a tanner, took his firstborn son as his apprentice, and sent Helmar, his second son, to Draconstead to be a dragon worker. That was two seasons ago. But in that time, Helmar showed such an affinity for dragons, that Master Boren quickly recognized his talents and gave him more and more responsibility.

When Daron Dracon, Master Boren's first and only son, refused his father's offer to become his novice, he turned to Helmar. If no one else understood Master Boren's selection, I did. Helmar is tall, strong, handsome, a natural leader with a warrior's spirit who gets the most out of dragons and men.

Daron is everything Helmar is not. He's moody, cruel, and not the least bit interested in dragons, or Draconstead. If I know that he's going to be at the stead, I do my very best to stay as far away from him as possible and with good reason.

It's no secret that he has a complete and utter disdain for those who he believes are beneath him. I remember well a vicious kick to my good leg that left me limping for weeks on both limbs because I didn't get out of his way fast enough.

Malo said that afterward, I walked as if I were a drunken sailor on the first night in port after being at sea for months. I wouldn't know anything about drunken sailors or being at sea, all I know is that from that point on, if Daron Dracon was anywhere near the stead, I made a point of being where he wasn't.

Helmar turns a serious face to me. "Let me ask you, why do you like Scamper so much? He'll never bring you any of those things."

My mouth works for a moment as I search for an answer. "Because . . ." I mutter and stop. "Because he's my friend. He makes me laugh and accepts me for who I am. He's special to me."

Helmar shrugs at my answer. "So are dragons, special I mean. Or, as Master Boren believes, magical." He pauses and runs a work-worn hand over the red's scales. He murmurs, "Sometimes I think he's right."

"Magical," I mutter. "Do you really believe that?"

"Magical," he answers, "in the sense that certain dragons can be worth their weight in gold."

"You mean like Wind Boomer," I reply, "and the golden?"

"Boomer? Perhaps," he states. "But the golden? She's another story in herself."

"Because of the legend," I respond.

He gives me a half smile. "Actually, it's legends. And the more the merrier, I say. Each just makes her that much more valuable." He eyes me sideways. "And the more valuable she is, the more the House of Lorell and our Dragon Master gain in stature."

And his novice, I think.

"So," I say slowly, "do you really believe that if a dragon ever cries its tears will turn into magical jewels?"

He pulls the red's head to him and inspects the creature's four stubby horns, large ears, and cat's eyes. None show disease so he gives the crimson a solid pat on its neck and shoos it away. He gives me a little shrug. "In all honesty, I don't know. I've never seen a dragon cry, and I've never seen a dragon gem."

He gives me a lopsided smile. "I know Phigby believes it's true. Last time I had dinner at Dracon Haus, he was there. I think he and Master Boren could talk for a fortnight on the supposed mystical qualities of dragons."

He says wistfully, "With all their talk, I hardly got a word in edgewise to Cara."

I feel a warmth creep up my neck, not from the sunlight's heat, but from his comment. He and the beautiful Cara Dracon together, in the same room, just a few hand widths apart for a whole evening.

Something I've dreamt about for a long time. However, I know that some dreams will never happen, and Cara Dracon is one of those.

Helmar starts to turn but then screws his mouth up to one side while he eyes me. With a hard edge to his voice, he says, "With the Wilder menace, I'm having the other workers practice their bow and sword skills. Since you're worthless at both, you're going to have to take up some of their workload, understood?"

I keep my eyes averted and duck my head so that Helmar doesn't see the hurt in my eyes. I swallow to get rid of the lump in my throat and mutter, "I understand, Master Novice."

With that, Helmar turns and strides away. My shoulders slump, and I glance over at the four sprogs who are springing up and down, trying to capture a large dragonfly that flits just above their noses. Of course, all they accomplish is to get entangled with each other and start squabbling among themselves.

I watch for an instant before saying to no one in particular, "Did you hear that? I'm worthless."

The sprogs ignore me, of course, as catching a fluttering, dancing, green-winged dragonfly is much more interesting than listening to me. I stare at the ground, my shoulders slumped, my eyes downcast.

"You know what?" I mutter as I slam my muck rake into the ground. "He's probably right, too."

4

I move from paddock to paddock, and though I hurry so that I don't miss my deadline to have the new sapphire's stall ready by sun high, I admit that I stop on more than one occasion to scan the horizon and the dark forest. My anxiety and overzealous imagination has me seeing a Wilder behind every tree and a horde of Wilder barbarians winging over the horizon, their scimitar swords gleaming in the sunlight and their scarlet drakes spouting dragon fire as if a waterfall of fire cascaded from the sky.

Fortunately, it's all in my imagination and my morning passes like most all of my dreary mornings. My very own dragon herd, tiny though it may be, follows me everywhere, underfoot and generally making nuisances of themselves. I'd like nothing better than to scoop all of them into my wooden wheelbarrow, dump them on the manure heap and leave them there.

However, that would probably lead to my head on a chopping block. And though I'm not overly fond of my unsightly face and scarred head, it's not like I have a spare lying around in case I lose this one.

Just as I'm about to scoop up another dung pile, Regal Wind starts sniffing at the same stinking heap. I'd like nothing better than to give him a good, swift kick to move him away, but it would be my luck that another worker would see me. You just don't kick a purple dragon that's bound for the royal stables.

You see, purple or violet dragons are rare and only royalty may own or ride a violet dragon once they're grown. When he's old enough and trained to Master Boren's satisfaction, Lord Lorell will present Regal Wind to His Majesty, King Leo. After that, Regal Wind will lead a luxurious life in the royal stables at Wynsur.

In fact, he'll live a better life than most commoners in the kingdom. Clean quarters, a giant paddock all to himself, all the goats and sheep that he cares to eat, regular feedings of sugar grass, workers who will scrub and polish his scales to a glimmering finish. Moreover, all he'll have to do is to be on a team of four or six purples that sky the royal family around in their carriages of state.

So, as I said, one doesn't kick a future addition to the king's stable. So I bend down, pick him up, and place him to one side before I can shovel up the mess. He chirps and chups at me, but I ignore him. When they're very young, sprogs sound like a cross between a bird and a bullfrog. To me, it sounds something like a warbling screeep or a chuuup.

Just as I set him aside, there's a loud, "Hooper!"

I turn at Malo's shout. "Yes, sir?"

He waddles through the corral gate and tosses a small chunk of goat's cheese and the butt end from a loaf of bread to me. My catch is a juggling act, but somehow I manage not to drop the food. "There's your mid-meal," he grouses. "Hurry up and eat. When you're finished, get to Boomer's stall, the sapphire's not coming in today after all. Once you have the dung cleared, wash him."

I give him a quick nod. "Yes, Barn Master."

"Good, I'll be by later to check." He leans toward me, his grizzled face less than a hand's width away. "And it had better be done right. Understand me?"

"Yes, Barn Master."

I stuff my meal inside my tunic, quickly scrape up the last of the manure, dump all of it on the dung pile, load my herd up in the wheelbarrow, and make for the birthing barn. Once inside, I deliver the four sprogs to their respective mothers and then head for my little corner that I call home. I reach into the straw, and my fingers run across a warm, furry body that's a bit longer than my forearm.

A little oval face pokes up through the straw and peers at me with two-midnight dark eyes.

Threeep?

I smile at him. "You can sleep some more if you want to, Scamper, but, just in case you're interested I brought you something to eat."

At the mention of food, he instantly pops his head up out of the straw. One thing about Scamp, he'll always wake up for food. I break off a thumb-sized piece of cheese and bread and hand those to him while I gnaw on what's left of my meal. It doesn't take long for the both of us to finish our meager portions.

Mrrrr? Scamper asks, as usual.

"Sorry," I say as I scratch him behind the ears. "That's all they gave me."

With that, he snuggles back under the hay, and I go off to do my chores before Malo comes looking for me to accuse me of not doing my work.

Wind Boomer is the second pride and joy of Lord Lorell. He's Draconstead's legendary red dragon; the biggest and most majestic crimson in the Northern Realm. Because the Dragon Knights covet his offspring for their size and ferocity in sky battles and jousting tournaments, he's given preferential treatment to keep him in prime shape; the biggest paddock, more food, lighter wing chains and only the Dragon Master skies him on exercise days.

That preferential treatment also means that along with the birthers', I clean out his stall every day, instead of the once- or twice-a-week cleaning that the other dragons get. As I approach the paddock railing I call out, "Hey! Boomer!"

He slowly unlimbers and lumbers over to where I'm standing. He gives me two quick sniffs and turns away. He knows me well enough that I'm surprised that he smelled me twice, as once is his usual. Unlike the golden, who followed my every move, Wind Boomer lowers himself back down and closes his eyes as if he doesn't have a care in the world.

Which, from where I stand, he doesn't.

Once I've shoveled up his mess, I grab several buckets of water, a long handled stiff brush and start scrubbing the beast. I no sooner finish under his bony left wing than he lazily lifts a rear talon to scratch at the place I'd just cleaned, leaving a wide, dripping streak of mud down his side.

I roll the brush handle in my hands, thinking how badly I'd like to smack the creature up side the head, but that wouldn't do, of course. Someone would see and I'd be feeling the Proga lance several times over. No matter how much you'd like to, you just don't go around clobbering Lord Lorell's dragons, at least, not if you're Hooper.

I finish with Boomer and move from paddock to paddock, shoveling dung, scrubbing dragons as needed while the sun lowers toward the horizon. The sun is almost to the tops of the high hills that make a long arc around Draconstead when I hear what seems to be wind rushing through the air and crane my neck upward.

Sapphire wings soar over the birthing barn's peaked roof. It's Helmar, on his blue dragon, Wind Glory. The dragon swoops over the corrals, makes a gentle left turn and comes to a soft landing just beyond the holding pens.

Helmar deftly jumps down from his dragon and strides toward Wind Boomer's stall. He's still carrying his bow and sword. I duck my head and say, "Good afternoon, Sir Novice."

Helmar frowns, apparently not pleased at my meager attempt at a joke. "I'm not a 'sir' as you well know, Hooper, so mind your words."

I duck my head again, apologetically. "I'm sorry, Master Novice, my tongue wanders at times."

"Then I suggest," he snaps, "that you keep it on a tight leash in the future."

He enters Boomer's paddock, stops, and does a slow scan of the meadows and forest around the stead like he did before. He's still worried about the Wilders, I think to myself. Well, so am I.

To try and get back in his good graces, I point at his sapphire. "Getting ready to sky down to Draconton and then to the Manor House? Do I need to get anything for Wind Glory? Water? Food?"

"No," he answers. "He's already well fed and yes, I'm about to sky down to Draconton, just checking on some last things."

I nod appreciatively. "That means that you'll dine with the master tonight."

His lips turn up at the thought as he eyes me. "Yes, and while you're here supping on turnip stew or potato slush, they'll force on me roasted venison, sweet squash, fresh bread with honey butter, and cinnamon apples for dessert."

He leans forward and murmurs, "And the worst part, Hooper? I'll have to sleep in a bed with a down mattress, pillow, and comforter."

He shakes his head and waves his hand in the air in a cavalier fashion. "It's going to be terrible, Hooper, absolutely brutal."

"Then," I reply, trying to match his jest, "it's a good thing that you're strong enough to endure such torture — a lesser man, such as myself, obviously could not."

His laugh is a sharp bark. "A man, Hooper? As I said before, you need to watch your words more carefully. Your tongue does indeed wander for there's no one around here that would call you such."

I bite down on my lip, trying to hold my face as impassive as I can, though it feels as if his words were a knife twisting into my insides. He walks over to Boomer's stall, makes a quick check of Wind Boomer's chains, inspects the paddock railings, ensures his water trough is full before he turns and glances at the forest, his eyes hardening. "Well, I'm off. You may not be carrying a bow or sword but I've ordered the other workers to keep a sharp lookout, and that goes for you, too. Understood?"

Pretending that his words didn't hurt, I snap my shovel up against my side as if it were a lance. "You can rely on me, Master Novice. My razor-sharp shovel and rake will always be at the ready, along with my trusted wheelbarrow steed. We'll protect m'lord's lands to our last breath."

Helmar snorts and laughs lightly at my mockery. "You do that, Hooper."

He turns and moments later, Wind Glory is winging back over the barn in the direction of Draconton, taking Helmar to his roasted venison supper. Not to mention that he'll be at the same table as the lovely and charming Cara Dracon.

I let out a long sigh. Venison, bread with honey butter, a down bed and comforter to match. A far cry from what I eat and sleep on. I admit, sometimes I dream about what I could be if I weren't here, if the dragons hadn't come on that horrid night so many winters ago.

Could I have become a Dragon Knight, or a man at arms for a Dragon Lord? Or, maybe a sailor, or a tailor, or a blacksmith? Perhaps a farmer? I would settle for being the lowest servant in a Great House.

Or, as I watch Wind Glory sky in the distance toward Draconton, I could have been Master Boren's novice and had the wonderful and giddy pleasure of being in the presence of his only daughter.

Could I —

No, I couldn't.

What other job can you do when one arm and a leg are scarred from dragon fire, and barely useful? In my world, that leaves cleaning out the muck from the dragon pens and paddocks as the measure of your worth.

That, and nothing else.

The sun is close to setting, and I've just returned my four always-underfoot, annoying, irritating drachen sprogs to their mothers when Malo finds me. He savagely tosses a large straw basket along with a small hunk of cheese and bread wrapped in a dirty cloth at me.

"Here's last meal," he grounds out in that wheezing voice of his, "go out in the far meadow, past the Bread Loaf rocks. Helmar says he saw a patch of sugar grass on the far edge that the dragons haven't found. Fill that up and give a portion to all the birthers."

He pauses, wags a finger at me, and then coughs out, "Give a double portion to the golden."

"Now?" I stammer. "It'll be dark by the time I get to the meadow.

There could be Nightfall Goblins, or Wood Trolls, or the drogs will —
"

"Be hunting for their supper," Malo cackles. "So you best be careful that they don't mistake you for a bony two-legged deer."

He gives me a hard look. "Just make sure that basket gets filled and the brood dragons get an ample share."

I can smell the strong barley ale on his breath. As they say, when the master's away, or, in this case, the master's novice, the workers will play. He and the cooks have brewed up a fresh batch and undoubtedly from the way Malo wobbles, he's had more than his share.

I can also see in his eyes that Helmar gave him the order to send me out much earlier in the day, but the ale made him forget about the task, until now. And, it doesn't matter to him if the drogs or trolls catch me or not. All that matters to him is that he can report to Helmar that he had me go search for the sugar grass.

He turns and over his shoulder calls out, "I'll check on you later."

I scrunch up my face in a mixture of anger and fear, mostly fear, as Malo plods away. I hate going beyond the paddocks and barn boundaries at night when we're in the high meadows. It's a perilous business. Not only is that when the drogs patrol, but there are other, hungry creatures that roam the forest, looking for a quick meal.

Like me.

I sigh, knowing I have no choice, pick up the basket, and make for the side door. As I open the creaky door, I'm surprised to find Malo standing just a short distance away. Hearing the door's squeak, Malo turns and gestures toward the paddock walkway that leads to the meadows. "Drogs," he mutters, "and would you look at what they've got."

A whole phalanx of warty, thick-bodied drogs are coming up the pathway. What they're herding causes my mouth to drop. Two lines of the gray-colored foul creatures are using their cruelly barbed dragon lances to prod an old emerald dragon up the slight incline.

"Isn't that something?" Malo snorts. "Don't see greens very often, they usually keep to the deep forest. But from the looks of that one, it wouldn't have taken much for the drogs to capture it."

I nod in agreement. Supposedly, no one captures green dragons. Nor do you find them on a dragon farm. That's why it is so surprising to see this one being driven up the paddock lane by the drog guards.

It's slow going for the old one, even with the brutes using their lances on almost every part of its body. Malo chortles as he watches the old one limp closer. "I don't think Master Boren will have to cull an oldster from the herd to whet the drogs' appetite, after all. That one will fill their bellies for a fortnight at least."

I wrinkle my nose at his comment. Dragons are nasty creatures, but drogs are just as bad. They're brutish, filthy beasts and for some reason, I'm extremely uncomfortable when they're around. Sometimes, I feel like they're sizing me up for one of their cooking pots, so I keep my distance whenever I can.

It's apparent where the drogs are taking the emerald dragon — to their nearby encampment of scummy mud-and-stick huts. And there's no guessing as to why. Drogs relish dragon flesh when they can get it, which isn't often enough to suit their cravings.

As they come closer, I can see that this dragon has turned very, very old. Three of his four top carapace horns are broken and missing. Most of his once thick scales are worn and battered, some are missing, and several are barely hanging on by a scrap of dragon hide.

One eye is entirely white, and a thick, yellow goo seeps from his other sunken eye socket. He limps on two of his four legs, and the long, spiked talons that once jutted from his hoofs are now mere stubs.

He can barely lift his head, and his long, sinewy tail drags behind, slithering from side to side in the dirt. Occasionally one of the two broken tail spikes, once formidable weapons that could rip a man wide open with one swipe, snags on a grass clump until it springs loose.

He once was a forest giant, feared for his fire, fangs, claws, and monstrous tail. Now, he's so feeble that he would have been an easy catch for the drogs. He painstakingly plods ahead, his head lowered to the ground, the fire and fight gone out of him as if he knows his grisly fate.

Nevertheless, every few steps or so, he lifts his head and peers around. The scrutiny from his one good eye and the way he acts make me think he's desperately searching for something. But what could a green dragon possibly be looking for on a dragon farm? I shake my head to myself as my thoughts don't make any sense at all. As if seeing an emerald dragon here makes any sense, either.

"Would you look at that," Malo breathes out.

I turn to where he's staring. From the paddocks lining the rutted road, I can see that the other dragons have come to the railing to watch the ancient one approach. As he begins to pass, each dragon slowly lowers its muzzle as if in homage to the old green dragon.

Even Wind Boomer.

The emerald gets halfway up the trail before he stops. The drogs don't waste a moment before each plunges a Proga lance into his scabby skin. He doesn't flinch, nor does he move. Instead, he raises his head as high as it can go.

For a moment, he holds it up, proud and composed, as though once again he's a forest monarch. Then he lowers his grizzled snout towards the other dragons on each side of the path as if he were giving them a small head bow.

I can't help but think that he is acknowledging the respect that the other dragons have shown him. But, of course, that's ridiculous, dragons are dragons; that's all they are, and nothing more.

The old one raises his head, swivels it around as if he's once again trying to spot what it is that he's looking for before he drops his once proud head and renews his plodding pace.

Dragons aren't immortal as some people believe, but they do live for hundreds of seasons. This one could have been walking the forest when the first Lord Lorell founded Draconstead almost ten generations ago.

I've seen a dragon be perfectly healthy one day and within a week be dead from old age. It's as though they live life fully, and when it's their time to pass on, they just die.

He reaches the incline's top, and for some reason stops. He raises his head as high as it can go and turns it in all directions. Again, I have the feeling that the old one is urgently searching, trying to delay the inevitable until he finds what he seeks.

Then his one healthy eye turns on me. I've never actually stared deep into a dragon's eye before. I haven't ever wanted to, but now I find that I can't turn my eyes away from his. For just an instant, I get the overwhelming feeling that I've seen him before and more so, that I know him and that somehow he knows me.

But that too is ridiculous, and I shake my head hard to rid myself of such a foolish notion. Then, something even more absurd happens. I have this almost overpowering desire to stop the drogs. That what they're doing is wrong and should not happen to this dragon. I can't help myself, and I take several steps toward the old green.

The drog pack is furious that they can't make the dragon move, no matter how much they thrust their spears and Proga lances into its sides. They yammer and bellow, dancing around the green while continuously plunging their lances into him. I hadn't noticed before, but Sorg, the Drog Master, is with this pack.

Sorg is more than mean and nasty; he's pitiless and bloodthirsty. I've seen him lop off the head of one of his own comrades just because the brute didn't carry out an order fast enough.

Did I mention that they're cannibals too?

Sorg charges around the dragon's tail and I don't see him in time. His meaty, beefy paw of a hand catches me just behind the ear. The blow is so vicious and hard that it sends me flying into a nearby mud puddle.

As I sputter in the slop, I hear a cackling laugh from Malo and then the barn door slamming. Malo is mean, but he's no fool; he snickered all the way into the barn scurrying out of Sorg's way and to protection.

Sorg stands over me, shaking his clawed fist in my face. His bulbous, pox-filled face, is now puffy and dark red, and his flabby neck jowls jiggle and bounce as he yells, "You, boy, stay away from drog meat. Or, next time I use something else on you, eh?"

His "something else" just might be the barbed end of the overly long spear he's holding. Supposedly, drogs have never killed one of us; that would break one the Forbidden Laws of the Great Houses and bring down the king's justice on him. Meaning, he would lose his head to the executioner's blade.

But there are whispers and rumors that they've gotten away with it more than once. I certainly don't want to be the twice so I numbly nod and stay put. I make sure that my eyes don't meet Sorg's; he'd take that as a challenge and forget about the King's Law.

If I was a Dragon Knight, I might have picked a fight with the whole lot. But I'm just Hooper and picking a fight with an armed, mad, and hungry drog mob, ravenous for dragon meat, is not something I want to do. Ever.

I hear a loud yell from the drogs and out of the corner of my eye, I see them scattering in complete disorder. Sorg is still towering over me, and he doesn't see the green change from just plodding along into a rampaging beast that's charging straight at him.

Something in my wide eyes must have warned him because at the last moment Sorg turns, but he's not quick enough. The oldster catches him with a wicked swipe of his massive head that sends Sorg sailing through the air. He hits the ground with a kind of squishy thud and rolls up against the nearest paddock fence, belly down.

I feel warm, heavy breathing and turn my head. I'm face to face with the old green. There's not a hand's width between us. They say that just before you die your life flashes before you. It's not true. I knew I was going to die right then, but my life didn't flash before my eyes. The only thing I saw was this enormous emerald dragon staring straight into my eyes.

And not just any dragon. This wasn't a Draconstead dragon, bred and trained to serve the Drachen Menschen. This was a wild dragon, fierce, proud, and untrainable. And, I'm sure, the killer of many Drachs in his time.

He didn't blink, and I didn't blink. I was too scared to blink. My eyes were so wide that I thought that my eyeballs would roll out of my head, down my cheeks, and plop into the mud.

But then, very gently, the old dragon put his muzzle in my lap. He closed his eyes and just for an instant, a crystal clear tear hung from the corner of his eye.

The tear slides down his face, but instead of falling from his scales, seems to float through the air until it settles on my tunic, right above my heart. I stare in disbelief until I remember to move and manage to reach up and clutch the jewel in my hand.

Grasped tight in my fingers, shaped in the form of a long, pointed teardrop is a colorless but radiant crystal — a dragon jewel.

The old green lifts his head and once again, our eyes meet for an instant. His expression changes from one of determination to one where he is at peace with himself and with his fate. My eyes are full of wonder and amazement at what has just happened between the two of us. I don't know what to do, what to say, what to think.

An emerald dragon just gave me a dragon gemstone. What I once considered as foolish folk talk has instead become very real and very personal.

The old one then lifts his head high and for some reason, stares long toward the birthing barn. Then, there's wild shouting and commotion from the drogs and in moments they're all over the old dragon, thrusting their lances into his sides, his legs, his neck. Sorg has risen to his feet and in a frenzy bellows at his followers before he begins to pound his fists on the old green's head.

The dragon gives me one last solemn look and turns away.

I know that expression all too well. It's the look of one who is about to die.

Thoughts of Golden Wind

Oh, that this time had not come. Oh, that my heart didn't overflow with anguish and fill my soul with agony's fiery tempest. My sun, my stars have fallen from the sky. Darkness descends.

What I've feared from my birth has started, and it began with death.

The death of one whose heart I knew oh so well and whose heart I will miss with every breath that I take. A noble spirit whose strength lifted me when I was weak, whose faith inspired me to face the horrors to come, and whose joy in living filled me with life's light.

Honor his name. Honor his memory. Honor his sacrifice.

Now I must be stronger than I've ever been and prepare for that for which I was born. The doors begin to open wide to unleash waiting, simmering evil. The time of blessed peace is over, and the thunder of war begins. No people shall be left unscathed. War's dark wave shall flow across Erdron and this time of creation will be filled with rage and ruin.

There will be those who will desperately seek a safe haven but will find only an instant of calm before the wings of dread pass over. They who think that they have found sanctuary will know but a moment of tranquility before scarlet arrows fill the sky and demons shall be unleashed to ravage the land. The innocent ones will try to flee to the darkest wildlands seeking refuge only to find that even there, terror stalks their every day, their every night.

Like a snake that slinks unseen in the leaves, evil will slither into the mind, heart, and soul.

There will be those who at first merely recognize its manifestation, then they will acknowledge its presence, then they will accept, and then embrace the evil, making it their own.

Few there will be who refuse to give up their hearts to wickedness. Will those few true hearts be enough to face evil's onslaught? Only the Fates know Destiny's End.

5

I wipe away the brown mud and water from my face to watch the ancient green plod down the lane. I stay in the sludge until the drogs crest the small incline and fade out of sight, still clutching the jewel tight in my hand against my chest.

I hear the creaking of the barn door opening, and I push my hand, with the gem held tight, inside my tunic, and hunch over as if I'm hurt. A shadow falls across me, and I look up to see Malo grinning at me from ear to ear.

"You're lucky to be alive," he hoots, "ol' Sorg was in fine form today. I thought he was going to land both feet on you. If he had, you'd be looking like one of the cook's flat cakes with your guts squished all over the ground like someone had stomped on a ripe tomato."

With another cackle, he bends down and splashes mud and goop on me. "And if you're trying to wash the dragon smell off, boy, I hate to tell ya, but, you're going at it the wrong way."

His face grows hard, and he kicks my bad leg hard. He waves his Proga lance in front of me while stabbing a gnarled finger at my face. "Now out of that slop and back to work. You can clean up, later."

I quickly roll over and stand, while still clutching the gemstone tight to my chest to make sure that Malo doesn't notice what I'm holding. He ambles away, and I glance all around to make sure that no one is watching.

I grab the straw basket and in spite of what Malo said, at my best lurching gait, I limp down to the creek. At the stream, a series of stepping-stones form a natural stone dam that backs up a small pool of water.

I toss the basket across the brook to the other bank and then I literally throw myself into the pond. I splash and splutter from the water's icy cold feel, but in a few seconds, most of the dirt and stink are gone.

Making sure that no one can see, I open my hand to stare at the jewel. I run my fingertips across its glistening surface. Once, Lady Lorell visited Draconstead, and the wind blew her silken scarf off her head. When I fetched it for her, it was as if the silk caressed my fingers, smooth and utterly soft.

That's how the jewel felt, silky, and cool to the touch.

It's barely bigger than my thumb and tapered on one end while the other end widens out like a tulip bulb. I thought it would be heavy to hold, but it's light, almost feathery, and so perfectly balanced that it sits upright in my palm.

I'm surprised that it doesn't sparkle. Instead, it's as if it soaks up the sunlight until there's a blazing clear radiance that fills the crystal from one end to the other. I suck in a breath as inside the jewel's center, I see the barest of movements. It's a tiny, closed plant that appears to be a water frond that sometimes edge the creeks and streams in the meadows.

The edges of the plant are laced in a bright emerald color and as I watch the plant seems to slowly twist inside the gem. I wait to see if the frond will unfurl, but it remains closed tight. I'm so mesmerized by the sight of the gemstone encasing the little plant that I get lost just staring into its depths and forget about the cold water's chill.

Abruptly, I realize that I've been sitting in the creek too long. I glance around, but fortunately, there's no one in sight. I push the gem deep inside my tunic pocket, wade out of the water, grab my basket, and head toward the far meadow. I push myself inside a dense thicket to make sure that no one will see me and sit on a small rounded boulder while I eagerly bring out the jewel, again.

In my hand, it doesn't seem warm or cool, heavy or light, it just feels perfect.

I can't help thinking that, for some unknown reason, the old green bestowed on me a wondrous and astonishing gift, a dragon tear jewel. But, why? Why me? I don't know the answer, but what if the legends are true?

What if I hold in my hand a magical crystal with incredible, even mystical powers? What could I do with such a thing? More importantly, what could it do *for* me?

My thoughts spin and my imagination gallops through my head as if it were wild stallion racing across an open field; unbridled, untamed, racing along faster than any storm wind.

Why, I think, this could change me into a mighty lord, a noble of regal bearing with fertile pastures and fields to call my own. I would have a great castle to live in, and dozens and dozens of servants to wait on my every whim and bidding. I could have a whole company of knights to do my fighting and my own dragon herd with the greatest Dragon Master in the land to watch over them.

Why, I could even have a lovely lady on my arm, someone who wouldn't scowl and turn her eyes away from me because of how I look. A sudden incredible thought fills my mind. Could that elegant lady be none other than Mistress Cara Dracon?

Yes, it could, after all, with magic, you can do anything.

Then my head stops spinning and I abruptly realize that yes, the old green has given me a great gift, but I have absolutely no understanding of how to make it work. Such things are a mystery to me, and I'm not sure how to unlock the inner workings of such a magical jewel.

For now, I can't let anyone know about this, especially not around here. The instant they find out what I have, the next moment will find me with a slit throat. I glance up and see Night's Curtain on the horizon and know that I'd better hurry or for sure I'll be spending time in the darkness looking for Malo's stupid sugar grass.

Reluctantly, I put the gem inside my inner tunic pocket and set out to find the patch of sugar grass before the last of the light is gone.

As I push out of the bramble, I'm torn between making noise to let the drog dragon guard know that I'm out here or being quiet so that a goblin or troll doesn't hear me. I decide to keep quiet, as there's no guarantee that even if I make noise that a drog won't send a lance my way.

I hurry across the first dell until I reach the far side and the Bread Loaf rocks, so called because the tall, smooth stones appear like slabs of thick, burnt baked bread stacked high. It's used by the dragon trainers to teach the dragons when and how to spew their dragon fire on their rider's command.

You always know when the trainers are going to be doing that particular training as they call it, "baking the loaves."

Once past the granite slabs I start looking in the knee-high grass for a patch of short, white grass, mosslike in texture. Of course, it's not where Malo said it would be, and I have to circle farther and farther out until it becomes almost too dark to see.

The four moons haven't risen yet, so I have only starlight to guide me. Fortunately, the King and Queen Stars are high above the trees, which gives me some light, but still I have to bend close to the ground to really see anything. I move slowly as sometimes sugar grass patches are small and set apart.

I lean closer to the grass when suddenly there's a pop! pop! pop! I catch the full blast right in my face and jerk away. I stumble backward before stopping to spit out tiny fluffy cotton seeds.

Poppin' cotton not only tastes terrible, it sets my nose to itching, and I vigorously rub it so as to not sneeze and alert anyone, meaning whatever hungry things are out here.

With my nose itching uncontrollably, I spit out the last of the seeds, rub the wispy cotton off my cheeks and chin and go back to looking for the sugar grass. I finally spot a soft white patch among the darker grass and hurriedly start pulling up handfuls of the velvety foliage and placing it in my basket. I'm almost done when at the very edge of the small patch I see a tiny dark flower, buried amongst the white of the sugar grass.

I bend down until my nose is almost against the ground. A soft hiss escapes my lips, and I stare wide-eyed.

Dragon bane!

The black petals edged in a crimson tint are unmistakable. Dragon bane is rare but lethal even to a full-grown dragon. If a dragon eats even one leaf, the flower's fatal poison kills the beast quickly, and as far as I know, there is no antidote.

Because of that, some call it, the Dragon's Curse.

I'm stunned at my find. Helmar and Panjeah, the Meadow Master, are so careful in searching out the lethal blossom that I know of only one dragon who's died from eating the bloom in the last several seasons.

I reach out with one hand, my fingers curling around the stem. A dark thought creeps into my head. All I would have to do is to hide the petals among the sugar grass and let the dragons in the barn eat. Eight heartless, evil creatures not only gone from my life but from the world.

My fingers tighten on the thin stem for an instant more before I stop and think. Just how long would I live after the dragons died? Master Boren, Malo, Helmar and everyone else would know in an instant who was responsible. What would they do? Give me to the drogs?

No.

The king's justice, death by the executioner's blade?

Perhaps.

More likely, since my crime was against their beloved dragons, they would find a wild green and feed me to its hungry mouth.

Is the death of that many dragons worth my life? Maybe —

I hesitate, but then pull the flower from the ground and shove it into my hip pocket.

With my basket full, I start to walk back to the barn when I stop in my tracks and stare at the sky. For the last month, every evening, I've watched the four moons grow closer and closer into forming a straight line up into the heavens. Now, they're rising over the horizon, just above Draconstead, and they're perfectly aligned, each behind the other.

The largest moon Osa, the First Moon, is leading the three smaller orbs, Eskar, Nadia, and Vay. Osa always rises first, always makes a grand appearance. Tonight, Osa, Eskar, and Nadia are bright, almost silvery white while Vay, the Dark Moon, seems even darker though its shadowy outline is plain to see.

Together, they resemble a giant mace, with Osa as the head, and the three smaller spheres forming the handle.

I can't help but stare at the incredible sight. Suddenly, a cold gust of wind lifts my tunic. I shiver just a bit from the icy feel. I hear a rustling in the forest behind me and think that the breeze is stirring up the leaves.

The sound comes again, and I realize that the breeze has died down; there is no wind.

I turn at a crackling noise. It's as though someone is dragging his feet through the dry foliage, crunching the tiny twigs and old leaf droppings from the past fall underfoot.

There's nothing there, just sharp shadows cast by the moonlight. I stand and stare for several heartbeats before I start to walk on.

The crackling sound comes again. I spin around. For an instant, I see what seems to be a shadow that glides among the trees before it's gone. I blink several times and rub my eyes to make sure I'm not seeing things.

I glance around one last time before I start to back away, only to stop as the swishing sound, louder this time, comes from behind. I whirl around and suck in my breath.

A shadow emerges from the darkness, blacker than any night, darker than all the forest shadows combined. It floats just above the ground, creeping closer and closer. As it moves towards me, the tree limbs bend and creak to give it passage through the forest as if they feared the thing's touch.

Its outline flows and ebbs like a tattered black robe that's been shredded by dragon claws, fluttering as if from a stiff breeze — only there is no wind. The specter has no face, no eyes, but I feel that the thing is staring straight at me, and I can't help the shudders that shake my body.

The woodlands have grown still and silent. No bird calls, no small animals rustle in the underbrush. All afraid, it would seem, to make their presence known to the shadowy apparition.

My heart thumps in my chest. My eyes widen, and my mouth sags so deeply that I feel my face stretching all out of shape. I've never seen such a phantom before and for the moment, I'm transfixed in place, unable to move. I know I should run, but I can't. It's as if the thing is holding me in place by its sheer presence.

The spirit moves toward me. It raises what I think is an arm and hand with wispy black tendrils for fingers. It stretches out its dark hand, and I feel as though icy skeleton fingers are slithering around my neck as if to squeeze the life out of me.

I try to yell, but the words choke in my throat, and all that comes out is a gurgling sound. I try to run, but my feet are seemingly rooted in the ground.

The shadow comes closer. I can hear what sounds like a thick robe swishing the dried and loose leaves as it floats above the ground. It seems as though both time and my heart stop. I'm completely frozen in place, unable to flee, to escape this black wraith.

The apparition raises its head, and I see a pale, haunting face that's distorted and misshapen in the robe's hood. A shadowy, sinister lady whose eyes flash like lightning, full of menace and malice. Her hair writhes and flows around her face as if she wears a nest of venomous asps. Her mouth is set in grim resolve as she advances.

This night demon is death, and it's coming for — me.

The shadow slowly floats forward until she's but an arm's length away, her wispy, clawed fingers outstretched, ready to pierce my body as an eagle's talons impale a hapless rabbit. I know that if she touches me, I die.

I'm not sure if it's the terror that binds me or some spell that this enchantress has cast that's holding me in place, but try as I may, I can't move.

Then, a soft, warm, green-hued light breaks the surrounding darkness. It reaches out in long gentle swathes that flow around and over me as if to hold me upright and strengthen me against my nemesis. The light seems to break the trance, and I manage to turn my head.

My eyes grow even wider. Walking toward me is a glowing, brilliant emerald dragon. It comes to stand behind me and opens its wings wide while its light fills the meadow and embraces me like a mother wraps her arms around her newborn baby.

The sound of a snarl of pure rage causes me to turn back to the dark lady. Her face is a mixture of astonishment and swelling wrath. She thrusts her claw-like fingers toward me, straining to curl her hands around my neck. Her mouth is open wide as if she is screaming, not in pain, but in rage and fury.

Only, there's no sound, no cry to break the stillness. It's as if the shroud of light emanating from the dragon is blocking her evil intent, and she can't break through the aura that surrounds the emerald dragon and me.

For an instant, the evil lady's darkness and the dragon's light battle and I'm caught in the middle, having no part in the fight, other than that of an unwilling and terrified spectator.

Then, the wraith draws back. She scowls at me in sheer hatred, gathers her darkness around her, and disappears.

For a moment more, the soft light surrounds me, but then the aura and the dragon slowly fade away, and they too withdraw into the night.

When the last ray of emerald-hued light fades, it's as if the radiance has been holding me up and I fall to one side. I don't know how long I lie on the ground when I feel a rough, gnarled hand on my shoulder, shaking me.

"Hooper," a voice calls from far away. Then there's a sharp, "Hooper!"

My eyes pop open, and I'm staring into a wizened, bearded face.

"Hooper," the man behind the beard grumps, "this isn't the best place to be sleeping, you know."

"Uh," I answer and let out a moan. "I wasn't sleeping Master Phigby, I — "

I jerk myself to a sitting position and frantically whirl around in all directions. Both the evil lady and the green dragon are gone. Phigby leans a little closer, both eyes squinting and his lips pursed together in open questioning. "Hooper, are you all right? Why are you out here practically in the middle of the night sleeping in the meadow grass?"

I shake my head. "I wasn't sleeping! She tried to kill me."

"Kill you?" Phigby grunts. "Who tried to kill you?"

"A witch," I sputter, "or a wraith."

I stop and point toward the nearby trees. In a rush of words, I say, "She came from the forest like some dark shadow, wearing this wavy black robe, though I couldn't actually make out her face, she was trying to wrap her claws around my neck, and — "

"Slow down, Hooper," Phigby interrupts, "before you swallow your tongue."

He pulls at his bushy beard as he peers at me. "I think you fell asleep. You've been dreaming, Hooper."

He reaches into his always present haversack that's covered with glowing stars and half-crescent moons and sparkling comets, and pulls out a water flask and a tiny, yellow bottle. He tips the bottle so that exactly three drops go into the flask. "Here, drink this, it'll clear your mind."

I take a little sip and sputter and spit. "Why can't you ever make a concoction that doesn't taste so terrible? You'd think you were trying to poison me."

"If I were attempting to poison you," he curtly answers, "then it would taste so sweet and delectable that you'd drink the whole flask, and I'd be done with you."

He tilts the container back and makes me drink the contents to the last drop. Surprisingly, my head does seem to clear and after a moment, I get to my feet. "Now," Phigby says, "let's try this again. Just what are you doing out here so late at night?"

I rapidly recount my search for sugar grass and then in slower words, describe my encounter with the foul apparition. As I finish, I draw in a deep breath and say hesitantly, "Maybe I did fall asleep. It must have been a dream, isn't that right?"

He doesn't answer, just strokes his long, gray beard as if he's deep in thought and doesn't hear me.

"I was looking at the moons and then . . . " my voice trails off before I whisper, "it was just a dream, wasn't it?"

"Eh?" Phigby replies. He pats me on the shoulder and mumbles, "Of course it was a dream, Hooper, nothing more than a bad dream."

His eyes are drawn to the moons, and he begins to speak, almost in a chant,

"Seven have come, seven are done,
Four did sleep, and now three will weep,
For now comes the eighth and open swings the gate,
On high the four shall align, a portent, an omen, a blazing sign,
That chains have burst, and the evil that thirsts,
Will walk once more, on hill, dale, and rolling moor,
As a seed, it will grow, up high and down low,
Rage and ruin, merciless death, pain will come with every breath,
All to slave, all to obey, all to serve the Domain of Vay."

His words cause me to shudder as if another sharp gust of cold wind had cut across my body. "Master Phigby," I say, "that sounded awful, what did it mean?"

"What?" he mumbles as if I've just disturbed him from being in deep thought.

"I said, what did that mean?"

"It means," he begins, then stops and gives me a scowl. "It means, young rascal of a Hooper, that I can't stay out here all night talking to you. I've got to go find a certain book that I haven't seen in many, many seasons."

He leans close and brusquely says, "It also means for you to stay inside at night and quit venturing out after dark if you know what's good for you."

"That's easy for you to say," I answer in as reasonable a voice as I can, "you don't have to answer to Malo."

He stares at me and then mutters, "No, I guess I don't. Still, it's not wise to be out at night, especially alone." He pauses and murmurs, "And especially not now."

I can see that I won't be able to convince him that I have no choice in the matter. Master Phigby doesn't understand that if Malo says "grasshopper" I ask him, "Do you want me to jump using just my legs or use both legs and hands?"

Instead, I say, "You didn't answer my question. Did I dream the whole thing? There really wasn't a dark lady and a glowing dragon."

He studies my face for several moments before he lays a hand on my shoulder. "Of course not, Hooper, it was all your imagination as if in a dream."

"Good," I say firmly. "The last thing I need is to be dreaming about dragons, especially a green glowing dragon."

Phigby studies my face briefly before asking in a knowing air, "You still don't believe dragons are special, do you?"

"No dragon is special," I state.

"Not even our golden dragon?"

"Especially our golden dragon," I snap. "She's no different than any other four-horn."

"Oh? Is that so?"

"Yes, that's so," I retort.

"I would be careful who you say that around, Hooper," Phigby cautions. "Especially Master Boren. I've heard him say many times that the golden is the royalty of dragons, an enchanting creature, and all dragons are of legend and lore."

"I know," I reply in a sigh. He's right, I do have to be very careful with what I say. But Phigby's known about my feelings for a long time, and he's never let on that I'm different from all the other Drachs.

I feel the dragon gem's hardness in my pocket and think that his finding me was actually a bit lucky on my part. "Uh, speaking of legend and lore, what can you tell me about dragon gems?"

"Tear jewels?" he grunts while giving me a quizzical stare. "Why would you want to know about dragon gems?"

"Oh," I say, "it's just that Helmar and I were talking about them earlier. Kind of made me curious, you know, if they're really magical."

"Hmmm," he answers. He glances from side to side, finds what he's looking for, and sits down on a tree stump. He fishes in his bag before hauling out a thin book that has a silver cover and sets it on his lap.

He reaches into his bag again and pulls out a long, thin stick that has a small rounded end. While I'm staring at the rod trying to figure out how it fit inside his bag, Phigby stabs the stick into the ground so that it stands upright. He then touches the bulb, and it bursts into flame, lighting up a small circle with Phigby in the middle.

"How," I sputter, "did you do that?"

"Do what?" he mumbles.

"The fire," I stammer. "How did you — "

"Simple alchemy," he quickly replies with a dismissive wave of his hand. "A few pinches of this and that mixed into a ball and plastered on the end of a little rod. That's all it is, Hooper."

He makes himself more comfortable on the stump. "Now, let's see, what was it you wanted to know about, again?"

"Uh, dragon gems," I reply slowly, as I'm not sure I believe Master Phigby's explanation about the fire. Sometimes, I think Phigby is more than he makes out to be. His full name is Professor Phineas Phigby, or the Book Master as some call him, or Master of Potions, or the Alchemist or — well, he has a lot of titles. But to everyone he meets, he'll typically say, "Please, my friends and acquaintances just call me Phigby," so we do, or Master Phigby on occasion.

I think he's a wizard of sorts, but I don't say that out loud. After all, wizards are known to turn people into toads or lizards if you cross them.

He owns a bookstore in Draconton, on one end of Merchant's

Square, just across from the tailor's, the shoemaker's, and the butcher's shop. I never go into any of those places because I don't have any money. Besides, if I tried to enter one of those stores, the owner would take one look at me and throw me out on my ear. However, there is one shopkeeper that does let me in — Master Phigby.

Above his shop's entrance hangs a faded wooden sign that spells out in large, dingy red letters: Professor Phineas Phigby — For Sale or Trade Books, Maps, and Scrolls. Underneath is a set of smaller words: Potions, Tonics, and Medicines. Made by Appointment Only.

His shop is always a bit dark and sometimes there's a light hazy smoke cloud that smells a little of sulfur, bitter wood, and other nameless scents. I like it best when the aroma is of ginger and cinnamon, scents that he uses in his potions and medicines.

He always wears a long, crinkled robe, but I can never quite describe the cloak's color. Every time I see him, his cape seems to be a different shade. Tonight it seems to be a dark green under the moonlight though when I last saw him in town it had a bluish tint.

At times, he can be utterly forgetful as if he's lost in thought and doesn't remember where he is or what he's doing. At other times, he speaks as if he's lecturing to a hall full of scholars. It's like he's been everywhere and seen everything there is to see in the world, though he claims that he's never really traveled that much or that far in his life.

He knows a lot about dragons, legends, and lore, potions, and ointments. And he makes grand fireworks for the children on Feast Day, even though he says he's only a shopkeeper who sells books, maps and scrolls, and sometimes medicinal tonics.

He's one of the few people in Draconton who actually speaks to me in a somewhat civil tongue instead of yelling or cursing at me. When I'm in his shop, for some reason, he seems to take an interest in my lowly world, especially when it comes to me and the dragons. He's always asking if I've learned anything new and exciting about the beasts.

I always reply, no, unless you want to count how many extra things I've learned to hate about them.

And every time I say that, Phigby frowns and gives me a little lecture about how I should pay attention to the dragons because there's a lot to learn about them that might come in useful someday.

During the long winter, when the dragons and the dragon workers stay in the lower meadows just outside of Draconton, as often as I can I sneak out at night to visit his shop. He doesn't mind and is always willing to let me in. Why? So that I can read his books.

You see, I've never gone to school, and I'll never be able to go. School is for those who can afford to pay, such as the villagers' children, and not for someone who hasn't a farthing to his name, like me.

My school is his shop at night, and Master Phigby and his books are my teachers. He makes me read to him and actually gives me lessons most nights. Thank goodness none of which are about dragons, or I'd never go back. The fact is, I may lose sleep in visiting his shop, but it's worth every lost moment of slumber. I just have to be extra careful not to get caught by Malo or another dragon worker. If I did, that would be my last night of visiting the book shop.

I once asked Master Phigby how he came to know so much. He swept his arm around his shop at the rows upon rows of books. "In here," he said, "I can take a journey to the farthest realms of Erdron; to Majorca and Keeni in the west to Homeron and Batel in the east.

"I can sail the Great Oceans and visit the Merpeople or walk the deserts of Faldron and see six-legged kamels lope across dunes that appear as giant waves cresting through an ocean of sand.

"I can visit the high north steppes and marvel at the grand lights that play in the night as if the gods were twirling their fingers in the heavens and making the stars dance."

He took a breath before saying, "From my books I can learn how to combine sulfur and saltpeter together with just a pinch of charcoal and dye to make sparklers for the children. Or, how to mix the leaves of dandelions and willow tree bark together to cure a fever or lessen the pain of a broken arm."

He swept both arms wide and bellowed, "And all from books, Hooper, that open your eyes, your thoughts, your hopes, your dreams, and your imagination to what can be instead of just what is."

I can't say that I've read all of his books, but when I started, I was reading the books on the lowest shelf, the children's section. Now, I have to get his tall ladder to reach the topmost row and the books I haven't read yet.

However, from early spring when the sunlight begins to return to the fading light of fall, we dragon workers work the high meadows and Draconton is too far for me to walk. So I have to wait for my once-a-month trip with the cooks into town to pick up provisions and after we've loaded the wagon, and the cooks are in the pub, I hurry over to visit Phigby.

He always seems to know when we're coming because he's waiting for me, thrusts a book into my hands, and sends me outside to lie on the grass beside the Mill Pond to revel in a few luxurious moments of nothing to do but read.

While I'm reading, Scamper typically takes a keen interest in the Whistle White Swans, the Anser Geese, and Maller Ducks that float and paddle through the pond's clear, smooth water.

Every so often, he tries to see if a lily pad will hold his weight as he tries to get to the birds, but, of course, it doesn't, and he falls into the pond. He scurries from the water, sputtering and chittering angrily because he's soaking wet and acts as if it's the fowl's fault.

I still haven't figured out if the swans honk and the ducks quack because they're laughing at him or warning him to stay away.

I always have to return the book, of course, because I have neither money to buy nor another one to trade. Besides, if the other Dracon-stead workers ever caught me with such a thing, they'd just take it away from me, whether I'd actually bought it or not.

"So," Phigby says, bringing my thoughts back to the here and now. "You want to know about dragon tear jewels." He holds the book up for me to see. "This little tome might tell us something about them."

"What's it called?" I ask.

He holds the book out so that I can read the title, *Dragon Tear Jewels, Moon Stones, Sun Gems, and other Crystals of Power.*

"Crystals of power," I murmur. "So a dragon jewel has some sort of magical ability?"

"Let's find out," Phigby answers and places the book in his lap. He opens the cover and mumbles, "Now, where shall we begin?"

A gust of wind comes up, ruffling the pages as if some invisible hand were turning them rapidly until they stop about midway through the manuscript. "Ah," he says and puts his finger on the page, "quite so."

"Master Phigby," I ask timidly, "did you do that?"

"Eh?" he answers as he peers at me. "Do what?"

"Make the wind turn the pages."

"Phhh," he replies with a dismissive wave of his hand, "of course not. Nothing more than a sharp breeze that ruffled the pages. Now, let's see . . . "

His voice trails off as his finger traces down the page while he mumbles, "Hmm . . . yes . . . "

He stops to run his fingers through his flowing beard while saying thoughtfully, "Of course, I can see why that would be so."

He keeps reading and then starts to chuckle. "Why, those silly dragons."

He flips the page while still pulling at his long beard, nods a few times, and then snaps the book shut. He tosses the book in his satchel, snuffs out the light stick, stands while stuffing the light rod in his bag, and begins to march away.

"Master Phigby," I yelp, "wait!"

He turns at my shout. "What is it, Hooper?"

"You never told me about dragon gems," I sputter. "Are they magical? If you have one, what can you do with it?"

"Of course, they're magical," he answers. "What makes you think they weren't? But first you'd have to have one to know just how magical it is, and since you don't possess a dragon tear jewel, it doesn't really matter, does it?"

I bite on my lip. I can't let him know that yes, I do have a dragon gem. Not yet, anyway. I have to bide my time, decide how I'm going to handle this extraordinary gift. "No," I mumble, "I guess it really doesn't matter."

Phigby starts to turn and then stops. He mumbles as if he's talking to himself before he gives me a sideways glance. "If, by chance, you see Cara Dracon, don't tell her about that book of mine that I mentioned. She'll be pestering me to let her read it from now until she's an old gray lady."

"I won't," I quickly reply.

Though Cara and I don't really know each other, I do know one thing about her. Phigby told me once that she loves books, even more than I do. While I can honestly say that I've read quite a few books, Phigby stated that Cara, on the other hand, has read every book in his shop at least twice, some three times and is always pestering him to get more new books. Ones that she hasn't read.

If she knows that he has a new book that she hasn't seen, well, from what I know, he's right, she will most likely bedevil him forever to get her hands on the thing.

Phigby turns and gestures toward the west. "Look, Osa's light on the Dragon Tooth Mountains, it almost appears like the Dragon Glow that you get on the mountains just before dawn."

I turn, and my eyes catch a soft pale pink radiance on the mountains far away. Dragon Glow, Phigby called the soft light. I call it Dragon Blood because of all the innocent lifeblood that the monsters have spilled; enough blood to cover the mountains in scarlet from top to bottom.

I turn back to speak to Phigby, but he's gone. I spin around looking for him, but he's nowhere to be found. I scratch my head trying to understand how he could have walked away so quickly, but I'm at a loss to explain how he just vanished like that.

With a start, I realize I've tarried far too long in the meadow. At my usual limping gait, I cross the fields with my basket load of sugar grass, afraid that Malo will be angry with me for my tardiness. If he asks why, I'll tell him about the evil spirit and the green, glowing dragon.

That brings me to a halt. No, I can't tell him that. He'll say I'm making the whole thing up to cover for my falling asleep instead of coming straight back to the barn. I'll have to say that it just took longer to gather the sugar grass than I expected — which is actually true — and hope that he believes me.

I hurry until I get to the stream. I sink to my knees and splash cold water onto my face, just to make sure I'm not asleep and dreaming. I rub my hand over my eyes and shake my head hard. It couldn't have been real, I think, I must have imagined the dark wraith. There are no such things as phantoms or glowing dragons that walk the night, I tell myself.

But, what about Master Phigby? Did I imagine him too?

I take a deep breath and hurry on, clutching my basket of sugar grass. I slip inside the barn and listen. I let out the breath I'd been holding. I'm lucky, Malo isn't to be seen. I stop at the first enclosure and let my hand slip inside my pocket to grasp the fatal petals. It will be so easy, I think, one tiny leaf per dragon. Why, I'll even hand-feed each one, just to make sure they eat the poison bloom.

I clutch the flower, my hand trembling at the thought. I stay that way for several heartbeats before I slowly bring my hand out. Empty. I can't do it. My life is one miserable day after another, but still, it is life, and I can't bring myself to face a death warrant.

I'm a coward, it's that plain and simple.

I reach into the basket and with a savage toss pelt the first sapphire dragon in the face with several handfuls of grass. I move from stall to stall, bombarding each dragon with the pale plants as I go along.

It doesn't take long to spread the foliage among the birthers. Then I reach the golden's stall, and stop to stare at her. The beast is lying down near the enclosure's farthermost wall, and no matter how much I would love to chuck the grass into her face, she's too far away for my puny throws. I dump the remaining foliage into the stall. She notices what I'm doing and with ponderous steps comes to the grass to eat.

The golden lowers her head and sniffs the stem deeply before she snorts through her nostrils. Abruptly, the ugly thing jerks her head up to stare at me and for a moment, I see what I think is surprise, maybe even bewilderment in her eyes. I shake my head and turn away thinking that I must be seeing things again because I know that dragons don't have feelings.

I hear her moving, following me down the railing. I look over my shoulder, and her eyes seem to stare straight at me. She hasn't touched the sugar grass and her gaze never leaves me. She's never done that before, and I grow a bit apprehensive so I turn quickly away. But for some reason, I stop and turn around after just a few steps.

The golden is standing at the corner of her paddock, still staring as if she were studying everything about me. Her intense stare is unnerving, so I whirl and hobble away at my best gait.

As I do, I shake my head, thinking the witch and the green dragon were just a dream, an awful dream, nothing more, just like Phigby said. Just as you're dreaming that the golden is examining you or showing appreciation for the sugar grass, you brought her.

Remember, I tell myself, it's all a dream and nothing more.

Hooper? No, it can't be, but it's true. I thought I had lost my senses, but I haven't.

Hooper carries the Voxtyrmen, the Jewel of Growth and Life. I can feel its essence, its radiance, even though Hooper believes he has it hidden under his tunic.

I admit, I have not known many Drachs, but of those, I would not have even begun to consider him as one fit to carry such a wondrous gift. I have a most difficult time accepting the fact that Hooper is the Gem Guardian.

Is it possible that Pengillstorr made a mistake? Could Pengillstorr make such a monumental error considering all that is at stake? My instincts say no. There is one other possible answer though it too would be unfounded speculation on my part — but it may make the most sense.

What if Pengillstorr, for some unknown reason, couldn't find the guardian and with death at hand had to find a caretaker, someone to protect the gem until the actual guardian appeared? It is the choice of last resort, and if Pengillstorr chose Hooper, he did so with good reason, for it is evident that Hooper is weak and not just because of his physical limitations.

His eyes do not see, his ears refuse to listen, and his heart, except for a few brief moments, feels only one emotion.

If he is to carry the Voxtrymen, then he stands on a precipice that could lead ultimately to the slavery of mind, body, and spirit. I wish that I could tell Hooper what he faces, but that is not yet possible. Worse, his carrying the Voxtyrmen along with his own unbending hatred will only draw evil to him.

Somehow, we must find the guardian and quickly for only he or she can wield the gem's power against the Wicked One.

6

The next morning, just as the orange-red sun slides over the horizon, I've finished with my kitchen chores and had my early meal. I managed to snag a second small flat cake while Marly the cook wasn't looking and shared it with Scamper. Even before he chomps down on the corn loaf, I can see that the little tub's tummy is nice and round, so I know he's had a successful evening hunting worms and crunchy beetles.

Me, I had a less than lucky night trying to make the dragon gem work. I spent half the night muttering what I thought were mystical words over the thing to see if I could get a response. Common phrases like "abracadabra" and "williewilliewish-mewishes."

I even tried saying the words backward but arbadacarba is even harder to say, and I stumbled over it several times, with my tongue all knotted and twisted before giving up.

The result? Absolutely nothing. Not even a tiny spark or flame out of the gem.

So I lost sleep and woke up grumpier than usual, but I did resolve to get a look at Phigby's book that he had last night. I'm positive it has the answer to how to unlock the jewel's secrets. Secrets that I badly want to learn because I just know that they will lead me away from this wretched life I lead.

Just at high sun, I'm finishing with the last outside paddock when Malo scurries up. He throws me a hunk of bread for middle meal. "Make for the top meadow," he orders bluntly, "and do a count. Everyone else is on guard, and Master Boren wants an accounting by the time he gets back. I'll take care of the lower two pastures."

He snaps his fingers at me and gestures at the nearby open glades. "Go! Make it fast and don't force me to come lookin' for you either."

"What about these four?" I ask, pointing at the sprogs rolling around in the dirt.

"Leave'em here," he says in an irritated tone. "I'll fetch'em back to their mothers."

"With pleasure," I mumble under my breath. I can't believe my luck. I not only get away from my dung duties, but I get to leave my pests behind, too. The world must be coming to an end. What else can account for such miracles happening all on the same day?

I hurry over the creek and hasten toward the meadow's center where the bulk of the upper dragon herd now roams. I pass by two drogs, who stand atop a small knoll, watching over the meadows. A bit farther down, I see two more plodding along the tree line.

I give them all a wide berth; nevertheless, the breeze carries their scent, and I scrunch my nose up at the odor. I stare at them and confirm my suspicions. Drogs never bathe and the olive-colored streaks running from their jutting jaws down to their protruding bellies is what I smell.

Dragon blood.

And I have no doubt where it came from, either.

I jerk my head away as I abruptly realize that I've gazed at the closest two for too long, and now they're returning my scrutiny with a hard, threatening stare. I scurry away and glance over my shoulder, once, to make sure they're not trailing. They follow me with their eyes, but thankfully, they stay where they are and let me continue into the meadow.

I hurry on till I'm wading almost knee-high through the pasture's lush grass. The high meadows are a series of three broad and spacious glens that step their way down from Draconstead toward Draconton, where the lower, warmer winter pastures begin.

Most of the dragons are lying in the soft new spring grass and not moving around, which will make my counting a bit easier. Folded tight against their bodies are their leathery wings, held there by body chains, making it impossible for them to fly, and the drog guards ensure that they don't leave the meadows and wander into the forest.

The dragons are free to roam throughout the three expansive green pastures, but the drogs prevent them from going anywhere else. Sometimes, a dragon will try to make its way down to the lower fields where the goat and sheep flocks are kept, but the drogs drive them back, usually.

Last season, a crimson dragon managed to evade the guards and made its way all the way down to the winter meadows. The beast had a grand feast of several heads of mutton, which, though bothersome to Lord Lorell, he wouldn't have minded all that much.

But when the dragon somehow caught m'lord's favorite black stallion for dessert, well, let's just say that we never saw that drog pack leader again. I suspect he became drog stew.

Not only do the drogs keep Draconstead's dragons in the meadows, they also prevent the occasional wild dragon from getting into the glades. The Dragon Master is very careful with his breeding and doesn't want any other dragons, especially wild ones, intermingling with his herd.

And lastly, the brutes ensure that no one but stead workers enter the pastures, either. Lord Lorell has made it known far and wide that if a dragon thief is caught by the drogs attempting to pilfer one of our dragons, m'lord will not turn him over to the king's High Sheriff, or to Draconton's Low Sheriff.

The drogs administer their own brand of justice.

It's been quite a while since anyone tried to steal one of Draconstead's dragons.

I catch sight of one big red moving ponderously near the tree line. It's Wind Thunder, one of Wind Boomer's offspring. Already his size is causing a stir among the Dragon Knights as well as some of the other Houses. They would like nothing better than to have a sire like Wind Thunder in their stables.

Crimson dragons have the hottest fire stream, able to set a grove of trees ablaze with a single pass, and their wings are the strongest and widest. They have the most stamina and are able to carry a Dragon Knight, sometimes two if necessary, far and fast.

Their dragon scales, from horned heads to their long, sinewy tails are akin to metal forged by a skilled blacksmith, and only the deadliest of lances or arrows can pass through and harm the dragon.

Pacing through the meadow, I use my short field knife to cut a large notch in a branch for each red I count. When I'm finished, I have four notches. Then I start with the sapphires. I make a smaller notch for each of those dragons so that I can show Malo the difference in the count.

Sapphires and violet dragons, or as most people call them blues and purples, are smaller than reds, but much faster in the air. Sometimes they're used in fighting, but more often they're used as speedy flyers to carry their riders swiftly to and from almost any point in the kingdom.

Some blues are almost turquoise in coloration. They're sea dragons and spend most of their time in water, usually the deep oceans. Slender and sleek for gliding underwater for long stretches of time, they can fly, but rarely do, preferring to spend their time in seawater.

Phigby once gave me a book that had drawings showing merfolk or MerDraken as they're sometimes called, riding water dragons in the South Ocean, but I'm not sure I believe the illustrations. After all, some books are pure fantasy, you know.

Only in the wild do you find emeralds or green dragons. They're as big as reds, and their dragon fire as powerful. They can fly, but they prefer walking in the thick forests. Sometimes they're called the Protectors or Friends of the Forest.

But that's not what I call them. For me, cold-blooded murderers is a more apt name.

Orange and yellow dragons are also known as sprite dragons, or just plain sprites. Some are not much bigger than my hand, some twice as big as Scamper. They live almost anywhere, forest, mountains, high and low meadows, forest glens and even along the seashore, but you never find them very close to where Drach or other folk live.

They can be shy one minute and intensely curious the next. If you see one in the forest, then quickly look around because there's a good chance that there's probably a dozen or more peeking out from behind the leaves and branches watching you.

Seven dragon types, each the color of the rainbow.

Then there's our golden dragon. She's as big as any green, supposedly as fast or faster than a blue or sapphire, and as powerful as a red. Whether she is or isn't, I really don't care. My hope is that King Leo sends for her quickly, and we're rid of her and the trouble she causes, at least for me.

Among the Great Houses, it is a Forbidden Law for a House to try and steal a golden from another House. If it happens, then there must be war and the remaining Houses will join the offended House's cause against the rogue House. This has happened only once, and the transgressor, the House of Radoc no long exists, and there is no hereditary line of Radoc, nor does anyone carry that surname.

A short while later, I've finished my count and sadly, head back to the stead proper. Even though I had to spend my time around dragons, still it was a bit of a lark for me, and I enjoyed being away from the dull routine of sprog sitting and manure slinging. It even gave me a chance to think about my dragon jewel, but other than getting ahold of Phigby's book, I still have no idea of what to do with the crystal.

After I finish giving my numbers to Malo, he throws my shovel at me and jerks his head toward the far row of stalls. The meaning is clear, get busy. Hooper, the lord and master of all that comes from the south end of a northbound dragon, is back in business.

I've just finished Wind Flame's corral, a crimson dragon who's finishing the last of his sky battle training and will soon go to the

Dragon Knights, when I hear dragon wings overhead. If you've spent practically your entire life around dragons, you know that the sound that each dragon makes while skying is distinct. Just as each person's voice is different, so is the beating of dragon wings.

It's Wind Song, Cara Dracon's sapphire dragon.

I quickly glance upward as Cara guides her dragon in tight circles over the paddock and barn. Her lithe body sits confidently in her saddle while her long, auburn hair streams behind her, whipping back and forth in the rush of wind. Even from here, I can see the gleam in her apple-green eyes as she guides her dragon as if they sky-danced in the air.

I hate looking at dragons, whether they're on the ground or in the air, but I fully admit, I could spend every moment of my day watching Cara on Wind Song.

And, I confess, my eyes wouldn't be on the dragon.

Cara brings Wind Song to a smooth landing and before her dragon has actually settled to the ground, she swings her leg over its neck and slides down its shoulder scales to the ground. My eyebrows go up at the sight of her longbow and quiver over her shoulder.

It's said that Cara is almost as good with a bow as Helmar, not to mention that she's a better dragon rider though he's loathe to admit that to anyone.

However, she typically doesn't take her bow unless she's going stag hunting in the forest and that she never does alone. She too must be carrying her bow because of the Wilder threat.

My eyebrows rise even more when I catch sight of a sword scabbard on her hip. Her blade is naturally shorter than Helmar's. Nevertheless, I can see the hilt's gleam. I knew she had skills with the bow as she and Helmar often hunted together, and from what I know, she was as successful as he in bringing home fresh meat.

But a sword handler, too?

With the nimbleness and grace of a doe in the woods, Cara briskly walks over to the paddock where I stand with my rake in hand. I stop what I'm doing and duck my head low as she approaches.

She opens the gate, steps inside, closes the gate and stands next to the railing giving Wind Flame the once-over before she turns and gives me a tiny nod in acknowledgment. It may have been an afterthought for her to recognize me, but even that small gesture makes me feel as if today is my Day of Miracles, and may it never end.

Cara, unlike her nasty brother, occasionally speaks to me, albeit it's always just a cool greeting. I raise my eyes and murmur, "G'day Mistress Dracon." I try hard not to be too overzealous in my greeting, but it's hard not to where Cara is concerned.

"And to you, Hooper," she answers in that low, husky voice of hers.

She settles her dark forest green tunic around her waist where it meets her even darker brown riding pants. She places her bow and quiver against the lowest fence rail before she climbs to the top rung. There, she sits by bracing herself with her soft, leather boots against the next lower rough plank.

Her eyes are very intent on Wind Flame, and she studies him from his four curved horns, clear to his spiked tail. I, of course, don't interrupt her and stand quietly to one side. "How's Wind Flame doing today?" she asks.

Her question catches me totally off-guard. She's never said more to me than a quick greeting. But to ask me about a dragon, that's a question for her father, or Helmar, or the Dragon Trainers. Not me. Then I remember that Malo said that everyone else is on guard, patrolling the boundary woods around the buildings. I glance around and abruptly realize that I'm the only dragon worker in sight.

I stammer for a bit before I gesture toward the scarlet and say, "Uh, he's fine, miss, just fine."

She's listening, but her eyes are still on the red. "Did he go through his training yesterday?"

That I can answer because I saw the trainers working Wind Flame and two other crimsons through mock sky battles early yesterday morn. "Yes," I quickly respond. "The trainers had him, Spark, and Flash aloft for quite a while before they took up their guard posts."

"Good," she replies. "While father and Helmar are away, I'm to get him ready to turn over to the knights in a few days."

She jumps down to stand next to me. "You can help," she orders.

"Uh, me, ma'am?" I stutter. "I'm not a — "

"I know you're not a trainer," she curtly replies, "but there's no one else and father explicitly ordered me to check on Wind Flame. Besides, Helmar says you know what you're doing around dragons."

I don't move. I'm too stunned. First, I've never been this close to Cara before. Her hair has a faint fragrance like wildflowers, and she and her clothes have the odor of honey-scented soap. She's clean, and her clothes are spotless, whereas I stink of — well, I just stink.

Secondly, Helmar Stoudtman gave me a compliment? I'm thinking that Cara must have heard wrong. But even if it's a mistake, if it gets me this close to Cara, may the mistakes keep coming.

"I want to check his talons first," she commands as she moves next to the red. "They need to be filed sharp as well as his tail spikes. Then we'll inspect his wings, make sure there's no lice in the skin folds' under wings."

I still don't move. She just spoke more to me in the last few moments than in the twelve seasons I've been here. I have one foot in heaven, and the other in hell. I've thought feverishly about having a conversation with her since I first noticed that girls are delightfully different, and Cara the most wonderfully different of all.

But now that the moment has arrived, I can't move, I can't speak, afraid that I'll make a complete fool of myself. I whip my head around, hoping that one of the trainers or even Malo has made his way back to the paddocks, but there's no one in sight.

I turn back to find her staring at me with a frown on her face. She cocks her head to one side and slowly says, "You do move, don't you?"

I swallow, place my rake against the railing and mumble, "Uh, yes, Miss Cara, I do."

"Good, now get over here and lift up his front talons so that I can see."

As I scurry over to Wind Flame's head, Cara commands, "Wind Flame, up!"

The big dragon obediently rises to his feet, and I duck under his neck to hold up the first of his three huge talons on his left foot. One by one, I hold up the other two, holding them until Cara nods at me. We repeat this with each sharply pointed and curved talon until Cara gives a final nod in satisfaction.

It doesn't take long for us to inspect his wings, his horns, his tail spikes, the fitting for his neck saddle and reins and finally his body rivets. Once finished, Cara gives the dragon a good scratching between his eyes while crooning, "You're a good boy aren't you, Flame?"

She steps back, gives him one last scuff between the eyes and announces, "He's ready. Tomorrow, give him a good washing with a stiff brush so that his scales shine."

"Yes ma'am," I dutifully answer.

She strides toward her bow and quiver, quickly dons them and says, "Thank you, Hooper."

"My pleasure, Miss Cara," I murmur.

She starts to open the paddock gate when she suddenly stops and turns back to me. She eyes me for a moment before saying, "Phigby tells me that you like books."

I can't tell by her tone if she's saying that's a good thing or not. I hold my gaze down as I mutter, "Yes, Miss Cara, I do." I raise my eyes and say, "But I don't get too many chances to read, not with the work here, and all."

I see a little gleam in her eyes. "He also told me that when you're down in the lower meadows during the winter you often come to his shop during the night, just to read."

Uh, oh. I've been caught. Master Phigby just opened the barn doors and let the dragons escape. I'm in for it now.

She must have seen the anxious look on my face for she laughs lightly and says, "Don't worry, your secret is safe with me. Besides, I know of only one other person who sneaks out at night to visit the bookstore just to read."

"Really?" I ask. "Who's that?"

"Me," she answers with a straight face. We stare at each other for a moment, before smiles creep over our faces that turn into wide grins.

"So," she asks, "what do you like to read?"

I shrug my shoulders in response. "Oh, most anything, I guess. Master Phigby and I have a deal. When I have the time, he picks out a book for me, and he lets me select one for myself. Of course, I choose those that have the most artist drawings and illustrations. He calls them children's storybooks but I like to look at the pictures."

I frown and grouse. "He chooses books that talk about math or science, or history. No pictures, either."

She throws her head back and laughs. Have you ever heard a beautiful melody that's carried on the wind? Or wind chimes in the breeze? Put the two together and that's Cara's laugh.

She delicately covers her mouth with one hand as she laughs again. "You too?" she says. "I thought I was the only one that Phigby pulled that stunt on. Drives me crazy, too."

I smile at her and say, "Well, since he told on me, I've heard that you've read all of his books, some two or three times."

She sighs in answer. "It's true, I have. I can't wait till he gets a new book so that I can get my hands on it."

"He has a new book," I immediately answer and stop with my mouth open.

I've gone and done the exact opposite of what Master Phigby ordered of me. He specifically told me not to mention that book of his to Cara. Helmar was right, I need a tight leash on my mouth. I'm doomed. When Phigby finds out that I've spilled his secret, I'll be lucky if he doesn't turn me into a pumpkin or a mush melon at the very least.

"He what?" Cara demands. "When did he get it?"

"Uh," I stammer, "well, uh — I — "

"Hooper," she says low, her eyes narrowed, her lips tight as if she would pounce upon me and batter the truth out, which she probably could. "What about this new book?"

I stand there with my mouth open as if I were one of the sprogs trying to catch dragonflies. Cara takes a few steps to stand just in front of me. Her eyes are intense. Beautiful, but intense as if she would bore a hole straight through me with her stare if I don't answer.

I gulp and say, "Well, actually it's not a new book, it's more like —"

"Like what?" she demands.

In a rush of words, I say, "It's more like a book that he's not seen in many seasons, and he needs to find it and read it because it has something to do with witches and an ode and the four moons and the Domain of Vay and — "

"Vay!" she explodes, stopping me with my mouth open, again.

This time, I only nod in answer.

She peers at me with a puzzled expression before she slowly asks, "Why were you and Phigby talking about Vay?"

I swallow and say, "Because I saw a witch in the high meadow last night. She came out of the forest and tried to kill me." I whine like a scared little boy. I'm probably acting like a scared little child too, I think.

Cara must have thought so too, for her eyes hold an amused look. "A witch? Really, Hooper? You think you saw a witch."

Again, I just nod.

Cara's face takes on a puzzled expression. "But you say the Book Master was out in our meadows last night?"

"He found me after that thing went away." I don't say anything about the green dragon, if she doesn't believe me about the apparition, she's certainly not going to believe me about a dragon spirit that glows in the dark.

Besides, I'm afraid that would just lead to more questions, and before you know it, I'll blurt out something about the dragon jewel.

At this point, I don't trust my mouth, at all, and for good reason.

She continues to stare at me before she firmly says, "Hooper, you shouldn't go around saying things like that. Not with this Wilder scare going on. Are you sure you didn't see a Wilder?"

I shake my head in answer. "No Miss Cara, she wasn't a Wilder, believe me."

She narrows her eyes. "Have you told anyone else about this?"

"Only Master Phigby," I reply.

She fiddles with a long strand of her lush hair, still peering at me. "The Domain of Vay," she breathes out. She crinkles her nose in a funny, but charming way that makes her appear as if she's thinking deeply. "And a book," she murmurs, "that talks about her."

She sets her feet and in a commanding manner says, "You stay here. When I'm finished, we're going to the village to see Phigby. We'll see about this witch of yours and that book."

She gets a little gleam in her eye. "Especially that book." She bites on her lower lip, and her voice has an excited tone to it. "A new book and one that I haven't read. And to think that old scoundrel has been holding out on me."

That tears it, I'm done for. This girl has more than a love for books, she craves them. And Phigby? Forget about being turned into a pumpkin. As soon as he finds out what I've done, I'll be a warty toad, or if he's really outraged, a slimy slug.

"Mistress Cara," I appeal, with a little catch in my throat, "I can't do that. You have to understand, Malo would have my hide if I left my work."

"You can if I say you can," she declares, her eyes flashing as if I've insulted her. "After all, I am the Dragon Master's daughter."

"Yes," I sigh, "you are the Dragon Master's daughter." I think to myself, I should be firm and say no because naturally Malo will be gracious and tell her, "Of course, Hooper can go."

However, once I get back, well, I'll be up all night to make up the work that I missed, and he'll probably double my workload tomorrow. Plus, he'll use his Proga lance on me to make sure that I move quickly and smartly about my tasks. Did I mention that I'd go hungry, too?

But I don't say no. Instead, I think of how wonderful it would be to be alone, for even a little while, with the most beautiful girl in the world. Is Cara worth losing a night's sleep over, and having to do double the next day's back-bending labor? Even enduring the Proga and missing a day's worth of meals?

Absolutely.

An idea slowly forms in my head of how I might avoid Malo's punishment. With some hesitation, I say, "I'll make you a deal. Don't say anything to Malo. He goes to bed early so I'll sneak out after dark."

I lower my gaze, as I'm embarrassed at what I have to say next. "It'll take me a little while to get into town, it's a long walk for me, but I'll hurry as fast as I can and meet you at Phigby's shop."

Cara shakes her head. "No," she answers firmly. "It's too long a walk there and back." She eyes me and cocks her head to one side. "You're kind of anxious about my speaking to Malo, aren't you?"

"Uh, anxious would be more than an understatement."

She crosses her arms, and I can see the fingers of one hand tapping on her forearm. They suddenly stop as if she's made a decision. "All right, we'll do it your way. I won't say anything to Malo. However, when it's fully dark, meet me by the stepping-stones that cross the brook. We'll sky down to Draconton together on Wind Song and afterward, I'll bring you back here."

She gives me a little smile. "You won't have to walk, Malo won't have to know, and we'll see Phigby together to talk about your witch." Her smile turns into a grin. "And I'll get a look at his new book. Deal?"

I let out my breath. I really, really don't want to ride on her dragon. Painful as it might be to walk the distance, I'd rather endure that than sky on a stinking dragon. However, she did say we'd ride together, and that means I'll have to sit very, very close to her. I might even have to put my arms around her waist to hold on. How can I say no?

"Stepping stones when it's completely dark," I answer. "I'll be there."

"Good," she replies and actually giggles. "This will be fun, sneaking out and all. Besides, we'll have Phigby all to ourselves, his shop will be closed, no customers to bother us and a brand-new book to explore."

She settles her bow and quiver over her shoulder and starts for the gate but stops. "And Hooper," she says, "stop with the 'miss' this and 'mistress' that. Just call me Cara, all right?"

I duck my head and smile. "Yes miss — I mean, yes . . . Cara."

With that, she smiles, lifts the gate bar and heads off through the paddocks, leaving me to watch the most beautiful, and perhaps the most stubborn girl in the world practically dance toward the birthing barn.

I pick up my rake and toss it into my wheelbarrow. Up until now, life hasn't seemed very fair, but starting tonight, maybe, just maybe life has decided that a little goodness should finally come my way.

Besides that, while Cara distracts Master Phigby, perhaps I can sneak a look at his dragon jewel book. If so, and it can show me how to work my jewel, then maybe more than just a little goodness will come my way after tonight.

Now, that would indeed be a miracle.

7

The rest of the day goes along like most of my days. I add more dung to the manure pile, feed and water dragons, and stay out of Malo's way as much as possible. Time seems to move more slowly than usual, though. I keep looking up at the sun, hoping to see it slide ever closer to the horizon, marking sunset.

Finally, the call for last meal sounds. I hurry through my food, the butt end of a loaf of bread, a small slice of goat cheese, and a bowl of thin soup made of carrots, potatoes, plus a tiny portion of meat that I can't identify. It may be a slice of rodent rump for all I know. When you're next to starving, you just eat, even if it's mystery meat that you're chewing.

I make my way to my little corner of the barn, thinking that with the sun setting Scamper will be there. He isn't, but I'm not too worried. Scamper lives by his own schedule, which means he comes and goes as he chooses. I put a small piece of cheese that I've saved from my meal in the straw for him and settle down to anxiously wait.

The evening darkens, and it isn't long before Malo comes through the barn making his final rounds. As he passes by, I pretend to be asleep, even though I am more awake and on edge than I've ever been before. It will just be my luck that Malo gives me some late evening chores. Moreover, that means he may just stay up later than usual checking on me.

Even with my eyes closed, I can feel his lantern's light on me. I hold my breath as he stops at the end of my straw bed and stays there for what seems like a thousand and one heartbeats. I just know he is going to kick me awake to go do some task, but miracle of miracles, he moves on.

I wait until I hear the side door close shut before I let my breath out in one long rush. My arms flop to each side in nervous relief, and I let my face break out in a big grin.

Since Scamper hasn't returned yet, I decide that the little tub is just going to have to be on his own tonight. I tiptoe to the side door and cautiously open it a crack. I peek out just in time to see Malo enter the far end of the long, low hut that serves as the sleeping quarters for the rest of the Draconstead workers.

Without making a sound, I step outside, scoot around the barn's near corner and keeping next to the paddock rails, hobble down the trail, and cross the stream. I'm not sure just how Cara is going to see me in the dark, but this is where she said to meet.

I don't have long to wait. I spot a dark figure gliding through the night sky, blotting out the stars as it silently sails toward me. Then comes the rustling of dragon wings and with a soft thump, Wind Song's talons bite into the dirt.

As fast as I can, I amble over to the sleek sapphire and smile up at Cara. "Smart, gliding your dragon through the air like that. I barely heard her land."

"Of course," she replies with a thin smile. "Don't want anyone to hear us, right?"

"Right," I answer.

Cara bends over to say firmly, "Wind Song, leg."

Her dragon juts out one leg and using it somewhat like a small ladder, one with scales, of course, I climb awkwardly toward the saddle. Cara reaches out with a hand to help me up the last bit, and I settle in behind her. There's not enough room for me to sit on her dragon saddle, so I sit just behind on Wind Song's neck scales.

Dragon saddles are very similar to horse saddles, including stirrups, reins, and saddlebags. However, a sapphire's saddle is a bit less broad than other dragon saddles as they're smaller beasts. Dragon saddles are also more supple than stiff horse saddles, so as to allow the dragon freedom to move its neck naturally.

I knew from seeing her sky before, that Cara dislikes reins and uses voice, hand, and knee commands to guide her dragon. I've even seen her ride Wind Song without a saddle, but tonight she has her saddle strapped to Wind Song's neck.

I'm not sure what to do with my hands, so I don't do anything with them. "Uh, Cara before we start, you need to know something. This is my first time to sky on a dragon."

She turns her head and in the starlight, I can see her amazed expression. "Are you serious, Hooper?"

I swallow hard. We're not even off the ground, yet we're already pretty high up, and that's causing my stomach to churn a bit. "Uh, no, I mean yes, I'm serious. Cara, your father doesn't let dragon workers take rides on his dragons, you know. Trainers do, but not someone like me. So, you'd better give me a few pointers, and I suggest that you start by telling me how to hang on."

I can see her frown and shake her head slightly as if she's now sorry that she suggested this idea. With a little sigh, she says, "Squeeze your legs against Wind Song's neck and wrap your arms around my waist. I'll do the rest."

I slide my arms around her slim waist but only partway. "Like that?" I ask.

"A little tighter and all the way until your hands clasp together."

I scoot closer and clasp my hands together in a tight grip. "Good," she says. "Just make sure you hang on." She eyes me over her shoulder. "If you start to fall, you're on your own, I'm not falling off with you."

I nod in answer, and she leans over to pat Wind Song's neck twice. Wind Song's ears flick back toward us and quietly, Cara says, "Sky, Wind Song."

Her dragon unfurls its wings, cups them high, and then seems to gather herself before she literally springs into the air. I close my eyes for several moments before I get up the courage to open them.

Instead of following the open meadows toward Draconton, Wind Song is winging over the woodlands. The trees are a dark, thick carpet below us, so close that I feel as if I let go of Cara I could step off her dragon and walk on top of the leaves.

The wind is cool, but not cold and Cara's warmth and my closeness to her is more than enough for me. Her hair whips against my face, but I don't mind as all I can smell is the aroma of wildflowers.

As far as I'm concerned, we could sky all night, and I wouldn't care one bit.

All too soon, the lights of Draconton come into view and Cara has Wind Song gliding down toward a meadow shrouded in shadow on the far outskirts of town. Wind Song hovers above the grassy earth and just by hand and knee signals alone, Cara has her dragon set us gently on the ground.

With Cara's help, I clamber down and wait for her to join me. "Now, that wasn't all that bad, was it?" she asks as she jumps off Wind Song's leg. "And you didn't fall off."

"No," I admit, thinking to myself, as long as I'm with you, there's nothing in the world that could ever be bad.

She adjusts her tunic and brushes back her hair. "Ready? We've a bit of a walk, but Phigby's shop isn't that far."

"I'm ready," I reply and then ask, a little puzzled, "Cara, why did we land here? You could've set your dragon down a lot closer."

She sniffs and begins pacing toward town. "Didn't want to be seen."

"Oh," I answer. She doesn't want to be seen with me, I think. She'd be embarrassed if it was known around town that she was with Hooper, the Dung Master. I hurry to catch up with her and mumble, "Any particular reason you don't want to be seen?"

"Actually, an excellent reason," she quickly answers while ducking low under a tree branch. "My father and brother aren't due back until morning. It wouldn't be seemly if someone spotted the

Dragon Master's only daughter out at night when neither he nor her brother was at home."

"Oh," I reply in sudden understanding and nod to myself. That was something I hadn't even thought about. Cara's mother died several seasons back when River Fever swept through the villages that dot the Lorell Valley. With her father and brother away, the expectation would be that she wouldn't leave the house without ample cause, or without a suitable chaperone.

And skying at night with a Hooper is not an adequate reason, nor would I be judged an appropriate escort. In fact, if that ever got back to her father, well, she would get a firm scolding. Me? I'd receive my reprimand in the punishment stocks for sure.

We slip around several trees and skirt a thistle hedge, careful not to hook ourselves on its thorns. Cara halts us beside a downed log to peer toward town. Only a few lights from cottage lanterns or candles show through the overhanging tree limbs. I can see her chewing on her lower lip before she glances at me sideways and murmurs, "Do you and Helmar talk much?"

My eyebrows come together as I frown. What kind of question is that? Why does she need to know what Helmar and I talk about? Then my eyes widen slightly in understanding. She wants to know if we talk about her. My eyes grow even wider as I realize that she doesn't want to know what I say about her, but what Helmar has to say.

As if the sun had suddenly popped up into the sky, it dawns on me.

Cara likes Helmar and in a way that tells me that she wants him to like her, too, and perhaps as more than just friends.

Once, Master Phigby had come to Draconstead to brew up one of his concoctions for a sick dragon. He'd poured various liquids, leaves, and tiny white granules that appeared like salt, but weren't, in a large swan-neck glass flask. A bubble formed at the bottle's mouth and kept growing larger. Phigby had turned to me with a little smile and asked, "Want to pop it?"

I quickly nodded, and he handed me a tiny needle. I poked the bubble and instantly it vanished with a big popping sound. That's how I felt right now. Cara had just stabbed my bubble of dreams, leaving me feeling empty and with my hopes vanished in an instant. A Hooper cannot and will not ever be able to compete against the likes of a Helmar.

Reality had just crushed my grand adventure with Cara. I glanced up to see her questioning expression. She expected an answer. "Not much," I truthfully answer. "But he did say that the other night when he had dinner at Dracon Haus, he wished your father and Master Phigby hadn't talked so much. He wanted to speak with you, but couldn't because of them."

I watch as a small, satisfied smile grows on her face. "Oh, he did, did he?" Her smile grows and then she waves me on with a quick, "Come on, it's getting late."

We pace a bit farther before she slows and raises a hand. I start to speak, but Cara quickly puts a finger to her lips. "Shush." She points straight ahead. We're at the very edge of town, and Phigby's place is directly in front of us. His home sits atop his store, and although the shop is dark, I can see a light shining through an upstairs window.

"Good," Cara whispers. "He's still awake."

Since she doesn't want to be seen, I say, "We'll knock on the back door, right?"

"No," Cara replies tartly. "We do not knock."

"Why not? How else is Master Phigby going to know we're here?"

"And have someone hear us and then peek out a window and see me? I said I couldn't be seen Hooper, remember?"

Oh. That's embarrassing. I can feel my face grow warm. I've done it again, said something that she considers stupid. "What do we do?" I mutter.

She points to the thick oaken tree that grows at one corner of the shop. Its thick limbs form a natural, if leafy, ladder up to Phigby's second-story window. "We climb."

"Climb?" I stammer.

"Sure," she replies and turns to gaze at me with an amused expression. "You do climb?"

I start to answer that I climb about as well as I ride a dragon, but this time I keep those thoughts to myself and instead reply, "Of course."

"Let's go, then." She dashes across the short open space between the forest line and the oak tree. I do my best to keep up, but I'm no match for her speed. By the time I'm at the base of the thick trunk, she's already scurrying up the tree as if she were part squirrel.

She gestures for me to hurry and I shake my head to myself, wondering why she's in such a rush. It's not like the Book Master is going anywhere. Besides, in my mind, what will happen is that we'll get to the window, knock, Master Phigby will open the window, see who it is and promptly close and lock the window shutters on us.

And that means Cara won't get a chance to read Master Phigby's new book, and I won't have an opportunity to get at his dragon jewel volume. Which will be disappointing, but at least, I got to be alone with Cara, even if I did have to ride on her smelly dragon.

Ever so slowly, I pull myself along, grabbing onto the smaller limbs and hoisting myself up to the next higher branch. I find that trying to balance on my bad leg while standing on a swaying tree bough while reaching for the next branch is close to impossible. I'm just glad that there's no stiff breeze because if the tree were swaying, by now I probably would have somersaulted to the ground.

And ended up with something broken, no doubt after nose-diving face-first into the short, prickly grass that surrounds the tree.

Cara is already at the top and peering into the window. I reach up to grab the next limb while tottering on the one I'm standing on when Cara drops some bark on my head to get my attention.

"What's wrong?" I mouth silently.

She anxiously waves for me to climb up to her perch where she's wrapped her stomach over one limb while leaning toward the window. Grunting to myself, I pull myself up until I have my belly on the same branch. With wide eyes, she points at the window. I manage to push myself up close enough so that I can peer through the square cut glass.

For a moment, I'm not exactly sure at what I'm looking. Then as if my eyes finally clear, I realize that I must be gazing into the room where Master Phigby mixes his potions and medicines.

Covering one wall is a large bookcase that has a combination of books, jugs, and small bottles on its shelves. Against another wall is a long, low table where several large flasks with thin, crane-like necks sit on round burners that give off tiny flames. From each curved bottle rise small wisps of smoke or steam that curl up almost to the ceiling.

In the room's center, Phigby is slowly moving his hands above a large, leather-bound book that sits on an ornate pedestal.

I lean even farther, to see better and then I realize that the window is slightly ajar, and I can hear Phigby's voice. First, it's quiet and deep, then it rises in pitch and loudness, then lowers again. It stays that way until his speech begins to grow louder and louder. I can hear what he's saying, but his words sound like he's speaking in some unknown language. It's pure gibberish to me.

He raises his hands high over his head, cries out in a booming voice, and in a blur of motion brings his arms straight down. There's a sound like lightning streaking across the sky and a great cloud of smoke rises from the floor. The smoky haze covers Phigby and most of the room.

When the fog clears, Phigby is holding the book in front of him. He stares at it, and then with an exasperated growl, starts to vigorously shake it back and forth as if he's trying to jiggle the book open. He does that for a bit before he stops and brings it closer, turning it over slowly as if he's eyeing every part of the cover and its edging.

As he turns the book on its side, my eyes widen. The pages are sealed. There's a silver-coated strip, two fingers wide in size that runs from the book's back up over the front edges where it slips under a gleaming, ruby-colored half orb. The half sphere seems to be some sort of locked clasp.

Phigby pulls and yanks at the silver strap and buckle, but it doesn't loosen, and no matter what he does, he can't pry the pages open. Apparently frustrated after several attempts to undo the binding and failing, he slams the book down on the pedestal, blows out his candles, and stalks away.

I wait a few moments before whispering, "What was that all about?"

"I don't know," Cara murmurs. "I've never seen him act that way before. Whatever it was, it has something to do with that book. And I've never seen anything quite like it, either."

She turns to me, and her eyes are full of a mischievous gleam. She breathes out, "A sealed book that he can't open."

She gives me a sly look and grins. "But maybe we can." She pushes herself up higher on the branch and reaches for the window edge. I almost fall from the tree as I gurgle, "Wait, what are you doing? You can't go inside, Master Phigby didn't invite us."

"Hooper," she whispers, "I've got to get my hands on that book. I've heard of such things, but I've never seen one before. Isn't this exciting?"

"Wait," I stammer, realizing just what she's saying. "You're going to steal it?"

"Keep your voice down," she orders. "I'm not stealing it, I'm borrowing it. Phigby lets me borrow his books all the time."

She gives me an impish smile. "Besides, I'm his best customer, he knows I'll bring it back first thing."

"Cara," I implore, "this is not a good idea. What if we get caught?"

"Oh, bosh," she replies. "I won't get caught. He's a sound sleeper." She stops and tilts an ear toward the window. "Hear that? He's snoring already."

I lean closer to the window and cock an ear toward the opening. "I can't hear anything," I say accusingly. "You're making that up."

She shrugs. "I can't help it if you can't hear him snoring, I certainly can." With that, she reaches out, puts her fingers through the small opening, and slowly pulls the window open. She has it almost wide enough for her body to slip through when the window lets out a loud creeeaaak ...

We both freeze in place, not moving, not daring to breathe. We wait. I'm entirely sure that Phigby will come roaring back into the room to see who's trying to break into his home. Once that occurs, I'm also quite sure that absolutely nothing will happen to Cara, but as for me, well, in all honesty, can it get any worse?

Yes, it could. I could be spending the next fortnight in the penance stocks in the middle of the town square. The villagers threw rotten tomatoes at the last fellow they had bound between the wooden planks.

I have a sudden image of me with my head and arms through the stocks' holes. I'm being pelted with spoiled fruit, it's moldy red pulp and slimy, foul juice flowing down my face and into my mouth.

I reach out to stop Cara, but before I can, she has the window wide open. Then, as if she's been a practicing burglar all her life, she's through the window and standing in the room. Silent as a cat, she tiptoes across the chamber until she reaches the pedestal. Her hands glide over the book as if she's lovingly caressing the leather covering. She picks up the manuscript and turns, holding it triumphantly aloft.

I frantically wave for her to hurry back outside as I'm certain we've pushed our luck to the very limit. She gives me that impish grin of hers again, retraces her steps back to the window and holds the book out for me to take so that she can clamber out. I hesitate, but Cara gives me a death look so I reach out with both hands and grasp the leather-bound volume tightly.

It's surprisingly light, which is good, because my balancing act on the limb is causing me to sway back and forth. I'm one misstep away from mimicking a baby bird trying its wings out for the first time as it heads straight down to the ground.

Cara climbs out, grabs the book from me, and practically races down the tree. My trip down is a lot faster than going up, mainly because I want to get out of that tree as quickly as possible. By the time my feet hit the ground I'm sweating and sucking in air as if I've just pushed a hundred wheelbarrows of dragon dung up a steep mountainside.

Cara isn't even breathing hard. She pulls at my arm, and at a stumbling pace, I follow her mad dash to the tree line. Once inside the first stand of trees, I huff, "Cara, where are you going? You said you just wanted to look at the book."

"I do, silly," she answers. "But in the light. It's too dark in here to see anything. C'mon, quit dragging your feet."

Actually, I'm only dragging one foot, but I'm not going to argue the point and follow her as best as I can in the darkness. It's not long before we push through the last bit of brush into the small meadow where Wind Song has lain waiting. She raises her head to stare intently at us. One good thing about dragons is that once a dragon bonds to its rider, they can somehow sense that person from a long way off.

If not, and Wind Song hadn't recognized us, there's a good chance that she would have done something bad, like whip her tail around and skewer us with her twin spikes.

I stumble over to the beast, breathing hard, and lean up against one leg, trying to catch my breath. Cara looks at me and laughs. "Now, that wasn't too hard, was it? We're a good pair of burglars, Hooper."

"Sure," I reply, "as long as you don't get caught, you're a great burglar."

She laughs again, but before she can reply, Wind Song suddenly springs to her feet, knocking me to the ground. Her ears and head swivel toward the town and from deep in her throat comes a menacing snarl. Cara's smile instantly evaporates. She puts a hand on Wind Song's neck. "What's wrong, girl?"

In answer, Wind Song rips up the ground with her talons and growls long and low again.

Then I hear it; the most dreadful, horrible sound in the world and the one thing that I never, ever want to hear in my life again.

Dragon fire.

And the screams of those caught in its fiery, scalding stream of death.

8

From beyond the dark line of spruce trees, a blazing crimson torrent spews from the sky, then another and another. The brilliant streams of fire cast the slim trees in garish, spiked shadows. A deafening hissing fills the night as if the dragon breath is scorching the very air. Fireballs of red and orange erupt from exploding buildings sending fiery fragments that arc outward like shooting stars before they sputter and dim as they float and waft over the treetops.

Cara doesn't hesitate but darts toward the village, leaving me to follow as best as I can with my limping gait. I push through a last overhanging branch to join her at the tree line where we both stare in shock and in disbelief.

Tongues of fire leap skyward from thatched roofs where an inferno of scarlet and orange flames consumes a whole row of side-board houses. Just moments before, they wore bright paints the color of red cherries, golden tassels of corn, and sky blue.

Now, their outsides turn black from the blistering heat. Charcoal-colored molten slag oozes to the ground from those few houses with actual glass windows. In the rooftops' spreading flames, I can see more dark shapes swoop down, spraying fire into the helpless town.

Cara grabs my arm, her fingers tight and hard against my skin. "Wilders! They're attacking the village!"

I can't tear my eyes away from the dragon fire, and my whole body starts to tremble. I can hear screams of pain, shrieks of terror, but they're not from the townspeople. Seemingly, in the distance, I hear a ghostly voice urgently calling, "Run, Hooper! Run!"

I whirl and dash back toward the meadow. I push through thicket after thicket trying to escape not just the firestorm behind but the inferno that fills my memories. I rush past a scraggly bush and from the shadows a hand grabs my tunic and spins me around.

Cara holds me in a fierce grip. I struggle to get away, but she won't let me go and tightens her grasp even more. Her mouth is moving, but I can't hear what she's saying. I know she's speaking, but I don't listen to a single word. My heart is pounding, I can't breathe, and I feel as if everything around me is whirling, spinning, and I can't make it stop.

I stare at Cara as if I don't recognize her before she shakes me so hard that my head snaps back and forth. Cara's voice is so loud that it startles me. "Hooper, what's wrong with you? We've got to get out of here."

"Out of here?" I murmur. "Yes, of course, we've got to run, get away."

"Run?" she snaps. "No, we've got to get back to Draconstead — now."

"Draconstead? No . . . No," I hurriedly mumble. "We've got to get away; the dragons — the dragons are coming for us."

Cara stares at me and shakes me again. Her lips are pinched together, and there's a hardness about her face that I've never seen before. "Hooper, I have no idea what you're talking about. The Wilders aren't after us, they're after the golden. C'mon, we've got to get to Wind Song."

Cara loosens her grip and races away. I try to keep up with her, but my stumbling steps are no match for her frenzied dash. I finally catch up with her in the meadow. I stop to catch my breath and run a hand over my face; it comes away so covered in sweat it's as if I'd dipped my hand in a bucket of water.

Cara's picked up Phigby's book that she dropped and is climbing up Wind Song's leg toward her saddle. "Cara," I call out, "what are you doing?"

"I told you," she snaps back. "I'm skying to Draconstead. The Wilders are here to steal the golden, but I'm not going to let them."

"The golden," I mumble, trying to clear my head.

"If you're coming," Cara orders in a no-nonsense tone, "then get up here. Otherwise, I'm leaving you behind." She slaps the book into the leather pouch that hangs to one side of her saddle, tightens down the straps that hold her bow and quiver, and peers at me. Her eyes are narrow and hard. She's determined to go, with or without me.

"Cara," I plead, "wait."

I hold up my hands, imploring, desperate to stop her. "It's one thing to sneak into Master Phigby's house, it's another to go against armed Wilders. We haven't got a chance. Don't do this, please."

I take a few steps forward, still imploring. "Besides, that's what the drogs and the king's knights are there for, remember? They'll protect the golden."

From Wind Song's saddle, Cara leans down, her long hair almost covering her face. "Hooper, I can't depend on the drogs or the knights protecting Golden Wind, so I'm going." Her eyes soften just a bit, and she murmurs, "I could really use your help to save her."

She pauses for a moment before saying, "And if I remember right, don't you have a special friend that you'd like to save?"

My breath catches. Scamper. In my confusion and fear, I've forgotten about Scamper. My own fright, the ghosts that haunt me, pushed Scamper completely out of my mind. By now, he should have made it back to the barn, the same barn where the rampaging Wilders will be if they're after the golden. Will he stay hidden or will his curiosity bring him out in the open, an easy target for a Wilder arrow?

In my mind's eye, I see Scamper's lifeless body, pierced by a Wilder shaft and left behind, perhaps to be found by a drog, who would think nothing of eating him on the spot. A flame of anger ignites inside of me.

I climb up Wind Song's leg and slide in behind Cara. "Let's go," I say firmly as I wrap my arms around her waist. "I have no doubt that we're both going to die, but I can't just leave Scamper. He wouldn't leave me . . . "

I suck in a breath. "I won't leave him."

Cara settles into the saddle deeper. "We're not going to die," she states, "but if I get the chance, I know some people that won't see another dawn." She strokes Wind Song's neck and commands, "Sky, girl, sky."

We shoot into the air, and Cara immediately dips Wind Song's wings away from the burning town so that we won't be cast in its blazing light. We flew just above the forest before, now we're so low that Wind Song's dangling talons slash through the topmost thin branches leaving a wake of shredded leaves and broken limbs behind.

I glance over my shoulder at Draconton. Against the red sky, I see dozens of dark crimson bodies and wings circling over the town, like vultures above a dead or dying animal. I pick out Master Phigby's shop. Roof, gables, walls, all are in flames. For several beats of Wind Song's wings, the fire mesmerizes me, as I know exactly what the inferno means. I drop my gaze in sadness at the loss of Master Phigby.

Cara has her eyes forward, guiding Wind Song over the trees. She must have sensed that I was looking back because she asks over her shoulder, "How bad is it?"

"Bad," is all I reply.

"Can you see my home?" she asks with a catch in her voice.

I glance back again. Dracon Haus, set apart with its manicured lawn and twice as large as any building in Draconton is easy to pick out in the firelight. "Yes," I answer. There's no need to say more, like everything else in the village, the Dracon family's ancestral home is burning from thatched roof clear to the ground.

I can feel Cara take several shuddering breaths and a little sob escapes her lips. Then her body stiffens, and she asks in a hard voice, "What about the Wilders?"

"They're everywhere, but, I don't think they see us, no one's following."

I peer ahead toward Draconstead. I'm grateful to see no fires and no dragons in the air, but that doesn't mean they're not there. Red dragons are very hard to see at night unless there's moonlight, which there isn't just yet.

"I don't see any dragons," I say into Cara's ear. "But to be on the safe side we shouldn't land too close, we might be seen."

"I agree," she calls back. "We're going to have to hike a bit."

It's not long before Cara points ahead. "There."

A small meadow, set a good piece away from the open space that surrounds Draconstead comes into view. It's a tight fit for Wind Song, but Cara skillfully guides her to a soft landing.

I slide off Wind Song, quickly followed by Cara. She shoulders her quiver, grasps her bow firmly and snugs her scabbard against her waist. "If we get separated, meet at the woodpile, it has the best-concealed view of the birthing barn."

I quickly shake my head in reply. "I don't plan on getting separated from the girl with the bow and sword."

"Then stay close and be quiet," she answers.

Cara sets a steady pace, and I follow right behind her. The shadows are so dark that the few openings between the trees are murky pools of ebony silence. I peer through the few breaks in the treetops for dragon wings, but the trees are too high and set too close together for me to get a good view of the sky.

I marvel how silently Cara moves through the forest while my stumbling gait is so loud it would wake a hibernating bear. After a bit, Cara stops and whips around with an exasperated sigh. "Hooper, I've heard rooting boars in the underbrush that are quieter than you. Watch where you step. Try to place your feet on grass, rocks, or bare soil, not branches, twigs, or leaves.

"Don't brush against the bushes or scrape up against the bark of a tree. If you push aside a branch, don't let it snap back, but ease it in place. Move your eyes back and forth between the ground and where you're going to step. Just think about your next step before you go there."

I lick my lips and murmur, "I'll try to do better."

She gives me a wan smile and turns. I follow and soon find that I'll never match her abilities, but using her advice, I'm much quieter and actually move a bit faster through the forest. We haven't gone far when I hear the loud rustling of dragon wings overhead.

I throw myself under a nearby tree's spreading branches and lie still, hoping that the Wilder rider doesn't spot us. The beating of wings moves off, and I crawl out from under the limbs. "Cara?" I whisper.

There's no answer.

I take a few tentative steps and murmur, "Cara, where are you?" I peer into the darkness while turning completely around, but she's nowhere to be seen.

She's gone, and I'm alone with rampaging Wilders nearby and only a tiny work knife for protection.

A cold, clammy fear grips my heart, and my breathing comes hard and fast. I sound like the cook's wheezing bellows when they stoke their fireplace so that the fire becomes bright and hot.

I crinkle my forehead remembering that Cara said that if we became separated, to make for the woodpile. I turn in the direction that I believe leads to the cut logs and slowly move forward. The trees start to thin, which is a good sign that I'm headed in the right direction and the open space lets in more starlight to see by, too.

In the near distance, I can make out a low-slung building. I stop to study it for a bit before I nod to myself. It's the meal house. I turn left, keeping the hut to my right. Just beyond the next stand of trees should be the woodpile and Cara.

A noise from the dark makes me stop dead in my tracks. What was that? I glance around, but in the gloom, I don't see or hear anyone. I take a few more steps when the sound comes again.

Someone's moaning in pain.

I suck in a breath. I can see a figure standing up against a tree at the very edge of the forest. I can't see a face, but for some reason, I think I know this person. As silently as I can, I creep closer to the still figure. I slide around the outstretched limbs of a small spruce and stop. I stand motionless, my eyes locked in horror.

It's Hakon.

There's a drog spear pinning his body to the trunk of a birchen tree. Dark blood streams from his ghastly wound, staining the white bark.

I stumble back; only to whirl around in terror when I hear a loud moan right next to my ear. It's Arnie. He too has a shaft in him, only this lance hasn't only pierced his body, it's gone completely through the birchen tree as well. Even as I watch, his chin drops to his chest, and a long, gurgling breath escapes his lips.

His last.

I can't move, I can hardly breathe, and I can't take my eyes off Arnie. He was mean and hateful to me, but even in my wildest imaginations, I wouldn't wish such an excruciating death on him or Hakon, for that matter. I don't know how long I stand there before I feel a hot, evil-smelling breath on my neck.

I spin around. Sorg is leering at me and behind him are a half-dozen drogs, their lances lowered straight at me. Sorg's face is in shadow, but his malicious expression is evident enough. I'm drog meat and before I can move a spear will run me through, just like Hakon and Arnie, who hang lifeless against the tree trunks.

A loud whoosh sounds right next to my ear, so close that I instinctively jerk my head to one side. When I turn back, the eyes of the drog standing next to Sorg stare straight ahead, but with an arrow jutting out between its sightless orbs. The brute doesn't move, just stands there.

He's dead, but he doesn't realize it, yet.

Like a great tree that topples over ever so slowly after a woodsman's sharp ax has split it open, the beast tips over backward. Stunned, the drogs don't move. Then, Sorg bellows but another arrow cuts the air and a drog shrieks in terror and spins to the ground.

The drogs frantically scatter but not before a third brute falls to his knees, clutching at the arrow embedded in his throat.

Ochre-colored blood spews from his mouth and he gurgles and gasps in his death throes. In the chaos and bedlam to get away from the unseen deadly archer, the drogs completely forget about me.

Seemingly from out of nowhere, Cara dashes into the fray, grabs me by my shoulder and shoves me so hard that I stagger and almost fall. "Run!" she orders.

She notches another arrow and lets it fly. A drog scream fills the night in answer.

It's amazing what terror can do to a person. Sometimes it can make every thought leave your mind, leaving you numb and frozen, unable to act, do, or even think. And sometimes it can make your body and mind behave in ways they never have before.

For once in my life, I'm able to run almost like an ordinary person. My bent leg is pumping right along with my good one. I scramble through the forest brambles, pushing aside branches and brush with both hands. I run hard and with a purpose.

I'm running for my life.

Head and stomach first, I roll over a long log that abruptly appears out of the darkness. I fall awkwardly to the hard earth and then scramble to one side where I push my back against the fallen tree's rough bark. I swallow hard trying to quiet my heavy breathing and thumping heart.

I sit for a moment, not moving, just listening. I hear drogs grunting and cursing in the distance but little else.

I anxiously look in all directions. Where is Cara? Did she not follow me? I bite down on my lip and taste dirt and leaves. I start to push myself up when my hand presses up against a stout limb that's come away from the fallen tree trunk.

I begin to toss it aside but stop. I heft it in my hand. It's not only solid, it's twice as long as my arm. I think to myself that something this thick will surely crack open the stoutest of drog skulls if one of them tries to attack me again.

I need to reach the woodpile as quickly as possible. I'm sure that's where Cara headed after saving me from those crazed beasts. The question is whether she's going to wait for me. I'm totally amazed and in awe of Cara. She's like an avenging warrior, only instead of using a sword to wreak vengeance, she's using her bow.

I can't hear the drogs anymore, but, that doesn't matter, their nauseating smell will undoubtedly alert me that they're nearby. I slip around the thick log's gnarled end and hunched over, make for the woodpile.

As I slide around a large tree trunk, like a viper's sudden strike a hand reaches out, grabs my tunic, and all but slams me against the tree. "Just where do you think you're going?" Cara whispers furiously in my ear.

I take one look at her beautiful face and let out a long breath. "It's you," I sputter and then state, "the woodpile. You said to meet there if we got separated. Well, we got separated."

Cara shakes her head at me. "You're going the wrong way, Hooper. The woodpile is in the other direction." She glances down at the stout branch I'm carrying. "What's that for?"

I hold it up and shake it a bit. "A drog head if one gets too close."

Her short laugh is sharp, unflattering. She points at my branch and cocks her head to one side. "You're going to take on a drog with that?"

I grasp my skull basher a little tighter. "If one gets too close, yes."

Cara shakes her head and slaps at my knobby branch, sending it tumbling from my grasp. "Don't be a fool, Hooper. You wouldn't get within two arm's lengths with that before they'd run you through like they did with Hakon and Arnie."

She reaches down and holds up a longbow and a quiver of arrows. She shoves them hard into my chest. "You want to kill drogs? Then learn to use this."

I stare wide-eyed at my bow. Me? Use a longbow? I peer at my supposed skull basher where she'd knocked it down into the crushed grass. She's right. If I tried to club a drog, I wouldn't get within five steps of one before they'd gut me with a lance, leaving my lifeblood to pool and redden the ground under my dead body.

"Where'd this come from?" I ask, holding the bow and quiver out.

"From a Wilder who won't need it anymore," she curtly replies.

"You killed a Wilder?" I sputter.

"Yes," she replies and leans in close to mutter, "and I'm going to kill more." She taps on the bow. "You might want to be more alert than its previous owner."

"So there are Wilders here," I say breathlessly.

Cara pulls me close, her eyes are centered on mine. "Listen Hooper, and listen well. We've been betrayed." She glances around to make sure that we've not been spotted. "The Wilders and the drogs are working together."

"No . . . " I breathe out.

I can see her bite down hard on her lip. Then she says with a catch in her voice, "And most likely the message for my father to meet at the Manor House was a ruse, to get him, my brother, and Helmar away from here."

I quickly grasp her meaning. "They were lured away on purpose?"

She gives me a quick nod and in the starlight, I can see the anxiety in her eyes. "Do you know if . . . " I start.

"No," she quickly replies, "and I'm not going to assume the worst until I know for sure."

I hang my head for a moment, my stomach is in a knot, but I have to ask, "The other workers?"

She shakes her head sadly. "From what I can tell, all dead."

It's what I feared. The Wilders and drogs have killed everyone. "Where are the knights? They should be here by now."

Cara shakes her head and mutters, "I don't know, Hooper. Maybe they're all dead too."

I draw in a deep breath and mumble, "So what do we do?"

She hesitates before saying, "We can't do anything for the dead. It's time for those who still live, to live still."

She places her hand on my shoulder. "The drogs know we're here and more than likely Sorg went to get reinforcements for a bigger hunting party — with us as the quarry. Are you still willing to help me save the golden, Hooper?"

My eyes meet hers. I'm trembling, shaking at the sudden realization that at any moment either a party of murderous drogs or Wilders could show up and kill both of us. Her face seems to first grow large and then shrink, and I'm none too steady on my feet.

Cara grips the front of my tunic, shakes me and hisses, "Hooper, are you still with me?"

I swallow and squeak, "I want to find Scamper."

"And the golden?" she presses.

I take a breath and though it pains me, I say, "You saved my life, I'll help you."

She gives me a grateful smile and turns away. "What now?" I murmur.

"We need to get a look at the barn," she answers. Her voice is harsh, guttural. "For all I know, they may have taken the golden already."

She points off to one side. "The woodpile is in that direction. It's the only place that we can see the barn from this side without being seen ourselves." She glances around first to make sure no one is nearby before whispering, "Let's go, and this time try to stay with me."

I nod, and just for an instant, glance back in the direction where Hakon and Arnie met their death. From here, I can't see them hanging lifeless, pinned to the trees, but I know I'll never forget the gruesome scene.

I can't stop the trembling that shakes my body. Is that how Cara and I will end our lives tonight? Our bodies splintered by drog lances and left to droop from a tree like some spent fall leaf about to drop to the ground, dead and forgotten?

I can't help but think that with only the two of us against a pack of savage drogs and the Wilder horde, that's the only way this night can end.

Thoughts of Golden Wind

Dreaded wings overhead.

Wings that I long feared to hear but knew that this night, this day would inevitably come.

The putrid aroma of murder and massacre wafts upon the wind. A noxious odor that taints my soul. It will not be the first, nor the last time that such a rancid fragrance will fill my nostrils. Its icy touch drowns the warmth of life and reminds one of how truly short are our days.

The foul ones have come for me.

Oh, the vainness, the cruelty of those who crave power over the lives of others. From their mouths come silken words that caress vanities, that hold up lies as promises, that move hearts, and minds to accept falsehoods as truths. Vows of healing when there will only be more wounds, more sorrow, more hopelessness.

My brothers and sisters here are lost. Their crime? Only that they were born in this day and time. I may well be lost this night, too.

If so, perhaps with it goes the hope of a world. But what is hope or faith without action? Emptiness. I pray that there will be some, if but a few, who do not cower and merely hope, but instead, push aside their fears and come forth. Perhaps they will work a miracle, wrest victory from what seems to be defeat. If not, then the Evil One shall win, and my birth will be for naught.

Oh, how I sorrow for the little ones, the innocents who are born trusting into the world. What do they ask of us at their beginning?

Only that the world we leave them will be better than the one we found at our own birthing.

Is that so much to ask?

Forevermore, it is not.

9

Cara blends into the forest's shadows as if she's a shade herself. She moves faster than before; slipping from one ebony pool to the next, a dark apparition in the night. Her quick pace makes it hard for me to keep up, but I push forward, skirting scraggly brush and cone-shaped trees in a dogged lope. I can tell we're nearing the woodland's edge when Cara abruptly brings us to a halt. "What do you hear?" she whispers.

I strain to listen. After a few moments, I put my mouth close to her ear, "They must be doing something to the dragons in the paddocks. I can hear the dragons stomping and the clinking of wing chains, sounds they make when they're awake, not asleep."

I stop, listen, and then murmur, "They're doing something with the chains, I can hear the links sliding through the rivets."

"That's what I thought," she replies in a soft, but grim tone. "The Wilders are stealing the herd. Some of them must be in the paddocks and in the barn while others are out in the meadows."

Crouched over, we slide from tree to tree. We both stop at a sharp noise, like the clanging of two swords together. Then I hear voices that carry on the night air, but I can't make out their words. Their speech is loud as if they're not afraid of anyone hearing. My mind goes numb with the realization that it's Wilders that I hear.

We cautiously tread forward. Cara has her bow up, and an arrow notched, but I carry an empty bow with quiver slung over my shoulder. To be honest, I haven't the faintest idea of how to notch an arrow and let one fly.

We slip past one last tree when out of the blackness a hand grabs my shoulder. I start to yelp, but another hand wraps itself over my mouth. I struggle against my unknown assailant before a sharp voice whispers in my ear, "Be quiet, you fool!"

I recognize that voice! I glance up to see Cara holding her bowstring taut against her cheek, an arrow ready to fly, but then her eyes widen, and she quickly lowers her bow. The strong arms release me, and I stumble backward. Cara however, moves closer and whispers, "Helmar," as if he's the answer to her prayer.

Well, maybe he is.

I can feel the heartfelt relief in Cara's voice, the way she croons his name. I admit, for the briefest of moments, in a way, I'm disappointed to see him, but I quickly shut that silly thought out of my mind. We desperately need him. "It's awfully good to see you," I say, "we thought that perhaps — "

"Came close enough," he brusquely answers, "but no, I'm alive."

Cara reaches out a hand to grasp his forearm. "Father? Daron?"

He shakes his head in answer as they gaze into each other's eyes. "I'm sorry, I wish I could give you better news, but the fact is, I don't know. Your father sent me home early."

Cara drops her head for an instant before she nods and gets back to business. "The Wilders are after the golden. Hooper and I were going to get her out of the barn and into the forest."

Helmar nods slowly before asking, "The other workers?"

"I fear all dead," Cara answers and then in an angry tone says, "the drogs are working with the Wilders. They killed Hakon and Arnie, perhaps all the others as well."

Helmar's face hardens, and he gruffly asks, "Any sign of the knights?"

"None," she flatly answers.

"You don't think they're in on this, too?" I ask.

Helmar hesitates before he sharply says, "No, but with or without them, we must act and swiftly at that. Your plan?" he asks Cara.

"Get to the woodpile," she answers, "see what's happening at the barn. After that . . . " her voice trails off meaning she hasn't thought past the stacked wood.

"Good first step," Helmar acknowledges. "Let's go."

He spins away, with Cara right behind him. Neither glances back to see if I'm following, but I understand. With Helmar here, Cara now has little use for me. Still, bent over as low as I can, I follow them to the last line of trees, just behind the heap of cut logs. The two slide down on their stomachs and wriggle forward.

I do my best to imitate them, but by the time I get to the cuttings, they're already peeking over the bark's top. I slip next to Cara and slowly raise my head to peer at the barn. The dragon doors are open and crimson-clothed men holding broadswords that gleam in their torches' firelight stand guard. As we watch, several more stride from the barn and one turns to gruffly call into the barn.

Helmar pulls us down and whispers, "I count eight outside."

"And obviously more inside," Cara answers, "but how many?"

The two peer at each other for a moment before Cara murmurs, "If we assume that there are about the same number on the inside of the barn as are on the outside, then I'm sure the greater number are in the far meadows rounding up the dragons there."

"Makes sense," Helmar affirms, "as it would take far more of them to round up the free roaming dragons than those already corralled."

He slides up to take another look at the barn. Cara and I join him just in time to see a tall, scarlet-cloaked Wilder step from the barn's dusky interior into the flickering torchlight. Helmar is studying something off to the side when I see Cara suddenly lean forward as if she's intently scrutinizing the Wilder newcomer.

She stays that way for several heartbeats completely absorbed in watching this particular Wilder, but why, I don't know. I tap on her forearm and point toward the Wilders. "What?" I whisper in her ear, but she holds up a hand to quieten me.

The tall Wilder speaks to the others, and Cara edges forward even more as if she would crawl on top of the log pile to discern what the Wilder is saying.

The man's voice carries, but I can't understand his words. Cara is so engrossed in this Wilder that she doesn't realize that she's raised her head up too high. Helmar reaches up to yank her down. "What are you doing? Do you want to be seen?"

She doesn't answer but slides down with her back to the rough bark. Her face is taut, troubled, and she's gripped her bow tightly with both hands. "Cara, what is it?" I ask. "You couldn't take your eyes off that Wilder."

Cara runs her tongue over soft, pink lips. "It can't be," she mutters. She draws in a deep breath and lets it out while running her fingers through her thick hair. "But, if that's who I believe it is, then this night is even more monstrous than ever."

"What do you mean?" Helmar questions.

She hesitates before waving a hand at him. "Later, right now, we need to get the golden out and away from the Wilders before it's too late."

Helmar peers at her for a moment before asking, "Ideas?"

"One," she answers. She turns to me. "Hooper, I'm going to ask you to do something that's far, far more dangerous than climbing Phigby's tree. Can I count on you?"

I hesitate before saying hoarsely, "I'm listening."

Helmar leans forward to hear as she motions over her shoulder toward the barn. "I'm positive that they haven't spirited Golden Wind away yet, and she's still in there. I think the Wilders are waiting until they can move the whole herd at once. That means we still have time."

"To do what?" Helmar asks.

"For you and me to distract the Wilders while Hooper sneaks into the barn and gets the golden out."

My mouth hangs open, but before I can even gurgle out a word of protest, Cara points at the log pile's end. "From there, it's just a short run to get behind the meal house. It'll hide you for most of way until you can get to the rear of the barn. For some reason, it looks like most of the Wilders are staying close to the front so there might not be that many toward the back."

"The side door?" I ask while swallowing several times.

"Exactly," she replies. She turns to Helmar. "Where's Wind Glory?"

"With Wind Song," he answers. "That's how I found you two."

Cara takes a deep breath before saying to me, "Helmar and I will make for our dragons. That'll give you time to sneak into the barn." She peers at me with solemn eyes. "Once inside, just wait, you'll know when to get Golden Wind out of there."

My eyes grow as big as Osa the moon. Does she really understand what she's asking of me? She wants me to sneak into a barn where there are sword-wielding, bloodthirsty Wilders. She leans close with a fierce expression on her face. "Hooper, remember, this isn't just for the golden, but for Scamper, too."

I gulp and feel a bit faint, but at the mention of Scamper I can't help but numbly nod in answer.

"Good," she replies. "Once you're in, don't worry about the other dragons, just get Golden Wind away from here as fast as you can." She glances at Helmar. "Fairy Falls?"

He shrugs in answer. "As good a place as any."

She turns to me to ask, "Do you know how to get to Fairy Falls?"

I shake my head at her. "I've heard of it, but I've never been there."

"Just follow the meadow creek into the forest for a quarter league," Helmar explains. "Then turn west toward the high hills. You'll come to the Dielong River, go upstream from there."

"How far up the river?" I ask.

"Just keep going," he answers, "you'll know when you're there."

I eye both of them suspiciously. "Just what are you two planning?"

"Never mind about us," Helmar returns. He must have sensed that I wasn't happy with Cara's idea because he leans close and mutters, "Hooper, I know how you feel about dragons. I've always known how you felt, but we're asking that just for once you put aside your feelings and think about what this means for all of us."

Cara puts her hand on my mine. "Draconton's villagers and our workers here at the stead died tonight because the Wilders want to take our dragons and especially Golden Wind. If we can do this one thing, just this one thing, Hooper to thwart their plans, then we will in some small measure avenge our people."

She doesn't say it, but I can see it in her eyes — and avenge my father, brother.

She goes on. "The meadows are lost, but, if fortune is on our side, then we may have this one chance to steal away the golden."

Helmar reaches out to turn me toward him. "We need to know, Hooper, are you with us on this, or not?"

I meet his eyes, and I have to admit, for an instant, the temptation to turn aside and say "not" is almost overpowering. Instead, I let my hand slide up and down my bow for a moment before I look at Cara. Her pleading eyes meet mine, and I feel like I'm melting inside.

"I'll do it," I answer. "Not for the golden, but for . . . " I stop, unable to go on, embarrassed to have let my affection for her come out so obviously.

Her hand squeezes mine gently. "Thank you, Hooper. Scamper is fortunate to have such a good friend."

I screw my mouth to one side. She thought I was talking about Scamper. Well, in a way, I was, but what I really meant was that I was willing to do it for her. Oh, well. It's probably for the best. What chance do I have with her, anyway?

Absolutely none.

I hold out my bow and quiver. "And if you're going to do what I think you're going to do, then these will be of more use to you two than me." I tap my waistband where my knife sits. "I'll make do with this."

Cara pulls my bow and quiver over her shoulders, gives me a tiny smile and then with Helmar leading, spurts away, crouching low, to disappear into the gloom.

I wait a few moments and then edge to the woodpile's far end to peek around the corner. Where there were eight or so Wilders before, there are only four now, and the tall one is not among them. I eye the distance between the cut wood and the meal house. If I were as fleet of foot as a deer, I could be to the hut in three or four bounds easily.

But I'm not a deer, and any bounding I could manage would make the waddle of a sprog look graceful.

Going straight across is out of the question, the Wilders would surely see me. I glance to my right. Several small bushes sit almost in a diagonal line that ends near the meal house's far corner. The bushes are skimpy and thin, but they at least provide some cover.

Hunched over as low as I can, I slide out from behind the wood-pile and scurry across the short distance to the first bush. I crouch behind the thin limbs and the new spring leaves, clearly able to see the Wilders. Their torchlight outlines the bushes' stringy leaves in odd shapes and for a moment, I see a leering skeleton head with fiery eye sockets looking straight at me.

I pull my eyes away and think, if I can see the Wilders, surely they can see me. Nevertheless, no flight of arrows speeds through the air in my direction, so once again I gauge the distance to the next bush. This space is almost double the length. The one redeeming feature is that I'm going away from the Wilders though not far enough that a red arrow from one of their longbows couldn't pierce my thin body.

I rock back slightly on my heels, gather myself and rush out from behind the shrub. At any second, I expect to hear a cry of discovery and moments later the muted twang of longbows releasing their arrows.

I'm behind the next-to-last bush, breathing hard and somewhat surprised to still be alive. I glance back at the Wilders. Their heads are turned away. Two are staring into the barn while the other two are peering toward the meadows. This is my chance. Without hesitating, I dash from behind the waist-high leafy bush and rush headlong for the low-slung cookhouse.

I dart around a corner and lean my back against the rough log walls. I take several deep breaths and listen. I hear nothing that would indicate that the Wilders saw me so I follow the wall until I reach the end. I peek around the corner, but I can't see the Wilders.

Almost tiptoeing, I hastily cross the open ground until I'm behind a haystack that's several heads taller than me. The smell of newly cut hay, rich and strong fills my nostrils as I hurry along. The paddocks on this side are empty and using the railings for cover, I scurry between the enclosures until I reach the trace that leads to the barn's end.

In the darkness, I crouch low and ease my way until I'm at one corner. I reach out and rub my hand across the sidewall. The barn's planks are smooth and even, the only building in the upper meadows with such even-textured siding, painted barnyard red.

I slide down to make myself as small as possible in hopes that it will lessen any chance of the Wilders' discovering me. I place my ear close to the barn and listen. Startled, I jerk my head back a little. The dragons are letting out deep growls, and I can hear them stomping and clawing their talons against the bare ground.

They're obviously agitated but from what? I push around the corner and slowly open the small side door. I step over the threshold and slip into the barn. I ease down behind one of the posts that hold up the enclosure railings and make myself small.

The Wilders have placed sputtering torches inside to light up its interior. At the building's other end, in the torchlight's glare, I see several swordsmen standing around the tall Wilder. There's a muttering of voices, but they're too far away for me to make out their words. I know that Cara and Helmar want me to do whatever it takes to get the golden out, but there's something I must do first.

I have to make my way to my corner and see if Scamper, perhaps frightened by all the commotion, came back to his straw nest. If he did, and the Wilders found him —

I don't want to think about what would happen if they had, I can only pray that he stayed quiet and hidden and is still alive. I duck under the lowest railing, crouch against the barn wall and almost crawling start to cross Golden Wind's paddock. My hunched over posture is agonizing to my leg but my eyes never leave the Wilders. I hear Golden Wind's tail scrape across the ground as she moves around but I ignore her. I'm sure she'll recognize my scent as I've cleaned her enclosure enough times.

I'm not quite halfway when I feel a warm, almost steamy breath on my head and shoulders. I glance over my shoulder. The golden's muzzle is so close that if I rose up even a tiny bit, I'd bump my head against her. She's watching my every move. It's clear that she recognizes me, which is good, but what if the Wilders get suspicious of why she's standing and staring toward the back end of her stall?

I reach up with my hand and try to push her away, but she stands firm. "Go," I furiously whisper, "you're going to give me away." She doesn't move. Like the big, dumb beast she is, she just stands there staring at me.

I grimace to myself. I recognize that expectant look on her idiot face. She thinks I have more sugar grass and is waiting for me to bring it out and feed her.

Then, she comes even closer. I've nowhere to go, she has me pinned against the back wall. I start to panic, she's never shown hostility before, but there's a first time for everything. All she has to do is place one of her huge clawed feet on top of me, put her weight down and —

But she doesn't. Instead, she brings her muzzle close and starts gently nuzzling my tunic, right where I've stashed the dragon jewel. Wide-eyed, I stare as she swings her muzzle back and forth, barely touching my tunic.

I can't help the feeling that she knows what's inside my pocket. She raises her head and stares at me for a long moment before she takes several steps back.

Movement near the barn's middle catches my eye. Oh no. The tall Wilder and another are slowly making their way toward the golden's pen. They're engaged in some quiet, but earnest conversation and haven't spotted me. I hesitate, unsure of what to do. I still have over half of the enclosure to go.

It won't be long before all the two Wilders have to do is lift their heads in my direction, and they're bound to see me before I can get to the next stall. I've got to go back. I can't make it to my little place where Scamper and I live.

My hands curl into tight fists of anger. Now, I may never know whether Scamper's alive or dead. With the golden still watching me, I silently creep back to the dark corner where I started.

Just as I sneak under the bottom railing, outside the barn's immense dragon doors, the sky lights up with a scarlet stream of dragon fire. I hear screams and wild yelling from the barn's fronting. Cara and Helmar must have caught those Wilders in the open before they could dart for safety inside the barn.

There are loud shouts and the tall Wilder and his companion spin around to run toward the shrieks of pain and rage. Overhead, I hear the whistling of dragon wings — it's Wind Song and Wind Glory flashing by, barely skimming over the barn's pitched roof, before they separate to go in different directions.

I listen to the sound of a longbow, followed by an anguished cry. Whoever loosed the arrow, their aim is perfect. Then, from near the barn's front, I hear the thruung of Wilder longbows as they send a flight of arrows skyward, searching for Cara and Helmar. The Wilders are fighting back furiously at the assailants who've turned the tables on them in a surprise attack that most likely killed several of their companions.

I sneak across the golden's stall until I'm near the front so that I can see down the barn at where the Wilders are yelling, cursing along with the almost constant thrumming of longbows. Their attention is centered on what's happening outside the barn, not inside.

Now's my chance. I start to rise from my crouched position but stop halfway up. I hear a familiar fluttering and scratching coming my way. "No . . . " I groan. It can't be, but it is.

Moments later, I'm surrounded by the four sprogs. Regal starts to screep, but I wrap my hand around his muzzle. I lean down, face to face with the four and angrily whisper, "No noise! None!"

They seem to understand because they all promptly plop down on their backsides and stare up at me expectantly. I raise my eyes and stare at the ceiling while shaking my head. "This can't be happening," I mumble in disbelief.

I have no choice. If I leave them behind, they'll start squawking and will certainly attract the attention of the tall Wilder, who's now retreated from the barn's front and stands almost midway to the golden's stall.

He's stopped and has his back to me, watching the other Wilders unleash more arrows into the night sky. In one hand is a thin, slender sword that he holds point down. I raise my eyebrows at that. From what I know, such a weapon is not the typical sword carried by fighting men.

This blade seems meant more for thrusting at an opponent from a distance rather than the close infighting dictated by a broadsword that warriors use. It's much like the type of sword that Lord Lorell carries, the kind that gentlemen and royalty of the realm use in mock duels.

Either way, my little field knife will be no match against the Wilder's blade.

Time's running out. I've got to do something, now. Neither my luck nor that of my two companions overhead will hold forever. I shepherd my little dragon troop over to the side rail. I then step over to the rope that runs through several pulleys overhead and lifts the huge crossbar that secures the dragon doors at this end of the barn.

As quiet as I can, I begin to pull the thick line down, watching the bar rise ever so slowly. It finally stands straight up so that when I'm ready, I can push the two wide doors open.

I turn back. There is still the matter of getting the golden out of her enclosure. Not to mention the Wilder, who's standing nearby still gazing outside. I have a feeling that he's not going to leave his post and will leave the fighting to the others.

I push my body into a little stoop and silently step to the stall's side postern nearest the barn doors. The bar that holds the gate in place is smaller than the barn door rod, but it's still heavy for me to raise, especially when I'm trying to remain unseen and not heard. I lift it up and over the stanchions that hold it in place and turn to set it down.

A sword point appears less than a finger's width from my face and leveled exactly at my right eye.

The Wilder is standing a sword's length from me. Covering his face and head is a turban wrap-around, only his fierce eyes show through a small slit in the cloth. "Put it back, now!" he hisses as the tip of his sword dances just in front of my nose.

I draw in a deep breath and nod. I raise the bar up as if I'm going to replace the grainy shaft so that it's once more cradled in the two braces. I hesitate, and the rod wiggles in my grasp as if I'm having trouble lifting it up. I step back, wobbling until I have the thick board right where I want it.

Then, with every bit of strength I can muster, I shove the wooden beam straight into the Wilder's chest. The bar's blunt end catches the man just below his throat. With a grunt, he stumbles backward but doesn't fall to the ground. Before I can turn and fling open the gate, the man rushes me, swinging his sword in a high arc toward my head.

I fumble with the knife in my belt. For some reason, it's stuck, and I can't get it out. My eyes catch the sword's dull glint, and I try to jump aside, but my heel finds some unseen object, and I fall, landing on my back. The Wilder's foil hits the stony ground next to me with a muffled clank, but he whips the blade back up again and raises it high.

I try to squirm away, but it's no use, I can't escape.

The sword starts to slash downward, but before it can land its deadly blow, a great golden muzzle swings over the stall's top rail. A fang-lined mouth opens, and a scream echoes through the barn. I look up, gaping at the sight above me. Swinging in the air, his arm gripped between the golden's jaws is the Wilder.

He shrieks again, his voice filled with pain and terror. For another second, he hangs there before the golden tosses him aside where he hits the ground with a thump. He rolls over and becomes still on the floor, his bloody arm beneath him.

I pull myself up and swing the enclosure gate open. I stumble over to the barn doors; place both hands on the planking and start to push. Before I can get them to move a finger's length, the doors shatter in a burst of planks and splinters from a dragon head-butt, and the golden lumbers past me into the night.

Behind me, there are shouts, yells and the sound of boot steps pounding, racing toward me. I start to run, but then I hear the fluttering of tiny wings and stop. I wave frantically at the four sprogs, "If you're coming it's now or never," I yelp.

The four dash past the door, waddling along like ducks out of water. Without looking back, I make a run for it, with the sprogs right at my heels. I never knew they could move so fast.

A sudden realization hits me. The golden will almost surely be able to get away. Though her wing chains prevent her from flying, even in her condition, she can run as fast as a horse. The pursuing Wilders, being on foot, will never catch her.

I, on the other hand, can barely outrun baby dragons. Without wings to carry me away to safety, the Wilders will surely find me long before I can reach the forest. I don't have a choice; I'm going to have to make a final stand.

I'm past the cookhouse, so I can't stop there. The woodpile. Can I make it to its relative safety; use the cords of wood as a barrier against the Wilders' arrows? I stub my toes against a rock, and I fly forward. I don't catch myself in time, my head plows into the ground, and I put a face-sized furrow in the grass.

I turn over and spit out dirt and grass. The sprogs are all over me, their little talons scraping at my tunic in panic. I push them away, pull myself up, and stare wildly at the woodpile. I'm too far away. I'll never make it before a Wilder arrow finds my back.

I glance behind and see several Wilders stop just beyond the meal hut. One drops to one knee and draws back his bow, his arrow point aimed straight at me.

Then like a spear of light, a flash of dragon fire streams down on the Wilders. It catches the one who knelt and in an instant, he's a human torch running and screeching in the night. The others break and make a run for the barn's protective cover.

I glance up to see Wind Song hovering over the meal hall. Cara pulls back on her bow and sends an arrow flying. A scream of anguish fills the night, and another Wilder falls dead. A second later, Cara sideslips Wind Song so that she hovers over me, the powerful downdraft of her wings almost bowling me over.

"Go!" Cara shouts. "The Wilders are skying their dragons. We won't be able to hold them for long!"

She tosses my bow and quiver to me. Wind Song dips her wings, heels to one side and then speeds away into the darkness. Clutching the bow and arrows, I spin around and trundle for the log pile, the sprogs running right along with me. I stop long enough to catch my breath before I make for the tree line.

I slow as I slip past the first tree trunks, not wanting to trip over the gnarled roots that spread from the trees to catch the unwary toe. I keep going, deeper into the forest, the sprogs trailing right behind me. I have no idea why they sought me out instead of staying with their mothers, but I have the feeling that if I left them behind, Cara would never forgive me.

I slow long enough to sling both the bow and quiver across my back before I take up my stumbling run again.

Nothing is familiar and in the darkness, every tree looks the same, every bush has limbs reaching out like skeleton claws to grab and pull me down. My eyes take in the gloom, and my imagination sees a drog or a Wilder hiding in every shadow, just waiting to leap from the blackness to run a lance or shoot an arrow into my body.

Or worse yet, the night specter will reappear, only this time, there won't be a Phineas Phigby or a ghostly emerald dragon to save me from a grisly death.

I have to stop to take in a deep breath. As I bend over, hands on knees and sucking in great drafts of air, the sprogs crush up against my ankles. "You know," I gasp between breaths, "running away from death is hard work."

Though the night air is cool, nevertheless, I wipe sticky sweat from my brow. Straightening, I plunge farther into the murky woodland, the sprogs staying right with me. Now that I'm not stumbling along, I can hear the rustlings of small animals, field mice and rabbits, and overhead the occasional fluttering of wings in the tree limbs.

The sprogs want to cluster around my feet, and I almost trip over them several times. The purple voices a plaintiff screeep and I bend down and furiously whisper, "Be quiet, all of you."

We tread deeper into the forest. I believe I'm heading towards the stream, but I'm not entirely sure. I've never had to go this far into the woods at night, and there are no landmarks to guide me. I'm positive the golden is in here somewhere as this would be the best place to hide, but where is she?

You'd think that with something that big moving in the woods, you could hear it, but I don't. It's like she disappeared into nothingness or was swallowed up after falling into a giant hole in the ground.

I stop to get my bearings. There's a tree stump nearby, and I sit down to rest for a bit. The little dragons press up against my legs, their heads turning anxiously in every direction. There's not much light to see by, but from the look in their eyes, I can tell that they're scared.

I wonder if my eyes have that same frightened expression. Probably.

I bend over and run a hand through my hair. The sprogs turn their heads hopefully up to me. "I'm not lost," I mutter to them as if they can understand what I'm saying. "I just don't know where I am, that's all."

I hang my head down and bite down on my lip. I grip the bow so hard that I feel pain in my knuckles. Was Scamper in the barn? If so, did he make it out and make a run for the forest? Maybe he never went back to the barn but was so afraid that he stayed hidden in the dark? Maybe he's out here in the woods like me, lost, scared, alone and wondering what to do in a world gone mad.

I pound a fist on my thigh. But what if he didn't make it out of the barn and lies dead from a scarlet arrow? Did I sacrifice my friend to save one stinking dragon?

If I did, it will haunt me for the rest of my life.

I stand and continue walking; turning my head in every direction, trying to find Golden Wind but it's the same wherever I look, trees and dark shadows. "This is impossible," I say to the sprogs. I turn in a big circle, my arms held out wide. "How do you lose something as big as a full-grown dragon? Losing one of you, I can understand, but something as huge as the golden?"

I stop to watch and listen, but to no avail. I say to the sprogs, "It's like she's vanished. She's in here somewhere, but she must be invisible. I can't hear her, and I can't see her."

I peer down at the baby dragons. "What about you? Any idea where she's gone?"

They sit down on their rumps and just stare at me. Obviously, they're not going to be any help, either. "Wonderful," I mutter to myself, "just how do I explain to Cara and Helmar that I've misplaced a golden dragon?"

I do another slow circle trying to spot the golden, but I see nothing that even remotely resembles a dragon. I let out a long sigh and throw my hands up in frustration. After we three risked our lives in the desperate battle against the Wilders, to lose the golden after all that!

It's not fair!

A dark thought enters my head. "What if the Wilders recaptured her?" I mutter. I shake my head, pressing my lips hard. "No," I state. "I'm not going to believe that they found her first, not after all we did. She's in here, I know it, I just have to find her."

I keep walking, stopping every so often to listen to the woodland noises. I've never been this far into Dielong Forest before, and my head starts to fill with the stories I've heard about its shadowy depths. Wood trolls and goblins that set traps for the unwary and eat alive those they capture, or green dragons whose fiery breath can scald the flesh off the unlucky.

And other — scary things.

I push aside several low-hanging tree limbs and pause to listen. Except for the rustling of small animals, the cheep of an occasional bird, and the scrabbling sounds of my companions, I can't hear anything that would indicate that a dragon moved nearby. I start to push aside another limb when a long, low, mournful howling in the distance causes me to suck in my breath.

Dreadwolves!

I've only seen the night stalkers once, and that was from a far distance. Sleek and powerful, with a flame-red mane against pitch-black hides, a pack of such vicious animals could bring me down in seconds.

I'm alone and somewhere close is a hunting pack of hungry wolves. I need to retrace my steps, go back. Not into the Wilders' hands but close enough to Draconstead where wolves won't go. I start to twist away but hesitate. I haven't seen or smelled any drogs, but if they're around, most likely they're close to the stead too which means if I go back, I could easily run into Sorg and his bloodthirsty pack.

Besides, if I turn tail now, not only would I never be able to face Cara, I might not ever be able to face myself again.

I'm not brave or courageous like Cara, or Helmar, or the king's knights, and I'll never be like them. But, still, tonight, for once in my life, someone thought of me as more than just Hooper, a manure mover, a dung driver. Moreover, for a little while, I really was more than that. Did I really want to throw that feeling, that sense of pride away?

And what of little Scamper? If he died at the Wilders' hands, then as Cara said, this would be at least in part, a way to avenge him.

I snug my knife tight in my belt, swing my bow off my shoulder and grip it tight along with an arrow. I glance down at the sprogs who've stayed quietly at my side. "All right," I whisper, "I'm going on, anyone who wants to go back, now's the time."

They just raise their heads and wait for me to make my move. We tread through the grass and leaves and haven't traveled far when I stop at a noise. I wait and listen, but whatever made the sound doesn't move. I take a few steps forward. It comes again. My eyes widen and my breathing quickens.

Did the wolves pick up my scent on the breeze? Are they even now closing in on me, their scarlet eyes fixed in hunger on my body, their lips drawn back over their cruel, sharp fangs?

Or, could it be a drog? I shake my head at that, given the circumstances I doubt if Sorg would send any of his troops into the thick forest after me. To seek out the golden, yes, but they wouldn't waste time on me. Not until they found Golden Wind.

I take a few more steps, stop and listen. The same sound floats through the air again. Only this time, it's much closer. The night stalkers are behind me, slowly trailing their prey, which I'm sure is me. I can't see them; their sinewy, slinking bodies must be close to the ground, moving unseen from shadow to shadow. I run my tongue over dry lips and try to slow my breathing.

My hand trembles as I slowly notch my arrow. I'm not sure what one arrow will do against a whole pack, but it's all I have.

I take another step forward. So do the wolves. I take a deep breath, pull the bowstring back, and spin around with my arrow pointed straight at the things.

And stop; my hand quivering with the strain of pulling the sinew taut.

A large, ponderous shape moves out of the shadows.

It's Golden Wind.

So — the Gems of Power and Righteousness begin to come forth.

From the dark now comes the light. From death comes life. Is that not the way it is with a sacrifice of the heart?

They are as small as tears, but mighty in the mind, heart, spirit. A gift long ago crafted for just this day and time.

May these gifts be received with all the reverence due to a lasting sacrifice and may they always be used with purpose, courage, and honor.

Small they are but is it not true that from the tiniest of seeds grow the mightiest of dragon heart trees whose crown of leaves paint the clouds like a brush upon an easel?

Does one's stature always denote the size of one's spirit or capacity to fashion great deeds or even miracles? There are those who are large in importance but entirely bereft of any living spirit and filled with nothing other than darkness. They wreak havoc and destruction, crushing dreams, hopes, lives.

Then there are those who must look up to the great in body as if they were staring skyward at a towering treetop. They are small in size but have noble spirits that are as a fountain welling over with an endless flood of goodness.

They are the ones who we remember, they are the ones whose works and achievements flourish throughout the ages. They are the ones who do not diminish us but uplift and cause our minds, our hearts, and our spirits to soar.

To be better than we are.

Who then is the mightiest among us?

10

I let the arrow slip from my bow, bend over in relief, and nervously chortle. I straighten and shake a fist at the golden. "You dumb hunk of dragon lard, you almost got an arrow up your nose, sneaking up on me like that. You know that don't you?"

The small sprogs trundle forward, bumping up against the golden's legs and making their usual screeping sounds. I don't try to stop them. If I were a baby dragon, I'd probably let out a loud, happy screep myself to see a mama dragon.

The golden lowers her head and nuzzles the sprogs before she comes close to me. She lowers her head so that her eyes and mine are almost level with each other. I'm face to face with a beast that could swallow me in one bite, well, maybe two, burn me alive with just one burst of dragon fire, or whose tail spikes could rip me in half with one swipe.

I can see her nostrils quiver, we're so close. Suddenly, she snorts. Her breath is a gust of wind that smells of long digested slimy grass, mutton, hay, and with just a hint of sulfur. Her splutter lifts the front of my hair, and I jerk my head back from the blast.

We stare at each other for a moment before I say, "I never thought

I'd say this to a dragon, but, believe it or not, I'm actually glad to see you."

I take in another breath and mumble, "Better you than a pack of wolves, for sure."

I swivel my head and peer at the surrounding trees. For some reason, they seem so much taller and bigger in the dark than in the daytime. I let out a little breath. "To tell you the truth, I'm lost. We need to get to Fairy Falls and meet Cara and Helmar, but I'm not sure which direction is which anymore."

I notice that the woods are starting to brighten, and I turn toward the east. Through the surrounding spruce and a few birchen trees, I see a pale light from the rising moons. Since we're deep in the woodland, and there's no sign of Wilders, I'm grateful for the moonlight as it will make my going a little easier.

I take several steps away surveying the forest, trying to decide which way to go. I say to the golden, over my shoulder in a half-joking manner, knowing that she's not going to answer, of course, "You wouldn't know the way, would you?"

The golden raises her head to peer through the break in the trees at the moons. Something in the way that she gazes at the moons — it's almost a reverent, imploring expression. Abruptly, the whole meadow is lighted in a soft radiance. Then a brilliant shaft of moonlight bursts through the trees onto Golden Wind and then spreads to flow over me, bathing us both in a soft, golden aura for several moments before it fades away.

I just stand there, like a statue, not moving, just staring at Golden Wind who still has her head raised up to the moons. Finally, I swallow, take some deep breaths, and say, "Better that than a dark wraith coming out of the shadows."

I glance once more up at the moons, scratch my head several times and mumble, "I have no idea of what just happened or what it means but we still have to find the falls, and I have absolutely no idea which way to go. Too bad those moonbeams couldn't have formed a big arrow pointing the way."

I slowly swivel my head, staring into the gloom looking for any sign to indicate a trail to the falls when I hear, "I can find the way."

I whirl around, my bow up, and an arrow notched. I eye the nearby scraggly underbrush and trees, trying to spot who it was that answered my question. "Who said that?" I demand.

There's no answer and after a bit, I decide that there's no one there, either. "Perfect," I mutter to myself, "first, we get a moonbeam bath, and now I'm hearing voices."

I lower my bow. "Well," I let out, "we're not going to get anywhere by just standing here, so, let's go." I start to walk in the direction of the falls, or at least, I think it's the right way. I don't go more than a few steps when I notice that the golden isn't following. Neither are the sprogs. They're staying close to Golden Wind.

She's just standing there, watching me. She hasn't moved at all. "This way," I say and point with a finger. "We need to go this way."

In answer, she slowly turns, being careful not to step on the sprogs, and starts walking in the opposite direction with the little dragons waddling along behind her. "Hey," I yelp, "where do you think you're going?"

In a stumbling gait, I run after her until I catch up. I slap at her leg to get her attention. "Stop, you big oaf, you're going the wrong way."

I might as well be whacking a strolling boulder for all the good my swats do to bring her to a halt. One of her ears swivels toward me at the sound of my voice, but she doesn't slow or even acknowledge that I'm right beside her.

Now what do I do? It's not like I'm a Dragon Trainer with a Proga stick and I can prod her into obeying me and going the way I want to go. Stumbling along and after thinking about it for a while, I see I have two choices. I either strike out on my own toward where I think the stream is, or I go with her in whatever direction she's taking us.

In the distance, a low, mournful wail wafts through the night air. The call of a Dreadwolf. That makes up my mind for me. So much for striking out on my own. I don't have the faintest notion where the golden is headed, but I do know that at least with her it's doubtful that the wolf pack will attack. Whereas, if I were alone, well, I don't even want to think about what would happen if I were caught out in the open by a pack of ravenous wolves.

We haven't gone far when Regal and Sparkle get in a scrap over something or other. They tussle with each other, then draw apart and try to growl, but what comes out of their mouths sounds like a sick chicken. Then they start spitting tiny fireballs, no bigger than the tip of my last pinkie, at each other.

I stop and stare for a moment. "Huh. Never knew they could do that," I mutter, before stepping over to stop the two.

"Stop!" I order and shove the two apart, careful not to get my hands in front of their faces. The little glowing globes don't go all that far, but I suspect that they could leave a nasty burn if one splattered against my skin. I push them toward the golden, and I'm not at all gentle. The last thing we need is for Wilder eyes to see fire, tiny though it may be, in the forest where there shouldn't be any.

The golden stops, gazes at me for an instant, before she eases down on her belly and stretches out her neck and head on the ground. The sprogs waddle up, scratching and clawing, trying to climb up on her skull plate.

After a couple of attempts, mixed in with several head-over-tail falls from halfway up, I get the idea and one by one lift the sprogs onto her head, where the four settle themselves behind her carapace. They snuggle together and close their eyes. The golden slowly raises her head, rises to her feet, and plods on. I scratch my head and mutter, "Never knew they could do that, either."

I try my best to match the golden's speed but her four legs against my two are no contest, and it's not long before I'm lagging way behind. She stops to eye me as if she can't understand why I can't match her pace.

I catch up, but as soon as I do, she moves off again. This time, though, I notice that she slows her stride to match mine, which is good, because my scarred leg is hurting so bad that I have a tough time maintaining even a sluggish speed.

We haven't gone far before I'm limping more and more with each step and it's so painful that I have to force myself to keep moving. I'd like nothing better than to sit and rest but I don't think I could make the golden understand that I need to stop.

Besides, we need to keep moving, away from Draconstead and the Wilders. I'd like to think that we're making our way toward the falls, but I'm totally lost and have no idea where we are or where the golden is headed. Surprisingly, for all her girth, the golden moves quietly through the forest and seems to blend into the shadows.

After a bit, my bad leg is so sore and stiff that I can barely lift it over the occasional log we come across. The fact is, I've put my legs through a lot tonight, and it's obvious that they're just not used to all the walking, running, climbing, crouching, stooping, and yes, hiding that I've had to do.

If we are indeed heading toward the brook, at the pace I'm moving, it could be several sunrises before we finally arrive.

After struggling over several slanted and broken tree trunks, I have no choice but to sit and rest my leg. The golden notices I've stopped and comes to a halt too but remains standing on all fours. Her head swivels as if she's searching the forest, but for what I don't know. For some reason to have her so close is actually comforting.

I wipe away the sweat that beads my forehead with the back of my hand. The wetness is both from exertion and from the agonizing pain in my leg. I'm not sure how much longer I can keep going tonight before I absolutely have to stop and wait until morning.

My head droops and I realize just how tired I am. This night seems like it has gone on forever, yet I know from the moon's being almost straight overhead that it's not even half over. The golden swings her head down and stares at me before she lowers her body and thrusts one of her front legs out in a bent position. My eyes widen and my jaw drops.

I'm stunned that she would know that particular position since no Dragon Trainer has ever taught her riding or skying commands. So, how does she know to offer her leg to a rider? It's a puzzle for which I have no answer, and I can't help but stare in amazement.

When she was born, Lord Lorell decreed that the golden would never know rivets for reins or saddle. She would have wing chains, of course, but that would be all. He also commanded that no one would ever ride her, either on the ground or in the air.

But there is no doubt in my mind of what she is doing. She's offering me the chance to ride her, her legs to become mine. I hesitate and think, what if Master Boren finds out, or worse, Lord Lorell? What if . . .

I stop second-guessing myself and think, who's going to tell m'lord Lorell? Me? Certainly, not. Then I laugh at a thought. Would Golden Wind tell? And just how would she do that? By pantomime? After all, dragons can't talk.

My laugh turns to a grimace as another sharp pain stabs my leg. My leg always hurts, but it's been a long while since it throbbed this bad. I wonder if this is what it would feel like if a drog lance had pierced my skin. The burning shoots up my leg until it's like someone is drawing a knife through my flesh. I bend over from the agony, and I can't help the small moan that passes my lips.

The pain wipes away any hesitation on my part. "All right," I say to the golden, "you win. I accept your offer. If the sprogs can ride, so can I."

As with Wind Song, my climb to the natural saddle just behind the golden's skull plate is clumsy and slow. I finally settle myself in her neck notch. "Sorry for the delay. This is all new to me."

At a sudden thought, I say, "And I guess for you, too."

I make sure that my longbow, arrows, and knife are all secure. I shake my head to myself and draw in a deep breath. I'm not only riding a dragon; I'm riding a Golden Dragon. "Very, very new," I murmur to myself.

The sprogs are asleep and don't even stir from my awkward movements to seat myself. Without any prodding from me, the golden begins a steady gait through the forest. After a bit, I have to admit that the golden seems to know where she's going, as she's staying on a relatively straight line. Maybe she's thirsty, and her need to drink is leading us to the stream.

While I wouldn't mind a long drink from a cool, clear brook, that's not what's first on my mind. Now that I have time to think instead of having to concentrate on just moving, I realize that even if we do reach the falls, I'm being naïve and foolish in thinking that Cara and Helmar will be there.

I feel the bile rising in my gullet and a stabbing pain in my stomach. What was I thinking? Cara won't be waiting for us at the falls. There's no way she was able to escape from the Wilders with their dozens of dragons.

Cara died tonight, along with Scamper, Master Phigby, and most likely Helmar. They're all dead.

I can see Cara's face, every curve, every dimple. For just a little while, she was in my life. But now, I won't ever see her radiant face, her beaming smile, the delightful way she crinkled her nose, the gleam in her eye when she became so excited over Master Phigby's new book.

Never to hear her melodious laugh again.

In one brief, wonderful moment, she made me forget the harshness of my world just by being close. Just with a smile — the touch of her hand.

No more Scamper, no more laughing at his peculiar little antics, no more having the furry warmth of his body close when it's cold, or feeling the way his little paws tickled me when he searched my pockets for food. No more knowing that there's someone in the world who accepts me just the way I am.

I put my head down. I haven't cried in a long time, but I admit I'm having a hard time holding back the tears. It doesn't matter that I've found the golden — how could I have forgotten Cara, Scamper, and Master Phigby? Yes, and Helmar, too.

I stare straight ahead. My sorrow isn't done, there's still plenty left in me, but there will come a better time and place to let my grief wash completely over mind and body. Cara wanted me to get the golden away from the Wilders, I have to do that first, and then I'll let the anguish pour through my body, let the tears flood my eyes.

I study the darkness around me, only broken by the shadowy, dark forms of tree and brush. Then it hits me in a sudden realization.

I don't have to go to the falls now, there's no real reason to make for the river anymore. I could go somewhere else.

But where?

I've never been outside of Draconstead except to Draconton. Though I've studied some of the maps in Master Phigby's bookstore, I still wouldn't have the faintest idea of where to go or how to get there.

Unlike Phigby, who seems to be familiar with the whole world, Draconstead and Draconton are all I know. I finally decide that if the golden is indeed headed toward the falls, it's as good a place as any for now. At least, for the moment, I have a place to go, and that gives me purpose in what I'm doing if nothing else.

The dragon's walk produces a soothing sway that eases the pain in my leg. At her pace, it shouldn't take long to find the creek and then make our way to the falls. I wonder how many people have ever ridden a golden dragon? History doesn't say. Who knows? I might be the first and only Drach to have ever ridden on a one-and-only dragon.

I glance down, and my eyes catch a dull glint in the pale moonlight. It's the golden's wing chains. They're still on, constricting her wings into tight bundles at her side. I'm not sure why, but the sight of her chains causes me to ponder for a long time before I come to a decision. If the House of Lorell can't have the golden, then I'm going to do something that will fulfill Cara's last wish and ensure that the Wilders will not have her either.

I squirm around until I'm holding onto her by one horn and dangling over the side in an awkward fashion. I hope that she understands my message and stops. She does, and I drop to the ground, emitting another small moan from landing on my hurt leg.

"Hold on," I say to her. "I'm going to do something that I really, really shouldn't, but just in case the Wilders or drogs show up, you should at least have the chance to escape."

I don't mention that if the Wilders or drogs show up, I probably won't have an opportunity to escape.

I'm not sure if she'll understand my command or not, but I've got to try. "Golden Wind," I speak firmly, "down." To my surprise, she slowly lowers herself until she's lying on her belly. I work on the chain's link latch on one side until I'm able to slide the chain through the rivets and then completely off.

Her left wing spreads out slowly, and I trundle over to the other restraints. Moments later, the second chain falls to the ground, and the golden fully spreads both wings. She beats them up and down, and I can feel the rush of wind lifting my hair and cooling my face.

For a few heartbeats, I think that she might sky away, leaving me stranded on the forest floor. I wouldn't blame her if she did. Instead, after a few more beats of her leathery, batlike wings, she tucks them against her body. She swings her muzzle close so that we're practically nose to nose.

"Thank you, Hooper, that feels so much better."

I don't blink. I don't breathe. I don't move. I just stand there and gawk.

A dragon just spoke to me, and I understood every word.

First the golden aura and now this. It's too much for me. My knees buckle, and I slowly sink to the ground. "You . . . you . . . talk," I sputter.

"Yes," she responds. "I do."

It takes me a moment, but I finally gurgle, "But — But you're a — "

"Dragon and dragons aren't supposed to talk, is that right?"

I nod several times, unable to speak. It's a good thing the wind isn't blowing, or my mouth, which must be as wide as the dragon doors back at the birthing barn would catch every blowing leaf in the forest, and I'd strangle on the leaves.

She lowers her head a little more. I never noticed before just how big her golden eyes were. Up close like this, each one must be as big as my head. Maybe bigger. "Well, I do, and for now, only you can understand me."

I swallow and manage to gurgle, "Just me? Why — "

"Because," she answers, with what seems to be a smile. "You've got something hidden in your tunic, don't you?"

My hand goes to the hard lump next to my chest. I start to answer "no" but I can see in her eyes that she knows that I have a dragon tear jewel. "How — " I stammer, "did you know about the — "

"Dragon gem?" she replies. She seems to have a way of knowing what I'm about to say even before I can finish my sentence. "Let's just say that dragon tear jewels are unique and very special, Hooper. They carry the life-essence and the power of the one who gave it to you."

Her eyes become sad, mournful. "It is good that you carry it so close to your heart, for it was indeed a sacrifice of the heart from an honored one. And one whose life-force I knew well."

I blink several times, still not quite believing I'm having a conversation with a dragon. "You mean the old green dragon?"

She pulls her head back as if she'd just whiffed rotten, soured cabbages. "Old green dragon," she replies somberly. "You say that as if you've just bitten into a peeled lemon that's been sprinkled with salt."

I don't know how to answer her. She gazes at me for a moment before saying in a subdued tone, "Pengillstorr Noraven was an extraordinary dragon, a noble king of the greenery." She lowers her head until she is again less than a hand's width from my face. "And for all of his long life, a protector of the Drach Menschen."

"Protector?" I choke out. "You're not serious."

"I am most serious," she answers. She swivels her head around and surveys the dark forest. "We should go," she states. She rises and thrusts out her leg. "We've tarried too long, and we're still too close to those who would do evil to both of us."

She glances skyward before saying, "We'll have to stay on the ground. It would not be wise to take to the sky. I can hear other dragons in the far distance."

"Wilders?"

"That is my thought for they do not sound like the wings of those I knew at our home. And if so, then it would be wise for us to quickly continue our journey and not chance a meeting."

Mentioning the Wilders is like a slap in the face, it focuses my attention on what we're trying to do and for the moment, I put aside all my doubts and questions about a talking dragon. "I can say for a certainty let's not chance it," I respond. "I've had all the Wilders for one night, no, make that for one lifetime that I ever want to have."

I put a hand on her leg, but a sudden thought stops me, and I walk around to face her. "Uh, one thing. If you need to sky away to save yourself, then that's all right with me. Cara would want you safe and not a Wilder captive.

"So, if you need to leave me — " I take a sharp breath and let it out. "Then do it. She would understand. After all, that's what she . . . " I can't finish the sentence. I can't say, "died for." It's too painful, too hurtful to acknowledge that Cara's life is over.

And I can't let my anger and hatred of all dragons overcome Cara's last wish. Cara died saving this dragon, and I will do my best to honor her unselfish act.

Golden Wind swings her head down close, eyes me for a moment and then says, "That's very gallant of you, Hooper. But I don't think that I shall need to sky, as you call it, anytime soon."

"Well, I just wanted you to know, just in case."

"Thank you. Now, let us go, we need to get even deeper into the forest."

I do a better job of getting aboard this time and settle myself on her neck. She waits and then asks, "Ready?"

"I'm ready. I think."

She swivels her head around to gaze at me. "And Hooper, thank you for saving the babies, that's what their mothers wanted, you know."

"They did?" I stammer. "I thought that the sprogs were just following me because that's what they've been doing lately."

"No, the little ones' mothers sensed an evilness in those who were in the barn. They did not want their babies to fall into their hands."

"Oh," is all I can answer.

"And one other thing, Hooper," she murmurs. "For now, it is very important that you do not reveal that you and I can speak to each other. We both have been given a great gift, but it must remain hidden."

Her voice turns solemn. "Our lives depend on it. Can I trust you to keep this promise?"

I raise my eyebrows at that "our lives depend on it" statement. She sounded ominous, but I quickly say, "Oh, yes. You can count on it. People think I'm odd enough as it is but if I start claiming that you and I can talk to each other . . . "

My laugh is sort of a cross between a chuckle and snort. "They'll turn me out, and I wouldn't even have a dragon barn to sleep in."

"In that case," the golden answers, "we certainly don't want our secret out, the barn was a very comfortable place to sleep."

"Uh, huh," I respond. "Maybe for you."

She doesn't reply. Instead, she lumbers off, skirting around the trees and rarely brushing up against one which is remarkable considering how close some are together. After a bit, I ask, "Uh, Golden Wind, about this speaking business. What if we're around other people and you speak to me, will they hear and understand you?"

She chuckles. "They'll hear what you Drachs call dragon speak and not as we're talking this moment." She hesitates and then says, "At least, for now."

"Oh," I reply. "Dragon speak" is the clucks, snorts, rumbling growls, and other odd sounds that dragons make to each other that some people claim is a language that dragons use to talk to each other. Always sounded just like clucks and snorts to me and nothing else.

We go a little farther. "Uh, and skying?" I ask. "You can sky, can't you? I mean, I've never seen — "

She again chuckles in reply. "Of course, I can. Just because I haven't doesn't mean I can't."

I stay quiet for a while before asking, "The name that you gave the green dragon. What language is that?"

"Pengillstorr Noraven? It's Gaelian, the First Language of all dragons."

"Gaelian," I mumble and frown. "It doesn't sound like something I can wrap my tongue around very easy."

I can feel the smile in her voice. "Few of your people have ever learned to speak true Gaelian."

"Does his name mean anything? You said he was a special dragon."

We plod along a little farther before she says, "His full name is Pengillstorr Noraven Prottigr Vior, which in your tongue means Great King of the Mighty Forests. Or, by how you name us, he would be called the Wind King."

I raise my eyebrows at that. "King?"

"Yes," she answers and then in a small voice says, "and more."

I wonder what she means by "and more." How much more can you be than a king?

I touch my tunic where the gem sits in my pocket. So, a great dragon king gave me his tear jewel? I really don't care why — what I care about is what I can do with it. Since the golden knows about the gemstone and where it came from, maybe she can tell me.

"Golden Wind," I begin, "if a dragon king gave me his tear-gem, then that must mean that he wanted me to use it as if I were a king. Right?"

She lumbers along and doesn't immediately answer. Then she slows and then stops altogether. She swings her head around so that she's looking at me with one eye. Her words are slow, deliberate. "Are you sure the jewel was meant for you, Hooper?"

"Huh?" I reply. "What does that mean? Of course, it was meant for me, why else would he give it to me?"

She's silent for a few moments before saying, "It may be that Pengillstorr couldn't find the one he truly sought and was forced to give it to you before he died."

I'm at a loss for words. Is she saying that the jewel isn't mine — that it was actually meant for someone else?

She lets out a long sigh. "Perhaps your calling may be that you're only meant to carry the jewel, not to be its rightful guardian. After all, the one who carries the water bucket isn't always intended to drink from it."

I'm taken aback by her words and slow to respond. "Are you

saying I'm not? But I saw the old — I mean, I saw Pengillstorr act as if he were searching for something when he came up the paddock trail. And then, he even knocked Sorg off me, just to give me the jewel. Doesn't that sound like the crystal was meant for me?"

She begins to plod on, not answering, but then says, "A dragon jewel carries the life-force of the dragon it came from, and it will only work for the one who is destined to wield its powers and who is actually ready to use its powers."

Her steps slow. "Is that truly you, Hooper?"

Her answer angers me. "If it wasn't meant for me, then why do I have it? Answer me that."

"Have you considered," she quietly says, "that what Pengillstorr actually sought, he could not find in time, and was forced to give his jewel to someone else, before he was slain? Perhaps to someone who would hold it for safekeeping until the crystal found its true keeper?"

As if she could read my mind she growls, "Do you actually think that Pengillstorr would bestow his precious jewel on someone who was only interested in acquiring such things as lands, a castle, servants, and meadows filled with herds of dragons?"

She stops and swings her muzzle up so that she can eye me. "And do you think that a protector of the Drach Menschen would give his jewel to someone who would use it to have power over others? To enslave them so that they would obey your every command, your every whim, no matter what that may be?"

The tone in her voice makes me think she's the one who's bitten into a peeled lemon covered in salt. I screw my mouth to one side as I think to myself that she got it all right except that she left out one important detail. The one thing that I will never have now.

Cara.

After thinking about it, I defiantly snap, "So? It's a gem from a king, isn't that what kings do? Use their power to make others do things for them and gain more power?"

"Most, yes," she acknowledges sadly. "And that's what you'd like to do, too?"

For a moment, I let my silence be my answer. Then I murmur, "I don't see anything wrong with wanting to be a king. Especially when you've been little more than a slave for most of your life. Is it so wrong to want that, especially since it was . . . " I stop and don't say what I was thinking, especially since it was dragons who shattered your life in the first place?

"I see," she answers as if she knows my thoughts exactly. "And since you believe it was dragons who harmed you, then this gift of a dragon gem must be our way of making up for the dreadful wrong."

"That's the way I see it," I mumble.

"And you think that I can show you how to unleash its magic. Help you become this mighty Drach Mensch King."

I don't answer because it's obvious that she knows that's what I want.

Have you ever heard a dragon sigh? It's long and melancholy. When I was very little, I once asked a foolish question in front of Master Boren. His sigh was exactly the same. Then he went on to explain patiently how misguided and wayward my thinking was, and he did so in a way that even as a small child I could understand.

That's exactly how the golden sounded as if she were the master and I the child.

"Hooper, just to hold a dragon gem, even as its caretaker, is a great honor. It means that Pengillstorr entrusted to you a gift that is as precious as life itself. It is true that dragon gems channel power, but it cannot go against the purpose for which the jewel was given. In simple terms, Pengillstorr's jewel will not make you a king. It will not bring you lands or castles, or any of the trappings of Drachen royalty."

"Then what is it good for?" I ask harshly.

"Just that, Hooper. Since it's Pengillstorr's jewel, it must be used for good, because it came from a dragon who was both courageous and good."

"For good," I spit in contempt. I can feel my anger, my disappointment building. Then I have a thought.

"All right, you said it's to be used for good. Let's assume that I'm meant to be the gem's guardian, able to wield its power. If so, then I want to use it for the most good that I can think of. Tell me how I can use it to bring Cara back to life again."

Her head droops as if she is full of sorrow. "Hooper, neither can I show you how to do such a thing nor can even Pengillstorr's tear jewel accomplish that."

My anger boils over. I slide off her neck and fall to the ground. I stumble around to face her, my hand tearing at the inside of my tunic to get at the jewel. I rip it out and push it into her face. "Then what is it good for!" I shout.

She gazes at me, her eyes and expression patient and understanding at my outburst. "Hooper, sometimes the good in a thing is not immediately evident. You must wait for the good to show itself." Her eyes are gentle on me. "As it is with some people."

She hesitates a moment before saying, "But there is one other thing that you must know about the gemstone. As the caretaker, you may not be able to wield its powers, but that does not mean that its influence will not be felt, even now.

"Power always has two faces, Hooper, one for those who turn to the good and righteous, the other for those who would debase themselves in evil and wickedness. The gem will call to both; one to strengthen and reassure, the other to repel and disgust."

She pauses as if to go on but then simply says, "I have said enough for now."

I hold the jewel up. In the gloom, its clear radiance softly glows. Once I thought the gem was beautiful, now it's ugly and useless. I thrust the gemstone at her. "Here, you take it. If it's not mine and I can't use it to do any of those things, then it's not of any worth to me."

She brings her muzzle close and peers deep into the gem's depths. The jewel's soft luminance seems to fill her eyes as if she would drink in the radiance until it filled her completely. Then she lifts her head and meets my angry eyes. "No Hooper, Pengillstorr gave it to you, not to me. For now, you must carry it. It is your burden, not mine."

I hold the teardrop-shaped gem in my hand and stare hard at its smoothness. "All right, if you won't take it, then I'll sell it. Surely, someone will pay a bag of royal ducats for a genuine dragon jewel. Enough to get me far away from Draconstead and — "

"Dragons?" she asks.

"Yes," I reply bluntly. "And dragons."

"Then I am truly sorry, Hooper, for if that is your wish, then the jewel will not be of any help to you."

"It will if I sell it," I retort.

"No," she answers frankly. "If you were to sell the gem, or if someone were to steal it, they would quickly find that they possess nothing more than a shiny bauble of no value."

I grip the jewel harder, so hard that I want to crush it in my hand. For just a moment in time, I had a dream. A dream where I escaped from my wretched life; a dream where Hooper the Dung Master became Hooper, the Master of — of — what?

My head slumps as I realize that without Cara it really doesn't matter what I become master and lord over.

None of it really matters anymore.

I turn and trudge away, with the golden following slowly behind. In my anger, I decide to throw the jewel as far as I can reach. For a moment, I hold it as if I would toss it deep into the dim shadows. I stand there for the longest time, but I find I can't throw it, can't be rid of the useless thing.

Why? I don't know. Maybe I'm hoping that the golden is lying and that someday I will be able to sell it, to the highest bidder with bags and bags of ducats.

Silly dreams, of course, but that's all I have left, stupid dreams and shattered hopes, courtesy once again of a dragon.

11

We trudge along, neither speaking. Me, in a swirl of gloomy thoughts, the dragon — well, I have no idea what dragons think about nor do I care. Besides, in my foul mood, the only words I would utter would be insulting or hurtful and for some reason, I keep them to myself.

It's not long before I'm again in severe pain from the walking. I'm not even sure why I keep going, there's no longer any purpose. I spot a fallen tree alongside the trail and pull my weary body over to sit with my back against the rough bark.

The golden settles down on all fours. "Is your leg hurting again, Hooper?" Her voice has a gentle ring, but I don't care. I don't want anything from this dragon, or any dragon, especially not sympathy.

"No," I snap, "I just like to sit in wet grass and leaves with my back rubbing up against sharp bark and think about how wonderful life is." I stop, my eyes fill with tears, and I mumble, "And how tonight I've lost my best friend and . . . "

I wave my hand at her. "Ah, never mind, you wouldn't understand anyway."

She doesn't answer at first but then says, "Actually Hooper, I do understand your wounded heart for I too carry a similar hurt. I know how the pain seems to consume your whole being driving away all other thoughts and considerations. And if I could, I would lie beside you and let my own grief wash over mind and body.

"But neither you nor I can afford to wallow in our self-pity for we are still being hunted, and we can not allow ourselves to be caught up in the whirlwind of actions that have been started this night. Later perhaps there will be time to grieve, but not now."

She shuffles forward until her muzzle is almost in my face. "I would consider it an honor if you would allow me to be your legs for the rest of the way, Hooper."

I don't respond, I just sit there with my head down, kneading my bad leg, trying to lessen at least the physical pain. After a while, I clear my throat. "Back in the barn, if you hadn't grabbed that Wilder's sword arm, he would have killed me. Why did you save me? It would have been better if you had just let me die."

She had been surveying the murky woods, now she swivels her head around to peer at me. "Because you needed saving," she answers as if that explained everything.

"Hooper," she presses in an urgent tone, "we really need to keep moving."

"Why?" I answer curtly. "There's no reason to go on. It doesn't really matter if we're here or there."

"No. It does matter, greatly and I seem to recall that you said it was Cara who wanted us to go to the falls."

I jerk myself upright. "Don't you talk about her!" I shout. "You don't know anything about her. Nothing!"

My breathing is hard and my anger matches. The golden stares at me for several heartbeats. "But, Hooper, I do know Cara. She visited me frequently. She made sure that I always had enough to eat, that my water was always fresh and that my wing chains didn't chafe or were too tight."

She brings her mouth back in the semblance of a smile. "She would rub my belly and always speak in a soothing tone."

She moves her head a little closer. "Didn't you ever notice that my stall was always a little cleaner than the others? That you didn't have to do quite as much work there?"

She pauses before saying, "Cara did that, for me. Maybe even for you."

I don't know how to answer. I finally stammer, "She did?"

The golden nods. "You never knew, did you?"

"No," I murmur, "I guess I never noticed."

The golden is silent for some time before saying, "It would seem, Hooper, that you haven't seen many other things in your life, intentionally or not. Perhaps now is the time for you to start noticing."

My laugh is bitter. "Like what, for instance?"

"Like why would Cara want you, and me, to go to Fairy Falls? She must have had a good reason, you know."

I give her a little shrug. "Probably because it was deep in the forest and as good as place as any to get away and hide from the drogs and Wilders. At least that's what Helmar said."

"Perhaps," the golden acknowledges, "or perhaps there was something more. Wouldn't you like to at least find out? For Cara's sake? Or Helmar's?"

I draw in several deep breaths and face Golden Wind. "All right, for Cara's sake if for no other reason."

The golden thrusts out her leg and reluctantly, I climb up and settle myself into her neck saddle. We move off, and it's not long before the golden's swaying motion begins to rock me to sleep. I lean forward and find that by holding onto her horns, I can actually keep upright even if I'm dozing off.

I fall into a fitful sleep. Even in slumber, my mind feels as though my thoughts battle each other, from the joy of being in Cara's presence to the agony of knowing that both she and Scamper are dead.

I don't know how long I was asleep before I jerk upright. We've stopped moving. In my sleep-drugged state, I fumble with my bow thinking that something is wrong. I actually hit myself in the head several times with the bow's wood before I finally tug the longbow off my back. My eyes are puffy, and I have to wipe at them with one hand before I'm fully awake.

I can hear water. Not the hard, rock-slapping torrent from a rushing, spitting stream, but the sweet softness of a gentle brook whose water caresses the smooth stones that layer its streambed. I lean forward to gaze at the broad stream that flows just ahead.

"Well," I mutter, "it's not the falls. But at least you got us to the river, now all we have to do is figure out if we go upstream or down."

The golden turns slightly so that we're facing upstream. I take one look and say, "Oh."

Farther up, the water flows over three broad steps, one after another. Each ledge is at least waist-high in height and half as wide as the birthing barn. The gurgling water has a luminosity, like Dragon Glow, but a soft white instead of pink.

Each ledge is cracked and uneven so that the water has to bend and curl as it passes over the rock shelving, which makes for dark, wavy swirls in its radiance. After the very last step, the water drops into a full, deep pool where it slows to a meander and then spills out into the wide streambed.

The golden draws closer to the falls, slows, and then turns to one side. My eyes widen and a "Wha . . . " slips out of my mouth.

In the center of an almost perfectly oval glen, stand three dusky white spiral-like swirls that rise from the grass-covered ground to dragon height. The coiled earth is thick at the base, but slims and narrows as it rises until its point is as thin and sharp as any arrow point. I glance around, but the glade is empty except for the three towering pillars.

I've never seen anything like the columns, they seem unearthly, almost supernatural. I can't help but gawk at the spires, it's like I'm seeing an artist's drawing from one of Phigby's fantasy books. I slip down off the golden and take several steps toward the columns as if I'm drawn to them, my eyes riveted on their sweeping upward forms.

"I've never seen anything like that," I say, "They're — "

"The three Gaelian Fae," the golden murmurs reverently.

"Gaelian Fae?"

"Yes, three of the four Fairy Queens; Osa, Nadia, Eskar, and Vay

— the creators and guardians of all dragons. But these only represent Osa, Nadia, and Eskar."

I stare at the three monoliths. To me, they appear like cream-colored clay that someone has molded into shapes that resemble swirled butter when it thickens. "Uh," I ask, "are you saying that those three dirt columns created you?"

The golden doesn't immediately answer, but when she does, it's in a soft, melodious singsong,

> *"Four there were, the Gaelian Fae*
> *Osa, Nadia, Eskar, and Vay*
> *Given a place below the gods,*
> *Where neither Drach nor dragon trod*
> *The gods created all creatures both great and small*
> *Some to fly, some to walk, and some to slither or to crawl*
> *On worlds far below to the heavens high above*
> *Some in spite and some with love*
> *But of the dragon, the Fae lay claim*
> *Talon and tail, and fiery mane*
> *Brought them forth as to reign*
> *Over hill, forest, and starry train*
> *But Drach their equal was to be*
> *On land, sky, and deep-blue sea*
> *Gaelian Fae who set their scales*
> *Green to tread through forest dales*
> *Red to thunder in fiery fight*
> *Orange and Yellow to shimmer in flight*
> *Sapphire faster than even the wind*
> *Violet to royalty its knee will bend*
> *Blue to swim thru wondrous ocean*
> *Each creation most carefully chosen*
> *Seven of the bow that colors the rain*
> *Over hill, forest, and starry train."*

I close my gaping mouth before muttering, "You and Phigby must have read the same book. You sound just like him." I bite down on my lip, realizing that I've spoken of Phigby as if he's still alive, which he isn't.

I start to turn away from the columns, when, with a snort, the golden whips her head up and peers downstream. Her ears swivel as if she's searching the star-studded sky and a low, deep rumble comes from her throat.

My breathing quickens. From the way she's acting, whatever it is she's sensing, it's not good.

"What's wrong?" I ask, my voice rising in alarm.

"Dragons," she answers, "headed our way."

"Wilders!" I hiss. "They'll spot us!"

I frantically survey our immediate surroundings. Off to the left, a small hill rises with part of it carved out by stream floods of past seasons. There's an overhang of sorts, but it's too low for the golden to fit under. Just past is a thick grove of cone-shaped spruce, dark with shadows.

"There!" I cry. "Head for those trees, hide in there."

The golden remains where she is, staring up at the sky. "Move!" I yell. I push at her big body to get her running toward the forest, but I might as well be trying to shove aside one of the Dragon Tooth mountains for all the good it does me.

I put my back against her scaly stomach and push, but that doesn't budge her a gnat's width. In desperation, I run to face her and yell, "The trees, you fat butterball of a dragon, get into the trees!"

She gives me a hurt look for an instant before turning and lumbering toward the forest with me following as best as I can. We slip into the tree line just as I hear dragon wings in the distance.

I hastily slide down to the ground and hide under the over-hanging limbs of a good-sized spruce. The golden goes deeper into the grove, careful not to brush too hard against the trees and set them to swaying, a dead giveaway that a dragon is moving through the forest.

I wiggle forward and peek through the needle-like leaves to watch the open glen. Moments later, the pulse of dragon wings sounds through the night. I can tell by the slow beat of their wings that the dragons are gliding in for a landing.

And that's the last thing we need right now. After all, what good is someone, me, who can barely notch an arrow, let alone hit anything with it going to do against armed and angry Wilders?

Die, that's what.

I start to back out of my hiding place to follow the golden deeper into the woodlands when I stop and with a grin so broad that it hurts, I scramble to my feet. I know the sound of those wings! I'm almost choking as I stumble from behind the tree. It can't be, but it is.

Sailing just over the treetops comes a sapphire. It cups its wings before extending its hind legs and settles to the ground. A second later, a second dragon drops to the ground, and then a third. Three sleek sapphires, and to my eyes, miracle dragons.

By the time the second sapphire touches down, I'm already running at my best pace toward the first. It's Wind Song, and riding her is the beautiful, and very much alive Cara Dracon. She slides to the ground holding a wriggling bundle. She opens her arms and a dark-grey wad leaps to the ground and bounds toward me in that funny, sideways rolling gait that I know oh so well.

It's Scamper.

The little grub digger hits me in the chest, nearly bowling me over. I drop to the ground, and an almost childlike giggle escapes my lips as Scamper licks every bit of my face. I squeeze him tight in my arms. I've never been happier in my life.

Finally, Scamper stops giving me a tongue bath, puts his paws on my chest and juts his face at mine. *Grrwaaayyy*, he says in a stern and accusing voice. "Yes," I answer in my most apologetic tone. "I went away and left you."

I draw in a deep breath. "And, I'm very, very sorry I did. I didn't mean to, I — I tried to find you, but I couldn't. I promise I won't ever do it again."

He eyes me for a second, considering whether my apology was sincere enough. It must have been because his little nose quivers before he drops down in my lap and searches my tunic with his paws. *Eeeeet?* he asks.

I scratch him behind his rounded ears. "Sorry, fella, I haven't had anything to eat either. We'll have to find something later for the two of us." With that, he ambles off, no doubt to forage and find his own late-night meal.

I look up. Cara is standing nearby, a little smile on her face. I scramble to my feet and all but stumble over to her. There are so many things I want to say, but I fumble my words and sound like a gibbering fool. "Cara — you're alive — you're — I'm so — how — are you hurt?"

She laughs and throws her arms around me and to my astonishment gives me a hug. "Of course, I'm alive, silly," she says. "I told you we weren't going to die. And no, I'm not hurt, but Helmar is."

She steps back and with a serious look on her face asks, "The golden?"

I swallow and point. "In the woods, she's fine." I start to say, "But there's something you should know," when Cara draws in a deep breath and lets it out in great relief. She gives me another hug while whispering, "Thank you, Hooper." She lets go of me and runs back to the sapphires.

I quickly follow her to find Helmar easing himself down to the ground, grimacing in pain and holding his left arm. "You're hurt," I state.

"Just a nick from a Wilder arrow," Helmar answers bluntly. "I didn't duck fast enough."

"Nevertheless, even a nick needs tending," a familiar and welcome voice comes from the side.

"Master Phigby!" I yelp. "We thought you dead."

"Near enough," he answers, "but it appears my time is not yet."

Before he can say more, Helmar reaches out to turn me toward him. "The golden?" he demands.

"Safe," I reassure him and point toward the dark tree line. "I hid her in there when I heard dragon wings. I was afraid you were Wilders."

"Wilders there be," Phigby grumps, "but, for now, we've left them behind." He points to the hill's overhang. "Let's get Helmar under that so that I can brew up the medicine I need to tend to that wound. I'll get my kit."

Phigby stumps back to the third sapphire and my eyes widen when I catch full sight of the blue dragon. "That's Wind Rover," I stutter.

I turn to Cara. My announcement has brought a mist to eyes that turn sad and bleak. She holds a hand to her mouth before saying, "Somehow, she made her way back to Draconton, but father wasn't with her. Nor was there any sign of Daron and his crimson."

She takes a deep breath. "Phigby said there wasn't any blood on Rover, so that's a good sign."

"But where is — "

"We don't know, Hooper," Phigby growls as he rejoins us. "Save your questions for later." He motions for Helmar to follow and as they do, Cara says, "Hooper, bring Golden Wind over by the overhang, I'll get the sapphires in close."

I give her a quick nod and head for the trees. I push past the jutting tree limbs to find the golden lying on all fours. "C'mon," I say, "it's Cara, Scamper, Master Phigby, and Helmar. They're all right, except Helmar has an arrow wound."

"I know," she replies.

"You know?" I reply. "Then why did you stay hidden, why didn't you come out?"

"Because I wanted you to have your moment with your comrades and friends. I would have been a distraction."

She rises and together we walk back toward the small hillside. Helmar is sitting on a small log and Phigby is helping him get his tunic off. I can see the blood streaming down Helmar's arm from the puncture-like wound that still has the arrowhead and a shortened piece of the shaft sticking out of his shoulder.

As Phigby presses a cloth on the wound to stem the bleeding, he glances up and barks, "Get wood for a fire, I need hot water."

He tosses several water flasks at me. "Fill them, and hurry."

Helmar wipes at his sweating, grimy face and says, "The Wilders may see the fire's glow."

"Maybe they will, maybe they won't," Phigby grunts. "But, without hot water to brew the medicine I need, that wound of yours could fester and the poison will spread through your body. If so, then your life glow will surely end."

I glance around and say, "The dragons."

Cara turns and asks, "What about the dragons?"

"We could bring them in closer," I answer, "form a screen. The overhang will prevent the fire from being seen from above, the hill shields it to one side, and the dragons will mostly block it on the other."

Cara peers up at the overhang before she turns to Helmar with a questioning expression. He nods in return. "Put the golden in the middle," he orders, "she's the biggest and will block most of the light."

Cara says to me, "Get the water, Hooper, and I'll arrange the dragons. When you get back, help me with the wood."

I start to turn, but Helmar calls out, "Hooper."

I face him, and he says, begrudgingly, "Nice work getting the golden out of the barn."

I give him a sheepish grin. "All I did was get a barn door open, which I couldn't have done if you and Cara hadn't so thoroughly distracted the Wilders. Not to mention that there are a lot fewer of them going back to their lairs thanks to you and Cara."

I lean closer to Cara. "And I do thank you for saving my life back there."

She smiles in return, but the moment is quickly over as Phigby snaps, "Now that we've stopped patting each other on the back, Hooper go get the water. Cara get those dragons in place and then the both of you collect some wood."

Before I hurry out, I say to Cara, "Just so you know, the sprogs are asleep in the golden's carapace."

Her eyes grow wide. "You did save them!"

I give her a quick smile in answer and dash off to get the water. I hurry down to the river to fill the flasks and find that Scamper is fishing. "Having any luck?" I ask. His front paws are wet which means he's made at least one attempt to snag a fish, but missed.

Brrrrrt, he says and shakes a few drops off one paw. "Yes," I reply, "the water's cold, but keep trying, I hear brook trout are very tasty."

I rush back with my filled water flasks, squeeze past the dragons to find Cara pushing together a pile of small twigs and branches that she apparently found under the overhang. She reaches out for the water flasks, and I hand them over.

From his bag, Phigby pulls out a small jar, takes the lid off, and sprinkles some tiny gray pellets in his hand. He tosses them into the wood, mutters something under his breath, and the wood catches fire. I'm not the only one with an amazed expression at what just happened, but before I can say anything, Phigby points to the tree line. "More wood," he orders, "this little fire won't suffice for what I need to do."

Cara starts to turn, but I reach out to stop her. "Stay here and help," I say, "I'll get the wood."

She nods gratefully, and I can see the weariness in her eyes. I push past the golden who's lying with her head on her forelegs, eyes closed. The sprogs are still asleep, having slept through all the excitement.

It doesn't take long for me to gather a bundle of dried, broken limbs and branches and start back. I don't see Scamper anywhere, but I figure he's given up on his fishing expedition and is rooting in the hillside for worms and beetles.

I glance upstream to where the three pillars stand tall and dark. The clouds part and a beam of moonlight falls on the columns. I suck in a breath. In the pale light, I see three faces staring; their cool, blue eyes centered on me. The light passes, and they're gone. "No," I whisper to myself. "Please, please no more witches."

I scurry back with my load and quickly drop the wood by the small fire. I gulp and start to point toward the pillars. Phigby, who's laid out two gray, metallic cups and several jars, takes one look at me and snaps, "Well, what is it? You look as though you've seen a ghost."

My mouth works, but nothing comes out. Out of the corner of my eye, I see the golden raise her head, peering at me with an intent expression. Phigby glares. "Hooper!" he grumbles. "Out with it, or let me get about tending to Helmar."

I shrug my shoulders. "Nothing," I murmur, deciding that I must be seeing shadows in the night, faces that really aren't there.

"Humph," Phigby replies. "In that case, put more wood on the fire." As I do, Cara unloads the sprogs off the golden and places them near the fire for warmth. They're snuggled together, except I notice that Regal has wormed his way into the middle of the pack, gaining even more warmth off the other sprog's bodies.

Phigby dips two fingers into a lime-colored jar and pulls out a pinch of green-tinted flakes. He drops those into the first cup, adds water, stirs with a small wooden spoon and sets the cup next to the fire.

He pours water into the second cup, adds a sprinkle of fine granules from a white jar and a liberal amount from a small, dark red pot. After stirring, Phigby sets that cup, too, next to the fire. It's not long before steam begins to rise from the first cup and he pulls it away from the coals.

He stirs the olive-colored liquid, letting it cool before he hands the cup to Helmar. "Drink," he orders. Helmar brings the mug to his nose and sniffs the steam. He jerks his head back and wrinkles his nose.

"Phigby," he scowls, "if that tastes like it smells, I'm going to end up spitting it all out. What happened to that delicious cinnamon and honey molasses concoction you gave me when I had the cough?"

"I don't tell you how to train dragons," Phigby retorts. "Don't tell me how to tend arrow wounds. Now, drink."

Cara gently touches Helmar's hand. "Go ahead," she says encouragingly, "I know from experience it doesn't always smell or taste good, but Phigby knows what he's doing."

Helmar wrinkles his nose again. "I'm not so sure," he answers. He takes another sniff, grimaces, but then takes a deep breath and downs the liquid, making a face when he finishes. Seeing his expression, I know from experience exactly how he feels.

He coughs, gags, and says in a raspy voice, "I was right, it tasted every bit as bad as it smelled."

"Be that as it may," Phigby answers, "that will help defeat the poison, just in case there was any."

"Poison?" I ask.

"Wilders sometimes use the juice of the pison berry on their arrow tips," Phigby explains. "Even a tiny scratch results in a horrible death. Someone who has such a wound begins to writhe, foam at the mouth, and — "

He stops, seeing the distressed look on Cara's face. He reassuringly pats Helmar on the shoulder. "You show none of the symptoms, lad, so be at ease. I only gave that potion to you as a precaution."

He reaches over and pulls the other steaming cup away from the fire. He rummages in his bag and pulls out several long strips of cloth. He hands those to Cara and lifts up the cup to Helmar. "Drink just a bit of this but no more than one small swallow or you'll be sleeping for three days and that we can't afford."

After Helmar downs one small sip, Phigby holds the cup over the wound. "This," he says to Helmar, "is going to sting. But it will cut the pain while I get that arrow head out of your shoulder. Hopefully, if it hasn't gone too deep, your arm should practically be good in a day or so."

Phigby tips the cup, letting a good amount of the liquid pour into the wound. Helmar grimaces and says to Phigby, "You and I have a difference of opinion on what the word *sting* means."

Phigby ignores Helmar and goes to work on the arrowhead. Fortunately, the tip hasn't gone very deep, and it takes Phigby only a few moments to work it out. Cara pours the rest of the medicine into the wound and with Phigby binds Helmar's shoulder tightly with the bandage strips that Phigby has pulled from his bag.

I reach over, pick up Helmar's tunic, and hand it to Cara. With Phigby helping, Helmar manages to wiggle back into his tunic and pulls it down over his waist. Phigby fashions a sling and settles

Helmar's arm in the crook. Once done, Helmar flexes his fingers and peers at Phigby in surprise. He nods appreciatively while announcing, "The pain is all but gone. From now on, I'm going to call you Professor Medicine."

"Professor *Emeritus* of Medicine," Cara smiles.

Phigby lifts one corner of his mouth in a tight, satisfied smile while he points at Helmar's wound. "You were lucky, that arrowhead didn't even go halfway in. Your arm should be pain-free well past sunrise. So, was a few wee moments of pain worth a day or more of no pain?"

Helmar smiles back. "Of course."

"Good," Phigby says, "so from now on, you won't be questioning my medicines, now will you?"

Helmar shakes his head dutifully. "No, Professor Phigby. I promise to keep my mouth shut in the future."

"Wilder poison," I say to Phigby, "I've never heard of that before."

He turns stern eyes on me. "There are a great many things that you've never heard of before, Hooper. You should have studied my books more."

"I did what I could," I mumble in defense.

Phigby flaps a hand at me. "Never mind. I guess you were like most every other child in the village." He peers at me sideways, and his eyes seem to bore straight into my soul. "Except that I always thought you were different . . . "

He lets out a long breath. "Maybe I was wrong."

I hang my head in the uncomfortable silence that follows before I start to rise and murmur, "I'll go get more wood."

"Wait, Hooper," Helmar orders, "I have something to say to you, too."

His manner causes me to think, what else have I done wrong now? First, Phigby, and now Helmar.

He gestures with his good arm toward the golden. "Where are her wing chains?" he demands.

Cara jerks her head around, apparently unaware until now that the golden's wing chains were missing. "Did you remove them?" Helmar questions bluntly.

I take a deep breath and let it out before I answer. "Uh, yes, Helmar, I did," I reply truthfully. I hurriedly go on. "If we were discovered either by the Wilders or drogs, I wanted her to have the chance to escape."

He and Cara exchange looks. From Helmar's stern face and disapproving expression, I'm afraid that I'm in for it. I can only hope he understands my reasoning, even though he may disagree with my decision.

I wait for the tongue lashing that I'm sure is forthcoming while Helmar's gaze flicks from me to the golden and back again. He mutters slowly as if forcing each word out of his mouth. "I guess under the circumstances; it was the right thing to do, Hooper."

Not exactly high praise, but coming from Helmar, it's pretty close. I glance over at Cara, who gives me a small smile of approval, too. Cara's smile warms me more than any fire.

Phigby holds up a hand and says, "No need to get more wood, Hooper, we have enough for now. Besides," he says while glancing at the lot of us, "I suspect that we need to sort a few things out."

He points to the golden. "Especially about her. Obviously, the question is, what do we do now?"

"I agree," Cara chimes in. She nods toward Wind Rover before turning to Helmar, "And I want to know what you can tell me about how she found her way back here — without father or Daron."

I sit back down and almost tripping over my words, say, "And I want to hear how Master Phigby escaped the dragon fire in Draconton, how you two escaped the Wilders, how you found Scamper, what happened to — "

"Hooper," Phigby growls in an exasperated tone, "I've never known anyone to get so many words out in one breath as you."

I smile sheepishly. "Sorry, sometimes they just come flying out."

I glance over at Helmar. "I guess I need to put rivets and chains on my tongue."

Phigby strokes his beard before asking Helmar, "It appears we have several things to talk over, but first, are we safe from the Wilders here, or do we need to move on?"

Helmar considers Phigby's question, and I can see by his contorted expression that he's wrestling with several thoughts. "Safe enough for the moment," he answers. "But if we had the choice, I'd say we need to sky farther away. However, the sapphires are tired, and we'd have to ride double on one of them."

He takes a deep breath. "If we were caught by Wilder reds, especially fresh ones, while skying, they'd be able to quickly bring us down."

His hard eyes circle the group. "We need to give the sapphires rest, at least part of the night. Otherwise, everything we've done, everything we've fought for would be for naught."

Safe enough for the moment, I think.

Have you ever seen a storm brewing, with the dark clouds swirling and becoming darker as time passes? The lightning flashing as if the gods were throwing spears at the hapless beings below, the thunder rolling as if a thousand dragons growled in the swirling clouds?

You know the storm is coming, that it will unleash its roaring fury upon you, and there's absolutely nothing you can do to stop the oncoming tempest.

That's us, the storm is coming, and it's headed right at us with all its might and power. And like a fly caught in the raging winds, there's nothing we can do to stop from being engulfed in the ferocity and carried away to our doom.

12

A fter Phigby puts his medicines and utensils back in his bag, he turns to somberly say, "We must have a plan for safeguarding the golden. And I suggest that hiding her in the forest only works for the near future, particularly since the Wilders will be searching every bit of the countryside to find her."

He glances sharply at me. "And it goes without saying that they'll be more than eager to get their hands on those who were the instruments of her escape."

I can't help myself and swallow hard as a small tremor runs through my body. Phigby doesn't have to say it; his meaning is clear. If the Wilders capture us, our lives will be short, but the torture long.

"What about Lord Lorell?" I mutter. "After all, it's his dragon we're protecting. Let's get her to him — and quickly. Let him deal with the Wilders."

Helmar hangs his head down, and I can barely hear him say, "I don't think Lord Lorell will be able to provide any help. He may well have already had dealings with the Wilders."

No one speaks, waiting for Helmar to continue. He raises his head, and the firelight catches the shadows under his somber eyes. "It is my belief that Lord Lorell and his lady are dead. The Wilders have shattered House Lorell this night, and it has joined House Dornmuir as little more than ashes and painful memories."

Cara sucks in a breath. "Helmar, no," she all but moans.

Helmar stirs the fire with a little branch, sending embers upward that dance on the air like fireflies before their glow dims and dies. He remains silent a few moments more before turning sad eyes on Cara. "I'm sorry, but I think the attack on the stead and Draconton was only part of the Wilders' plan. I believe they struck the Manor House, too."

Cara's hand flies to her mouth. The firelight catches the tears welling in her eyes. "Are you sure?" she sobs, her voice sounding both desperate and hopeful that Helmar is wrong.

Helmar lifts the thin branch to stare at the glowing end. "For certain?"

He turns his eyes to the dragons and motions with the limb toward Wind Rover. "No, but it would answer why she returned on her own. She would not have if your father were . . . " his voice trails off, leaving the dire, unspoken thought hanging in the air.

I glance over at Cara. I can see in her eyes that she's thinking the same as Helmar. It's a painful, terrible idea, but it makes the most sense. Lost without her rider, Wind Rover would have returned to that which she was most familiar with; the stead and Draconton.

The flames light Cara's face. She's trying to be brave, but the tears, the quivering lower lip betray her anguish. I can't stand to see her like this but what can I do? Tell her to be brave, that not all is lost — that she still has Helmar?

I say none of those things. Instead, I stay quiet, watching the tears streak her cheeks, listening to her soft sobs and feeling my own insides wrench in torment at watching her agony.

Only the fire's sharp crackle breaks the silence that follows until Helmar says, "When your father, Daron, and I reached the Manor House, we found not only the captain of our knights' guard there but a good number of his knights as well. He told us that he was ordered to bring them as they might be escorting Prince Aster to Draconstead."

"That would explain," Cara murmurs, "why the king's knights weren't around when the Wilders attacked."

"Yes," Helmar replies. "When your father saw how many were absent from patrolling around the stead, he became uneasy and ordered me to return. That's why I came back early."

He pauses to shift his weight as if he's uncomfortable with his next words. "When I went to leave, I don't know why, but Master Boren and Daron got in an argument about me returning."

He turns slightly toward Cara. "For some reason, your brother argued against my going back, which I found a bit surprising."

"How so?" Phigby questions.

Helmar hesitates, gives Cara a quick glance before saying, "Well, it's no secret that Daron and I have not exactly been on good terms since I became Master Boren's apprentice. In all honesty, we've avoided each other's company whenever possible."

"Yet Daron wanted you to stay," Phigby muses.

"Yes," Helmar replies, "but Master Boren ordered me to leave, so I did."

His eyes never leave the flickering flames. "I arrived just in time to see the fires raging in Draconton."

He straightens and meets Cara's eyes. "Like you, I immediately knew that the Wilders were after the golden, and that's how I came to find you and Hooper."

Cara buries her hands in her face. It's obvious that she's tried to be brave and hold back the grief, the torment, but now the sobs rack her body as Helmar finishes his explanation. Her father and brother are most likely dead. Like so many others tonight, slain by merciless Wilders and their evil dragons.

I dare to slip closer to her, our bodies barely touching. It's the only way I know to comfort her, to let her know how badly I feel for her. Master Boren was practically a stranger, and what I knew of Daron, I thoroughly disliked. But Cara mourns for both of them, and I can't bear to see her pain and suffering; the sobs that now shake her body.

She hurts and that makes me hurt.

"Cara, I'm so sorry," I whisper.

For long moments, the grief flows over and through her, before she finally raises her head, wipes away the tears and sniffs deeply. "Thank you, Hooper," she murmurs.

A somber silence falls over our makeshift campsite until Helmar states, "The attack on Dornmuir was a ruse meant to get as many of the knights chasing them eastward, away from Draconstead. That's why they actually only needed a small contingent to take Draconstead, especially as they had the drogs helping them, the scum."

"So what do we do?" I ask.

Helmar is quick to answer. "King Leo. We have to get the golden to him as swiftly as possible. There's no one strong enough to stand against the Wilders but he and his Dragon Legion at Wynsur Castle. It's the only answer."

"It would have to be a long and circuitous journey, Helmar," Phigby observes. "We simply cannot sky straight from here to there as the Wilders are most certainly between us and the castle. I suspect the clouds will be filled with their crimsons and the reward to the Wilder who brings in the golden will be literally her weight in gold."

I blink hard several times and my jaw drops. "Wait, that's just not a saying? There's really that much gold in the world?" I sputter.

Before Phigby can answer, Cara declares, "We can't take the golden to Wynsur."

"Cara," Helmar explains, "I realize it's a long and dangerous sky road, but it's the only choice we have. There's no one else that — "

"No," Cara replies in such a determined manner that both Helmar and Phigby cock their heads toward her with a puzzled expression.

I'm as baffled as they for I agree with Helmar, if Lord Lorell is indeed dead, then it makes the most sense to take the golden to the king and be done with her.

Let King Leo worry about her safety, after all, he has a whole Dragon Legion at his command plus cohorts of men-at-arms and archers, not to mention that he can call on the Great Houses to supply fighters as well.

"My dear," Phigby says in a soft tone, "the way you answered

Helmar tells me that there is more behind your reply than the mere fact that it's a perilous journey to Wynsur."

He leans toward Cara, the fire catching the gleam in his eyes. "You know something."

Cara hesitates, lets out a deep breath and says, "I'm not sure what I know but even if it weren't a long journey, I don't believe that we should try to get Golden Wind to King Leo — not just yet anyway."

I can see her biting down on her lip before she murmurs, "Not until we know for sure."

Phigby and Helmar exchange quick, puzzled glances. "Know what for sure?" Helmar questions.

Cara is staring deeply into the dancing flames as if she's drawing up some distant memory. "Of whether or not it's just the Wilders who are after Golden Wind," she answers.

At her reply, Helmar's eyebrows furrow together so deeply that his skin makes a big bulge over the bridge of his nose. "Cara," he stammers, puzzled. "You're making no sense whatsoever. Who else would be after Golden Wind but the Wilders?"

He points at his wounded arm. "That was a scarlet arrow that Phigby pulled out of my shoulder, remember?"

"I know, Helmar," she murmurs, "believe me, I know but you're just going to have to trust me on this."

Phigby mutters, "Cara, you're not thinking that another House was part of what happened tonight?"

"But the Forbidden Law," I protest, "it — "

Phigby cuts me off by saying, "Means nothing in the eyes of some if the risk is worth the prize. And the golden could well be worth the risk. Think of it, if the world faces some calamity that only Golden Wind's sprog can stave off, what price would we pay to whoever controls that very special dragon to save us?"

"Anything and everything," Helmar bluntly states.

Phigby strokes his beard, and his long sigh blows the fire's flames sharply to one side. "And as far as the Great Houses or King Leo are concerned, after all, it's well known that kings and lords make, change, or ignore the laws, even their own, at their whim."

He smiles grimly. "Even good kings seldom let laws stand in their way to achieve their goal, even if it's dastardly in nature."

Cara remains mute, nor does she raise her eyes to even acknowledge Phigby. My head is reeling from Phigby's remarks. A Great House in league with the Wilders?

Unthinkable.

Or is it?

Phigby's voice is cold, toneless as he goes on. "After all, Golden Wind is the greatest treasure in all the land and the House or whoever controlled her could dictate terms to every kingdom, nation, or dominion that exists on Erdron."

His eyes narrow and he turns to Helmar. "Which brings up a question that I've had in mind for some time but felt it wasn't my place to challenge Boren. Why wasn't Golden Wind taken to Wynsur Castle sooner? After all, she's been fully grown for some time now."

Helmar looks decidedly uncomfortable, and his answer is hesitant, halting. "It is not in my nature to speak evil of my former master."

Phigby leans closer, his eyes boring into Helmar. "Ah, you too know something."

Helmar takes a breath and gives a little shrug with his good shoulder. "Like Cara, I'm not sure what I know, but I will say that you're right, the House that has a golden dragon could indeed dictate terms even to a king."

He draws in a breath. "Which is why I suspect there was more than one reason that Prince Aster was at the Manor House."

Phigby leans back, and his face holds a triumphant expression. "I knew it. Just as I suspected. That wily fox of a Lorell was negotiating with King Leo over Golden Wind. Looking, no doubt, to add to his already fat purse."

He slaps his knee and points at Helmar. "And Prince Aster was there to seal the deal on behalf of the king, no doubt. And if he were bearing a chest full of gold nuggets, or perhaps royal jewels, then yes, a company of knights would indeed be required."

His eyes are alight for a few moments more before his shoulders slump and his mouth skews to one side. "Though it would appear that Lorell's greed earned him nothing but death and for his lady as well."

"Not to mention," Cara chokes, "that it cost so many innocent lives at Draconton and Draconstead."

Phigby turns sad eyes on Cara. "Yes, and those most of all for they truly were innocent in the games that kings and lords play in their cold marble halls."

"And it would appear in their cold hearts," Cara answers. "If they had moved her long before this we wouldn't be sitting here, my father and brother would be alive, this horrible night would never have happened, all those poor people — "

Her voice chokes and her usually soft face has turned to stone while her eyes are fixed and lifeless as they stare at the crackling, dancing flames.

A sudden thought strikes me, and I lean over to ask, "Cara, you're not wanting to take the golden to Wynsur Castle, does it have anything to do with the tall Wilder at the barn? You said that if that's who you thought it was, this night was even more monstrous."

It takes her a moment but then she nods slowly in response. "Yes," she replies, her eyes never leaving the fire, "and I meant every word."

"What tall Wilder?" Phigby is quick to ask.

"While we watched the birthing barn from behind the woodpile," Helmar explains, "this tall Wilder came out of the barn. He seemed to be giving the other Wilders orders."

"He was definitely the master," I add.

Helmar motions toward Cara. "She practically went head over the woodpile to get a better look at him. I had to pull her back before the Wilders sighted us."

He shakes his head and sighs at Cara. "I don't understand what this one Wilder has to do with any of this, particularly your not wanting us to take the golden to Wynsur Castle."

Cara sits completely still, not moving, nor does she answer Helmar. Phigby looks first to Cara and then to Helmar before clearing his throat and muttering, "Helmar, the Cara Dracon I know is not one to hold back in word or deed unless it's absolutely necessary."

He pauses and in a softer voice says, "I suggest that for now, we trust Cara's judgment and do as she asks. No doubt, she has an excellent reason for feeling as she does and will tell us what it's all about at the proper time."

Cara gives Phigby a grateful smile and says, "Thank you, Phigby, that's exactly right."

Helmar stares at Cara for a bit more before shrugging and saying, "All right, for now, we'll assume that we won't make for Wynsur Castle."

"So where does that leave us?" I quickly ask and glance around. "Please tell me that it's not just the four of us against the Wilder horde, and we aren't all alone."

Phigby flicks his eyes toward Helmar as if waiting for him to speak but when he doesn't, says, "For now, that may well be the case, Hooper."

He leans toward Helmar. "Unless we consider seeking help from the closest strong House which would be House Falston, a day's skyride south as I recall."

Helmar shakes his head. "If I were the Wilders I'd be thinking the same thing, that we'd make for Wynsur or Falston and have a screen of reds between here and there."

He twiddles with a thin stick in his fingers and murmurs, "Even if we could get through, I'm not sure how much help the House of Falston would be."

He pauses as his face darkens in the campfire's light. "What if the attack by the drogs here was not an isolated event but widespread, an— "

"Uprising!" Cara's voice is sharp, incredulous.

"It has been several generations," Phigby muses while stroking his beard, "since the Peace of Oran's Dell—"

"The Peace of Oran's Dell? What's that?" I ask.

Instantly, Phigby eyes narrow and I can feel the retort coming so I quickly say in my defense, "Most of your history books are on the top shelf, I haven't gotten that high up yet."

To my relief, Cara explains, "Hooper, the Peace of Oran's Dell is a peace pact that came about during the drogs last rebellion at a place called Oran's Dell. The war with the drogs had been long and bloody so King Malory, Leo's grandfather, made a peace offering to Grug, the drog leader.

"In exchange for what was to be a lasting peace, the king agreed to let the drogs stay within the kingdom, specifically as dragon guards. Their payment was to come in the form of dragon flesh."

"From old dragons that die," I return.

"That's right," she replies. "In exchange—"

"The drogs promised not to rebel," Phigby takes up, "or to kill any Drachs and to be subject to the king and those for whom they worked."

"Like Lord Lorell," I say.

"Like Lord Lorell," Phigby nods. He almost growls while saying, "Why the king entered into that agreement and let the drogs stay in the kingdom is beyond me."

"His legacy," Helmar states. "Perhaps peace with the drogs wasn't enough."

"Or perhaps," Cara offers, "he thought that the drogs wouldn't keep to the high hills and would continually raid into the herds and this was his way of preventing that."

She gives a little shrug. "It would keep them in plain sight and satisfy their craving at the same time."

Phigby nods thoughtfully. "Perhaps that is the way of it, still, when you make a pact with the devil, you have to know that the evil one has no honor and will break whatever promises were made when it no longer suits them to adhere to the agreement."

He takes in a breath. "Or, when someone offers them more."

"And you think that's what happened now?" Helmar questions.

"Assuredly," Phigby replies. "It's no secret that the drogs have chafed under their bonds and their loyalties to anyone but themselves have always been suspect."

He leans forward, his eyes gleaming as if they were glowing coals. "What if," he whispers, "someone offered them more dragon meat than the occasional oldster that we cull from the herds?

"What if they were proffered an unending feast of dragon flesh? What would they do for the one who made such a proposition?"

Helmar lets out a long sigh. "Anything," he states.

I blanch as I recall the death of Pengillstorr. Would the promise of dragon flesh, and plenty of it be enough to cause the drogs to turn on their masters?

Probably? Almost certainly.

I'm the first to voice the obvious question. "But who? Who would have that much dragon flesh to offer?"

Phigby pinches his lips together, his eyes saying that he's deep in thought. "Of course, the Wilders come to mind immediately," he says.

"Yes," Cara murmurs. "But what if it's someone else, someone in league with the Wilders?"

Both Helmar and Phigby look at her in sharp surprise. "You're not implying a Great House is behind this?" Helmar says.

Cara slowly answers, "I'm not accusing anyone, I'm simply saying that I have the feeling that what happened tonight is beyond just Wilders and drogs."

I look at Cara's face. It's solemn and steadfast. She believes in what she just said.

If so, the horrific truth is that not only are we being hunted from the air by Wilder dragons and on the ground by murderous drogs, but we face an unknown enemy.

One whose power is such that they can have the Wilders and drogs do their bidding.

And we are but four against a malevolent force that apparently can command legions.

Thoughts of Golden Wind

Hooper is so young to be carrying a dragon gemstone as well as for the task that he faces.

So very young, and not just in body.

Of course, misplaced hatred always stunts the growth of mind and soul.

On the other talon, the youth have a resiliency about them, a strength that when called upon can carry them great distances and endure great hardships. Some among them are the dreamers who have visions and ideas of what the future may hold for them and others.

Wonderful visions to see what others do not.

Is Hooper one who can see what others cannot? Feel what others do not? Voice what others will not?

His decision may well depend on his ability to do just those things.

We can only wait and see.

But then again, the young have a tendency to be a bit on the selfish side, to worry more about themselves than others. Hooper has just such moments.

Then again, there are two others in our company that soften his heart, Scamper and Cara. Perhaps they can teach him how to grow his heart, too.

He does not yet truly understand what is at stake, nor does he know whom it is that we face — and why.

That which is to come may well change his mind and his heart. The question is, will he survive to do what only he can do? To make the decision that only he can make?

We shall see.

13

The mood around the campfire couldn't be gloomier. How can so few of us stand against the Wilder Horde and the drog packs? I don't think we can. We're doomed.

And it's not just that. Our world's shattered, everything we knew is gone. Cara stares at the fire, but I can see that both her eyes and her thoughts are far away — perhaps to a happier place and time of family and belonging.

The firelight starkly marks the tear streaks that snake down her dirty face. She fought bravely, ferociously tonight to save Golden Wind, and for the moment, we've rescued the golden.

But Cara couldn't save her own family.

Of all the things I wish we had in common, this is not one of them. To both be orphans.

I decide we need to change the conversation, get Cara's mind off her loss, away from her grief, if but for an instant. "Master Phigby," I ask low, "how did you escape the dragon fire in Draconton? I saw your shop go up in flames and thought you dead."

His face holds an odd expression as he replies, "Just after going to bed, I thought I heard noises and voices in my formulating room."

His words bring Cara back to the here and now; she gives me a quick, sideways glance and I return the look.

"But, being old and slow," Phigby rumbles, "by the time I got these cranky old bones out of bed and put my robe on, the first of the dragon fire hit the shops and homes farther down in Merchant's Square."

He pauses and sadly says, "If I hadn't risen just then, I might be still in bed, but as a smoldering corpse, as I'm afraid so many of our friends and neighbors are this night."

He tugs at his beard, staring at the flickering flames. "I grabbed my bag and decided not to chance the front door. I crawled out my second-story window, which for some reason I had left open. I scrambled down the tree, and my foot had just touched the ground when I heard the roar of dragon wings overhead.

"I ran just as a stream of fire hit my neighbor's shop. I ran as fast as I could, but it seemed as though the flames followed me just as quickly. It was all I could do to throw myself into the Mill Pond. The heat was so intense that if not for the water, I think it would have burned me alive.

"I swam to the other side and using the trees to mask my movements made my way toward Dracon Haus." He pauses and pats Cara's hand gently. "The house was completely engulfed in flames by the time I arrived."

He hesitates before saying, "I knew that Boren and Daron were away, and I thought that if Cara had managed to flee the flames in time, that she and anyone else who survived would be on the River Road heading away from the inferno."

No one speaks; like mine, no doubt everyone's mind has turned to the horrific destruction of Draconton. In a subdued tone, I ask, "Do you know if anyone else escaped?"

He shakes his head in answer. "I'm not sure, Hooper, because I never made it to the road." He nods toward Wind Rover. "I didn't find Cara, but I did find her. She was in the open meadow behind the house. She let me lead her away from the village, out of the firelight and into the lower fields."

He gestures toward Cara and Helmar. "Not long after, these two found me."

"Actually," Cara murmurs, "it was Rover that we saw first."

I ask of Cara and Helmar. "How did you escape? There were so many Wilders and only the two of you."

Cara motions to Helmar to begin. He rubs at his chin, the fingers making a raspy sound over his short, stubby beard. "The night and surprise made up for being outnumbered. The Wilders weren't expecting anyone to fight back and were so intent on stealing the herd and Golden Wind that the last thing they expected was dragon fire and expert archers in their midst."

He draws in a breath before saying with a grim smile. "Those on the ground didn't have their reds close by so they were easy pickings. They tried to fight back but trying to hit a sapphire in full flight is close to impossible, and none of their arrows came close."

He grimaces while pointing to his bandaged shoulder. "I got this after we flew down to Draconton." He nods toward Cara. "She wouldn't leave until she had seen with her own eyes what had happened to . . . " his voice comes to a faint whisper as he stares at the fire.

Cara takes up the story while turning to me. "I had another reason for wanting to sky to Draconton, and that was to lead the Wilders away from both you and Golden Wind. So, after I threw you the bow and saw that the golden had escaped, Helmar and I flew fast and low toward town.

"By then, some of the Wilders had made it to their reds and pursued, though like Helmar said, our attack caused lots of chaos in their ranks. We made for Draconton and passed close to Dracon Haus and were about to turn back toward the forest, and make our way here when Wind Song started speaking."

"Speaking!" I yelp a little too loudly for Cara gives me an odd look before saying slowly, "Yes . . . You know that clacking, snorting sort of sound that the dragons make back and forth to each other."

"Oh," I say and let out a breath. "That speaking."

Cara gives me another odd sideways glance before she goes on. "I realized that she'd recognized another dragon nearby and went to look. That's how we found Phigby and Rover. We landed just long enough to get Phigby on her, and then just as we lifted off, a band of Wilders attacked."

She motions at Helmar. "Before we could outrun them, Helmar took an arrow."

She hangs her head for a moment, her long hair, made stringy by sweat and the long skying, makes an oval of her face. "If there were any survivors in Draconton," she murmurs, "we didn't see any."

"And Scamper? How did you find him?" I ask.

Phigby points to Cara. "You can thank her for rescuing that beastie of yours."

I turn to Cara, and she says, "We swung wide of the lower meadows close to the Bread Loaf rocks."

"I know it," I answer.

"I merely glanced in its direction," she goes on to say, "when I saw movement on top of the rocks. It was Scamper. The poor little thing had his front paws up scratching at the air as if he were pleading for us to stop for him."

She dimpled slightly. "I couldn't help myself, he looked so sad and miserable, so I set Wind Song down."

"I didn't want her to," Helmar growled, "I thought we were taking an unnecessary risk, but she wouldn't listen so while she went to rescue your friend, Phigby and I kept watch."

"I no sooner set Wind Song on the ground," Cara went on, "than Scamper shoots up Wind Song's leg and settles behind her carapace as if he belonged there. Then we skyed here."

"Thank you, Cara," I mumble. "Thank you very, very much."

She pats my hand and says, "You're very welcome, Hooper."

She turns to Helmar, and her voice hardens. "Helmar, from what you've said, I can only think that the attack at the Manor House was a trap, to catch father, Daron, you, and the others."

Helmar reaches over, grasps a water flask, and takes a long drink. "And I think so, too. That message to meet Prince Aster and Lord

Lorell was the lure to get practically everyone charged with the golden's protection in one place."

Helmar's face is as hard as stone. "And I, for one, would like to know who sent that sky rider to bid us come to the Manor House."

In the silence that follows, Phigby mutters, "It would seem that the Wilders' tentacles may well reach far into the Northern Kingdom." He tugs at his beard while saying, "And the answer to your question Helmar, is not one that we shall find here."

Helmar nods in agreement. "You're right, and perhaps it's a matter we should discuss at first light. We're all tired, we should rest."

Phigby slaps his knees and rises. "And to that, I heartily agree. There is still some night left, and I suggest that we use it in sleep. Dawn's light will come soon enough and with it a fresh look at what lies ahead."

"I have the first watch," Helmar states as if the matter is settled.

"Your arm," Cara protests.

He pulls his sword out with his good arm and waves it around for a bit. "For now, this will be enough."

"I'll take the second watch," I quickly say.

"And I will greet the rising sun," Phigby rumbles.

Cara opens her mouth as if to protest, but Phigby is quick to hold up a hand. "You need sleep to ease your mind." His eyes grow gentle. "Take what time you can, Cara, you may not have the opportunity after tonight."

She nods and sniffs, as a tiny tear rolls out of the corner of her eye.

Helmar slides his sword back into his scabbard before striding out of the firelight. Always vigilant, I think to myself, he's not content to simply stay by the fire. Instead, he'll see what lies beyond the warm, friendly glow of the flickering flames. Helmar's nature is to be courageous, to be brave, and to protect the weak and vulnerable.

The weak and vulnerable; like me.

As he steps out into the dark, I think to myself, will I ever be as Helmar, able to face danger instead of wanting to flee instead? Will I ever be someone who can protect the helpless, or is brave and daring like him and Cara?

Phigby tends to the fire as Cara settles down on the ground, using her arm as a pillow. Watching the two, my mind wanders back to the night's events. This morning, I dared nipping an extra flat cake from the cooks without them seeing me and thought that it was such a brave deed.

I silently laugh to myself. To think that such a thing was so daring, yet compared to what Cara and Helmar have done it is so trivial as to be laughable.

Thinking over the recent past events, an ominous notion worms itself into my thoughts. I rise and go stand next to the dragons. I stare out into the darkness before I feel a presence and turn to find Phigby standing next to me, peering at me with a concerned look. "Something troubling you, Hooper?" he asks in a small voice. "You should try and get some rest."

I hesitate and then answer in a whisper, "The witch. I know you said it was a dream, but I keep having this feeling that it wasn't. Especially after — "

"Especially after what?" he sharply asks.

I can't hold it inside; I have to tell him. "Especially," I answer, "after I've seen three more."

Suddenly, Cara is beside us. "You saw more witches, Hooper? Where?"

I point toward the three columns. "There. As I was bringing back the water. I saw their faces peering at me from those spires."

Phigby slowly turns toward the glade and he stares for the longest time before he reaches for his bag and orders, "Follow me." Cara scoops up her bow and quiver and quickly falls in behind Phigby.

Me, I follow empty-handed and feeling a bit sheepish. I hadn't expected that this would turn into a witch hunt. I especially hadn't meant to wake Cara from the sleep she desperately needs.

We squeeze past the dragons, and Phigby strides ahead as if he's a soldier marching to battle. We're halfway to the spiral-like columns when Helmar looms out of the darkness. "What's wrong?" he demands.

"Hooper saw a witch — "

"Witches," I correct Cara, sounding a bit peevish.

She points ahead. "At the Fairy Pillars."

"Witches," Helmar snorts. "You three should be getting some rest instead of wandering around out here following Hooper's nonsense."

My face burns. That Wilder arrow may have punctured Helmar's shoulder, but it certainly didn't touch his temperament.

Cara ignores him and paces behind Phigby. Helmar lets out a long sigh in disgust, glares at me, and follows Cara. I trail behind as I don't want to get too close to Helmar, not in the mood, he's in now. Phigby comes to a halt a few paces from the dirt columns. Cara joins him to one side, and Helmar goes to the other.

I stand behind Cara, far enough away from Helmar's reach that if all of this is for naught, and his temper boils over, I might be able to duck his first blow. We stand there for a few moments, in silence, staring at the pillars.

I glance nervously around, my unease growing. "Phigby," I hiss, "what if that thing appears? It could be that it's not just Wilders, drogs, and wolves that stalk the night, you know."

Phigby holds up a hand to silence me. "In this place, we need not fear your phantom, Hooper, especially not that dark specter. For the moment, we are safe."

I hear soft, familiar paws, and surprised, turn to find Scamper scooting next to me. I reach down to scratch his head. "Humph," I grunt, "all we need now are the dragons." Though I say it in jest, I peer back at the dragons, and as I do, my eyes catch sight of the golden. Her head is up, and she's staring intently in our direction, her eyes wide and her gaze expectant, almost eager.

A sudden hush settles on the glade. Even the sounds of the nearby brook and the small stirrings of the trees as the breeze caresses their leaves becomes quiet and still. Overhead, what few clouds there are seem to whisk away letting the full light from the moons shine directly on the three circular towers.

I blink hard several times and rub my eyes, thinking I must be seeing things. From the base to the top, the pillars seem to be gathering the moonlight in long streamers that gently churn and swirl upward.

"What — " Helmar exclaims and takes a step backward as do Cara and I. Only Phigby and Scamper stand firm as a vortex of light gathers as if it's being sucked inside the twisted columns. I don't understand what's happening, but I certainly don't want to get drawn into the spinning whirlpool, so I keep stepping backward.

I start to yell at Scamper, to tell him to flee, to run for safety, but nothing comes out of my mouth. Cara and Helmar whip up their bows, but Phigby reaches out and pushes their bows down. "Hooper," he softly calls over his shoulder, not even looking at me, "come back here, there is nothing to fear."

Easy enough for Phigby to say, I think. He's a — he's a, well whatever he is, he's not afraid, whereas my heart is thumping wildly. I want to keep backing away, but I can't. It's as if unseen roots have come out of the ground to grip my feet and stop me. From out of the churning light, invisible hands push me forward, and no matter how hard I struggle to get away, they don't release me.

I'm pushed and pulled until I'm next to Cara. Whereas my face must be a mask of terror, hers appears to be fascinated by the aura. Her eyes are alight, just like when she held up Phigby's sealed book.

Suddenly, the vortex slows, stops, until only a misty glow surrounds the pillars. Then, the mist curls in on itself before turning into wavy, glowing swirls that flow outward into the glade.

The shimmering haze floats up and over me and seems to soak into my very being. A soft, white radiance fills the glen just like the light that covered Golden Wind when we were in the forest. My fear slowly ebbs out of me, replaced with a sense of wonder and a feeling of . . . Serenity? Peace? Power?

The glowing vapor is so thick that Cara reaches out with a cupped hand as if she could actually hold the light in her hand. I glance down at Scamper. He's sitting on his hindquarters, pawing at the glow, causing a radiant eddy to spin and swirl in front of his face.

Phigby reaches up, and with a finger, writes strange letters and characters in the misty haze. Where his finger pass, they leave a lustrous trail in the air that lingers before the odd-looking shapes fade away to nothingness.

The pillar's sharp edges soften as if the columns are melting. Like a soft wind that rustles through the trees, I hear a ghostly, *Velkommen Geyma.*

I swallow and turn to Cara. "Did you hear that?" I whisper. She barely nods in answer.

The velvety, almost ethereal voice comes again. *We welcome the friends of the Golden One.*

The glowing pillars fade and three beings take their place. The light seems to flow through them and then outward in weaving, shining wisps. Long, silver robes hang from their shoulders to the ground. Their slim arms are bare from elbow to their narrow, graceful fingers. Their blond, straight hair falls over their shoulders, gently lifting at the ends as if a tiny breeze were blowing it about.

Their eyes barely move as if they need but a glance to take it all in. At first, I thought their eyes were blue as before, but now I'm not so sure. They seem to change from moment to moment, just like Phigby's robe appears to shift from one hue to another. However, meeting their eyes is like holding one hand in icy cold water, while the other hovers over hot coals.

That they are female in form and with perfectly sculpted faces, I can see for myself. Moreover, there is no doubt that they are beings of power, of authority, and of regal bearing.

Though I was fearful, no, downright afraid before, nothing in their expressions now causes me to feel threatened or frightened. Besides, what good would any of our arrows do against someone who seems able to control the elements?

"Phigby," I ask in a tiny voice, "Who — "

His hand is quick to stop me. "This is a time to listen, Hooper, not to speak."

At that, the three begin to speak, their voices in perfect unison and sounding both sorrowful and hopeful.

Vay it was who broke the trust
Brought forth the golden to slake her lust
For greed, envy, fear, and power
So that oe'r all she would tower
One dragon to rule them all
One Queen, to her we'd fall
The dragon to rule over its own kind
But to Vay, she would bend the mind
Of the Drach and dragon too
That to her only they would be true
One Dark Queen upon her throne
Seeds of evil she has sown
And of the moment, we did partake
Now the right we must make
From heaven above to that below
The gods will grant that we will go
To set the right
In fiery fight.

The three raise their arms, their hands barely apart. A sparkling ball of light forms in the air, and then they spread their fingers, and the light changes to a rainbow that flows through the air and arches high above us. For a moment, I feel a warmth against my chest where the dragon gem sits.

The three speak again in unison, their voices part soft breeze, part whirlwind.

Bring the bow that colors the rain and lights the sky from horizon to horizon. It will quell the tempest, still the storm that comes to sweep across your world.

Their faces soften, but their eyes are still piercing, and their voices seem to fill mind and body. *To the one who will wield the tears of sacrifice, remember, remember, Vald Hitta Sasi Ein, Power Comes to this One.*

In a rising, commanding tone they say, *Never forget you are called to Ride the Rainbow.*

They slowly turn and point in the direction of the sun's setting. *Your journey continues there.* They turn back and the shimmering haze begins to fade until only the three's shining faces are left in the air. *Remember always that you are called to Ride the Rainbow . . . Ride the Rainbow,* they whisper so low that I must strain to make out their words.

A moment later, the pale moonlight is gone, and the glade is once again in dark shadow.

I peer at the three stonelike pillars, but Cara beats me to the question. "Phigby," she whispers reverently, "what did we just see?"

He turns to us. "Them whom I am both sad and glad to see." His eyes fix on me. "And who confirm my suspicions, unfortunately."

"What do you mean both sad and glad?" Helmar questions.

"Come with me," Phigby orders, "all of you."

Cara and Helmar dutifully follow. Even Scamper tags along with Phigby. But I stand staring at the pillars, struggling with my thoughts. I can feel the jewel in my pocket, and I can still hear the three's words, "To the one who will wield the tears of sacrifice . . . "

Tears of sacrifice? Were they referring to the gem sitting against my breast? And if I am the one who is to wield the gemstone, wouldn't they have called me by name?

I bite down on my lip. Maybe Golden Wind was right, after all, perhaps I am just the jewel's caretaker. But they didn't call anyone by name, they just said that we were the friends of the Golden One. Yet, if the golden is right, and I'm not the guardian, then who is? Helmar? Cara? Maybe Phigby?

After all, it is Phigby who seems to know who those three are. And what about the shimmering strange letters and characters he wrote in the air? Just after he finished, the three beautiful ladies appeared as if he had called them. Maybe the odd characters are a key of some sort, a key that opens a door to another world, a magical world.

A key that only Phigby, among us four, can turn.

The golden was right. I was given the gem only to temporarily hold until the guardian appeared. Where I would have run from the light, Phigby bravely stayed. Where my knees buckled, Phigby stood firm. Where I whimpered in fear, Phigby's voice was strong, steady.

The others' footsteps fade away, and I stand staring at the pillars. A bitterness fills me as I realize that what little hope I had is utterly gone. More than likely, Pengillstorr was searching for none other than Professor Phineas Phigby, Book Master, Alchemist and now, most certainly, the Gem Guardian.

All I can do now is to deliver the gemstone to its proper owner and go back to being only a Hooper. Just like I've always been.

My head droops, and I turn to walk away, my eyes on the ground.

And bounce off a big, fat, protruding stomach.

Do you want to know the difference between a drog and a Night Goblin? The goblin is twice as big.

I'm lying on my back looking up. A bulbous face with an evil grin descends until it's just above my head. I'm eye to eye with the hobgoblin. I never thought it possible but he stinks worse than a dragon. He draws in a deep, loud sniff. His eyes grow wide, and he raises his huge, knobby club.

I can't move, my eyes are held by his head-basher. In a moment, I'm going to know exactly how the fly feels when the fly-swatter lands.

Flat and dead.

14

Out of nowhere, a squalling, furious ball of fur shoots up the goblin's leg, runs along the thing's hunched back, and chomps down on an ear. The goblin springs back, bellows, and grabs at Scamper. But my little friend is too quick. He ducks under the beast's thrashing hand, darts around the gnome's face as if he's a squirrel racing around a tree trunk and bites down squarely on the monster's slime-filled nose.

The brute lets out another roar and tries to claw at its bulbous snout with one hand as Scamper feverishly tears at flesh with sharp claws and even sharper teeth.

From far away I hear, "Run, Hooper!"

The potbellied beast still holds its club high as if it wants to bring it crashing down on my puny head. It hesitates as if it can't make up its mind to either squash me or knock Scamper off its face. Then there's a gust of wind, and powerful talons grip the brutish gnome's deadly cudgel. Wings beat down so furiously that the rushing squall sends small rocks and dirt flying into my eyes and face.

The golden and the slobbering fiend are battling over the thick truncheon, he with both hands on the club's handle, she with her rear talons set deep into its fat end. Her broad wings beat at the thing's head and shoulders until he lets go of the mace and throws up both hands to protect his bulging head from Golden Wind's fierce onslaught.

Out of the corner of my eye, I see Cara, Helmar, and Phigby racing toward the battle royal. Cara and Helmar both have arrows notched in their bows while Phigby is clutching at his bag and trying to reach inside.

I finally get my wits about me and jump to my feet. I turn and shout at Cara and Helmar who are about to launch their arrows, "Wait! You might hit Scamper!"

Scrambling backward, I yell, "Scamper! Let go!"

For the first time ever, I think, Scamper obeys me and using the brute's oversized nose soars off the ogre. He hits the ground running, away from the fight.

I'm still backing away, but I see Phigby pull from his bag what looks like a wispy ring of coiled, shiny white smoke. He twirls the smoke around his head several times before he lets it fly right at the grunting gnome. In an instant, the smoke becomes a solid, gleaming rope.

The line seems to take on a life of its own and slithers through the air before it wraps itself completely around the creature's body pinning its bulging arms to its sides. The golden springs skyward with the mace dangling from her talons.

I hear Phigby shout, *Formulas slithern.*

Wide-eyed, I watch as, instead of a lasso, the rope transforms into a giant sparkling serpent.

A scarlet head with ruby-red glowing eyes appears. It opens its mouth wide to reveal two monstrous fangs. The goblin and the snake are but a few hands width apart. Then the glowing serpent rears back and unleashes a hiss that fills the glade.

The beast abruptly stiffens as if the serpent had squeezed the very life out of him. His eyes roll back in his head, and he starts to sway as if his legs will give out at any moment.

Phigby runs a bit closer and with upraised arms shouts in a commanding voice, *Slithern beway!* and poof! The glittering, giant snake fizzles away in a loop of wispy, silver smoke that rises until the wind blows it away.

The Night Goblin sways again as if it's suddenly lost all its senses. Of course, it doesn't help his cause when the golden drops the brute's mace squarely on his head. Abruptly I realize that if I don't move, that monstrous, bulbous form could fall on me and what its club didn't do, its enormous plump body will.

"Hooper, move!" Cara shouts, but at that point, I don't need her encouragement. I'm already stumbling away from the staggering goblin as quick as I can, but it's not fast enough. Like a tree totters before it falls to the ground, down come the giant gnome's knees, then its stomach, and finally its chest and ugly head with a dull thud.

Just when I think I'm in the clear, one flailing hand catches me square in the back sending me cartwheeling over the ground.

I end up lying on my back staring up at the sky. The monster's blow has knocked the wind out of me, and I gasp for breath. Scamper jumps on my chest, which doesn't help my breathing any and puts his face close to mine. *Hrrrrt?* he asks.

Cara's head appears in my line of vision and then Phigby's. Cara bends down and asks, "Are you hurt, Hooper?"

I shake my head and suck in a deep breath. "Just need to breathe," I gurgle. I push Scamper gently to the side so that I can sit up.

After making sure that the goblin is out cold, Helmar walks over and gives me a quick, curt glance. "You know, Hooper, if you would just do as you're told . . . " his voice trails off, but I can tell by his exasperated expression that he'd like to say a lot more, a lot louder, and with perhaps a bit more colorful language added.

Before he can get started in on me, I quickly ask Phigby, "Was that another little demonstration of simple alchemy?"

Phigby purses his lips together and shrugs. "Mmm, you might say it was a form of alchemy, yes. But simple? No."

He reaches down and grabs me by the shoulders. "Up you go, Hooper."

"Thank you, Phigby," I say with a rush of air, "thanks to all of you."

Phigby nods toward Scamper, who's sitting nearby licking his paws as if what he had just done was an everyday occurrence. "Thank your furry companion," he replies, "and Golden Wind. If those two hadn't gotten here first, my little effort would have been too late, and that goblin's club would've made your head look like a splattered pumpkin."

With that, he turns to study the golden who stands to one side, looking as if absolutely nothing untoward had happened. "I've never seen a dragon act quite that way before," he murmurs.

"Neither have I," Helmar says, giving me a funny, quizzical look before he points to the sleeping, slobbering brute. "What exactly did you do to him, Phigby? Not only have I never seen a dragon act that way, but I've never seen a Night Goblin go down like that, either."

"Oh, that," Phigby replies with a dismissive wave of the hand. "That was nothing. Goblins and their troll cousins are deathly afraid of serpents. They'll run from even the smallest, harmless grass snakes. But faced with a glowing, serpentine creature almost as tall as he was, well, you can see the results for yourself. He'll stay that way for quite a while."

"That's good to know," I respond. "Next time I meet either I'll be sure to have a snake in my pocket to throw at the thing." I reach over and scratch Scamper behind one ear. "Thanks, my friend, you saved my life."

I turn back to Phigby. "How did you know that goblins are so afraid of snakes?"

Phigby glowers and leans in close. "From books, Hooper, from reading books. There's more to reading that just silly illustrations of clowns juggling circus balls, you know."

Cara speaks up and says, "A better question is why was that goblin here in the first place? They normally don't get near dragons."

Helmar turns to peer at the neighboring forest. "She's right, goblins and trolls know they're no match for dragon fire and usually stay away from dragons."

Phigby slowly turns to survey the surrounding dark forest. "A goblin chances an encounter with not one, but four dragons." He turns to eye me. "And all for such a scrawny meal as Hooper."

"What are you saying, Phigby?" Cara asks.

"Either," Phigby says as he scratches at his cheek with one finger, "that was one famished goblin, or, Hooper had a delectable odor about him that the thing couldn't resist."

I glare at Phigby, but before I can respond, he again scans the wall of darkness that marks the tree line. "Or, there is a power at work here that caused that king-sized gnome to overcome its natural fear of dragons and attack Hooper."

"Power?" Cara asks.

Helmar steps in and says, "We can discuss this power or whatever later. But thanks to Hooper and your light display, Phigby, we can't stay here any longer. If the Wilders didn't know where we were before, they probably do now."

"Oh," Phigby answers apologetically. "I am sorry, Helmar, I didn't think about that. I was a bit rushed, you know."

"Understandably," Helmar is quick to answer, "but we've got to get out of here before we have more company, and it won't be goblins either."

"What about the dragons?" Cara asks. "They've not had much rest."

"And neither have we," Helmar answers gruffly. "I'm sorry, but we have no choice. We can neither stay here nor will it take long for the Wilders to get here if they saw Phigby's fireworks."

"As I said," Phigby tartly answers, "I'm sorry about that. But you have another problem." He motions toward the dragons. "One of the sapphires has to carry a double load, and she'll be no match for a red if the Wilders find us."

Helmar turns hard eyes on me, and I can see in his scowl that he has the thought of leaving me behind. In a way, I wouldn't blame him — it was my fault for tarrying behind the others. If I had stayed with the group, the goblin might not have appeared, and Phigby wouldn't have lighted up the whole forest.

Cara must have noticed Helmar's glare for she quickly says, "Wind Song can carry the load, she's strong."

Helmar works his mouth, but before he can speak, I volunteer in a small voice, "Perhaps the golden and I should walk. That would lessen the load on at least one sapphire, and what about the sprogs? They can't fly, but the golden can carry them."

"More nonsense, Hooper," Helmar states with an emphatic shake of his head. "Golden Wind being on the ground would make it that much easier on the Wilders to capture her."

He lets out a deep sigh, a sign that he has to face the inevitable, but he doesn't like it. Sort of like when you're starving and all you have is a thin slice of moldy bread to eat. You'll get it down, but you'll gag on it all the way down your throat.

I know.

"We'll have to take the chance," he says, "that the sapphires can deal with the load and that the golden will sky with us. We can put the sprogs in saddlebags. It'll be a tight fit, but they won't fall out."

"What if the golden doesn't follow?" Cara asks, evidently concerned that after all we've been through to get the golden away from the Wilders she might refuse to trail us.

"I think she will," Phigby says, giving me an appraising look as if he's musing over his thoughts before he speaks. "After all, she came to Hooper's defense. I think she may have an affinity for him."

"No," I sputter in protest. "She has no attraction to me, and I certainly have none for her."

"That may be so for you, Hooper," Phigby replies. "I'm not sure that applies to the golden." He turns and gestures to Helmar, "Let us make haste while we still have time to make haste."

We make for the sapphires, who are milling about, having no doubt risen when the golden took to the air. Even from here, I can hear the sprogs screeping. You'd think you were listening to a bunch of sheep bleating in fright.

I purposefully let the others get ahead of me. As I pass the golden, I slow, and my whisper is brusque, "I guess that answers whether you can sky or not. But you can stop saving me now. I have no desire to be in your debt."

Without answering, the golden follows me back to the campfire where Helmar is tossing dirt on the fire to put it out. Cara is on Wind Song adjusting her saddlebags so that they'll be able to carry the four sprogs while Phigby is doing something to his threadbare bag.

As soon as the sprogs see me, they waddle over and cluster about my ankles. I contort my mouth in consternation. I had hoped that after the golden had carried them that they would attach themselves to her, but that doesn't seem to be the case or my luck.

Cara calls out to me. "Hand me the sprogs, one by one. We'll put two sprogs in each pouch. That should balance them out. Scamper can ride up front with me, and you'll sit behind." I grab my bow and quiver in one hand, Regal in the other, and scurry over to Wind Song, with the other sprogs following close behind.

Dragon saddlebags are a little tricky. Each bag is connected to the other by a broad strap that fits over and under the dragon's neck. Then a much thinner strap ties into each bag and then to a rivet at the base of the dragon's throat.

But you don't want to overload the bags or have them unbalanced, causing the thin tie-down strap to chafe against the dragon's scales while skying. If that happens, the scales could cut clean through the slender strap, causing your bag to slip off to one side and dangle in the air. Worse, it could fly up and wrap around you, and if the contents are heavy, knock or pull you off your dragon.

None of which would be good if you're skying high above the ground. Someday, I just know that someone's going to invent a device that'll allow a dragon rider who falls off a skying dragon to float gently down to the ground. Someday. But until then, if you fall while skying you usually end up being very dead.

Cara and I hurriedly get the sprogs settled in Wind Song's saddlebags. They all object, but we ignore their bleating. "You'd think they wanted to stay behind," I say to Cara as I push Regal down into the bag for the third time. Squirming sprogs do not make it easy to stuff them into the bag and then cinch it tight.

She gives me a wan smile. "They don't understand that they should just enjoy the ride. It won't be long before someone's riding them."

We get the sprogs settled in, tie both arrow quivers to the saddle-bags and sling our bows over our shoulders. Cara will have to wear her wood shaft to her front, and I'll have to wear mine to the rear. If we're attacked, neither of us will be able to get to our bows quickly. Which really won't matter if we're attacked by a pack of Wilders, anyway.

Finished, I look around for Scamper. He's close by, digging into the hillside. I start to whistle for him, but just then Helmar and Phigby come striding up.

"Are you ready?" Helmar asks Cara.

"Except for Scamper, yes," she answers. She leans down. "Are we headed west? The direction the fairies pointed?"

"The Wilders are raiding to our east," Helmar replies, "and their lairs are to our north. If we assume that the Wilders will be expecting us to go south, then what's left?"

Helmar and Phigby exchange a glance as if they've had a quick discussion on this subject already. Phigby speaks up. "We really have no choice but to go west. I believe that's why the three pointed us in that direction. For now, it may be the only place where we can hide both ourselves and the golden."

Cara leans a little farther and asks, "How far west?"

Helmar and Phigby again exchange a quick glance. "Far enough," Helmar mutters. "Let's go." He dashes to Wind Glory while Phigby hurries over to Wind Rover.

Something in Cara's tone prompts me ask, "Cara, why did you ask about how far west we were going?"

She turns her head slightly, and I see her run a tongue over her lips. "Let's just say I've seen enough of Phigby's maps to know there's a certain point to the west where the maps have three sentences, and then there's nothing beyond that. The maps just stop."

"They just stop? What does that mean?"

She gives a little shrug. "That either no one has ever gone there, or maybe they have — and never returned to tell what lay beyond."

"What do the maps say? The three sentences, I mean."

She hesitates and then says, "The Golian Domain. Beware. There be giants in the land."

"Oh," I answer quietly and lean back. If there was something in Cara's voice before, I know what's in her tone now. Apprehension. And for a girl who's just taken on a slew of Wilders, that's saying something.

Cara settles onto Wind Song's neck, and I whistle for Scamper. He comes bounding up, flashes up Wind Song's leg and leaps into Cara's lap as if he knew that was his spot. He puts his paws on Wind Song's carapace and leans forward, pointing his nose into the wind.

Cara glances back at me. "I think Scamper is telling us it's time we leave."

Cara scoots forward just a bit and says, "All right, Hooper, settle in."

I squeeze myself behind Cara and murmur, "Do I hold on like I did before?"

"Not if you think you're going to fall off," she answers, "otherwise, yes."

I wrap my arms around her waist. I have no intention of falling off. But I have every intention of holding on tight.

Phigby hefts himself up onto Wind Rover and waves to Helmar that he's ready. Cara nods that we're ready, too. Wind Glory plods out into the clearing, and I hear Helmar's firm voice, "Sky, Glory, sky." The sapphire spreads her wings wide, beats them a few times, and then with a downward thrust of her wings leaps upward to catch the wind. Right behind is Phigby on Wind Rover.

"Here we go, Hooper," Cara says, "and make sure you hang on, this isn't going to be like our little flight from the stead to Draconton. Keep an eye on the golden, if she doesn't follow us, we're going to have to go back for her."

She leans down, strokes Wind Song's scaled neck, and says, "Sky, girl, sky."

Wind Song spreads her wings, beats them once before crouching and then lunging upward. If I hadn't known what was coming and holding on to Cara, I would have fallen off right then. Wind Song's upward stab into the air is so powerful and quick that it almost throws me off.

In moments, we're winging through the early morning darkness. We join Rover and Glory in circling the glen while all eyes are on the golden below. She trundles into the meadow, spreads her wings, beats them several times as if testing the wind, and then leaps into the air.

It doesn't take her long to catch up with us, and she rides the night air just off Wind Song's right wing. She's having no trouble keeping pace with the other dragons. Cara says over her shoulder, above the rush of wind, "Dragons take to flying like fish take to swimming."

"Still," I answer, "that was a huge chance Helmar took, thinking that she'd stay with us once we took to the air."

"He didn't have much choice," Cara replies. "We couldn't stay here any longer and besides, he's trying to honor Lord Lorell's decree that no one shall ride the golden on the ground or in the air."

I swallow, but this time I keep my mouth shut. If Helmar knew that I rode the golden, he'd definitely leave me behind. "Besides," Cara says over her shoulder, "see how she's staying close to Wind Song and you? I think Phigby was right. Golden Wind likes you, Hooper. Must have been all that sugar grass you've been feeding her."

I have no answer for her, but I do touch the dragon jewel and wonder if there's some bond between the dragon and the gemstone. I blanch as I suddenly realize that in all the excitement, I forgot to give the gem to Phigby, or rather, the Gem Guardian.

I look ahead to where he's skying Rover behind Wind Glory. It's not like I can ask Cara to have Wind Song catch up to Phigby, take the gem out and toss it to him, while saying, "Here! This belongs to you. I'm sorry I kept it so long, but this was the first chance I could deliver it."

As if she was reading my mind, Cara squirms in her saddle and says, "Hooper, what's that hard thing you've got in your pocket? It's rubbing against my back."

"Uh," I stammer before I ease my hold on her waist and lean back so that my front no longer touches her back. "Sorry, is that better?"

"Yes," she replies, "but what is that? It feels like a rock."

"Uh, that's pretty much what it is," I mutter. At least to me, I think.

"You're carrying a rock," Cara states.

"Never know when you'll need a good stone," I answer. "Might want to knock a squirrel out of a tree and there's no rock to be had."

Cara just shakes her head at my answer, and I can tell that she's thinking that it's just more Hooper nonsense.

The wind rushes past my ears, and Wind Song's leathery wings seem to whistle through the air with every stroke. Cara was right. This isn't like our first flight. I put my mouth next to Cara's ear. "We're really moving!"

"Helmar is keeping us at a good pace and low," she replies. "We could go faster, but he doesn't want to wear the sapphires out, and he's using the darkness of the forest to cover our movement. If we were higher, there's a chance we'd be spotted against the moons."

"Smart," I reply.

"Yes," Cara answers quickly, "that's Helmar. A very clever man."

I think to myself that she didn't have to agree quite so fast or readily to my comment. But who am I kidding? It's obvious how she feels, and there's no doubt about the depth of Helmar's feelings for her.

The forest is so steeped in darkness that there's not much to see so I gaze upward. The stars are more numerous than grapes in Draconton's vineyards and seem so close that I feel like I could reach up and pluck one from the night sky.

We fly low for some time before I notice a brightening at our backs. The night is passing, and it's one I never, ever want to repeat. With just a little anxiety in my voice, I ask, "Do you know where we are?"

She shakes her head in reply. "I'm not sure, Hooper, it's been too dark to see anything."

Scamper, who had been napping, is now awake and chittering madly as if something is bothering him. Cara asks over her shoulder, "What's he saying?"

"Like me," I answer, "he wants to know where we are and where we're going."

She points at two strikingly bright stars that are so close together that they seem almost to touch and blend into one. "Helmar's been using the King and Queen Stars to guide us west."

"West," I answer, "to the edge of that map you talked about where there's nothing beyond except giants."

"Quit worrying, Hooper. Helmar and Phigby know what they're doing."

That may be so, but I don't like the sound of not only not knowing where we are, but that we're headed toward a land of giants. As puny as I am, I already feel like I walk in a land of giants. And to go to a place where someone like Helmar is considered small, what does that make me?

A teeny, tiny gnat among dragonflies.

"Cara, these giants, do you know anything about the Golian Domain?"

"Some," she replies. Her matter-of-fact answer is too casual for me. There's nothing matter of fact or casual about giants.

I wait, but she doesn't answer. "Well? What do you know?"

She glances back at me. "That they are a race of warrior giants who are very willing to lop anyone's head off who sets foot in their territory without permission."

She pauses and then says, "Phigby has a history book that says that many seasons ago, the Wilders sent a large raiding party into the giants' territory. Only a single Wilder dragon and rider made it back alive. And they were allowed to live only to deliver a message to the Wilder chieftain."

"What was the message?" I ask.

"One word," she answers. "Don't."

"Oh." Hooper, I say to myself, never ask a question you're not ready to hear the answer to, especially if it concerns getting your head lopped off.

We go on a bit farther, the sky becomes lighter and lighter, and then both Rover and Glory slow and wing next to us. With a wave of his hand, Phigby gestures at what lies ahead and shouts across, "Those are the first of the Dragon Scale Lakes. Beyond that distant line of high hills are the Colossan Mounts. We're getting close to the Golian Domain's eastern boundary."

I admit, skying on a dragon is an incredible adventure and now that I've gotten over my fright, in a different place and time it might even be fun, especially sitting so close to Cara. However, it's not that wonderful when the dragon is flying you straight toward a realm of giant soldiers.

I'm not one to challenge Phigby or Helmar on their decisions, but this strikes me as sheer lunacy. The Wilders are vicious and blood-thirsty, but if Cara's story is true and the Wilders with their armor, bows, and mighty red dragons didn't make it out of the giant's domain alive, what chance do we have?

None.

After thinking it over, I call out, "Phigby, are you sure this is wise? From what Cara has told me, the giants don't take kindly to anyone entering their land."

Phigby smiles in return. "Cara's absolutely right, but don't worry, Hooper, we'll soon turn south. We're not going into Golian, but make for Woodsdale, a village which lies a bit farther onward."

With a large amount of relief, I give Phigby a little wave. Shortly after, our dragons dip their wings and in a slow arc, we put the brightening dawn on our left shoulder and turn south.

I lean forward and ask Cara, "Do you know why we're going to Woodsdale?"

She shakes her head, her hair whipping at my face. "I'm not sure. I know it lies at a crossroads where trade caravans meet. Maybe Phigby and Helmar are hoping to hear news of what is happening in the realm, and of the Wilders."

"News?" I reply and snort. "Me? I'd like news about a warm bed and some hot food. Right now, I'd be happy to have the butt end of a loaf of bread to gnaw on."

Her answer is quiet and forlorn. "Warm bed and hot food. Especially if the bed were yours, and the food from your own kitchen."

I've done it again. Opened my mouth and said something that reminded her of her destroyed home and dead family. I'm excellent at displaying ill manners. Of course, when you've never been taught any manners, it's hard to know good from bad.

I glance around, but of course, I don't recognize any landmarks except the Dragon Tooth Mountains far, far off in the distance and to our right. As the dragons right themselves on a southward course, I gaze off to the east. On the horizon, the early morning light is growing. Dawn is almost here and with it, a new day.

Movement in the distance causes me to immediately stiffen. Dozens and dozens of black, tiny dots fill the sky behind us.

I almost jerk Cara out of her saddle in my hasty attempt to get her attention. "Look behind!"

She twists her body, takes one look at the onrushing dragon army, and immediately prompts Wind Song to a greater speed. We come even to Wind Glory, and Cara thrusts out an arm to point at what follows us. "Wilders!" she shouts to Helmar.

Both Helmar and Phigby crane their necks to stare behind at our pursuers. But there's no doubt. A crimson cloud of scarlet dragons is bearing down on us. While we've been lazing along, their reds have been racing toward us. Now they're so close that I can easily make out their scarlet-clad riders. Their dragons are huge monsters; it would take two of our sapphires to make one Wilder red. Our attempt to escape has failed; somehow, the Wilders have found us.

"What are we going to do?" Phigby shouts to Helmar. Before he can answer, the golden suddenly bolts ahead of us. Her burst of speed takes us all by surprise, but not for long.

Helmar yells, "Follow her!"

He and Phigby scrunch down on their dragons while Cara shouts over her shoulder, "Hold on, Hooper! We're really going to sky now!"

The three sapphires pull their wings inward, and they seem to gather themselves like a coiled snake in midair. Then, like a striking serpent, they spurt forward, slicing through the air faster and faster in pursuit of the golden. I hunker down low behind Cara, the rushing air is incredibly powerful, and almost feels like it will blow me off Wind Song's back.

Scamper, on the other hand, has his paws on the edge of her carapace with his little nose pointed into the gale. The rushing wind makes his lips curl and flap together like the beak of an angry, quacking duck though his eyes are bright and eager as if he's enjoying our sky race.

Golden Wind makes a sharp turn in the air, her wingtip almost catching the treetops as she flashes above the forest. She's turned toward the west and the distant mountain peaks that are alight with the early morning dawn's pale radiance. Dragon Glow.

"She's headed west!" I shout to Cara.

"That I can see," she answers back above the roar of dragon wings and whipping wind.

I manage to turn my head to peer behind and what I see is not good. "The Wilders are gaining!" I yell.

"They're only burdened by one rider," Cara replies grimly. Her meaning is clear; our sapphires could outpace the Wilders' reds if they didn't have to carry the extra weight. I look around to see if there's anything that I can throw overboard to lighten Wind Song's load.

There are only two things that I can toss away into the morning air that would be of no consequence. The sprogs and me.

For just an instant, I loosen my fingers around Cara's waist as if to untie the straps that cinch the leather bags. It wouldn't take but a moment to loosen the knots and send the little dragons flailing to the ground and their deaths below.

I shake my head at the dark thought. Cara would never speak to me again, never look at me, and never, ever forgive me. That I could not bear. I push my hands together. In fact, I hang onto Cara that much tighter. "Where is the golden going?" I yell into her ear.

She points ahead. In the distance, I can see the mountains rising sharply to form snow-tipped towering peaks that seem to march from one horizon to the other.

"We can't fly over those!" I shout into Cara's ear. "They're too high."

"I know," Cara calls back, "but that's where the golden is leading us."

The sapphires are beating their wings furiously to keep up with Golden Wind and to stay ahead of the trailing Wilders. We're nearing the mountains and to me, they look like an impenetrable stone wall.

Cara abruptly raises herself in her saddle and jabs a finger into the rushing gale. "Look!"

I peer ahead and blink back the tears that form in my eyes from the wind's force. Though my vision is blurry, below us I can just make out a white-laced stream that's sliced through the mountains to cut a sharp, narrow valley. It's what lies across the gorge that causes me to press forward against Cara's back to try and see better.

Giants.

A line of warrior giants, twenty times taller than any one of us stands on a massive wall as if guarding the gap through which the rivulet flows. The Titans stretch completely across the vale from one mountainside to the other. Sharp tipped arrows, notched in enormous bows point right at us. The golden is following the stream straight up the valley toward the glowering giants. And we're following the golden.

"Turn her, Cara, turn her head!" I yell. "We're headed right for them!"

Instead of turning Wind Song away from the goliaths, Cara snaps out, "And fly into those bloodthirsty Wilders that follow? I'd rather take my chances with those stone giants and what lies beyond."

"Stone?" I choke out and peer harder at the towering titans. It's then that I notice that the giants haven't moved. They're standing absolutely still as if frozen in place. It dawns on me that I'm staring at colossal stone statues. Like sentinels, they stand as if to guard this valley against intruders. I start to ask Cara what good are rock giants when a crimson arrow flies by my ear.

Then another and another.

The Wilders are coming within longbow range. I look back, and I all but stop breathing. The sky is full of red dragons with their riders pulling on the sinews of their longbows to unleash a hail of deadly arrows at us.

We've lost the race. The Wilders are upon us.

15

My eyes grow wide, and I suck in a breath as I see the Wilders rise from their dragon saddles to take better aim at us. They're so close that I just know they can't miss — not at this distance. Just as they're about to loose their arrows, I hear a loud whoosh and an enormous iron-tipped bolt splits the air just over my head — coming from the opposite direction.

There comes a piercing screech, and I look back to see a red dragon thrashing in the air, an arrow shaft longer than I am tall protruding from its neck. A stream of green dragon blood spurts skyward. The red's neck snaps back, and his Wilder is catapulted out of his saddle. His arms and legs flail helplessly in the wind as his dragon begins a death dive to the ground far below.

More giant arrows fill the sky, each a lethal missile that impales a crimson, sending rider and dragon plunging downward to the boulder-strewn valley. I peer in the direction of the arrow's flight and stare in absolute astonishment.

From the shoulder of each stone giant runs an enormous bridge that connects each statue to its neighbor. Standing on the connecting spans are flesh-and-blood giants.

There must be at least several dozen, maybe more, each armed with a longbow that makes my bow look like it's made from a twig. Their aim is deadly; each arrow they launch brings down a Wilder dragon. They haven't fired upon us yet, and the only reason I can think of is that our sapphires don't present the same threat as the Wilders.

For once, luck seems to be on our side, and I'm not going to question why.

More Wilders fall from the sky, but now they're fighting back. Swarms of scarlet-clad Wilders turn their attention away from us and fill the air with hurtling arrows that fall on the Golians. Most of their arrows bounce off Golian shields, but I see two giants stagger on the stone ledge with Wilder arrows piercing neck or eye.

One giant falls onto the bridge and lies still, the other sways, trying to hold its balance before finally tipping forward and falling off the span. The giant's body somersaults through the air until it crashes onto the rocks below.

Even though they're taking losses, the Wilders press on, trying to overtake us, but they have to do a sky dance to throw off the giants' aim. The Wilder archers no longer have a clear bead on us. Nevertheless, our three sapphires are twisting and weaving their way through the sky, not giving the Wilder bowmen a clear target for long.

There are so many of them that their arrows seem to be like a black blanket over our heads. Once, a thundering storm caught me out in the open and I was pelted with sharp hailstones that bruised and cut flesh when they struck.

However, those chunks of ice didn't kill. I would gladly trade being in that hail tempest again for this storm of death arrows that rain down on us and from which we can't seem to escape.

I've long since lost sight of the golden, I have no idea if she's still skying or if she lies on the ground with a Golian arrow protruding from her neck. I know Scamper is still with us because I can hear his high-pitched squalling as he hunkers down under Wind Song's skull sheath. He's spitting mad and letting the Wilders know that he doesn't appreciate being their target.

I have no idea how I've managed to hang on and not fall off. Cara moves naturally with her dragon, seemingly knowing when, and which way Wind Song is going to twist and places her body in the right position at just the right time.

Not me, one instant I'm pitched to the right, the next I'm hanging off the left side. Then, we zoom straight up, and my head feels as though someone is trying to yank it off my neck, then we're spiraling downward, and I'm doing everything in my power not to lose my grip and do a header over the top of Cara.

I know it's only a matter of time before either a Wilder or a Golian archer skewers us with an iron-tipped bolt or I'm flung off Wind Song and die on the sharp rocks that litter the ground.

Helmar seems to be trying to get us away from the fight, but each time we turn in a new direction to escape, the Wilders cut us off with a flight of arrows or a phalanx of dragons that rush at us. We're caught in the middle of the battle between the Golians and the Wilders. A sudden desperate thought stabs at me, and I yell, "Cara, take Wind Song up! Go up!"

"What?" she shouts back.

"Up," I cry. "Straight up!"

Without knowing why Cara tugs on Wind Song's head, and she instantly responds by skying upward and away from the Wilders. We flash toward a layer of thin clouds, which stream high in the air above us. I still can't find the golden anywhere, but I see that Helmar and Phigby have their two sapphires pacing us as we climb higher and higher.

For the moment, we're clear of the clouds of arrows, but it won't be long before the Wilders catch up.

I glance over my shoulder. Far below, dozens of Wilders are still exchanging arrows with the Golians. At this height, they look like a swarm of angry bees attacking a marauding bear who's sniffed out their honey-laden hive.

To my disappointment, a dozen or more Wilders have followed our sapphires and those that trail us are pumping legs and arms in a furious attempt to gain more speed from their reds. I can feel Wind

Song begin to labor and slow. Having to carry the two of us to such heights is too much. She can't last much longer.

Cara senses the same because she calls over her shoulder, "It's too much for her, she's lagging."

I had hoped that the massive bodies of the Wilders' crimsons wouldn't be able to sky this high, but I was wrong for they still follow. Even at this height, we haven't cleared the mountain peaks that rise on each side, and the air is so thin it's hard to get a full breath. Cara calls over her shoulder. "Hold tight, Hooper, we're going to dive straight down."

My eyes grow wide as I understand what she's about to do. She's going to plunge her dragon right through the Wilders at such speed that hopefully they won't be able to hold their arrow points on us long enough to let loose.

My next thought is what will kill me first, a Wilder arrow through my body, or falling off Wind Song during our wild dive and plummeting to my death?

Wind Song seems to loll in midair as if she's skying over a gentle hill before she points her nose straight down. I decide that I'll know the answer to my questions within a few moments.

Wind Song, Wind Glory, and Wind Rover are wingtip to wingtip as if in a race to hit the ground first. One part of me wants to close my eyes shut, but I keep them wide open.

The sprogs' screeches of disapproval fill the air before they delve deeper into their saddlebags, the wild ride obviously not to their liking. I'm in total agreement and wish that I could burrow in alongside them.

For an instant, I see the whites of the Wilders' eyes as we speed past. They're as full of astonishment as my own. We split the Wilder dragon pack and the Wilder riders desperately pull on their reins, trying to get their dragons turned to follow us.

They're so busy with the reins that they don't dare try to draw their bowstrings. And they can't unleash dragon breath as we're so close that their own fire streams would scorch their fellow riders. At this point, they can only turn their dragons and follow us down.

The wind is roaring in my ears. Wind Song has her wings practically tucked against her body, and we're in a headlong rush to the boulder-packed ground below. I have no idea if she will be able to pull out of this dive or not.

If not, then we will make one large hole when we smash into the ground.

In our upward sprint, we actually crossed over and past the Golians' statue barrier and now we're falling on the far side. Below and to my left, I can see the Wilders and the Golians still battling. The fight is taking its toll on both sides, with fewer Wilders than before, but fewer Golians as well.

Helmar and Wind Rover pull ahead. The ground is so near now that I think I can see individual stones on the ground. I close my eyes. We've waited too long to pull up. We're not going to make it; we're going to hit so hard that we'll be splattered across the countryside.

With an upward jerk that is so forceful that it feels as if my head will snap off my shoulders, Cara pulls Wind Song up and to the left. We're skimming just above the stream. We're so close to the water that we leave a spray behind us that looks like a rooster's tail.

"Cara," I yell, "Helmar's leading us back toward the other Wilders!"

In an incredibly calm voice, she answers, "That he is."

In just moments, we flash past the Golian archers, directly at the remaining Wilder horde. Blood-red arrows whiz past to the right and left. One comes so close to my head that I'm positive I have a new part in my hair, straight down the middle.

Just ahead, I see a horde of Wilders bring their bows down with the arrow's knife-sharp tip aimed right at us. Their arrowheads glint in the day dawn's golden burst of light and look like Phigby's tiny Feast Day sparklers.

However, these aren't harmless sparklers that make a child dance and laugh with glee, these flickers of light are meant to kill.

I can see the Wilders pull their bowstrings taut, and my muscles grow as tense and tight as the sinews of their bows. We're headed straight for each other. They can't possibly miss. My jaws clamp down, my grip on Cara tightens so much that I fear I'll squeeze all the air out of her, and she won't be able to breathe.

I take a quick peek behind. The Wilders that followed are still with us, but the Golians' arrows are deadly and accurate. Fewer Wilders trail behind, but there are still more than enough to knock us out of the sky.

The distance between the Wilder pack to our front narrows. I suck in my breath. A thunderous twang of unleashed bowstrings fills the air. A barrage of arrows flies toward us, so thick that it seems as if I'm staring at a solid dark wall.

For an instant, time seems to come almost to a standstill. I can see the mass of arrows moving toward us, but it feels as if they're moving more slowly than a rising moon. Wind Song's wings barely beat the air. I think to myself—this must be what happens just before you greet death.

Everything comes to a halt and then you just . . . die.

I'm abruptly jerked out of my reverie by Wind Song's sudden rush skyward. Her drastic move catches me totally by surprise. We're skying upward again, but I've lost my grip on Cara. I'm falling backward, pushed by the roaring wind, my hands and arms flailing helplessly in the air. Only at the last instant do I manage to grab hold of an edge of Cara's dragon saddle.

I'm lying belly down on the back of Wind Song with both hands gripped on the decorative edging of Cara's saddle. Its thin lace and beadwork are not going to hold me long. As the sapphire beats her wings, her powerful back muscles throw me up and down as if I were on the back of a bucking horse.

"Hooper!" Cara shouts above the gale. "Hang on!"

"What do you think I'm trying to do?" I gurgle in reply.

Wind Song crests at the top of her upward rush, and we flatten out for a moment before we're speeding downward in a shallow dive. I can't see a thing. My face is pressed against dragon scales, and my body streams behind like the House of Lorell's pennant that flies on the flagpole above The Common back in Draconton.

I have no idea where we're going or what happened to the

Wilders. Are they still following us? Are we still trying to get away? Are we high in the sky or down low? I have no idea. What I do know is that as Wind Song twists one way and then the other, I can feel the decorative frill on Cara's saddle fraying and ripping.

My weight is too much. At any instant, it's going to tear loose, and I'll go flying off Wind Song's back. I desperately push my head up, looking for something else to grab ahold of, but there's nothing to grasp.

"Cara! The lacing's tearing!"

She looks back with real fear in her eyes as she realizes my precarious predicament. For a moment, she turns, does something with Wind Song, and then twists her body around and reaches out. "Grab my hand!" she shouts.

I loosen the grip of one hand and frantically try to catch her fingers. Just then, the lacing tears away. I have nothing to hold onto. I begin to slide backward from the wind's powerful push. Somehow, my fingernails grip one of Wind Song's scales and stop my slide, but only for an instant. I can't hold onto the scale, I'm not strong enough.

Cara leans out farther and farther, stretching her arm toward me. She's bent over almost backward with one hand just out of reach. I grip the tough dragon scale with every bit of strength I have with my right hand, take a deep breath and lunge with my left hand.

I touch Cara's outstretched fingers just for a heartbeat and then I'm torn away.

I'm falling, tumbling through the air.

Ground and sky spin through my vision. In one of Phigby's books, I once read where a maiden dipped her hand into the "gentle, soft waters of a lily pond."

Gentle? Soft?

Pure fantasy.

When I hit the water, it felt like Sorg the drog had picked me up and thrown me against the wall beams of the birthing barn back at Draconstead.

The only good part was that the water wasn't too deep, and the bottom was mud.

Gentle, soft mud.

I lay, dazed, my body half embedded in the brown, soupy goop which swirls up and over me. Little bubbles dribble out the side of my mouth. A demanding voice inside my head is yelling at me that I'm drowning, but I'm too shocked, too stunned to move. My mind keeps floating in and out of darkness.

With a swiftness that jerks me awake, I'm yanked from the bottom goo. Great blasts of wind beat at my body, and I can feel the sunlight on my face. I'm sputtering and spitting out gobs of water and sucking in huge drafts of air, trying to breathe again. Now I know what a fish feels like when an eagle snatches it out of a lake.

Then, there's ground underneath me. I hear faint, running footsteps and then dimly, "Hooper! Hooper!"

Hands are on my face, cupping my chin. Someone rolls me over, pounding my chest as if they would beat the life back into me. "Hooper, spit the water out. C'mon, you can do it."

I spit, sputter, and cough up more water, and then still more until no more water comes out and I'm sucking in huge drafts of air. Someone holds me so that I'm more on my side and my stomach until my breathing is almost normal.

Then I'm rolled on my back, and I open my eyes. An angel is floating above me, complete with halo and a serene, beautiful face. I can hear her delicate lacy wings rustling.

Wait, those are dragon wings and they are not delicate.

Two dark, solemn eyes, a button nose, and little paws that pull at my lips replace the angelic face. *Gwaaaake?* Scamper asks as he nips at my nose. *Gwaaaake?* he asks again in a very insistent manner.

"No, Scamper," I gulp and sputter to my furry friend. My words sound muffled in my ears as if my mouth is full of hay. "I'm not awake, I'm dead, can't you tell?"

"Hooper!" Cara yelps and gently pushes Scamper to one side. Her eyes are actually genuinely concerned. "I'm so sorry, Hooper, I tried to reach you, but I just couldn't."

Somehow, I manage to wave a weak hand at her. "I know," I answer. "If I could have held on just a little longer . . . "

"For what it's worth," she says, "in a way it was good that you fell off when you did."

"Really? It was good that I fell?"

"No, silly," she answers with the hint of a giggle. "It wasn't good that you fell off Wind Song, but if you had held on much longer and then fallen, you would have hit the trees. I think that might have been far worse than landing in a shallow, marshy pond."

I take a deep breath. "Let's see, dying by drowning versus being impaled on a tree limb. Yes, I guess there is a slight difference there."

Cara just shakes her head and with her help, I manage to sit up and look around. I see the golden and Wind Song, but not the others. "Helmar? Phigby?" I ask.

"I'm not sure," she answers anxiously. "I lost sight of them while I was trying to help you stay on Wind Song."

"The Wilders?"

She glances upward. "They may have followed Helmar and Phigby. I think they lost track of us."

I glance at the small pond. A few dark green lily pads float near the shore. Some of them appear to be mangled and torn, courtesy of my back-flopper entrance, no doubt. "Thanks for pulling me out," I say gratefully. "I don't think I would have lasted much longer."

"Don't thank me, "Cara replies. "I didn't get you out of the drink."

She gestures toward the golden. "Thank her. I think you've got a guardian dragon, Hooper."

The golden is sitting on her haunches, staring off into the distance, seemingly unconcerned as if nothing unpleasant had happened. "Just what I need," I mutter, "a guardian dragon."

"Actually, Hooper," Cara answers, "it seems that lately that's just what you need. For whatever reason, she appears to be watching over you, and you should be very grateful. Who wouldn't want a guardian dragon? Especially, if it's a golden."

I turn away and mumble to myself, "Me, for one."

Abruptly, both the golden and Wind Song come to all fours and stare toward the mountains on the horizon. Cara quickly glances up and peers at the two dragons. "They're not acting uneasy as if they're hearing Wilder dragons," Cara murmurs, "but let's not take a chance."

She nods toward the woodlands behind us. "Let's all get in those trees, just in case."

"Why not sky out of here?" I question.

"Because," she says, "if it is Wilders, Wind Song is too tired to try and outsky them with the two of us, and you're in no shape to ride a dragon right now."

I can't argue with her reasoning as when I stand, the ground wants to slide away and my legs feel like they're made of mush melons. Cara pushes me toward a nearby forest of tall pine trees. "You, in there," she orders, "while I get the dragons."

I hobble toward the thick woodland. It's a good thing I'm not in a race with a snail. The slug would win handily. I'm still a good two rods' lengths away from the greenery when Wind Song and the golden lumber past me, with Scamper right behind.

Cara comes up, grabs my arm and pulls. "Move, Hooper, we don't have much time."

I do my best to pick up the pace, but I'm still woozy and weak from almost drowning. As it is, Cara is all but carrying me the last little distance into the trees. We stumble into the tree line, and while Scamper and the dragons go deeper into the woods, Cara and I slide behind a thick trunk and peer toward the meadow we just left.

Faintly, I hear dragon wings. I listen intently and whisper to Cara, "They're skying low and pretty slow." I cock an ear toward the sound of beating wings, listen, and then say, "They're getting closer, and they're hardly moving as if they're searching the ground below them."

Cara grimaces. "It's Wilders, looking for us. They must have seen us land, but they don't know the exact spot."

She jumps to her feet and reaches down to pull me to mine. "C'mon, Hooper, we need to get farther into the forest, where there's more overhead. The tree branches are too thin here, they'll spot us."

I start to turn with her but stop. She takes several steps, turns, and hisses, "Hooper, move! They'll be over us in no time!"

I raise a hand to quiet her, listen some more and then turn. Wind

Song and the golden have stopped too, turned with their heads up, gazing at the treetops in an expectant posture. That only confirms what I'm hearing. "Wait, Cara, look at our dragons, see how they're acting?"

She looks over her shoulder at our dragons. "It's not Wilders," I state with a relieved grin. "It's Wind Rover and Glory. I recognize their wings and so do Wind Song and the golden."

"Helmar!" Cara cries and darts past me.

I push around the tree to hobble after her, but she's already to the open field. Moments later, I hear the rush of dragon wings overhead and at the same time, I hear Cara shout, "Helmar!"

The beating of wings slows, and through the thin line of trees that stand between the meadows and me watch a sapphire hover above the sawgrass for an instant before putting talons to the ground, followed by a second sapphire. Cara is pumping her legs as fast as she can go toward Wind Glory and Helmar.

I turn and hobble back to the golden and Wind Song. "Let's go," I mutter to the golden. "Cara has her Helmar back."

"And Phigby, too," the golden answers.

"Uh, huh," I answer as I gaze toward the meadow. "And she's certainly paying a lot of attention to Phigby, now isn't she?"

Scamper chatters at me and I say with a wistful smile, "Yes, I know, why would I want Cara when I have you."

I lead the golden and Wind Song toward the meadow, where Cara, Helmar, and Phigby are guiding their two dragons toward me. "Hooper," Phigby calls out with a wave of his hand, "it's good to see you, lad. We thought we'd lost the two of you."

Helmar ignores me and goes over to the golden to give her a quick inspection. Once he's finished, he gives the golden a gentle pat on the neck. "She appears unharmed," he mutters in a relieved tone.

"Well," Phigby smiles wide, "by some miracle we all appear none the worse."

"But we could have been," Helmar states. He slides his hand over the golden's scales and says, "I don't know how she knew to lead us to those giants, but if she hadn't — "

He doesn't have to say more as we each share a quick glance, knowing how fortunate we are that not only is the golden safe, but we're alive.

Phigby steps closer, his eyebrows furrowed as if he's just noticed that I'm dripping wet. "Hooper," he asks gruffly, pulling at my tunic, "have you been swimming?"

I let out a long sigh. "In a manner of speaking, yes."

"You should have seen it, Phigby," Cara gushes. "Hooper fell off Wind Song. Fortunately, we weren't too high, and he landed in the pond with a huge splat."

She shakes her head, her eyes wide. "Before I could get Wind Song turned to get to him, the golden came along and scooped him off the bottom, just like an eagle plucks a trout from a lake. She set him down, and it took a while for him to cough up all the water, but I think he's all right now."

"Is that right, lad?" Phigby asks. "Are you all right?"

I nod and say, "A little water-logged, but I'm good."

"He's lucky to be alive," Cara goes on, "he sank clear to the bottom."

I shrug and say, "So I swim about as good as a rock, what of it?"

"And the golden pulled you out . . . " Phigby murmurs while giving me an odd look. "Very interesting, indeed."

Helmar quickly steps in and says to Cara, "Interesting or not, we sighted a woodsman's hut, not far from here and almost due south." He motions to the dragons. "The dragons are tired, and I don't want to chance skying during daylight, so we'll walk from here."

He turns to Glory and commands, "Leg, girl." His dragon thrusts out her leg and like the skilled rider, he is, Helmar quickly clambers to his saddle. Phigby turns to Wind Rover, and Cara nods to me. "Let's go, Hooper."

Before I've even gone a step, the golden is next to me and thrusts out her leg. Cara gives a little laugh and points. "Would you look at that, she's imitating Glory."

I just stand there, unable to move, staring at the golden's leg. Out of the corner of my eye, I see Phigby turn, his face showing marked surprise. I raise my eyes to Helmar. The expression on my face and the golden's extended leg says it all.

Helmar literally jumps off Glory and in three steps he towers over me. I can't help but cringe. He stares at the golden and then turns to me, his face hard and sharp as if made from cut granite. "You — rode — Golden Wind!"

His words are so piercing, so cutting, that if they were a sword, I would be lying in several pieces on the ground, now.

Then comes the hiss of his blade from his scabbard, seemingly louder than Phigby's smoke snake back at Fairy Falls. And like the goblin, I know I should run, but I'm frozen in place.

His drawn sword gleams in the sunlight, a deadly blade ready to cut cleanly through weak flesh. My flesh.

The golden may have saved me from death by drowning, but in the next instant, the sheen of Helmar's blade will be dulled by my blood dripping off its knife-sharp edge, and I shall be lying dead at his feet.

16

"Helmar! Hold!" Phigby roars.

"Helmar, what are you doing?" Cara's voice is close to a scream. Scamper appears out of nowhere, putting himself between the big man and me, furiously chattering at Helmar with his little lips curled in a snarl.

Me? I stand mute, unable to raise a single word in my own defense. I cower before Helmar and his sword. The man seems to be a giant in his own right. He looms over me but it's more than his height, there's a power, a force about him that is riveting and holds me in place.

Have you ever been caught in a raging storm? You know that the tempest could easily kill you; still, you are awed by the sheer power of the thundering storm. That's how I felt about Helmar just at that moment.

Cowed and afraid, yes, but awed by his towering strength and commanding presence. Then, Phigby's hand slaps hard against Helmar's wrist, holding his sword arm in place.

Helmar growls at Phigby and Cara, "He broke Lord Lorell's decree, he rode the golden. You know the penalty."

"So?" Phigby bristles. "You said it yourself, Helmar, Lord Lorell is dead, and the House of Lorell is no more. Would you slay him over a dead man's declaration? I remind you, sir, that the King's Law says that such pronouncements are null at the death of the issuer, in this case, Lord Lorell."

"But we don't know — " Helmar begins, his lips curled back and fierce eyes never leaving my face.

"You were pretty confident last night of his death," Cara breaks in before she says with a catch in her voice, "and my father's."

Helmar swallows and glances from Cara to Phigby and back. I can see in his eyes what he's thinking, his own words have trapped him. To kill me while Lord Lorell lived would have been expected, but now? Now, under the King's Law, it would be murder.

Helmar is no murderer, of that I am sure. But, in his eyes, I have broken the law and his trust.

I finally find my voice. "Helmar," I whisper, "I'm sorry, but it was dark, I was lost, and the golden seemed to know where she was going. Just like she did when she led us to the giants to escape the Wilders. My leg was hurting terribly, I was slowing us down, and I could hear the howls of Dreadwolves in the distance."

I take a breath. "She offered," I all but whimper, "like now," pointing at the golden as if that made my decision and actions acceptable.

Helmar glares at me for a moment more, his face still stone hard before he gives a curt nod to Phigby, lowers his arm, and scabbards his sword. "Lord Lorell may or may not be dead," he spits out, "but until we know for a certainty, no one, especially you, Hooper, is to ride the golden."

He jabs a finger in my face. "Is that clear?"

I swallow and nod. My legs, none too strong before, now feel as if they'll give out and I'll sink into the ground, never to rise again.

Helmar spins away and stomps back to Glory. Cara slips next to me, and our eyes meet. The angelic, concerned face is gone, replaced with a hard, cold expression. She opens her mouth as if to speak but then brushes on by and heads for Wind Song, leaving me with Phigby.

He stands eyeing me for a moment before he turns to gaze at Cara's rigid back and murmurs, "I suggest you ride with me, Hooper. It would appear that you are persona non grata, at the moment."

"I'm what?" I mumble.

"Persona non grata," Phigby finishes. "It means that you've just fallen into a barrel of rotten fish, and no one wants to be near your stink."

"Oh, well," I sigh. "That's nothing new."

He leads me over to Wind Rover, and we clamber aboard. Helmar and Cara are already pacing their dragons away, leaving Phigby and me behind. I whistle for Scamper, and he flashes up Rover's leg and settles behind Rover's carapace.

Phigby prods Rover and we slowly trundle off, the golden following behind. We plod along for some time in silence, with only the fluttering of morning birds to break the quiet. I'm deep in thought, thinking of Helmar standing there with his raised sword, his eyes flashing like lightning bolts, his face set and stiff.

Yes, he scared me so bad that I thought my heart would stick in my gullet. Yet, I have to admit, even though I was incredibly afraid of him there was something about the way he stood. There was a presence, an aura that seemed to surround him as if the morning sunlight had melted and left its sheen glowing on his body. The muscles in his neck had bulged and rippled and he had towered over me like a god, full of power and strength.

Murderous power and strength. Still, even as he was about to lop my head off I couldn't help but feel his commanding authority.

I stare at Phigby, his unkempt hair, scraggly beard, and rumpled robe. Yes, he had stood firm when the three had appeared at Fairy Falls, and Helmar had given ground.

But after seeing Helmar in all his impressive ability, I have to wonder, is Phigby really the Gem Guardian?

Or, was it Helmar that Pengillstorr searched for at Draconstead? In a way, that makes more sense. If Pengillstorr was searching for Phigby, he would have lumbered onto The Common at Draconton, or stood in front of Phigby's shop. And after this morning, with Helmar appearing as he did, commanding, larger than life, and appearing as powerful as a torrential tempest, I can't help but wonder, is he the guardian, and not Phigby?

I shake my head to myself, deeply troubled and confused. How do I know which of them is the guardian? Or, is it still possible that the guardian is yet to show? My head is spinning, trying to decide who I should give the jewel to, or should I wait? After all, the guardian may yet appear at some point in our travels.

I let out a long sigh. I can't decide on my own. First chance, I've got to speak with the golden, she has to help me. For the first time, I feel a weight on my shoulders. With all that's happened, the power of Pengillstorr's jewel may just be the thing to help us. I absolutely can't give it to the wrong person.

Phigby says over his shoulder, "What was that deep sigh all about, Hooper? You sounded as if you'd lost your best friend. But, you haven't, he's right here." He chuckles lightly and points to Scamper, who's curled up in sleep. A corner of my mouth lifts up in a little smile. He'd been so ferocious back there, certainly braver than I, willing to take on Helmar and his longsword.

I abruptly realize that Phigby is waiting for an answer. "Uh, Phigby," I slowly ask, "have you ever faced a question that you didn't know the answer to or a problem that you didn't know how to solve?"

"Since just a few moments, ago?" he snorts. "Never."

I can tell he's teasing so I go on. "Seriously, what do you do when you're so perplexed that you can't think straight, yet you know that you've just got to find the answer to your question? And it absolutely has to be the right answer."

He's silent for a moment before he mutters, "Sounds serious, Hooper. Just what is this taxing question that you face?"

"Umm," I answer, "I'm sorry, but I'd rather keep it to myself for now."

"I see," he murmurs. He gives a little shrug and then says, "What little advice I can give you is that I've found it quite useful to ponder over the question for some time, formulate several possible answers and then decide which of those answers feels most right to me."

He pauses before saying, "Then I do the most important thing you can do before making the final decision."

I lean forward and ask. "What is that?"

"Sleep," he answers. "A good night's rest does the heart, mind, and soul good. Never make a critical decision, if you can help it, without sleeping on it first."

"Sleep," I mutter, a little disheartened by what seems to be an overly simple solution to a most vexing problem.

"Absolutely," Phigby replies and then says, "Barring that, flip a coin and pray that it comes up right."

"Oh, that's a big help," I retort. "I haven't a farthing to my name."

He glances over his shoulder and grins. "Don't worry, if you come to that point, I'll lend you a coin, with the stipulation you return it, of course."

"Of course," I mumble.

We ride on in silence for some time before I say, "Uh, thanks for standing up for me back there. I thought for sure that Helmar was going to slice me in half."

"That man," Phigby growls, "like too many, acts before thinking."

"Well, I guess I deserved his anger," I mutter.

"Nonsense!" Phigby is quick to say. "Under the circumstances, I would have ridden the golden too, and Helmar for all his sanctimonious prattle would have done the same if it meant saving the golden from the Wilders."

He stops and lets out a long sigh. "I suppose, though, that Helmar is having a hard time accepting that all he knew, his world has been lost and with it, his dreams, too."

Not all of his dreams, I think. He still has Cara, and she would gladly be his world if he would just let her.

"For him, I guess so," I reply.

"But not so much for you?" Phigby questions.

I shrug and say, "Oh no, my world has hardly changed at all. I don't have to shovel manure all day, but I do have a dark witch chasing me. I don't have to worry about Malo stabbing me with his Proga lance, I only have to worry about drog spears and Wilder arrows piercing my body. Or maybe Helmar slicing my head off if he gets angry enough again.

"And at least before I had a barn with a roof overhead, straw to sleep on and a meal house with food, even if it was barely enough to survive on." I raise my arms toward the sky, "Now I get to sleep on dirt and rocks and wonder where my next meal will come from, if ever."

I pause and then say, "No, my world has hardly changed at all."

"You still have Scamper," he points out.

"That's true," I answer, eyeing my little friend who's curled up in sleep. "And that's the best part of my world that hasn't changed."

"And all thanks to Cara," Phigby is quick to say. "You owe that girl, Hooper. You know that, don't you? If it hadn't been for Cara, Helmar would have left your furry friend sitting on those rocks."

I gaze ahead to where Cara sits upright in her saddle, never once glancing back. It's apparent she shares Helmar's feelings about my blunder with the golden. I crossed the line and for now, I'm that persona non whatta that Phigby called me.

"I am deeply, deeply grateful," I murmur. "I'll make it up to her, somehow, I promise."

"And I'll hold you to that pledge," he replies.

My eyes go from Cara to Helmar, who seems to sit rigid in the saddle. Still getting over his mad, I think. "I guess you're right about Helmar," I say. "He did have big dreams, and now it's all gone. Draconstead, I mean. The buildings, the dragons, his chance as he put it to climb up the ladder of success."

Phigby is slow to answer, but when he does, his voice is quiet and mournful. "Yes, Draconstead is gone, and not just the herd, or the buildings, Hooper, but the good people who worked at the stead and those who lived in Draconton. That's the greatest loss. You can replace mere things, but lives you cannot."

He lets out a breath. "Nothing left of Boren Dracon's legacy but these four dragons and the four sprogs in Wind Song's saddlebag. A sad ending to a good man and a great Dragon Master."

"You're forgetting Cara," I murmur.

"So I am," he replies, "and perhaps she is his greatest legacy. After all, our children are a part of us, and we are a part of them, down through all generations."

I bite down on my lip. If that is the case, then my family's heritage stops with me.

We plod along a little farther before I ask, "Phigby, what happened back at Fairy Falls? Who were those three?"

He's quiet for a bit before saying, "Someone whom I dreaded seeing, and yet, in a way, glad as well."

"Their poem or chant," I say, "it sounded like the one you spoke the night I saw that witch thing."

"It's more than just a poem or chant, Hooper, it's part of an ode," he replies.

"An ode . . . " I've never heard of an ode. "What's that?"

In answer, he says, "What they and I recited is part of a lengthy poem that tells a story." His tone lowers as if he's recalling a memory. "Of creation, of life and death, and perhaps the future, as well. It's part history, part prophecy, part answers to many questions."

"They kept mentioning something about riding a rainbow," I point out. "How do you ride a rainbow? It's just colors in the sky, or so say your books."

Phigby grunts. "Did I not say that odes often present mysteries as well?"

"Well, you mentioned Vay," I reply, "and so did they. Who exactly is Vay?"

He's slow to answer. "Someone that we need to discuss among the four of us and not just between you and me."

He turns back to face forward and from his posture, I can see I've gotten all that I'm getting out of him, for now. I glance up at the swaying treetops. The wind rises, causing the new spring leaves to rustle together.

Abruptly there's a *caw, caw* . . . from overhead. I find the source of the noise and see a bird, its feathers as dark as night, hovering high above.

Phigby stops Wind Rover dead in her tracks. The bird whirls over us for a moment, its eyes on the dragons, before it dips its wings and speeds away. Phigby's body is stiff, and he's staring at the bird as it disappears through the treetops.

"Phigby, what's wrong? It was just a bird."

"Not just any bird, Hooper," Phigby rumbles. "That was a black crawven, strictly a night bird. It should not be out this late in the day."

I shrug. "It probably fared poorly in its night hunting and was searching for one last bit of food."

Phigby shakes his head. "Its eyes were on the dragons, especially the golden, and dragons are not part of its diet."

"Then what are you suggesting?"

"Nothing," he snaps and urges Rover onward. "Hooper, stay quiet, I need to think."

We're soon marching next to a series of tall, rounded hills. We climb up a small knoll and stop. Below us, set just inside the tree line formed by a mix of forest glens and stands of birchen trees is a broken-down cabin. We peer down into the little dale, which is covered mostly by short grass and tree stubs.

Helmar gestures. "From the looks of those cut trees, I'd say it was a woodsman's hut."

"It's not much more than a shanty," Cara murmurs. "How do we know it's empty?"

"No smoke from the chimney," Phigby observes, "and from the looks of the roof's thatching, I'd say that either the owner doesn't mind getting wet, or it is indeed deserted."

"I think the latter, Phigby," Helmar answers and prods Glory down the slope. We follow Helmar cautiously until he calls a halt. Helmar slips off Glory signaling for us to stay where we are and to be silent. He quietly draws his sword and warily approaches the cottage.

Cara notches an arrow and holds her bow at the ready, just in case. Helmar stops at the hut's front corner and seems to be listening. After a few moments, he steps to the door, which seems ajar, and slowly pulls it open. He guardedly sticks his head inside, then all of him disappears into the shanty. Moments later, he steps out and waves for us to join him.

As we bring the dragons up, he says, "It's long empty. There's a dirty makings of a bed, a small, rough-hewn table and chair, and a hearth with a bit of wood. The cuttings are so dry that they'll give off little smoke. I think we can chance a fire. Phigby, would you get one started?"

"Certainly, my boy," Phigby answers and clambers down to the ground.

Helmar points to the woodland past the hut and says to Cara, "The trees thicken just beyond. Let's get the dragons under cover and let the sprogs out of their cocoon. Before we let them graze, though, we'll search the ground for dragon bane. This is still dragon country, and there might be some just sprouting."

At the mention of the poison petals, I blanch. I'd forgotten about the flower in my pocket. My hand starts toward my tunic, but I stop as I don't want to draw any further attention to myself, especially not about that and particularly not from Helmar. If he knew I had poison petals on me, not even Phigby and Cara combined could stop him from slaying me on the spot.

As soon as I can, and in a safe place, I'll get rid of it. Helmar hasn't given me any orders, so I reach for the two water flasks that are tied to Rover's saddlebag and mutter, "I think there's a stream over that way. I'll fill these and try to find more dry wood."

"You do that," Helmar growls, "and if you do find water, let us know so that we can take the dragons for a drink."

I give him a quick nod and Scamper, and I slide off Rover. I start to walk off, when Cara says sharply, "Hooper, aren't you forgetting something?"

I raise the water flasks to peer at them and do a quick once over of my tunic and threadbare pants, but I don't see anything missing.

Cara stands there watching me with an irritated expression. I glance up and give her a questioning shrug. "A bow," she says, "without arrows is like a sword or knife without an edge. Useless."

She points at Wind Song's saddlebags where my quiver of arrows is tied tight. "Oh," I say meekly and hurriedly retrieve the arrows. I scurry away, but I can feel Cara's and Helmar's glowering stare on my back the whole way. Scamper is already off searching for food, and Phigby has disappeared into the shanty.

As I pass the tiny cabin, I give it a quick once-over. The walls are cut tree trunks and strips of bark hang loose, exposing the pale, bleached wood underneath. Unfinished logs notched at the ends and set ten to a side make up each wall of the rectangular structure while old, stringy darkened yellow hay thatches the roof.

Carved out of one wall is a window with thin shutters while the rough-hewn door is slanted and partly open. The sagging thatched roof and the door that tilts to one side, as Helmar stated, signal that the previous occupant abandoned the cabin some time ago. Still, it is out of the weather, and out of sight, which is good.

I start to slip past the door but stop. I can hear Phigby inside fussing with the kindling, scraping at the hearth with an edge of some kind and muttering under his breath.

My hand goes to the jewel. It would be so easy, with Cara and Helmar out of sight, to march in, hold out the gem and declare, "Phigby, you are the guardian of this dragon gemstone. Keep it safe, keep it hidden, and I know you'll soon be able to wield its powers."

I'd hand him the crystal, I'd stride out, my duty done, and go back to what I'm good for and meant to do in this life. Draw water, collect firewood, and most of all, shovel dragon dung.

I hold my hand over the jewel for a moment more, before my shoulders droop, and I pace past the cabin door. Hand the gem over to Phigby is what I should do, but I can't. Not without talking with the golden first. She'll be able to tell me if my suspicions are correct; either Phigby or Helmar is the Gem Guardian.

It has to be one of them, I'm all but certain it can't be anyone else.

A sudden chattering startles me. I spin to see what's making the noise. Evidently, a squirrel has come down from the treetops to investigate Scamper's activities. Now the two are engaged in a furious back and forth of chattering and chittering at each other.

From what I can tell, the squirrel is letting Scamper know that this is his tree, and Scamper had no right to strip the bark away.

Scamper, on the other hand, seems to be saying that squirrels don't eat termites, so why is he so upset?

Knowing that my attempt to skewer the squirrel with an arrow would be a waste of a perfectly good bolt, I glance around to see if I can spot a rock. He's only one squirrel to split among the four of us, but still, we could make squirrel soup. It would be short on meat, but it would fill our empty bellies for a time.

Before I can find a rock, the squirrel, still angrily chattering at Scamper, darts back up the tree and disappears into the branches. I shake my head in disappointment. Even if I could find a suitable rock, I'm not sure I could throw it that high with enough force, to knock the squirrel out of the tree. I resolve to tell Cara about the animal, maybe she can bring him down with an arrow.

If she'll listen to me, which is not a good bet right now.

I make my way out to a small open meadow and hold my right hand straight out and up so that the fingers are horizontal between the horizon and the sun. I put my other hand and its fingers on top of my right hand and count between horizon and the sun's edge. "Eight fingers high," I mutter, "and no sleep last night."

I stifle a yawn. "No wonder I'm so tired." I glance back toward the hut just in time to see Cara and Helmar come from the tree stand and head for the cabin.

Cara walks exactly beside Helmar, close enough that her arm and shoulder brush against his. They're talking to each other, but they're too far away for me to hear. However, it must be an earnest conversation because Cara appears quite animated, her hands out front making quick, small gestures and her eyes centered on Helmar.

"Probably talking about me," I mutter. I put a hand on my hip and pretending to be Cara, say, "Helmar, what shall we do about Hooper? He's making a mess of things. First, he rides the golden, then he gets us in a battle with a goblin that leaves us running from the Wilders, then he falls off Wind Song and nearly drowns himself."

"I know, I know," I answer, imitating Helmar's deep voice. "He's nothing but trouble, spouting nonsense, costing us valuable time. He can't use a longbow or a sword, he can't sky a dragon, and with that leg of his, he can't keep up. Frankly, my dear, he's not worth our time. We should get rid of him."

They're almost to the cabin when I see Cara point back at the dragons. "Now she's telling Helmar, that there's only one reason to keep me around. To water, feed, and pick up after the dragons, and oh yes, be a mother duck for the sprogs."

I see Helmar shake his head and wave a dismissive hand before he and Cara enter the hut. Obviously, I think to myself, Helmar must believe that I'm not even good enough for that.

I whirl around, my anger and hurt building inside me. I'd like to see them get lost in the dark, with wolves and trolls lurking in every shadow, ready to sink their fangs in them. Or, worse, a witch just waiting to wrap her claws around their throats and strangle the life from them.

Oh sure, they wouldn't have gotten up on the golden to ride, they would have stayed loyal to Lord Lorell's stupid decree to the very end. Well, I'm not one of them. I may have a miserable, rotten, go-away-and-leave-me-alone life, but it's all I have, and I'm not going to give up on my life. Not for some stinking dragon.

I kick at a clump of grass and trudge toward what appears to be a line of treetops that snake behind a rolling ridge. I hear a snuffling behind me and turn to find Scamper following behind, poking his nose into this and that. He seems to have resolved whatever his argument was with his adversary because his fur seems intact, and I can see that his tummy is a bit rounded, meaning that he's found something to eat, somewhere.

I'm glad he's eaten, I just wished he'd shared. My stomach feels like one gigantic empty cavern and at this point, I'd even consider some fat worms dug up by Scamper to fill it.

I make my way up the small hill and stop. At the knoll's base runs a tiny stream that meanders between two little hillocks before it wanders out of sight. I pick my way down the modest incline and find a small pool where I can dip the flasks under the water.

While the deer hide containers are filling, I set aside my bow and quiver while I cup the water to my mouth and drink deeply before I splash a little over my cheeks and neck. The coolness calms my anger and the flush on my face.

The bubbles escaping from the containers as they fill are almost gone, and I'm about to draw the pouches from the water when a dark shadow falls across the stream.

I try to leap away, but I'm too clumsy. I awkwardly trip and fall before rolling onto my back. Silhouetted in the sun's glare is a large, dark-skinned man. His open leather jerkin hangs over bulging chest muscles. With arms and hands that look the size of trees, he shoulders a gleaming two-edged ax. I have no doubt of his ability to wield the fearsome blade.

Moreover, I have no doubt that he's about to wield it on me.

At that moment, I resolve that if I live through this, I'm going to learn how to use a bow.

The question is, am I going to live through this?

17

I reach for my bow, but I'm too slow and fumble away my chance to bring the longbow to bear. The ax swings through the air straight at my head. I can't help myself, I close my eyes and let loose a scream of sheer terror. Instead of slicing my head open like a sharp blade through a watermelon, the edge of the ax barely kisses my forehead and nose.

I wait a moment before I'm able to open my eyes again, only to find the ax wielder bending over, his eyes fixed and hard while he keeps the blade centered on my face. He leans closer before his mouth slowly turns up into a smile and his chuckles turn into a deep belly laugh.

His smile abruptly ends with a yelp when a gray ball of flailing fury flies out of the air and lands squarely on the man's broad shoulders.

Scamper sinks his tiny teeth into one ear. The burly man lets out a cry, reaches up, and grabs Scamper by the scruff of his neck.

He swings Scamper around so that the two are eye to eye. Scamper's four paws are furiously scratching at nothing but air and his black lips curve back in a vicious snarl. Well, as ferocious as he can, which really isn't saying much. From his mouth comes a throaty growl intermixed with high-pitched chitterings of anger.

The man holds Scamper out, turning him from side to side. "Humph," the man growls. "You're small but plump. With a good roasting, you might be worth eating."

That does it. Before he can stop me, I roll away, scramble to my feet and charge straight at the bare-chested man. I don't even remember to draw my knife as I'm so enraged that he'd want to hurt Scamper.

Before I get close, the man lifts his ax up and holds it out level with the short, pointed wooden end aimed squarely at my gut. I manage to stop and suck in my stomach before he can twist the handle and have the blade bite into my flesh.

His brown eyes are like stone as he stares at me. "Hold, boy," he rumbles in a deep, bass voice, "before you find yourself missing body parts."

He cocks his head to one side as he sizes me up. "You be no Wilder, and this," he says as he gives Scamper several hard shakes that sets him off to chittering again, "is no Wilder dragon."

Holding a snarling Scamper out to one side, he asks, "What you be, boy?"

I take a deep breath and lick the sweat off my lips before I stammer, "I be a Hooper."

The man grunts at my response. "And what exactly be a Hooper?"

I eye his double-edged ax. He holds it straight out as effortlessly as if he were holding no more than a dandelion. But I'm sure that if I make the wrong move, he'll have it slicing through my flesh before I can take two steps.

I decide to take a chance. "I, uh, well, a Hooper is someone who lives deep in the forest many leagues from here." I swallow and go on in a rush of words. "We Hoopers are fearsome warriors and we don't take kindly to one of us being hurt or killed, you know."

I gesture toward Scamper. "That is a symbol of our tribe — a sacred symbol that we hold in high regard."

The man snorts, eyes Scamper and then me. "Seems your tribe takes to liking things on the small size if you ask me."

I manage to muster the sternest expression I can. "Maybe, but, just so you'll know, there are lots more Hoopers just over that hill. That yell I let out was our war cry, calling for hundreds of warriors to come to my aid. If I were you, I'd best be going before they show up. And, oh, without killing or hurting me, or our sacred symbol, of course."

The man stares at me for a long moment before his face cracks into a grin so wide I think it's going to split his face in half. His laugh is more of a roar that starts deep in his belly and ripples up and out of his mouth. He lowers his ax and steps back, all the while letting out one rolling belly laugh after another.

After a bit, his guffaws simmer down to loud chuckles. I always thought of Helmar as being a big, strong man. However, this fellow is a Helmar and a half. I feel like a tiny twig next to a giant oak tree.

Scamper is still furiously wriggling in the man's grasp. He's not used to being handled in such a rough manner. The man glances at my bow and knife while firmly saying, "Now, boy, tell me the truth. I've walked this forest from one end to the other, and unless they're invisible, there's no 'Hooper' warrior clan."

I start to stammer, but just then my eyes catch movement over his shoulder. With as much bluster as I can, I say, "Well, you might want to rethink that because our clan elder and two of our warriors are on the hill behind you with arrows pointed straight at your back. And most likely there are more on their way."

Without letting go of Scamper, he turns halfway around so that he can see who's on the knoll's crest. Phigby, Cara, and Helmar stand almost shoulder to shoulder. Cara has an arrow notched while Helmar and Phigby stand with swords in hand.

Phigby stares down into the little vale and then, for some reason, reaches out and pushes Cara's arrow down before his sword disappears under his robe.

The big man seems to study the three for several moments before he turns back to me. "You say the long-beard up there is your clan leader?" he asks.

"Yes," I reply stoutly. "And he's a very powerful wizard, too. Why just last night he slew a huge goblin with just one of his mighty spells."

"Goblin, eh?" the man says. "And a big one, too? Well, now, I've always wanted to meet a powerful sorcerer."

He takes his ax and points up the hill, his meaning clear. He holds a still struggling Scamper off to one side as we trudge up the small knoll until we reach the top.

"Your warrior here tells me you're a great shaman," the muscular man says in a mocking air to Phigby. "Able to slay a good-sized goblin with one spell. I have to admit that's quite a feat, it usually takes me a half dozen good swings of my blade before I can bring down one of the bigger brutes."

He gives Scamper a little shake causing him to start chittering loudly again. "He also says that this is a sacred symbol of your tribe."

He casts a sideways glance at me. "What did you call it, again? Oh yes, the 'Hooper warrior clan.'"

He snorts and says, "So, magician, give us the truth, did you actually slay that oversized barrel of pig's fat with one spell? As I said, it takes me a few swings before I can cut one down to size."

Phigby stands a little straighter and says, "Then maybe you should sharpen your blade so that it cuts better."

The ax man lifts his blade up as if to inspect the edge. "Hmmm," he replies. "You may well be right; it does look as if it's getting a bit dull."

He smiles at Phigby and points his ax at him. "Maybe I should sharpen it on your scraggly, old beard. It looks as rough and coarse as any grindstone."

"You, sir," Phigby answers as his fingers stroke his whiskers, "would find my beard to be more than a match for that thin, rusty blade you claim to be a goblin slayer."

Uh, oh, I think to myself. That does it. We're all dead. Neither Cara nor Helmar are going to get their weapons up in time, and

Phigby isn't going to be fast enough to dip into his bag of tricks before the ax man lops our heads off with one swing.

As if reading my mind, the man lifts his cleaver, no doubt readying it for the fatal blow. Who will be the first to lose his head? Me, no doubt.

Phigby and the axman stare hard at each other, their eyes locked as if blinking would somehow show a lack of courage. Neither speaks, both stand glowering, less than a body's width apart. Then, the big man starts to chuckle. A moment later, Phigby is chortling.

Then, broad grins appear on both men's faces along with gales of laughter. Helmar, Cara, and I exchange puzzled glances. A moment ago, I was sure that Phigby had provoked this man into attacking us, now they're laughing as if someone had told an excellent joke.

The man holds Scamper up. "Professor, what am I to do with this ferocious beast? He almost left me with but one ear!"

"Hooper," Phigby orders, "retrieve your beastie. It's not polite to gnaw off a friend's ear."

"Friend?" I choke as I gather Scamper in my arms.

"Friend, indeed," Phigby replies. "And well received, too."

He spreads his arms wide and says, "Amil!"

"Phigby!" the man heartily replies and gives the old man a bear hug. It's so enthusiastic that I'm afraid he's going to snap Phigby in half. Both men are laughing as Amil lets Phigby go and stands back.

"So," Amil says as he nods his head toward me, "this one tells me that you are now the grand chief of the entire Hooper warrior clan, and here I thought you had retired to the quiet life of reading books and mixing your potions."

Phigby's eyebrows rise noticeably. "Chief of the Hooper warrior clan?" he asks me in a long-drawn-out questioning tone.

With my head lowered, I can barely meet his eyes as I mumble, "Had to say and do something, I was afraid he was about to slice me open with that huge ax of his."

Phigby shakes his head as if he can't believe what he hears and gestures towards me. "Amil, this is Hooper, and that furry rascal he's holding is Scamper. And these two are Cara, daughter of Boren

Dracon, and Helmar, novice Dragon Master to Boren Dracon. All good and true friends of mine."

He pauses before saying in a more serious tone, "We've come from Draconstead."

Amil's face turns serious and he eyes the three of us. "Draconstead," he murmurs, shaking his head. "There was a news crier in the village. I wasn't sure if he was telling the truth or spreading rumors, even if he did wear the king's colors."

"Unfortunately, they are not rumors," Phigby answers. "And it is amazing how fast news can travel, especially bad news. The Wilders attacked Draconstead and left it burning, forcing us to flee."

Phigby eyes the lot of us before he gestures to Amil and says, "There is more to tell, but not here." He glances upward. "We're out in the open, let's get back to the cabin." He motions toward the stream. "Hooper, retrieve your flasks, I, for one, thirst."

Phigby whirls, his robes swishing around him and heads back to the hut. I grab the full flasks, and hurry after them. I notice that Phigby's route avoids the thick grove of trees that hides the dragons. Amil may be Phigby's friend, but he's not revealing that we have a golden dragon, at least not yet.

We enter the cottage and Cara, Helmar, and Phigby sit on the makeshift bed while Amil takes the chair. I get the bare ground to rest upon.

Phigby is quick to ask Amil, "By any chance do you have any food to share? We're a bit on the hungry side. Besides, I would consider it an honor to break bread with you again, old friend."

Amil shakes his head. "Sorry, no. I came into the forest hoping to find a fat rabbit or two, but I've come up empty-handed."

"And we haven't had a chance to hunt either, I'm afraid," Phigby answers. He then asks, "Is there a village nearby that we might find food?"

He pauses before saying, "We had to run before a pack of Wilders early this morn and to tell you the truth, I'm not exactly sure where we are."

"Yes, there's a small village about a league from here, Deerfield, but I would not be so hasty to enter it," Amil quickly interjects.

Phigby leans toward Amil. "Why is that, old friend?"

Amil stares at Phigby for several moments as if making his mind up about something before he gives a slight shrug and says, "Well, you might as well hear it from me, rather than the sheriff. There's a King's Warrant on your heads. All except you, Phigby."

"A King's Warrant?" I sputter. "What is that?"

"We've been declared criminals and have a price on our heads, Hooper," Cara answers dryly. She peers at Amil and asks, "And no doubt the warrant makes no distinction between being brought before the king dead or alive?"

"That's right," Amil affirms.

I can't help but notice that as soon as Amil mentioned the warrant that both Helmar and Cara's hands went to their sword hilts. Amil, no doubt, sees the same thing for he lays his ax on the ground and raises his empty hands. "I am not here to collect the bounty," he says reassuringly.

Without looking at either Cara or Helmar, Phigby orders, "There's no need for swordplay here, you can rest easy."

"But — " Helmar begins but Phigby is quick to say, "I trust Amil, Amil trusts me. I owe my life to him — "

"And I him," Amil adds emphatically. "If you are Phigby's friends, then I am not your enemy. Phigby does not easily call anyone friend, but those he does are honest and trustworthy. Which causes me to wonder about that warrant."

Cara and Helmar glance at each other before they ease their hands off their sword hilts. Cara mutters to Phigby, "A King's Warrant. How did the king issue such a document so quickly? It's not even been a full day."

"An excellent question, Cara," Phigby replies and eyes Amil.

In answer, Amil's eyebrows furrow and he says, "A dragon rider came through Deerfield at dawn's light. I was under the impression that he had ridden through the night. He read the proclamation, it bore the King's Seal but was signed by Prince Aster on the king's behalf.

"Once he finished, he stated that his next stop was Brayton at the head of Thomson's Valley. From what he said, I'm under the impression that His Majesty has news criers, riding sapphires, going to every corner of the Northern Realm."

Phigby let out a long sigh while saying, "Which means that news of that warrant will be known throughout the kingdom in just a few days."

"But why?" Helmar growls. "We've done nothing wrong. Why would the king post us after we — "

Phigby holds up a quick hand, stopping Helmar from speaking further. "Amil is a commissioned Traveler of King Leo," he rapidly explains, "and as such is considered to be one of the King's Own."

"A Traveler?" I ask. "What's that?"

"Amil is a representative of His Majesty," Phigby explains, "and journeys both within the Northern Kingdom and to other lands. He sees what there is to see and then reports what he finds back to the king."

"Oh," I answer, "you mean he's a spy like those I read about in your books."

Amil and Phigby share a sideways glance. Phigby murmurs, "Amil carries out his tasks in many ways for the king." He pauses before hastily saying, "But most importantly, be assured that the Amil I know is a good and trusted friend of mine."

"All right," I mutter, not entirely convinced by Phigby's explanation as what little I know of spies and such are that they are devious whether what they do is in the open or not.

"Amil," Phigby presses, "this warrant, did it mention why we were posted?"

I notice that Phigby uses the word "we" even though he's apparently not named on the document. Phigby is loyal to his friends; that I can certainly say of him.

"It did indeed," Amil is quick to reply. "And I must say, that it will do nothing but provoke the whole countryside to be out looking for the lot of you."

He presses his lips together. "Stealing a golden dragon that is both the dread and hope for us all is no small matter, Phigby."

The dragon is out of the bag. We're doomed. Who's going to take our word against the king's?

Nobody.

We may be breathing at the moment, but as soon as we're captured, our heads will roll. Cara is quick to say, "We didn't steal Golden Wind. Besides, as my father's heiress and with Lord Lorell dead, I had a legal responsibility and obligation to protect her against those who did try and steal her, namely the Wilders. They're the ones who should have a King's Warrant on their heads, not us."

Amil uses two fingers to purse his lips together, "An interesting argument, mistress, but I'm neither a magistrate nor in a position to speak for or against you in the matter."

Out of a sense of morbid curiosity, I just have to ask, "Just how much is the price on our heads?"

Amil grunts and points to Cara and Helmar. "Each of you is worth your weight in gold." He turns to me. "You're only worth your weight in silver."

"But I — " I stop and shrug. Even though I was the one who actually stole the golden, it figures that I'm worth less than anyone else.

The room is silent for quite a while before Phigby says, "Well, that certainly changes my thinking as to what to do next."

Cara murmurs, "It appears that we not only have to run from the Wilders but now the whole kingdom is after us."

"But we've done nothing wrong!" Helmar explodes.

"No, we haven't," Phigby murmurs, "yet it is what it is."

My head is spinning. We face not only a horde of Wilders but now the whole kingdom, too. And there's only four of us, whereas there's a — a — well, a whole horde of them.

Phigby eyes Amil and mutters, "Amil, old friend, you and I have walked many trails together, entrusted our lives to each other. Would you not judge us before you hear our story? I suspect it is quite a bit different than what you've heard and what that warrant states."

Amil returns Phigby's stare for several heartbeats. He gives a little nod. "I'm listening Phigby, and if it will ease your mind, I know that you're not one to go around stealing dragons, especially a golden one."

His mouth upturns in a small smile. "Still, from sitting around many a campfire with you, I take it I'm about to hear a fascinating story?"

"Indeed," Phigby answers, "and now with this latest news you've brought, a story that I'm beginning to think has more twists and turns to it than I believed possible."

Amil's eyebrows rise a bit at that, and he motions with one hand. "Go ahead, I'm still listening."

"Helmar," Phigby orders, "tell your part, first, then Cara."

I notice he doesn't include me, which in a way is good. No telling what my undisciplined tongue will utter.

Helmar is quick to recount his story, the order to meet at the Manor House and then his return to a burning Draconton. Phigby stops him and has Cara begin at that point. Phigby halts her when she starts describing her part in the attack and turns to me. "Hooper, tell us what happened in the birthing barn, we've not heard from you yet, this would be a good time, I think for us to hear all of it."

I nod and as detailed as I can, recall the events in the barn. When I begin to describe my nemesis, Helmar, Amil and Phigby lean forward with intense expressions on their faces. "Hooper," Helmar orders, "repeat what you just said."

"I said," I reply, "that the tall Wilder drew his skinny blade, but he stayed well away from the fight. The other Wilders did the fighting."

"Skinny blade," Amil is quick to say, "describe this sword that he carried."

I shrug and hold my arms out wide. "The other Wilders had these long, large broadswords while his blade was . . . " I hold out one finger. "Not much wider than this."

Helmar leans even farther, his eyes questioning. "He was carrying a rapier?"

I shrug at his question. "I don't know what they're called, I just know that his sword looked like the one I saw Lord Lorell carry when he was at the stead last summer. If the golden hadn't chomped on his sword arm, he would have run his blade through me when he caught me opening the golden's paddock gate."

"The golden did that?" Phigby questions with widened eyes.

"Yes," I answer, "she brought her head clear over the top railing. And just when he was about to skewer me with that rapier, or whatever you call it, she clamped down on his arm and threw him to one side."

"Hmmm," Phigby muses quietly while he strokes his beard and peers at me with an intent look. "She's saved your life three times now. Fascinating."

Amil has an elbow on one knee, his chin in one hand. "A Wilder would no more carry a foil than a pig would go romping with a pack of wolves."

He looks at me, his eyes like stone. "Are you absolutely sure of this that he didn't carry a Wilder longsword?"

"And am I absolutely certain that he almost killed me with that 'foil' of his?" I retort. "Absolutely."

Amil begins to shake his head from side to side as if he doesn't quite believe me but can't discount what I've said either. Slowly he says to no one in particular, "Only royals and landed gentry carry rapiers."

His heavy breathing is like a giant bellow going in and out. He peers at Phigby. "Do you know who was in that barn?"

Phigby shakes his head in answer. "No, but now that I've heard Hooper, I certainly would like to know for I suspect that whoever it was is also behind this King's Warrant."

Amil gives Phigby a sharp look. "You're not suggesting — "

"I'm not suggesting anything," Phigby is swift to respond. He gives Cara, who's remained silent this whole time, a quick glance. "Other than it may well be that it wasn't a Wilder clan chieftain who led the

attack on Draconstead. Besides, none of us would make such an accusation without more proof than the fact that a supposed Wilder
carried a rapier."

Phigby gestures to me. "Finish your story."

I shrug one shoulder and say, "There's not much more to tell. I
ran from the barn into the forest, found Golden Wind and eventually
we made it to Fairy Falls. After that, you three showed up."

Of course, there's much more to tell than that regarding Golden
Wind, but I've a promise to keep, and keep it I shall.

Phigby then says to Amil, "When we met up at the falls, and after
discussing it at length, we decided that the Wilders were between us
and both Wynsur and the nearest Great House, so we flew west to
obtain some space and time.

"We were looking for a safe way to get the golden to Wynsur, but
we were attacked by a swarm of Wilders early this morn and let's just
say that through a miracle on high made our escape to this place."

"So you do have the golden?" Amil bluntly questions.

Phigby eyes us all before shrugging as if it didn't matter that he
revealed the golden's presence here. "Yes, we have her. For the
moment, she's safe." He stops and murmurs, "But for how long . . . "

Helmar clears his throat and says, "There's one more thing. I'm
convinced that the attack at Draconstead wasn't isolated. I believe the
Wilders also attacked the Manor House where Cara's father and
brother were, not to mention the captain of our knights' company as
part of their overall plan."

His voice becomes almost toneless. "It may well be that Prince
Aster was there as well though I didn't see him before I skyed back to
Draconstead."

"He's safe and unharmed," Amil returns. To Helmar's questioning
expression he adds, "The King's Crier said as much that Prince Aster
had escaped the attack unscathed."

Cara reaches out a hand, and I can see in her eyes the question
she wants to ask but can't bring herself to voice.

As if hearing her unspoken question, Amil turns sad eyes on Cara
and says, "Mistress Cara, I cannot confirm that your father or brother

are dead, but I can say that Lord and Lady Lorell plus every knight that was at the manor died in the attack. It was part of the proclamation that the rider read."

He then points at Helmar and says, "And it names you as the conspirator who organized the ambush and fled just before the attack. Thus ensuring your own safety."

He pauses before saying, "And it proclaims that those who stole the golden are in league with the Wilders and, therefore, their lives are forfeit to the crown."

He lets out a breath and jabs a finger at us. "Meaning, all of you."

18

"**W**hat!" Helmar thunders and jumps to his feet his fierce glare centered on Amil. I hope he's not foolish enough to attack Amil in such close quarters, but his bulging neck muscles, his face as red as a ripe tomato makes me scoot as far away from the two as I can. Swords and axes swinging in such cramped quarters is going to get someone entirely innocent hurt or killed. Like me.

"Helmar!" Phigby's voice is sharp, commanding. "Amil is not the one doing the accusing. You don't sword-gut the messenger, lad. Now, sit down and let's talk and think this through."

For a few more heartbeats, Helmar stands glowering before his face finally softens a bit and he mutters, "My apologies, Amil. Phigby is right; I should not be angry at you. But to be accused of such . . . That anyone could think I was capable of such a traitorous act against Master Boren . . . "

His voice chokes and for an instant, I can see that Helmar may not have loved Master Boren as Cara loves her father, nevertheless, his respect and admiration are real for the man, and Boren's death has struck deeper than I suspected.

It's a revelation to me that outside that gruff, hard shell of his, Helmar can actually feel, for others other than himself and Cara.

Amil holds up a hand. "No need to apologize, I would be angry too, if I were suspected of such."

"It makes no sense at all," Helmar growls as he slowly sits. His face has gone from bright red to a dark almost purple hue. "We risked our lives against the Wilders, we're the ones who saved the golden from them and if it weren't for us, Golden Wind — "

"Would be in the hands of whoever led the Wilders," Cara murmurs softly.

Cara is pressing her face into her hands. Amil's news has reopened the still fresh wound, and I can hear the soft sobs. Phigby drapes an arm across her shoulders. "Perhaps, this is actually good news, my dear."

She lifts her tear-stained face. "No news is good news, Phigby?"

"Perhaps," he shrugs. He glances up at the big man. "Amil?"

Amil shakes his head. "I'm sorry, that's all I know."

We all fall into a deep silence. A king's bounty on our heads, I think to myself, and now not only accused of stealing the golden but of being in league with those monsters, the Wilders.

I break the silence by whispering, "Can it get any worse?"

I glance up at Phigby. His expression is honest, frank. It says, that yes, it can, and may even become ghastlier. I shake my head at Phigby. "Please don't tell me that — "

He holds his hand up, palm out. "Let's save that discussion for another time, Hooper," he replies softly. "For now, we have enough spoiled meat on our plates as it is," he finishes.

He takes another breath, gives Cara's hand a gentle squeeze and stands. "Amil, we four have been up all night and between fighting off the Wilders and your news, I'm afraid that we're exhausted in body and spirit. We need to sleep and let both mind and body refresh themselves."

"Say no more," Amil replies. "I rested well enough last night. I'll stand guard. Get some sleep."

"The dragons — " Helmar begins, but Phigby quickly says, "Are safe enough for now, and I doubt highly that they'll wander off. Now, let's take Amil up on his gracious proposal."

For me, Amil doesn't have to offer twice. I think I'm asleep before my head even hits the ground. At some point, I feel a furry, warm body curl up against my stomach. I reach out a hand and pull Scamper close. I admit, caring for someone, and having someone care for you, makes the world a little easier to take.

Even if that same world has Wilders, witches, and now a whole kingdom out to get you.

A soft hand pushes me awake, and an angel voice sternly says, "Hooper, wake up."

I open my eyes just long enough for Cara to thrust a cup in my hands. "What is it?" I ask groggily, not entirely awake yet.

"Squirrel soup," she answers.

"Oh," I reply. Well, I think, at least, Scamper has that particular tree to himself, now. I see that the fire is a bit brighter than earlier, and someone has gathered more wood. I'm surprised, but grateful that I wasn't woken to fetch the wood. I take a sip of my broth and then in one gulp down half the cup. It's bland as there's more water than squirrel meat flavor, but at least, it's filling.

I glance around, the shanty is empty except for Cara and myself. "Where are the others?" I ask.

"Helmar and Amil are taking a quick swing through the forest," she answers, stacking some wood next to the small hearth, "hoping to find something more substantial than a squirrel. Phigby's out searching for nuts or berries."

She turns and motions at me. "We're to take the dragons to the brook so that they can drink, so be quick about downing the rest of that."

My eyebrows rise at her answer. They let the Hooper sleep longer than the others? Unheard of. Two more swallows and I'm done with the thin broth. Cara takes the cup, quickly rinses it out, and without another word to me, slings her bow and quiver and is out the door.

I hobble after her, rubbing at my eyes in the late afternoon sun. I take a quick glance around the glade but don't spot Scamper. He might have gone with Phigby. While nuts and berries are not high on his list of what he considers good eating, he'll eat them when nothing else is available.

We trudge up the small incline behind the hut and slip into the thicker stand of trees where Cara and Helmar settled the dragons earlier. Except for Rover, who's contentedly munching on a beech bush, the rest of the dragons are resting or sleeping. Cara motions to the left, "I'll gather up Wind Song and Rover, you get Glory and the golden. On our way to the creek, keep an eye out for dragon bane."

Perfect, I think. This will give me a chance to speak with the golden about Phigby and Helmar, one of which, in my mind, is the Gem Guardian. But which?

I no sooner turn from Cara, then I'm stampeded by a tiny herd of lively baby dragons. The sprogs cluster around me, screeping and chubbing. I have no idea why they're so excited to see me. Surely, they must know how much I dislike being around their ugly toad bodies.

Trying to look as if I'm studying the ground in search of the poison petals, I slowly amble toward the golden. When I reach her, I take a quick glance at Cara. She's on the meadow's far side and disappears behind Wind Song. No doubt, looking her dragon over before getting her up to move to the stream. Now's my chance.

I slide up next to the golden. "Pssst, Golden Wind, wake up."

"I'm awake," she answers, though she keeps her eyes closed.

"Phigby or Helmar," I state, "one of them is the Gem Guardian. Right?"

She slowly opens her eyes and stares at me. "What makes you think that?"

"Phigby at the falls," I quickly reply, "he drew magical characters and symbols in the air that called to the three fairies, and when they appeared, well, the rest of us were scared, but he stood strong, unafraid.

"Besides, he knows about dragons and dragon gems, in fact, Phigby knows just about everything. If anyone can make the gemstone work, it would be him."

I stop and then in a rush of words say, "But, then again Helmar is strong, powerful, a warrior. He'd be able to protect the jewel against anyone who would try to take it. Especially when he's mad."

I shudder, thinking of Helmar standing there with his blade held high, looking like some majestic god with a thunderbolt in his hand, ready to spear me.

"A warrior," I go on, "such as Helmar or one who holds a great store of knowledge, like Phigby, armed with a dragon jewel would make a powerful combination to do this 'good' that you're so concerned about."

My shoulders slump, and I murmur, "I'd hoped that I was the guardian, and it'd change my world, give me the things that I've always wanted — "

"But since it won't," Golden Wind says, "you're now more than willing to give it up." She brings her head a little closer, her eyes never leave my face as if she were searching for something.

I shrug. "I'm certainly not doing any good with it, just hauling it around. Besides, if anyone can make it work, it's Phigby or Helmar. I'm sure of it. I just don't know which one."

"I see," she replies. "Phigby holds a vast store of knowledge and Helmar is imbued with power. And such attributes are the key to wielding the gem wisely and bringing about the most good, is that it?"

"That's the way I see it," I answer. "Now all that's left is for you to tell me which one gets the jewel and I can be done with the whole thing."

She considers my reply for a long moment before saying, "Hooper, knowledge and power without the wisdom or desire to use both righteously are a dangerous combination. Even the wickedest among us can garner those traits, but they choose to use them for their own selfish desires, having neither true wisdom nor the inclination to seek righteousness."

"But," I object, "Phigby's good, he's smart, he'd know what to do with the jewel. I certainly don't. And Helmar is already powerful in a sense, he's used to using power, though I admit I think he needs to work more on the 'good' part."

I screw my mouth to one side. "All I'm doing is lugging the thing around until I deliver it to the right person. I don't see me doing much good in that."

"As I said, Hooper, being the — "

"I know, I know," I snap at her. "Being Pengillstorr's jewel care-taker is a great honor and I should be proud that he chose me."

Disgruntled, I say, "Being the custodian is one thing, but finding the real guardian is another. Why can't you just tell me who it is and be done with it?"

She gazes at me for a moment and then asks, "What of Cara? Why haven't you considered her as the guardian? She's smart, brave, there's a sense of power about her as well."

She pauses and then says, "Is it because she's a girl?"

I glance down at my feet, hesitate and then say, "No, it's not because she's a girl. She's all that you said and more."

I fidget a bit and then blurt out, "I don't want her to be the guardian because, for me, she's *the* girl. If she's the guardian, you've already said that more danger would come her way. I don't want that for her — I want less danger, much less for her than anyone else, including me."

The golden peers at me for a moment before saying, "I under-stand. You're trying to protect her. That's very chivalrous of you, Hooper, but you must accept the fact that if Cara is the guardian, for the world's sake, you must hand over the gemstone to her. No matter your personal feelings."

I bite down hard on my lip before I nod and mumble, "I understand."

The golden's gaze is gentle, but her words are firm. "Hooper, when the time comes you shall know for a surety who the guardian is and who should wield Pengillstorr's jewel, and its power. But that time hasn't come."

This conversation isn't going in the direction that I thought it would. I fully expected the golden to say, "Congratulations, gem care-taker, you've chosen well, now deliver the gem, your task is over, the burden lifted."

Instead, I have the distinct impression that while she hasn't come out and directly squashed my announcement that Phigby or Helmar is the Gem Guardian, she hasn't exactly given either one rousing approval.

She breaks into my thoughts by saying, "I thirst, as do the others. Come, Hooper, I believe you are to take us to water."

I duly point toward a far line of treetops. "Over there," I mutter, "there's a small brook."

Cara has the other dragons filing along in a single line and the golden falls in at the tail end. I glance down at my little milling mob of sprogs. "C'mon," I grumble, "you too. Let's go."

I stump behind Cara and the dragons, and it's not long before we have them at the water. The four adult dragons spread out. Otherwise, they'd drink the water dry if they stayed in one spot.

The sprogs jump into the stream, splash about, and plunge their heads down into the water, coming up with a bit of bottom grass each time. Naturally, Regal and Wind Glow get into a tussle, fighting over the same piece of soft moss and end up kicking and scratching in the mud. I let them have at it as I'm not inclined to get wet separating two squalling dragon brats.

The golden eyes the sprogs while she gulps down great drafts of the liquid but she lets them be too. She raises her head and water spews out the side of her mouth while she chews on some bottom grass that came with the water. Cara is at the far end, standing next to Wind Song. I can hear her softly humming to her dragon.

After thinking a bit, I slip to the other side of Golden Wind and whisper, "So, is that how I'll recognize the true Gem Guardian, someone who won't misuse the jewel's power?"

She chews the grass slowly as if she's a cow chewing her cud. She takes so long; I think she's not going to answer me. Then, she murmurs, "Hooper, a truly wise and good person will choose the right over the wrong, even if it means making a sacrifice of their own heart; in other words, giving up their greatest desires for the good of others."

She pauses and then whispers, "Take out the jewel."

I duck my head around the golden to make sure Cara can't see but she's out of sight. I quickly bring out the gemstone. "Look inside," the golden orders.

Peering at the gem, my eyes widen. The tiny frond, closed tightly before has uncurled just a bit, its leaves becoming more distinct. The jewel itself now has a slight green tint to it, ever so slight but noticeable nonetheless.

I point to the plant whose leaves sway just a tiny bit as if there were a gentle breeze inside the gem. "It's beginning to open, what does that mean?"

"It means that you are closer to finding its guardian," Golden Wind answers. "The jewel's power is starting to awaken."

She dips her head to the water and drinks again. For some reason, I know the conversation has ended, and I tuck the jewel away.

When the dragons are done, Cara motions that she's filled our water flasks, and we're to take the dragons back to the sheltered glade.

After Cara and I herd all the dragons back to the meadow, we return to the glen to find Amil and Phigby off to one side having a quiet conversation.

Entering the hut, I glance around, hoping to see deer meat roasting in the hearth or perhaps rabbits, but it's obvious that Helmar and Amil came back empty-handed, as did Phigby.

A moment later, Amil and Phigby enter and once again Cara and the others settle themselves around Phigby, but I find my corner, away from the others and sit, unsure of my place among this small company.

Phigby catches my eye and motions me over. "Come closer, Hooper," he instructs, "you're a part of this, and you need to hear what we have to say."

I scoot closer, and as I do, Amil clears his voice and says, "While you slept, I pondered deeply over your story." He takes a deep breath. "Though none of you said it, nevertheless your unspoken thought hangs as heavy over our conversation as a river fog in the dead of night."

His eyes turn hard. "You believe that someone in the royal family is behind the attacks and the attempt to spirit Golden Wind off to the Wilders' strongholds."

Surprisingly, at least, to me, none of my companions speak, nor do they challenge his accusation. My eyebrows rise at that, and I sit a bit straighter. Are they really thinking that the king or some other royal is actually conspiring with the Wilders? My head buzzes at the thought.

Like distant thunder, Amil's deep voice is a low rumble in the hut. "I am not convinced that King Leo had any part in the evil that's occurred, that's just not the king I know. However, as far as the king's brothers go — "

"Or his sons . . . " Cara's voice is hardly more than a whisper, but her bold statement holds me nonetheless.

Amil hesitates before saying, "Or his sons, well, that's another matter."

"A golden dragon," Phigby pronounces, "would be a powerful asset for one who sought a crown."

"Aye," Amil acknowledges, "that it would. Powerful enough that it would make allies out of those who have been enemies for generations."

I glance from face to face with the stark realization of just what they're alluding to. "Wait," I breathe, "are you saying that — "

"What we are saying, Hooper," Phigby interrupts sharply, "is that in the games that the high-born play they believe that the rules do not apply to them but only to us little people."

I open my mouth as if to speak but Phigby leans forward and snarls, "And that's all we're going to say about that."

He motions to Amil and then says, "As Amil does, we too take our fidelity to King Leo and the royal family seriously, and that is a sufficient enough explanation for now."

I promptly shut my mouth as I recognize the warning. Treason, even disloyalty can be a serious crime and royalty thoroughly dislike having their words or actions questioned by us "little people."

Amil swings his arm around at the lot of us while saying, "I'm not doubting yours or anyone's fidelity, Phigby. But I admit, your story leaves me with more questions than answers. For now, I will accept that all that I've heard is the truth."

He glances around, and his voice deepens. "The question is what do we do about it?"

"Thank you, Amil," Phigby acknowledges. "At this point, we can use any friend that we can find."

He pulls at his beard for so long that I begin to think that the conversation is done without us resolving anything. Then he starts up again, solemn and slow.

"I've shared with Amil our experience at Fairy Falls, and of Hooper's encounter with his apparition at Draconstead. I will hold, for the moment, my pronouncement of who that is. Instead, it would be best if you first learned just who the three were that appeared to us in the glade."

I lean forward, eager to hear. "But not here," Phigby states and waves a hand at the hut's inside. "Not where it's dark and gloomy. This needs to be outside in the light of day." He jumps to his feet, grabs his bag, and orders, "Follow me."

Surprised, we rise and follow. He marches us out and into the glade where the dragons are resting. I spot the sprogs curled up asleep next to the golden. I guess our march to the stream tired them out. I look around for Scamper, but he's nowhere to be seen. We find some fallen logs to sit on, and Phigby stands before us as if he's about to deliver a lecture.

"The beings that we saw at Fairy Falls," Phigby announces, "were none other than three of the four Gaelian Fae, Osa, Nadia, and Eskar."

Phigby's words instantly bring Amil's intense gaze from the golden. I wouldn't have thought that a King's Traveler who's seen so many things would be impressed by anything but it's obvious by the way his eyes gleam and his face holds a certain eagerness that Amil is awed by Golden Wind.

"The Fairy Queens," Cara murmurs.

"Yes," Phigby acknowledges. "Or as some call them, simply, the Fae."

At Phigby's declaration, my head jerks up. So it was the Gaelian Fae we saw, the same ones that the golden spoke of when we first entered the glade. Phigby must have seen my startled reaction for he asks with a narrowing of the eyes, "And what do you know of the Gaelian Fae, Hooper?"

"Uh," I reply slowly, trying to think how to respond. I certainly can't tell him that the golden told me about the fairies and their part in creating dragons. "I probably read about them in one of your books. The falls are named after them, right?"

"Hmmm . . . " Phigby murmurs. "Yes, the falls are named after them, but no, I don't believe I ever gave you a book that spoke of the Fae."

I'm stuck. I don't have an answer for Phigby, and he's peering at me at me like a hawk that's hovering over a rabbit hole, just waiting for the rabbit to stick its head out.

"I think I may have told him, Phigby," Cara abruptly says. "When we were discussing where to take the golden after Hooper got her away from Draconstead."

I turn toward Cara, but she's not looking in my direction. Instead, she has her eyes on Phigby. I don't know why she spoke up for me, but I'm grateful she did. For the moment, it gets me out of Phigby's noose.

Phigby gives a little nod, but before he can speak, Helmar asks, "Phigby, Cara may know something about the Gaelian Fae, but I don't. Just who are they? What exactly did we see, and why?"

"I'm not sure I can entirely answer the why," Phigby replied, "but I may have something that will address some of your questions."

He reaches into his haversack, rummages around a bit before he draws out a thick manuscript. Its rumpled binding seems to glow in the lowering sun's light.

He hands it to me. "Here, Hooper, a book that really does speak of the Gaelian Fairies, and not one you imagined reading."

Cara is amazing. Phigby no sooner plops the book into my lap, then she's off her log like an arrow shot and slides next to me. She runs her hand over the book's covering and wags a finger at Phigby. "You've been holding out on me."

I'm surprised she doesn't add an "again" to the end of the sentence, but she doesn't. Phigby sniffs in retort. "An old man is entitled to some secrets, young lady."

"Oh, bosh," Cara answers. "That's not how you should treat your best customer, and you know it."

She nudges me with her elbow. "Hurry up, Hooper, open it."

The book is heavy, quite thick, and so broad that it covers my whole lap. I shake my head at the size of the thing. How does Phigby carry all of this in his bag and yet be as spry as he is? If I were carrying just this, I'd be straining under the weight.

Cara gives me another impatient jab with her elbow. I run a hand over the cover. The soft and pliant leather is timeworn, so I know it's been opened many, many times.

Helmar and Amil come to stand behind us, and glance over our shoulders. With Cara's help, I hold the book up so that they can see the front cover's lettering. Cara reads aloud, *Fantastical Creatures, and other Myths, Lore, and Legends.*

She gives me an eager smile, and her eyes gleam. To Cara, it would appear that a new and unread book is as exciting as a previously unknown treasure map is to a pirate.

To me, well, though I wish Phigby had explained it himself, I'm glad to see Cara with a smile again, and her eyes clear and bright instead of dull from harboring tears.

I open the volume to the first page and find it's an alphabetical index. I run my finger down the listing while Cara reads aloud. "Angels, Balrogs, Centaurs, Demons, Empousai, Fairies or Faeries in Old Tongue."

She nudges me again. "Page forty-seven, Hooper."

I turn the pages until I come to the part about fairies. Cara reads aloud while I read along with her. The book describes woodland and mountain fairies, fairies that live in people's homes, invisible fairies, and cloud fairies, the ones that make white, fluffy clouds.

Then we come to the part on the Gaelian Fae or as Cara called them, the Fairy Queens. Cara reads aloud in a small voice, "During the Time of Creation, the four Gaelian Fae sisters, Osa, Eskar, Nadia, and Vay were favorites of the gods and given the privilege of creating dragons."

She stops and points. "Look, a drawing of the four."

Bending over our shoulders to see better, Helmar mutters, "Either the fairies drew that themselves or the artist had his own visitation, I would say, at least of the three that we saw."

I have to agree with Helmar. The faces in the illustration are remarkably similar to the faces that we saw emerge from the pillars.

"Perhaps," Phigby mutters, "but as I mentioned, those who appeared to us are Osa, Eskar, and Nadia. The one set apart is Vay."

Behind Osa, Eskar, and Nadia is a subdued glow that seems to highlight and soften each face. But not Vay. Her expression is hard and dark. She stands apart from her sisters and where they have light behind them like a velvety aura, not Vay. There is no radiance to shine on her, no glow upon her haggard face, no serenity or peace as in the other three.

Instead, above her are gloomy, roiling clouds as if she were about to bring a tempest and darkness upon the land. I can almost feel the thunder and lightning that would come from such storm clouds.

"Why is Vay's face so dark? She looks mad," I say to Phigby, "and so different from the other three."

"Turn the page," Phigby instructs.

I flip the page over. Cara reads, "A fragment of the Ode of the Gaelian Fae, said to come from the Parchment of Soracles."

"Soracles?" Amil asks.

"A historian, long dead," Phigby quickly replies. "Who, it is believed, gathered together the histories and writings of the ancient ones, kings, rulers, everything he could get his hands on. He compiled those documents into a running parchment supposedly a thousand rods long. It had to be wound together on a giant spool like some enormous paper barrel."

"A thousand rods long," Cara breathes.

"Yes," Phigby returns. "It would take even you, Cara Dracon, several cycles of the moons, maybe even a full season to read it all."

"Oh no," she quickly responds, "a few fortnights perhaps, but not an entire season."

She bends her head to the page and begins to read aloud,

> *Vay it was who broke the trust*
> *Brought forth the golden to slake her lust*
> *For greed, envy, fear, and power*
> *So that she oe'r all would tower*
> *One dragon to rule them all*
> *One Queen, to her we'd fall.*

"Wait," Cara declares, "isn't that part of what the three said to us?"

"Yes," Phigby answers, "but if you'll remember, they had a fuller version than what's written there."

"That's right," Cara breathes. "I remember it filled me with both hope and dread."

"Do you remember any of it?" Phigby asks.

Cara shakes her head. "No, not really."

"Hooper? Helmar?" Phigby questions.

We both shake our heads in answer. He nods in understanding and says, "Then let me help you."

> *Vay it was who broke the trust*
> *Brought forth the golden to slake her lust*
> *For greed, envy, fear, and power*
> *So that oe'r all she would tower*
> *One dragon to rule them all*
> *One Queen, to her we'd fall*
> *The dragon to rule over its own kind*
> *But to Vay, she would bend the mind*
> *Of the Drach and dragon too*
> *That to her only they would be true*
> *One Dark Queen upon her throne*

Seeds of evil she has sown
And of the moment, we did partake
Now the right we must make
From heaven above to the earth below
The gods will grant that we will go
To set the right
In fiery fight.

After Phigby stops, I ask, "What does it mean?"

"It means," Phigby answers, "that the seventh epoch is over, and the eighth has begun."

"Wait," I quickly point out, "didn't you recite or chant something about the eighth epoch the night the evil spirit attacked me?"

"Yes, Hooper," Phigby replies, "I did." He again begins to chant low,

Seven have come, seven are done,
Four did sleep, and now three will weep,
For now comes the eighth and open swings the gate,
On high the four shall align, a portent, an omen, a blazing sign,
That chains have burst, and the evil that thirsts,
Will walk once more, on hill, dale, and rolling moor,
As a seed, it will grow, up high and down low,
Rage and ruin, merciless death, pain will come with every breath,
All to slave, all to obey, all to serve the Domain of Vay.

"The evil that thirsts," Cara murmurs and shudders. "Is that Vay?"

"It is," Phigby replies. "And the chains that held her and her sisters for seven epochs have been torn asunder, and they are now free to roam Erdron. Vay to work her wickedness, her sisters, evidently to fight against that evil."

"And that's why," Cara replies softly, tapping her finger on the page, "in the drawing, Vay is apart from her sisters and cast in such a dark and foreboding light."

"Exactly," Phigby affirms.

Amil shakes his head and mutters, "I don't understand. Why would the fairies be held in chains for all that time and why does Vay want to enslave us? We're a mortal kingdom, she belongs to — "

"The enchanted, immortal world?" Phigby finishes.

Amil nods in answer. Phigby slowly replies, "It may be that she cannot or perhaps will not be allowed to rule over anything in that kingdom, so — "

"She would have her own world to rule over and to enslave all those who live upon it," Amil returns.

"That is my thought," Phigby replies.

While pointing at the book, I ask, "Is that all there is? Is there more to the story?"

Phigby wrinkles his forehead for a moment as he runs a gnarled finger over the book's edge. Wistfully, he says, "There is a companion book that adds to what's there."

He breathes deeply, sighs and says with a frown, "Unfortunately, it's been lost."

"Lost?" Cara moans. "Don't you know any of it?"

Phigby takes a finger and twirls several strands of his beard together as if he's thinking to himself. "Only from what we can gather from the parts of the ode that we have, and what little I can remember. But as the legend goes, when the gods created Erdron, our world, it was to be a world of magic, with sorcerers and wizards, enchanters and — "

"Witches?" I ask pointedly.

He gives me a little nod. "And witches, too. But also fantastical creatures such as — "

"Those in the book," Cara eagerly answers, laying a hand on the thick manuscript.

"Yes, yes," Phigby grumps, "like those in the book. Now quit interrupting me. Because the gods favored the fairies, they allowed the Gaelian Fae to create dragons. The Fae in turn — "

"Set the colors of their scales," I say, "to match the bow that colors the rain."

I blanch. My mind has gone for a walk in the woods, leaving my mouth to march alone and speak for itself.

Cara looks at me with wide eyes. "Where did that come from?" she asks.

"Indeed," Phigby agrees in surprise, "just where did that come from, Hooper?"

"Uh, I must have read it," I answer, hoping that Cara will save me again, but when she doesn't speak, I murmur, "Or, heard it somewhere, maybe?"

"Really?" Phigby grumbles apparently not accepting my explanation.

I glance over at the golden and find that her eyes are open, and her ears cocked in our direction as if listening to every word of the conversation. Gazing at her, I seize on a way to turn this discussion away from my big mouth having a life of its own.

I point at the golden. "So, if the dragons were to be the colors of the rainbow, why did Vay create a golden dragon? That color's not part of the rainbow."

"Weren't you listening, Hooper?" Helmar snaps. "'One dragon to rule them all, one queen, to her we'd fall.' The golden must be the dragon meant to rule them all."

He peers at Phigby. "The golden is tied to Vay's power in some way, isn't she, Phigby?"

Phigby slowly nods and says, "If you had a golden bow in the sky and measured it against a rainbow's brightness, which of those two is the brightest?"

"Gold," Amil instantly answers.

"Yes," Phigby murmurs low. "What does the king wear on his head and what does he hold in his right hand when he's on the throne?"

"A gold crown and scepter," Amin again answers.

"Yes," Phigby affirms, "and as today, gold is an ancient symbol not just of wealth, but of great power and authority."

He gestures toward where the golden lies. "And Golden Wind is the embodiment of power, both here, and in the enchanted world."

Suddenly, it all fits together. "Phigby," I whisper in a voice so small that I can barely hear myself, "you're suggesting that it's not just the Wilders who are after the golden, it's Vay, too."

He doesn't answer, he doesn't have to. His solemn eyes say it all.

I remember thinking that when Amil announced that we had a King's Warrant on our heads that was bad. Add that to the Wilders trying to kill us and things were looking awful. But I honestly didn't think it could get any worse.

Cara's hand flies to her mouth, and I can feel both Amil, and Helmar abruptly stiffen behind me. Phigby turns grim eyes on us. "It may not be 'too' Hooper. It may be that the Wilders are under Vay's grotesque influence."

"Phigby," Cara says in a shaky voice, "you can't be serious."

"I'm very serious," Phigby utters. He turns his eyes to me. "And Hooper's witch?"

He shakes his head. "It wasn't a witch. It was Vay, herself. For some reason, she's not only after the golden, she's after Hooper, too."

I was wrong.

It just became much, much, worse.

Thoughts of Golden Wind

Drachs are such unusual creatures. They believe so much in what their eyes see, their ears hear, their sense of taste, smell, and touch.

Unable to accept beyond what their puny senses tell them they live such meager and limited lives. It is a wonder that any of them have survived this long.

So many turn their sight inward, caring only for the pleasure of the moment.

A few among them, such as Professor Phineas Phigby, he of the inquiring mind, understand that there is much beyond this world, much beyond what he sees and hears.

So much more.

Even when presented with the three queens, Hooper and the others still doubt. Granted clear direction, they waver. Given answers, they still question.

Even when faced by Vay herself, Hooper refuses to believe that which is happening around him, rather, he turns inward, in many respects a scared little boy.

The gemstone is his to carry, but he must face his task clear-eyed and not be clouded by pride, or vanity, jealousy, or greed.

He must begin to have faith, to believe in more than just himself, to want more for those around him, for those he knows and those he doesn't. His vision must grow.

For some, faith is frail, easily slain by the slightest adversity. That cannot be in this company. Their conviction must never waver; tested by hardship, yes, but met by confidence in each other, faith in themselves, and a firm belief in the promise that what they do is for the right and good.

Not just for today, but always. If not that, then what is the purpose of faith?

19

I shove the book into Cara's lap and jump to my feet. I can't help it. Terror sweeps over me, and I want to run, to hide. My adversary has gone from being a simple witch with skeleton claws for hands, eyes that glow like coals, riding on a broomstick, and eating little children, to being a wicked, powerful fairy "just below the gods." I'm doomed. I'm more than doomed if such a thing is possible.

Phigby is quick to my side and grips both of my shoulders in his strong hands. "Easy, Hooper, she's not here. Of that, I can assure you."

Helmar snorts with a crooked grin. "Oh come now, Phigby, just what would an evil fairy want with Hooper, other than to eat him, maybe. And even then, he'd be a pretty scrawny meal."

"That's not funny, Helmar," Cara retorts and turns to Phigby. "Seriously, Phigby, what would Vay want with Hooper?"

Phigby peers at me with a questioning, concerned expression. My heart is still thudding in my chest, and my hands have suddenly gone cold, even in the day's warmth. I manage to swallow, give him a weak nod that I'm all right, and sit back down.

He steps away, draws a breath and as his usual custom when thinking through a problem he tugs on his beard. As much and as often as he pulls on his shaggy whiskers, it's a wonder he has any hair left.

"I don't know," he rumbles and vehemently shakes his head. "But Vay would not waste her energy on Hooper if he were as insignificant as you assume him to be."

He steps back to scratch at his head as he peers at me. "Still, there must be a reason but for the life of me, I don't know why Vay would have such an interest in Hooper."

He begins to pace in a tight circle, his robe swirling about him. Today, it seems to have an azure color to it that almost blends in with the sky. "There is so little that I can remember," he mutters as if to himself. He stops and lets out a long, melancholy sigh. "That companion book I mentioned, it might hold a great many answers."

He whirls around, the hem of his robe scattering bits of leaves. Amil points at Phigby's oversized haversack. "You seem to carry your entire library in there, you don't have it with you?"

"No," Phigby growls. "Of all the foul luck, I had it and then lost it."

"Lost it?" Cara questions with a sideways glance at me. "How did you lose it?"

"In the fire," Phigby snaps. "I forgot to grab the book when I fled my shop, and now it's little more than ashes."

He gestures wildly and says, "And I had it sitting right there, on my pedestal and I ran right past it. All I had to do was reach out . . . " his voice ends in a groan, and he stands there, angry and upset at himself.

Cara and I stare at each other. I lean toward her and say firmly, "You have to tell him."

"Eh?" Phigby mutters, peering at the two of us. "Tell me what?"

Cara and I lock eyes in a hard stare and stay that way for several heartbeats before she abruptly jumps to her feet. "I'll do better than that."

Cara marches over to her sapphire, who's lying down while Phigby turns and watches her. He turns his head to me with a quizzical expression, but before he can say a word, I answer, "Just wait, she'll show you."

Cara rummages in her nearest saddlebag before she withdraws the sealed book and comes striding back. She hands it to Phigby while his eyes widen in amazement and an enormous smile cracks his face. His grin is so big, I'm afraid that if he breathes in too deeply, he'll suck in his beard and suffocate.

He holds the book up and turns it over in the sunlight beaming in delight as he holds the hefty manuscript. He continues to smile and then as quickly as his grin appeared, it disappears. He peers at us with a deep frown and glowering eyes.

"Wait," he rumbles, "how did you — "

Then he gapes at us, his eyes growing so large that I feel as if the moons Nadia and Eskar have taken their place. "You!" he sputters, his finger jabbing at the both of us. "It was you that I heard in my formulating room!"

"It was my fault, Phigby," I quickly say. "I goaded Cara into sneaking into your house and taking the book. I'm the one you should be mad at, not her."

"Oh, bosh," Cara replies, giving me a sharp elbow in the side. "Phigby, it was no such thing. After Hooper told me that you were going to find an old book that you hadn't read in a long time, I just had to have a look at it. Yes, I slipped into your house while Hooper kept watch, and borrowed your book."

"Borrowed!" Phigby thunders. "You mean stole, young lady."

"No," Cara answers primly and brushes at her tunic as if she'd just found some imaginary dirt, "borrowed. When I don't have the money to buy, you always let me borrow your books, knowing that I always return them."

"That's true," I quickly add. "Remember, she was, uh, is, your best customer."

"That's right," Cara huffs. "And what I borrow, I always return. So there."

Cara is holding her head and nose up a little higher than usual as if Phigby's accusation is somehow insulting and outrageous.

I keep my eyes on Phigby, just in case I need to leap away from his backhand. He wouldn't hit Cara — I, on the other hand, am a different matter.

He's never struck me before, but to Phigby, stealing a book is second only to murder. Then again, murder might be a close second.

Still keeping my eyes on Phigby, I hang my head low, like a cur dog with its tail between its legs.

Phigby's eyes, narrow and hard, flick from Cara to me and back again. He stays that way for several moments before he starts to chuckle, then laughs, holding his hand to his mouth to muffle the sound as if he's afraid to disturb the sleeping dragons. "Borrowed," he laughs out loud. "They borrowed it."

He reaches out and sweeps us both together in a bear hug. I look at Cara. Her smile is genuine. But not for me, for Phigby. I, on the other hand, I'm thinking Phigby may be laughing now, but it's like the calm before the storm. When he lets go, I'm still going to keep my head low, just waiting for his backhand to land.

Phigby releases us and to my surprise, declares, "Bless you both. I don't know what prompted you to do what you did, but I am grateful."

He lifts the book up. "This, I believe, holds many secrets, perhaps even the answers as to why we find ourselves in these circumstances and my heart was heavy with its loss."

"But it's not lost," Cara replies. "You have it back now. Can you open it, Phigby? We watched you try before and you couldn't."

At that, he turns a severe eye on her so she shrugs and says, "We were in the tree outside your window watching you try to open the book. We were going to knock for you to let us in but you were in such a foul mood when you went to bed that we thought better of it."

Phigby stares at us both for a moment and then, seemingly accepting Cara's explanation, sits on the log and Cara and I slide in next to him.

He runs his hands over the book's shiny surface. In the dying sunlight, the cover seems to change color in the sunlight, almost as if a rainbow played across the top.

His fingers tap on the orb that holds the clasp and he says in a distant voice, "Once I knew how to open it, but I can't quite remember now . . . "

As Phigby is speaking, I notice something unusual about the book.

"Phigby," I say, "it doesn't have a title. What's it called?"

"Eh?" he replies and shakes his head. "I can't recall that either."

Cara leans forward eagerly. "A mystery book! Phigby, you've just got to remember how to open it."

Curious, I run a hand over the front binding. "Phigby, what are these rounded depressions?" I count to myself. "There's seven all total, and they make an arch from one corner across the top and then to the other corner. Are they significant in some way?"

I run a finger on the inside of one of the shallow scoops. There is something vaguely familiar about the indentation's size and depth. Phigby lets out a long sigh. "Alas, Hooper, I'm afraid I've forgotten much. It's been too long, but, yes, I believe that they're meaningful in some way."

"So you really can't open it," Cara says in a disappointed voice. "And that means we can't read what's inside."

Phigby straightens himself and gently runs a hand over the book's cover. "It will come to me, I'm sure of it, just not now."

Helmar lets out a little grunt. "I'm sorry, Phigby, but frankly, I think you're filling our heads with more mystical nonsense. The Wilders, they're real, as are our dragons and the golden. Not some mumbo jumbo fairies from fairy folk land."

"It's not nonsense," Phigby retorts. "To every legend and lore, there is always a bit of fact, Helmar. Vay and her sisters are real. What? Do you think that what you experienced at the falls was, as you put it, some 'mumbo jumbo'?"

"And as I recall," Cara says curtly, "that 'mumbo jumbo' had you stumbling backward with your bow up."

"As it did you," Helmar returns.

"Oh, yes," Cara answers. "I fully admit that I was close to running. Wilders are one thing, they're from my world; fairies are not."

"No — " Phigby begins when abruptly, the dragons are on their feet, snorting and pawing the ground.

I snap my head up. "Dragon wings!" I yelp.

Helmar is quick to action. "Get deeper in the woods!" he orders. "Move!"

Cara springs away, with Phigby and Amil in close pursuit. I start to run, but Helmar's hand flashes out, grabs my hood, and jerks me back so hard that I stumble backward. He holds me up so that I'm practically on my toes. "Where's your bow and quiver?" he demands.

I swallow and point back at the cabin. "Get them," he orders.

"But — " I waver.

"No buts, Hooper," Helmar growls, his hand on his sword hilt, "we may just need that bow and those arrows. Go!"

He shoves me toward the hut. I stumble forward, hesitant and unsure, trying to choose between Helmar's sword and unknown dragon wings. Helmar is closer than the oncoming dragons, which makes up my mind for me, and I spin to scurry toward the shanty. An uncertain future death is better than a certain death standing in the form of Helmar.

Behind me, I can hear our dragons lumbering away as they make for the thick forest. I swing my head around in every direction, trying to find Scamper, but the little tub is nowhere to be seen. I'm at the cabin door when I hear the dragon wings almost overhead. I duck into the cottage, grab my bow and quiver before peering outside.

Wilders!

Six reds are landing in the far meadow, their crimson scales shimmering in the sun's last light. I start to ease outside when I hear *Eeeett?* behind me. "Scamper!" The little chunk has been sleeping under the bed the whole time. I snatch him, and bolt through the door, praying that the Wilders don't see us.

I charge around the cabin to hide behind the back wall. I peer around the corner. The Wilders are talking among themselves. One points toward the creek, and while he leads several Wilders toward the hut, the others take the reds toward the stream.

That's all I need to see. Using the shanty as a shield, I scramble low up the gentle slope, juggling Scamper, bow, and quiver. I slip behind the first large tree trunk I can find and peek out. The Wilders are almost to the tree line.

I put Scamper down and whisper, "Run!" He darts away, and I'm right behind him, trying to stay low and keep the tree trunk between the Wilders and me.

Scamper darts across the glade as if he's scented a honey hive in the far trees. I finally manage to struggle into the first thick grove and just as I pass a large, knobby tree, a hand shoots out, grabs me by the front of my surcoat and hauls me behind the tree.

"Wilders," I gulp to Helmar, "they're headed toward the cabin."

"I have eyes and ears, Hooper," he mutters and peers around the tree trunk at the hut. "We left warm ashes in the hearth, a dead give-away that someone's been there."

He scowls at me. "And fresh dragon dung in the meadow." He says it in such a way as if to imply that I should have done my job and cleaned it up. "They'll know we were here."

He pauses and then says, "Did all of them make for the hut?"

"No, four to the cabin, and two took their reds to the stream to drink."

He smiles grimly. "They split their forces, and they're off their dragons. Just the opening we need."

He pulls at me. "Let's go, we need to find the others, and quickly."

For me attempting to keep up with Helmar is like the sprogs trying to keep up with the golden when she's on the run. It's all I can do to keep his broad back in sight.

By the time I push through a last line of scraggly bushes, Helmar has already gathered the others together. Winded and out of breath, I stumble over to sink next to Scamper, who's sitting next to the sprogs.

I only catch the last part of Helmar's instructions, " — when we see the smoke, that's the signal for me and Cara to attack."

The group splits apart, each evidently with a part to play in Helmar's plan. "Helmar," I croak, "what do you want me to do?"

He turns, disdain evident on his face. "Guard the golden and the sprogs, stay here, and keep out of sight," he orders.

Helmar whirls away, and he, Cara, and Phigby climb aboard their dragons while Amil strides away in the cabin's direction, leaving me behind without another backward glance.

"In other words," I mutter to myself, "you'll be of no use to us in the coming battle, so stay out of the way and let real warriors do the fighting."

I hold up my bow. "Then why did I risk my life to go back for this?"

I reach over and scratch Scamper behind the ears before shrugging, "Oh, well, I guess he's right," and I set the long shaft aside. "I can't even use this thing."

The golden settles down next to me and swings her head around. "Not all warriors carry swords or bows, Hooper. There are other ways to be courageous that don't require the use of armaments, you know."

"Humph," I reply. "Not in Helmar's world."

I take in a breath and mutter, "Or Cara's, for that matter. To her, you're not a real man unless you can sky a dragon, wield a sword, shoot a bow — "

"Or read books?" the golden murmurs.

I raise my eyes at that. Suddenly, the golden is on her feet, lifting her head. "Smoke," she states.

I whirl around to gape toward the deserted cabin. "Helmar said that when they saw the smoke they'd attack. I — "

Abruptly, the golden snorts and takes several steps forward, her head and ears turned in a different direction. She raises her head as high as it will go, staring and listening so intently that it's as if she's frozen in place.

She spins around to me and orders, "Hooper, get the sprogs."

"Wha — "

"Get the sprogs, now!"

You don't argue with a fire-breathing dragon, believe me, you just don't. I scurry over and grab a sprog under each arm. The golden dips her head. "Under my carapace, and hurry."

I hobble as fast as I can, deposit the first two and grab the other two. "What is it?" I gurgle as I shove Regal and Sparkle in with Strider and Glow.

"I'll tell you in a moment," she responds. "You and Scamper, climb aboard." Scamper takes a running leap, bounds off her leg and lands smack in the middle of the sprogs. That sets them to screeching at him and squabbling but I ignore them as I hesitate.

Helmar's warning was clear. No one, especially me was to ride the golden. If I did . . .

Seeing me standing there, not moving, the golden swings her head around and demands, "What are you waiting for, Hooper?"

I can feel the urgency in her voice but I still don't move. All I can hear is the hiss of Helmar's sword leaving its scabbard, see Helmar standing large and menacing with his blade ready to deliver my death blow.

"Hooper!" Golden Wind's roar is so loud and powerful that it not only shatters my trance, it sends me stumbling backward a few steps. "Your friends are going to die unless we go help them. For the moment, isn't that more important than Helmar's threat?"

I shake my head. Cara in danger? She might die? I set my face and climb up on Golden Wind's neck and settle in.

She immediately whirls and gallops off in the opposite direction of the cabin. We crash through tree limbs, breaking branches right and left. "Wait, why are we heading in this direction? I thought you said that Cara was in trouble."

"She is," the golden answers. "As are the others. Serious trouble."

That makes me sit upright. "From what?"

"Wilders," she answers. "There are a good two-dozen coming low and fast from a different direction. They'll catch Cara and the others unawares."

"A trap?" I sputter and bend low under a sweeper, a branch low enough that if I didn't duck, it would brush me right off Golden Wind.

"I'm not sure," she replies. "I do know that there are more than just the six Wilders back at the hut."

"So why are we going the opposite way?"

"We'll catch those oncoming Wilders by surprise," she answers. She takes a few more steps and then comes to an abrupt halt. She pushes herself into a dark thicket and lies down. "Keep the sprogs quiet," she orders. "They're coming."

I lean down and whisper to Scamper, "Wilders, everyone stay quiet."

He wiggles his button nose at me, and I swear, he glares at the sprogs, just daring one of them to let out as much as a tiny screep.

Moments later, I can hear dragon wings beating furiously overhead. They're flying so low that the force of their downward beats sets the treetops to swaying. They rush overhead and then they're gone.

The golden waits for a few moments more and then bursts out of the thicket. Galloping at full speed, she sprints through a tree grove until she breaks into the clear.

"All right, Hooper," she commands, "hold on tight, we're going to sky."

"We're going to do what?" I yelp. "I thought we were staying on the ground. You have no saddle, and there's nothing for me to hang onto, I'll fall — "

"Hooper, just squeeze your legs tight around my neck and hold on to my horns. You won't fall off."

"Oh, yeah," I retort, "that's what Cara said too, and look what happened. Or don't you remember plucking me out of the pond goop?"

My hands stretch out partway and stop. Skying behind Cara is one thing, skying by myself with practically nothing to hang onto?

"Hooper," the golden growls, "Cara and the others need us. We have to go swiftly, now!"

I take a deep breath. "Look," I say to Golden Wind, "I've never done anything like this before and without a saddle or reins to hold onto, this could be a very short flight, and I could end up with a broken neck.

"So that 'swift' part you talked about — is there an unswift speed that we could start out with until I get the hang of this?"

"Hooper!" I can feel the exasperation in her tone. "Just squeeze my neck with your legs and hang onto my horns. Tight!"

"All right!" I snap and grab her horns. I no sooner latch onto her closest curved horns than she vaults into the air. Her leap pops my head back and for an instant, I'm a little dizzy, and I sway on her neck.

"Hooper, don't you fall off on me," she rumbles.

I blink hard and finally I can see clearly. And wish I hadn't. The pack of Wilders, their crimson corsair tunics and pants flapping in the wind, are bearing down on Cara, Helmar, and Phigby. They have their backs to the Wilders and don't see the danger swiftly approaching from behind.

Even at this distance, I can see Helmar and Cara releasing their arrows at the Wilders below them. I can't see what Phigby is doing, but it doesn't matter. There's no way we can beat the Wilders there in time to warn Cara and the others.

Underneath me, I can feel the golden gather herself and then, as if she were a speeding shooting star in the dusky sky, bolting forward.

Faster and faster we speed. The wind is a roar in my ears, and I have to hunker down as low as I can to withstand the gale.

I thought Wind Song was fast. Compared to Golden Wind, she is a plodding plow horse, and the golden is a sleek thoroughbred. Golden Wind angles swiftly upward for several wingbeats before she levels off and spurts through the sky.

Before I know it, we've caught up with and passed the trailing Wilders, and the golden is still gaining on the leaders.

We flash above the main group, and just ahead, I can see who I assume to be the leader. He's a big man, as large as Amil, and the scarlet he rides is enormous.

For an instant, I think that his red dragon looks familiar but then my eyes catch what he's doing. His longbow is notched, and his arrow is trained squarely on Helmar.

But neither Helmar nor the others have spotted the danger. They're too intent on their exchange with the Wilders on the ground. I lean forward and have to shout above the wind, "The lead Wilder, he's got his arrow trained on Helmar, and Helmar doesn't see him."

The golden's sudden downward swoop not only takes my breath away, she almost loses me again. Now, we're in a headlong dive, and I quickly understand what she's doing. She's putting her hard scales between the Wilder's arrow and Helmar's thin skin.

From the corner of my eye, I see the Wilder pull his longbow as taut as he can, and then he unleashes his arrow. It's flying straight and true toward the unsuspecting Helmar.

Time seems to slow, almost stop. No sound comes to my ears, it's as if all sounds have disappeared and I hear only silence.

I can see the arrow's feathering flutter as it passes through the air. Helmar is turned away from the lethal bolt and slowly draws back his bow, his eyes centered on some target below. His arrow speeds away, and I can see his bowstring vibrate from the power of his bowshot.

The Wilder's arrow closes on Helmar. We're diving straight between him and the lethal bolt, but if we don't get there before it does, Helmar will never see the arrow that takes his life.

At the last instant, Golden Wind puts on an extra burst of speed, and she's between Helmar and the scarlet arrow.

I don't know if it was a sudden gust of wind or the beating of Golden Wind's wings but at just that moment, instead of the arrow bouncing off her scales, the arrow tips upward in flight.

Have you ever tried to elude an arrow while sitting on a dragon in midair? It can't be done. Trust me, I know.

I don't remember screaming when the arrow pierced my body. What I do remember is an agonizing, shuddering pain that shoots tremors of torture rippling up and down my body before I bend over in pure torment.

Somehow I know that unlike the arrowhead that barely penetrated Helmar's shoulder, this bolt has all but gone clean through my puny body.

I waver in the saddle, barely hanging on when from far away, I hear Cara scream, "Hooper!"

My last thoughts are that Helmar may not ever see the arrow that takes his life, but I've seen mine.

20

I don't remember much after that, except for the searing, lashing pain — pure agony filling mind and body. I couldn't think of anything else except to somehow ease my suffering or better yet, take the torment away.

I recall grabbing the arrow that stuck out of my shoulder so that it wouldn't move. I could feel the arrowhead scraping across bone and every time it did, it was like old Malo stabbing me with his Proga lance.

Sharp, piercing torture and a feeling of the arrowhead digging deeper, slicing into tender flesh every time the golden's wings beat.

I slump forward, trying to ease the pain, but then I felt myself start to slide off Golden Wind's neck. Through the anguish, I heard, "Hooper, grab my horn — take my horn, Hooper!"

I lolled back, at the same time grabbing for a horn. I managed to wrap my fingers around a knobby curved spike and steadied myself. I knew there was a battle of sorts going on around me, but at that point, I didn't care. All I wanted was to hang on and make it to the ground.

The golden was weaving, coursing through the sky, and somehow I held on while she twisted and turned. I could hear Scamper chittering at me, but I ignored him. The sprogs were screeping as if they were on the brink of death, not me, and I definitely ignored them.

Suddenly, even though my eyes were closed, I could feel, not see, a wave of bright light sweep across me. I didn't know what it was. However, after that, the golden stopped her twists and turns, straightened, and flew level and fast, slicing through the air.

I don't know how long I stayed that way, eyes shut against the pain, swaying from side to side in the saddle, moaning. I swallowed and asked, "Where are we going?"

"To the only place we can go, now," the golden replied.

"What about the Wilders?" I groan.

"Scattered and far behind," she answers. "For the moment, we don't have to worry about them."

Ever notice that sometimes when you're really hurt you say the silliest things? I answered the golden by saying, "In that case, just find me a pond and drop me in, only this time make sure the water really is soft and gentle."

She didn't respond to my stupid comment, of course.

Then I hear a second set of dragon wings close by and Cara imploring, "Hooper, hang on, just hold on for a little while longer!"

What did she think I was doing, I wondered, dancing a jig on the golden's skull plate?

I'm not sure how long we sky before the golden goes into a long glide and then I feel her talons thump against the ground. By then, I'm so groggy that I keep going in and out of consciousness and only catch snippets of the conversation around me.

"Easy with that shoulder, the arrow shaft is still in."

"He's got a death grip on her horn, I can barely prod his fingers off."

"A good thing or he would've fallen off."

"Even so, how he stayed on her is beyond me. Cara, slowly swing his leg over — right, now Amil, Helmar ease him down."

"Easy . . . easy. Good. Let's get him under those trees. Cara, grab my bag and then get a fire going. Helmar, you get the dragons under cover — Amil, water and lots of it."

I try not to moan as they lower me down from the golden and place me gently under the limbs of a wide-spreading tree. Even so, every so often I can't help but let a whimper pass through my lips. Well, even Helmar let out a groan from his arrow wound, so I'm entitled to a few moans.

After a bit, I find I'm lying on what feels like leafy boughs and decide I've earned a good, long rest and go back to sleep. I don't know how long I nap before Phigby rouses me with a cup to my lips. "Here lad, get this all down, you're going to need it because that arrowhead went deep."

I don't argue with him over his sour-tasting concoction because if Phigby says I'm going to need all of his potion, then I have a feeling that what's coming next is going to be bad, really bad, and far worse than a foul taste in my mouth.

It is bad, and that's all I'm going to say about it other than at some point I totally black out because when I wake up I can see that the moons are just rising which means that several hours have gone by since we landed.

I guess I must have moaned or something when I stirred because Phigby is instantly by my side. "Easy lad," he orders, "I don't want you moving around just yet. We've got to give that wound of yours time to heal."

I put my hand on the thick bandage. "You got the arrowhead out?"

"Yes," he replies, "and before you ask, no, there wasn't any poison. Fortunately though it went in pretty deep, if you're going to take an arrow, you picked the right spot. It didn't do a lot of damage."

"Thanks, Phigby, for taking care of me. I really appreciate it."

"You're very welcome, Hooper. I'm just glad it wasn't any worse and for what it's worth, your comrades are still talking about how you managed to stay on Golden Wind with that arrow in you. That was a very impressive feat."

I raise my head up to see that there's a little fire going, and the others are sleeping close to the flames. "Is everyone else all right?"

"Thanks to you and Golden Wind," he answers, "we are. If you two hadn't busted up that ambush, well, I'm pretty certain that not all of us would be sleeping around our campfire."

I glance at the moons. "For some reason I thought it would be later, but the moons are just rising."

Phigby chortles. "My potion knocked your senses a little off kilter, lad. The moons are setting, not rising. Dawn's not that far off but for you, your job is to do exactly nothing but sleep and hopefully we'll get some food in you first thing tomorrow. Understood?"

"Understood," I answer and close my eyes. It doesn't take much for me to drop off to sleep.

My slumber is strange and unpleasant, not from the pain from my wound but it's as if I'm in my body, yet I'm not. I float in dark places and feel as though foul, unseen hands are reaching out to pull me into a never-ending darkness of lost souls.

I groan and twitch from the eerie touches when from far away I hear a ghostly, *Run, Hooper, if you can, but I shall find you and have what is mine.*

At that, my eyes pop open with my heart thudding in my chest. It's early morn with just a bit of pale sunlight upon the glade. I turn my head to one side to see Cara adding a few small twigs to the smoldering fire. My movement must have caught her eye for she hurries over and kneels beside me. "Hooper, how are you feeling?"

I don't immediately answer as I can still hear the unnerving voice in my head. Then, I nod and say in a croaking voice, "Better, but thirsty."

"Easily solved," she quickly says and holds the leather water jug to my lips.

I drink long and deep to quench my thirst. "Thanks, Cara."

She nods and then says, "I wish I could offer you something to eat, but we don't even have squirrel soup. Sorry. Amil and Helmar have already gone out to see what they can bag; perhaps in a bit, we'll have something to munch on."

She leans a little closer, her eyes suddenly concerned. "Hooper, is your wound worse? You look a bit feverish."

"No, I just didn't get much sleep is all."

"In that case, go back to sleep but if you need something, let me know. While Phigby's napping I've got camp duty."

I lie back, and it's then that I notice that I'm actually lying on a bed of leaves that cushion and soften the ground.

My wound aches but I have to admit, being tended to by Cara and not having to sleep on the hard ground goes a long way toward easing the pain, especially the part of being tended to by the most beautiful girl in the world.

It almost makes it worthwhile having taken that Wilder arrow. Wait, what am I saying? Even having Cara tenderly look after you is not worth taking a Wilder arrow in the shoulder.

I close my eyes and try to doze off, but I'm not feeling all that well. I'm feverish, and my shoulder has begun to throb, waves of pain that seem to be building by the moment. I don't want to appear to be an absolute coward to Cara, so I don't say anything.

I drop in and out of slumber but each time I begin to relax the dark dreams come again and each time the feeling of being pulled into a black abyss becomes stronger.

At some point, I'm awakened by Scamper, who bounds up to me, putting his paws on my chest with his face practically against mine.

His eyes are anxious, and he chitters sympathetically. I knuckle his head weakly and say, "I'm all right, Scamper. Go find some nice juicy grubs or worms."

He hesitates before his stomach wins the moment and he's off. I lean back and drift off to sleep. In my dark dreams, I'm running, stumbling through the forest. Behind me is a woodsman's hut. Fire leaps from its thatched roof and from the flames come fiery arms, reaching out to grasp me in their writhing tentacles.

I stumble through the trees only to fall painfully to the ground. From behind I hear, *Run, Hooper! Run!*

I glance back and in the roiling black smoke, Vay stands with a chilling, triumphant smile on her face. *Oh yes,* she sneers. *Run, Hooper, only you can't for I shall find you each time you flee!*

She glides through the air, reaching for me. I try to run, but I'm too exhausted. I ready myself for the death that I know is coming from her evil hands.

Suddenly, at the last instant, three emerald dragons appear. They stand between Vay and me before they turn and fix their cruel green eyes on me. I understand. It's not Vay who will slay me but these three emissaries of death that she's called to do her dirty work.

"Hooper!" the blast of sound jerks me awake. I open tired eyes and peer upward. The golden is standing over me. "Hooper," she says urgently, "try to stay awake until Phigby returns."

I try to keep my eyes open, but it's no use, and I drop back into darkness. My nightmare forms again, only this time it's not a dragon that sends spears of dragon fire into the cottage, my former home, it's Vay.

She rides the clouds, fire spewing from her ghastly hands. Once again, I'm running, but it's not my mother's voice urging me on, it's Vay's laughing cackle, *Run, Hooper, run. Run as far as you can . . . Only, I'll still find you.*

I jerk awake to find the golden, her head lowered, and her cat's eyes peering intently at me. My face is covered with beads of sweat, and I'm trembling. My body is on fire. I moan and clutch at my shoulder. I glance around, but other than the dragons, no one else is in sight.

"Where is everyone?" I rasp.

"Helmar and Amil," she answers, "search for food. Phigby and Cara seek water."

She comes closer, her eyes clearly concerned. She sniffs at my shoulder and her head jerks back as if she's breathed in the smell of a week-old goat carcass that's been left out to rot in the sun and is full of maggots.

A low growl rumbles from her throat. "Hooper, you've got to get up, find Phigby."

I wave a hand at her. "Go away, I'm not going anywhere. If Phigby wants to find me, he knows where I am."

I drift off to sleep. My nightmare comes again. I'm running, stumbling through the forest. The woodsman's hut is a heap of shattered, smoking ruins that I'm trying to escape.

I stumble through the trees only to fall a last time, exhausted from my effort and the pain. I hear a noise and lift my head, only it's not three dragons that come for me, it's Vay.

She glides across the ground, her claws outstretched, and this time, I know that no green dragon is going to save me.

"Hooper!" the blast of sound jerks me awake. I open groggy eyes and peer upward. The golden is still standing over me. "Hooper," she says desperately, "listen to me. When Phigby returns, you've got to say to him,

Foul worms there be, both land and sea
That claim the mind and to it bind
Away life's spark, forever in the dark
Until the light shall end the blight.

I have no idea what she's talking about. "Go away," I demand, "and leave me alone. Can't you see that I'm sick?"

I shiver one moment, and then I want to throw off my tunic the next as I feel as if I'm on fire. I writhe in pain, the agony coursing down my arm and through my shoulder as if Malo is piercing me with a dozen Proga lances.

Waves of darkness pass through my mind, but I fight them off, not wanting to face Vay again, even if it's but a dream.

I hear voices. It's Vay, she's coming for me. Somehow, I rise to my feet. I try to run but all my legs can manage is a staggering, stumbling gait. Vay's behind me, coming closer. I can hear her footsteps crunching leaves under her clawed feet.

I can't move fast enough; I can't get away. All around me is darkness, closing in, pulling at me as if to suck me into the blackness.

Then Vay's claws are on me. I try to fight but I can't. She spins me around to face her, and I know it's the end. Here, in this place far from Draconstead, I die.

"Hooper!" I struggle against her grasp. "Hooper!" I try to push away, but I'm caught fast.

"Phigby! Come quick, he's delirious!"

"Hooper," the voice is gentle, soft, definitely not Vay's harsh cackle. "Hooper, open your eyes, and look at me."

I keep my eyes closed. It's a trick. Vay has turned herself into appearing as Cara. If I open my eyes, she'll have me. "Let's get him back to bed," another, deeper voice says.

A moment later, I'm back on my leafy bed, twisting, turning in my torment. A gentle hand presses on my face. "Oh, Phigby," Cara murmurs, "he's burning with fever."

Phigby is kneeling beside me. His hand is rough on my face. I reach up to push his hand away. "G'way," I mumble, "leave me alone." I much prefer Cara's smooth, tender touch.

I retch, sending another painful round of Proga lances coursing through me. "Hooper, look at me," Phigby demands. Cara has a wet rag on my cheeks, my neck. The coolness feels good, but only where she touches, the rest of my body burns as if I were walking across a fire pit.

I barely open my eyes against the light. I can see the golden standing, peering over Phigby's shoulder. Her eyes are imploring, fearful. I can tell she's not going to leave me alone unless I repeat her silly ditty.

I wet my lips, trying to remember what she said. "Worms," I mumble.

Phigby leans closer, his eyes big and round. "What did you say, Hooper?"

"Something about worms," I repeat, trying to recall the golden's lyrics. If I can just remember, they'll all go away and leave me alone.

Abruptly, I can see the words, glowing gold and bright in my mind. Another wave of darkness starts to close in on me before Phigby's rough shaking brings me back to the light.

"Hooper, what's that about worms?" He's practically yelling at me. I get mad. He shouldn't be bellowing at me, I don't deserve to be shouted at, and I'm sick and tired of it; especially the sick part.

With lips and jaws set tight, I grind out,

Foul worms there be, on land and sea
That claim the mind and to it bind
Away life's spark, forever in the dark
Until the light shall end the blight.

Phigby's intake of breath is so loud that it makes me open my eyes a bit wider to stare at him in surprise. "Phigby," Cara demands, "what is it?"

"I'm a fool!" he bawls. "A complete utter, doddering fool. Get more wood," he orders. "I need a fire, now."

I close my eyes tight as the sunlight is now too much to bear, but I hear the fear in Cara. "Phigby, what's wrong, what are you going to do?"

"Something," Phigby replies, "that I haven't done in quite a long time. But if I'm successful — "

"Successful at what, Phigby? What's happening to Hooper?"

Phigby's voice is worried, anxious. "Hooper's dying. His body holds a Wraith Worm. If I don't remove the vile thing in time, he'll turn into a wraith and become a slave of Vay."

That opens my eyes.

21

"I need water and wood for a fire," Phigby snaps at Cara. "Leave the one leatheren with me that still has some water in it and get the others filled. Now!"

Without another word, Cara snatches up the water flasks and heads off at a dead run. I raise a weak hand to Phigby. My voice gurgles from the foam that forms on lips and tongue. I don't know if it's the spittle or my natural inability to speak clearly, but out of my mouth comes, "Wraaath wrrrm?"

Phigby eyes me, and takes a cloth and quickly wipes my mouth. He shakes his head in answer to my question and holds my head up for me to drink from his flask.

My throat feels as if I've a dirt clod stuck in it, and I choke and sputter, but somehow I get some of the liquid down. The rest just drools off to one side of my mouth.

Phigby sets the flask down and begins pulling objects out of his bag. I try to raise my head to see what he's doing, but then the darkness comes at me again. I know what will happen if I succumb so I fight back.

I'm not sure how I know that if I give in, I will no longer be

Hooper, puny and low as I may be, but something — someone else entirely and under Vay's dominion.

I'll become Vay's slave, and she'll grind me under her feet until I'm less than the maggots that burrow into rotted, stinking meat.

I grab leaves, dirt, anything I can lay my hands on to give me a feeling of something real, something firm to hold onto. I thrust my feet into the ground and with what little strength I have left, try to push myself away from Vay's dark world.

But it's no use, the darkness starts to close about me, swallowing me up in its infernal ebony curtain.

Somehow, I reach out to Phigby, clawing at him. Phigby jerks around, takes one look at me and places his hands on my shoulder. His face looms close. I can see his mouth moving, but the words are faint, distant. "Hooper, hang on, don't give in . . . "

Through blurry sight, I see Cara running up to dump her firewood. She takes one look at me, her mouth sags and her eyes go wide as if she's seen Vay.

She throws the wood together for burning and this time, Phigby doesn't toss anything into the kindling for it to catch fire. His hand makes a chopping motion, I hear, *"Blazen!"* and the arm-sized branches burst into flames.

Then Cara and he are tearing at my tunic. They practically rip it off, but at this point, I don't care, I just want the pain, the anguish to stop. It's stronger than I am, it's beating me down until I have nothing left, no willpower to fight back.

I wish I were stronger and had Helmar's or Amil's, or even Cara's strength. But I don't.

I — can't — do — this. I can't save myself.

If entering the bliss of Vay's shadows is the answer, then that's what I want. I stop squirming, stop fighting and lay my head back to let the darkness, let Vay claim me so that I can be forever rid of the pain.

Cara's slap across my face is every bit as rude and hurtful as Malo's swift kicks to my backside back in the barn. My eyes pop open, and Cara's angelic nose is practically touching mine.

An angry angel, nevertheless, a saving angel to me. "Hooper!" she yells. "Don't you dare leave us!"

That I heard, loud and very, very, clearly.

I think to myself, "Don't you dare leave us," is nice, it means that Cara believes that I belong in our company. "Don't you dare leave me," however, would have been so much better.

It means I belong to her. But still, "don't you dare leave us," must mean that she cares, right? And if Cara cares even a little, then that's important.

A quiet voice, sounding remarkably similar to the golden's, interrupts my thoughts; *If you won't fight for yourself, then fight for Cara.*

The darkness pushes at me again, stronger, harder. I feel myself slipping back into the blackness. I'm standing on the brink of a swirling, ebony whirlpool.

One more step and I'll drop into the void and be lost. Whatever and whoever I am will be forever gone, swallowed by Vay's dark will.

I hear Phigby's voice — it's powerful, forceful, calling me back from the edge. With every bit of self-will I can muster, I slowly turn from the spinning blackness. Parting the churning black clouds is a sliver of light, it grows, changing into a shining arch; a rainbow arch.

Striding through the colorful bow are Phigby and Golden Wind. Phigby's dark robe is gone, replaced by a brilliant silvery mantle that billows as if from a breeze. In one hand he holds a gleaming staff with a knobby end that he holds out as if to push away the roiling, dark curtain.

The golden's eyes are on me, they hold me so I can't move, keeping me from toppling over into the black pit of doom. Phigby reaches out, and his voice is like thunder and lightning combined, *Summonis, abjurate, Hooper — to me!*

His free hand touches my tunic right on my arrow wound. For an instant, I feel as if a lightning bolt had pierced through my body and I jerk upright. I suck in breath after breath as if all the air had been forced from my body.

It takes a moment before my eyes clear and then I see Phigby, standing over me, but what he holds causes my heart to almost stop beating.

He's holding long, blackened, smoking tongs as far away from his body as he possibly can. Caught in the pincers is a writhing, tiny wormlike creature. I watch wide-eyed as Phigby turns and strides a few steps out into the open meadow.

From the tree line, Cara appears, holding dripping wet water flasks. She stops to gape at Phigby for an instant before she starts to take another step.

Phigby's voice booms in the glade, seeming to echo off the swaying trees. "I told you to stay away!"

He swings his arm at her as if he would push Cara out of the glen. Then he commands, "Get back, for this brings the living death."

A shaft of morning sunlight breaks through the overhanging tree limbs to form a bright beam in the meadow's center. Phigby paces to the brilliant ray of sunlight and holding the tongs in one hand, reaches up with his other hand as if he were trying to touch the sun.

Then he cups his hand between the squirming wormlike thing and the sun and holds it there for a moment. *Ljos Hata Mykyr!* he exclaims in a loud, penetrating voice.

Either my eyes deceive me, or I see a beam of light shoot from the sky into Phigby's open palm. Then, as if his hand were channeling the light, the ray bursts out of his fingers with such brilliance that I have to jerk my head away.

As the light dissipates, I turn back to see that all that's left of the wormlike creature is a small, dark, wispy column of smoke that rises into the air until it entirely disappears.

When I look back, Phigby has lowered his pincers and is slumped over as if the exertion had drained him of every bit of energy in his body.

Cara hurries over and asks anxiously, "Phigby, are you all right?"

He straightens, and glowers at her. "I told you to stay away. Someday your curiosity will be the death of you, girl."

"I'm sorry, Phigby," she replies meekly and holds the water flask up. "I thought that maybe you or Hooper needed more water."

"Humph!" he answers before his face softens and he directs her towards me. "Go to Hooper, he needs to drink deeply."

Cara hesitates for a moment before she hurries over, kneels, and holds the water skin for me to drink. I practically down its contents in one swallow.

"Here," she says, "let's get your top back on. After what you've been through, the last thing we want is for you to catch the shivers." With her help, I slip my tunic over my scrawny ribs and lie back.

"How's the shoulder?" she asks.

"Much better, thanks," I reply.

She reaches out to lightly touch my wounded shoulder. "That's amazing," she murmurs. "Hooper, I saw your wound." She makes a face as if she's just stepped on a squishy bug. "It was ghastly, like a big black spider with yellow pus, and — "

"I get it," I quickly answer, my stomach rolling at her description. "When Phigby was getting that thing out, did you see — "

No," she instantly replies. "He shooed me away. Told me in no uncertain words to stay in the woods until — well, his exact words were, until the day had come and gone or he was come and gone.

"And then he said, no matter what I heard, even if was the most forlorn pleading or begging that I've ever heard, not to come back into the glade until he called for me."

She took in a deep breath. "He whispered that my very life depended on my heeding his words."

"What do you mean?" I stammer.

She bites on her lip. "I think," she begins softly, "that whatever he was dealing with was so deadly that he either succeeded or the two of you died."

My head spins and I feel a little woozy. Cara reaches out to me. "Hooper, you're not going to faint on me are you?"

In a moment, the world stops spinning and just after, Phigby joins us. He holds the tongs up and peers at them with lowered eyebrows. Whatever Phigby did, the pincer ends are now fused and blackened together.

"I admit," he says with a sigh, "it's been a long while since I had to do anything like that. I don't remember it being quite so hard before."

He tosses the charred nippers aside and goes to one knee next to Cara. Great drops of sweat run down his forehead and onto his cheeks to disappear into his beard. He's breathing heavily, his face drawn and his expression is one of exhaustion, but his eyes tell me that the victory was his.

I hear anxious chittering coming from nearby, and Scamper breaks through some tangling under limbs of a nearby bush and spurts to my side.

Cara quickly reaches out to stop him before he can jump on me. She holds him firmly with one hand and arm wrapped around his chest while her expression turns from deep anxiety to relief as she studies my face.

I reach out and knuckle Scamper as Cara eases him onto my lap. He raises his head to peer intently at my face. *Arrriiiite?* he asks.

I swallow, take another deep breath, and murmur, "I think so, Scamp."

He bumps his nose against mine, and then satisfied that I'm indeed all right, darts away, only to return a moment later with what looks like an acorn between his teeth. He stops to put an end of the husk on one side of his mouth, trying to use his heavier back teeth to break open the shell.

"Hey," I say and reach out with my good arm. "Wouldn't want to share with us would you? We haven't eaten in a while, and even a piece of acorn sounds good."

He peers at me, breaks the shell, and spits it out. His little paws push the kernel into his mouth and before I can take another breath, he's eaten all of the nut's meat. He tosses the remainder of the shell off to one side, grooms his face with a paw, and then waddles off.

"That would be a definite no," Cara states. "And it appears that he's off to find more acorns not to share with us."

I stare at the shell remnants and then to where Scamper disappeared into the thick underbrush. "You know, if he can find acorns to eat, so can we. Maybe a whole hoard of nuts for the finding?"

Cara looks at me with a skeptical expression. "Really? You don't think Scamper wouldn't have found such a treasure trove by now?"

"Never mind about acorns and such," Phigby grumps. "Hooper, your wound, the shoulder, how does it feel?" He leans close to whisper, "And inside your head?"

I take stock of my shoulder, the rest of my body, and most importantly, my mind before I whisper, "The blackness — it's gone. She's gone."

"She?" Cara asks. She gives Phigby a concerned look. "Who's she?"

I glance over at the golden who's watching with both gentle and relieved eyes. I bring my gaze back to Phigby. His eyes are impassive, but he doesn't answer, just returns my stare and gives me the tiniest of shakes with his head.

I lick dry lips and mutter, "No one, Cara. I was just having dark dreams, that's all. Talking out of my head with the fever, you know. It can do that to you."

She gives me a small smile of understanding and then holds the water flask up for me to drink again. This time, I do empty the water skin in one swallow.

"Phigby," Cara asks, "what was that you had in those tongs of yours? Was that thing in Hooper?"

Phigby scratches at his cheek for a moment before saying somberly, "That was a Wraith Worm, my dear." He lays a gentle hand on my hurt shoulder. "And yes, I removed it from Hooper, but he should be fine, now."

Cara gazes at me with an uneasy expression before she asks Phigby, "A Wraith Worm? What's that?'

"A form of the deepest, foulest magic that I know," he answers. He stares off at the nearby trees as if his mind is far away. "And something I've not seen in a long, long time."

He shakes his head as if to clear his thoughts, takes a piece of rough cloth, wets it from a water flask, hands it to Cara and motions toward me. "The coolness will do him good," he instructs her.

After several dabs with the cloth, I hold up a hand to stop her.

"You didn't answer Cara's question," I say to Phigby, "and as the one who had that horrible thing inside me, I want to know, just what is a Wraith Worm?"

"Yes, Phigby," Cara says, "I'd like to know, too."

I can see that Phigby is hesitant to answer, but he reaches over and picks an arrow out of Cara's quiver. He holds the plumed bolt up to the light. "When I took the Wilder's arrow out of you, Hooper, I thought it was a simple shaft of wood, feathers, and iron point."

He shakes his head in a forceful manner. "Fool that I was, I did not carefully inspect the tip." He holds the point up. "A necromancer cast a spell on the arrow, and inside the tip placed the Wraith Worm."

He again shook his head. "The arrow was not meant to kill. Instead, once it struck, the spell released the worm, in this case, into Hooper. The foul thing's sole purpose was to take over his mind, his body, eventually turning him into a wraith under the necromancer's influence who created the spell."

Cara's gasp is sharp. "That arrow was meant for Helmar, not Hooper."

Phigby gives me a quick sideways glance and says, "So it was."

I stare at Phigby with wide eyes and a thudding heart. I'm sorry now that I goaded Phigby into answering Cara's question. Some things are best left unsaid. Nevertheless, I ask, "Phigby, I thought a wraith was like a ghost, a specter. How could that happen to me?"

Phigby shakes his head and explains. "There are many types of wraiths, lad. In this case, the intent wasn't to turn you into an apparition but to keep you alive and under the evil one's spell.

"To us, you would seem to be Hooper, but in actuality, that which makes you — your personality, your traits, and most importantly, your ability to make your own choices and decisions would be gone.

"In all appearances you would be Hooper, but your every act would be only to serve your master or mistress who controlled the spell. And there you would have stayed until the evil one had no more use for you and then you would have faded away into oblivion."

Cara shudders at Phigby's grim words. "For what purpose? What would this necromancer want with Hooper?"

He holds up the arrow to peer at it before he gives me another sideways glance. "That I can't answer, but I can tell you that it takes a powerful wizard or sorceress, one who is steeped in the dark arts to do such a thing."

He draws in a deep breath and grimly says, "Indeed, a formidable dark lord or lady of the shadows."

For a moment, my head swirls and the thought comes unbidden in my mind, *One Dark Queen upon her throne, seeds of evil she has sown.*

I must have muttered something for Phigby leans close and asks, "Hooper, what is it? You suddenly look ill. Has the fever or pain returned?"

"What?" I mumble. "No, I was just, uh, thinking about what might have happened if you hadn't gotten that thing out of me."

Phigby gives me several gentle pats on my forearm. "Yes, we were fortunate. But, you fought a good fight, Hooper. Many have lost the battle against the likes of that. And the fool that I am, I might not have recognized it in time if you hadn't warned me."

"Yes," Cara pipes up and leans down to stare at me. "I'd like to know where that came from? You keep making some very surprising statements."

Cara cocks her head to one side, her eyebrows raised and waiting for me to answer. I rapidly think to myself that I'm caught between two awful choices. If I try to lie, they'll catch me in it and demand to know what I'm hiding.

If I tell the truth — I'm not sure what they'll think, maybe that I've gone insane?

Phigby clears his throat and says, "Let's talk about that at another time, Hooper needs his rest, and so do I for that matter."

Cara hesitates before saying, "You're right. You two both look like you've been through a war. We'll talk after you've had some sleep."

I think to myself that Cara doesn't realize how true her words are at the moment. It was a war, maybe not with swords or bows but a battle nevertheless in every sense of the word.

I meet her gaze, and I can see in her eyes that she's willing to forgo my answer for now, but this conversation is not completely over.

She gives me a soft pat on my shoulder. "You lie still, I'll get some more wood and water. Do you need anything else?"

"You wouldn't happen to have a well-cooked, well-seasoned venison haunch or roast lying around would you?" I ask.

She dimples and her eyes gleam. "How I wish I did! I'd start eating at one end, and you could start at the other!"

We share a little laugh before Cara turns to Phigby. "When I get back, you can have your nap, sir, and I'll stand guard." With that, she bounces to her feet and heads toward the trees.

I watch her go, my eyes watching her every move. Phigby rumbles, "Quite a girl, that Cara Dracon."

"Yes," I sigh. "If ever there was a blessed man, it's Helmar. I wonder if he knows just how fortunate he is." I think to myself that if I were Helmar, I would never, ever, take her for granted.

As she disappears behind some thick bushes, Phigby turns from his small, smoldering fire and hands me a steaming cup. "Drink. All of it."

I take a sip and immediately screw my face up. "Yuck! That's definitely not poison, it tastes awful."

"Drink," he commands.

Somehow, I manage to quaff the dark liquid down and from what I can taste it seems to be made of one tart lemon, a pint of brine, and green Bitter Berries. "Couldn't you have at least used ripe berries instead of green?"

"Couldn't find any," he shrugs, "had to use what was on hand. Doesn't matter, they work just as well, just leaves a little aftertaste in the mouth."

"A little aftertaste," I grump. "Is that what you call your tongue tasting like it's rotting in your mouth?"

But I have to admit, within a few moments, my wounded shoulder feels amazingly good. I hardly notice what little pain there is, and I can actually flex my arm.

I start to hold it upright to show Phigby but at a sudden thought, I quickly put it back down and snuggle deeper into my leafy bed.

Can't let Cara know just how well I actually am. After all, how often do I get pampered? Until today, the answer was never and the fact is, I really like it.

"Phigby?"

"Eh?" he mutters. "What is it, Hooper?"

"Who are you?"

He glances sharply at me. "What do you mean? I'm Professor Phigby — "

"No, Phigby," I answer, "I know your name, but you're not just a mere shopkeeper who sells books and makes potions and medicines, by appointment only. You're more than that, much more."

I again turn my eyes to the golden. She has her head on her forelegs, apparently asleep. "In my dreams, I thought I saw — "

"What you saw, Hooper," he says tersely, "doesn't matter."

He pauses and then murmurs, "What is important is for you to rest and to heal. And as for me?" He gently squeezes my arm. "I am who I am, and nothing more."

He turns away to place his pots and medicines back into his bag. On a hunch, I ease the gem out and take a quick look. It's exactly what I expected to find. The little frond has opened even more. I hurriedly put it away, but my suspicions have been confirmed.

Cara was right. That arrow was meant for Helmar. Why? Because he must be the Gem Guardian. That could be the only answer. Vay was trying to put her Wraith Worm into Helmar to control the Gem Guardian, but something went wrong and instead it ended up in my body.

But thanks to Phigby, I'm rid of the dirty thing and Vay's plan was thwarted. This time.

I lay my head back and for the first time, a peaceful, calm feeling flows over me. I've done it, I've found the Gem Guardian. I don't even have to ask the golden, there's no doubt in my mind.

My work is finally finished, and I can rid myself of this burden. I let out a satisfied sigh and snuggle even deeper into my leaf bed.

"Hmm," Phigby says, turning to eye me. "For someone who almost met a most unpleasant end, you sound quite content."

I can't help myself and laugh. To his bemused expression, I say, "You have no idea, Phigby. No sir, you have no idea at all of just how content I am."

22

I sleep so long after that, and without any dark nightmares that when I finally rouse, it's night again and from the shafts of pale moonlight that break through the boughs overhead, the moons must be rising. No sooner do I open my eyes than Cara, who's sitting cross-legged next to me, smiles and calls over her shoulder, "He's awake."

Two sets of heavy footsteps approach and I glance up to find Helmar and Amil standing next to Cara. Helmar has an odd expression on his face, but Amil's grin matches his size.

"You had the Hooper warrior clan pretty worried there for a while," Amil smiles. "But it's good to see you with your eyes open, even if they are a little droopy."

"Yes, Hooper," Helmar murmurs, "it's good to see you awake." He shakes his head as if in disbelief. "How you held onto the golden all that while with that arrow stuck in you is beyond me."

I shrug and immediately wince. Shrugging is not a good thing when you've just had an arrow dug out of your shoulder. "Too afraid of falling off," I answer. I bite down hard on my lip. "Helmar, I'm sorry about skying the golden, but — "

To my surprise, he quickly kneels next to my side and puts out a hand to stop me. Even more astonishing, he says, "Hooper, we'll speak no more about you riding or skying the golden. You did what you had to do."

His hand rests on my good shoulder, and he leans a little closer with a sober expression on his face. "If you hadn't, then more than likely, not only would I be dead but perhaps all of us."

"That's right, Hooper," Cara says softly, "you and the golden saved us. If you hadn't shown up when you did, the Wilders would have caught us completely by surprise."

In a gruff, raspy tone, Helmar says, "You took an arrow for me, Hooper, saved my life, and I'll never forget that."

Helmar's hand, his words ease the pain more than Phigby's potion. I don't know what to say, and I'm a little embarrassed to have so much fuss made over me so I duck my head, just a little, careful not to move my shoulder.

I mutter, "How did you get away from the Wilders? There were a lot more of them than us."

Just then, Phigby walks up and Helmar gestures past Phigby to his nearby bag. "That old, scruffy-looking haversack holds more than just potions, medicines, and books. I still think we're in the company of a powerful wizard or sorcerer."

"Wizards and sorcerers," Phigby splutters, "it was nothing."

"Nothing?" I ask. "What was nothing?"

Helmar turns to me. "As you know, the Wilders ambushed us with a host of reds but the golden's appearance seemed to throw their whole plan off. After you were hit, though, the golden tore out of there faster than any dragon I've ever seen.

"There was no chance that any Wilder crimson was going to catch her. As I said, how you hung on to her is beyond me. Anyway, seeing that they weren't going to catch you or Golden Wind, the Wilders closed on us, trying to ring us in.

"Their leader, a big man, is shouting orders, and it's clear we're in trouble. Their arrows are like a scarlet hailstorm filling the sky but somehow our sapphires weave through their barrage of arrows, and none of us get hit.

"But we're still in trouble, so Phigby reaches into his bag, mutters something loudly into the air, and then throws what looks like a coal-hot spear, directly at the Wilders. It splits the air like a bolt of lightning. There's a clap of thunder, and the whole sky lights up as if the noonday sun had suddenly appeared in our midst.

"Though my eyes are dazzled with colors I've never seen before, I can see plain enough that the Wilders' reds are tumbling about as if some giant had belted them from the sky. I don't know how many toppled out of their seats and fell to their death, but what I do know is that the rest of them turned tail and fled."

I look at Phigby with wide eyes. "You brought sky lightning?"

Phigby waves a hand in dismissal. "Just the right combination of a few simple chemicals Hooper, that's all there was, nothing more."

"Alchemy, again. Just like the other night with the goblin?" I ask.

"More or less," he mutters.

I glance over at Helmar, who shakes his head at me. "Uh huh," he mumbles, implying that he doesn't quite believe Phigby before he says, "I had Wind Glory swoop down, Amil climbed aboard, and we sped off."

He glances at Amil and mutters, "Leaving behind a host of dead Wilders on the ground, thanks to his prowess with that ax of his."

"Wilders," Amil rumbles while looking at me with lively eyes and a smile, "only take one swing to bring down, not three or four as with trolls or goblins."

"The golden led us here, Hooper," Cara murmurs softly. "For some reason, she wanted us to hide ourselves in this stand of dragon heart trees."

"Dragon heart trees?" I mumble as I glance around, not recognizing the giant trees beforehand.

"Yes," Amil replies as he motions toward the looming trees. "A whole stand, in fact. In all my travels, I've only seen a few of them, and always they grow singly, never together like this."

A grove of dragon heart trees, I think to myself. My head is resting up against one of the giant trees, so I reach up with one hand to touch the bark. The tree's outer covering is rough to the touch, and the bark seems to be split into pieces as big as dragon scales.

However, from what I understand, tear away the bark and underneath is wood that is incredibly strong yet in the hands of an expert craftsman is supple enough to be fashioned into powerful longbows.

I have to wonder, it seems that the golden does things for a particular reason, so what could be her purpose in leading us here?

A shaft of moonlight suddenly appears through a break in the trees and catches my eye. I turn my head slightly, and my breath almost catches. The moon's glow falls directly on the golden. She gleams a burnished gold, an aura that seems to shine and wave in the night.

I follow the shaft up to the three moons. They look so close together as if they were one in the sky, shining brighter than I've ever seen. And then, just for an instant, three beautiful faces are in the moonlight, smiling. They give me a small nod as if to tell me it's time and then disappear.

I glance back to Phigby. "Phigby," I ask gruffly, "how close did I come to dying?"

"Well . . . " he begins hesitantly, "you — "

"Phigby, how close?"

Cara answers gently for Phigby. "Very close, Hooper. I helped Phigby dig that arrowhead out."

She draws in a sharp breath. "I saw what he had to do. You're lucky to be alive." Her face takes on an odd expression. "I guess it sort of evened out, you saved ours and Phigby's life, he saved yours."

I let out a breath, give Phigby a small smile. "Thank you, Phigby."

He waves a hand in acknowledgment but knowing how close I came to dying has made up my mind. That arrow was meant for Helmar with its Wraith Worm, the golden led us to a grove of dragon heart trees, there was that aura surrounding the golden and the Gaelian Fae appeared as if encouraging me to act.

It's time.

I must deliver Pengillstorr's tear jewel to the guardian before it's too late.

I try to rise, but Phigby puts a hand on my chest to push me down. I push his hand away. "No Phigby, I've got to get up. It's important that I do, more important than any of you realize."

He and Helmar exchange quick, surprised glances. "Is he — " Helmar begins before Phigby quickly shakes his head and answers, "No, once he became fully awake, that meant the potion had worn off. He's lucid, even though he's not making any sense."

"I am making sense," I grumble, "now either help me or get out of my way."

The two of them put a hand behind my back and ease me into a sitting position. "Now, help me to stand, please." They push and pull me to my feet. The pain's returned a bit, and I grimace, but I nod toward the small campfire. "Over there," I whisper, "in the light."

With Phigby on one side and Helmar on the other, I manage to shuffle over to a smooth fallen log that's close to the fire. I ease myself down and look around to make sure everyone is close.

"All right, Hooper," Phigby asks sternly, "what's this all about? And by the way, if you start bleeding again, don't blame me, you should be lying down."

"I know, Phigby," I answer soberly, "and believe me, if it weren't so important, I wouldn't leave that bed for a fortnight, or longer."

I gesture with my hand toward his bag. "Phigby, the sealed book, would you bring it out, please?"

He gives me a sharp, questioning look before he opens the bag, reaches deep inside, and brings out the mysterious book. He hesitates for a moment before he begins to slide it onto my lap.

I shake my head. "Would you hold it, instead? I don't think I can with this arm."

He hesitates, then sits down, holding the book tightly. Cara quickly takes a seat next to him, no doubt anticipating that something is about to happen with the book, perhaps even, that we'll be able to open the thick manuscript.

With Amil's help, I stand, take a few steps forward before I turn and face my companions. I take a deep breath, reach into my tunic, fumble for a moment before I bring out the gemstone.

In the firelight, its hue seems to spread from my hand to illuminate all of our faces in a soft radiance.

Cara utters a little, "Oh . . ." and both Helmar and Amil suck in quick breaths. Phigby's wide eyes appear as if they're in a trance and his mouth sags just a bit.

I hold the gem out and start to speak when suddenly, I hear the plodding footsteps of the dragons. I peer upward, and now my own eyes go wide.

The four adult dragons, led by the golden, along with the sprogs, lumber over to form a semi-circle behind us, each gazing intently at the jewel.

They're drawn by the dragon gem, just as Golden Wind was attracted to the Gaelian Fae pillars; the gemstone calls them.

I've never been to church, but I've heard that it's solemn and reverent. In this moment, I can't help but feel that we and the dragons are in a sacred place. The night air grows still, with only the small fire's crackling disturbing the silence. Even Scamper joins the circle, his eyes on the crystal, too.

I glance at the gem and see that not only has the tiny frond fully unfurled, but the gemstone itself now radiates with an emerald hue, which to me is the final sign that what I'm about to do is absolutely correct.

"This is a dragon tear jewel," I whisper. I stop and glance at the golden. "Given to me by a very special green dragon just before he died."

I take in a deep breath and let it out. "I've had it for some time, but," I choke, "it's not mine to wield its powers. I was called to be merely its caretaker, to carry it until I found its guardian."

I hold the gem a little higher. "Why I was asked to carry it I don't know, I only know that this belongs to the true Gem Guardian, the one who can exert its powers."

I take in a breath, hold it for a moment before saying, "Which isn't me."

My companions' eyes are questioning, puzzled, even a little fearful, and flick between my face and the jewel. The gem's soft glow seems to fill the small glen.

"In my own way," I give the golden a quick, little glance, "and with a little help, I've been searching for the guardian and now I've found him."

I can't help myself and laugh lightly. "Believe it or not, thanks to that cursed arrow, it pointed me straight to him."

I take in another deep breath, take two steps and hold the gemstone out. "Helmar," I murmur, "you are the Gem Guardian."

His mouth parts and I can see his breathing quicken. His eyes hold a certain eagerness, and he starts to grab the jewel from my hand. At the last instant, he hesitates with his fingertips just touching the gem. "Are you sure, Hooper?"

"I am very sure," I answer and cock my head toward my injured arm. "And this proves it."

I lick dry lips and nod toward the dragons. "Just as the gem draws them, the jewel draws other things — " I glance at Phigby with my mouth screwed to one side.

"Like an arrow with a Wraith Worm spell meant for the Gem Guardian. For all intents and purposes, it was an accident that I got between you and that shaft, nevertheless, it proves to me that you are the guardian.

"When I woke, I suddenly realized that through all this, if I had died before I delivered the jewel . . . " my speech trails off almost to nothing before I can go on.

"If I died before I had the chance to deliver the jewel, then perhaps the gemstone would be lost, and we would not have its great power to counter Vay and her evilness."

I point at the seat I left and almost command, "Helmar, sit down, for there is one other thing. In my dreams, I saw how the jewel and Phigby's book go together."

I glance first at Phigby and then at Cara. "I know how to open the book, or rather, I know how the Gem Guardian can open the book."

I meet Helmar's eyes. Mine are firm, knowing, while his — well, even with the eagerness, there is the tiniest hesitation, born perhaps from confusion, or even fear. A look I know all too well, but one I'm sure will pass once he holds the gem in his hand.

He sets his face in the firm features of the Helmar I know, and with quick strides, makes his way around the log's gnarled end and plants himself into the spot I vacated.

Phigby's expression is troubled, questioning, nevertheless, he passes the book to Helmar. Helmar, in turn, peers up at me with his own quizzical look.

With one last look at the gem, I slowly hold it out and point down at the book. "It goes in the first hole," I instruct, "like this."

I bend down and place the gemstone in the first depression on the left-hand side. It fits snug as if it and the book were made for each other. For a heartbeat, nothing happens, and then a warm light spreads from all sides of the book.

Cara gasps and points. On the front, shimmer the words, *The Ode of the Gaelian Fae.* The glimmering grows brighter and then with a loud crack the clasp in the orb pops up, the strap snaps back, and the book opens — to blank pages, and even then, only a few; the rest of the book remains sealed.

All of us exchange quick glances before Cara scrunches closer to Helmar to get a better look. Even the dragons stretch out their necks to peer at the pages. All except the golden. She just stands there, stoic and impassive.

The jewel glows a little brighter in its depression, and the page shines with an almost blinding light. Then, floating above the pages, letters appear, each colored a light gold and each shaded by deeper, glittering gold. The letters hover for a moment before they snap onto the page.

No one says anything for several heartbeats before Cara nudges Helmar and murmurs, "I think you're supposed to read it." Helmar takes a breath and in a rumbling tone, reads:

Four there were, the Gaelian Fae
Osa, Nadia, Eskar, and Vay
Given a place below the gods,

Where neither Drach nor dragon trod
The gods created all creatures both great and small
Some to fly, some to walk, and some to slither or crawl
On worlds far below to the heavens high above
Some in spite and some with love
But of the dragon, the Fae lay claim
Talon and tail, and fiery mane
Brought them forth as to reign
Over hill, forest, and starry train
But Drach their equal was to be
On land, sky, and deep-blue sea
Gaelian Fae who set their scales
Green to tread through forest dales
Red to thunder in fiery fight
Orange and Yellow to shimmer in flight
Sapphire faster than even the wind
Violet to royalty, its knee will bend
Blue to swim under wondrous ocean
Each creation most carefully chosen
Seven of the bow that colors the rain
Over hill, forest, and starry train
Vay it was who broke the trust
Brought forth the golden to slake her lust
One dragon to rule them all
One Queen, to her we'd fall
For greed, fear, and mighty power
So that o'er all she would tower
The dragon to rule over its own kind
But to her, she would bend the mind
Of the Drach and dragon, too
That to her only, they would be true
One Dark Queen upon her throne
Seeds of evil she has sown
And of the moment, we did partake
But now the right, we must make

From heaven above to the world below
The gods will grant that we must go
To set the right
In fiery fight
Seven have come, Seven are done,
Four did sleep, Now three will weep,
For now comes the eighth, Open swings the gate,
On high the four shall align, A portent, an omen, a blazing sign,
That chains have burst, The evil that thirsts,
Will walk once more, On hill, dale, and rolling moor,
As a seed, it will grow, Up high and down low,
Rage and ruin, merciless death, Pain will come with every breath,
All to slave, all to obey, All to serve the Domain of Vay."

"Phigby," Cara says, "you must have read this book at some time, how else did you know the words?"

"Yes," Phigby slowly acknowledges, "but how and when? Truly, I don't remember."

"So," Amil rumbles, "you were right, Phigby, the Dreaded Age has begun. Vay is unleashed on our world, to rage and bring ruin and destruction."

Phigby brings a hand up to stroke his beard. "Yes," he murmurs, "but there is another name for your 'Dreaded Age' Amil, and that's the Age of Magic, when magic returns to our world."

"For both good and evil, I presume," Helmar says.

"I'm afraid so, Helmar," Phigby acknowledges. "Magic is like anything else, there will be those who will use it for good, and there will be those who use it for wickedness."

He draws in a breath. "It's all a matter of choice, and Vay and her minions have chosen the evil path."

Phigby pauses before saying, "There is also this, the portal is widening, but it does not mean that it is entirely open."

"So are you saying," Amil asks, "that like a door opens with just a small crack, it must be swung completely wide for the full measure of Vay's power to come through?"

"That's right," Phigby nods in assent. He flicks his eyes my way and then says, "For sixteen seasons, at springtime, the time of new birth, the moons have been close to aligning."

He pulls at his beard. "Throughout those seasons, a little more each time as the moons grew closer, Vay's evilness and influence have seeped through to our world."

"And now," I whisper, "they're fully aligned. The door is opening wide."

"But," Cara says, "doesn't that also mean the same thing for Osa, Nadia, and Eskar? That, their power is pouring through too?"

"It does," Phigby sighs in response. "Fortunately, for our sakes."

"Is Vay stronger than the three?" Helmar asks. "Is that why she's appeared more?"

"No," Phigby answers firmly. "Her magic has no more power than her sisters'; at least for the moment."

"For the moment?" Helmar questions. "What does that mean? Are you saying that she could grow in strength to do more than she has?"

Phigby reaches down and picks up four small stones, all practically equal in size. He holds three in one hand and one in the other hand. "When the gate opened, and the four came forth, their power was the same, like these stones, are close to the same in size."

He reaches down and adds small pebbles to each hand. "Good or evil," he says, "only grow when you and I first acknowledge them, then accept them, finally embracing them, and acting accordingly, either for the good or for the bad."

He shakes the pebbles in his hand holding the one stone so that they clump together as if he would make a larger stone. "Vay's power increases when others join her cause, choose to follow — to embrace her dark arts.

"Or, if," he mutters low, "she uses vile methods to bring others under her influence."

"And we, Phigby?" Cara asks in a small voice. "What have we chosen?"

He drops the stones representing Vay and holds out the hand

with the three stones. "We have chosen well and good, my dear," he answers Cara, "and unless we have a change of heart, we shall continue to do so. And because of our choices, and others' who will reject Vay and join our cause, the three will grow stronger to counter Vay."

As Phigby finishes, I take a step toward the log's end. My charge is over, I've completed my task, delivered the jewel to the guardian, and my burden is lifted. But then, I hesitate and turn back to the others. A feeling that I'd left something undone sweeps over me. But what?

"Phigby," I ask, as a sudden thought enters my mind, "we've already heard most of what was written there." I point to the book. "Is it possible that there's more?"

"Eh?" he replies and bends over to peer intently at the book. Suddenly, there's a gust of wind, and just as back in the forest when Phigby had held his book in his lap, the page abruptly turns.

Instead of being blank, these pages glow in a light green luminance. Lifelike illustrations of trees, bushes, plants of all sorts, adorn the page, all of them swaying as if a gentle breeze ruffled their leaves. Small, green dragons seem to move in and about the foliage, lifelike in their movement and mannerisms.

Then, amazingly, rising from the page, an image begins to take shape. It wavers for a moment before it grows bright and sharp.

My eyes grow big and round, and I take a step forward. I can't help the sharp intake of breath as the form raises its head and gazes at me with a kindly expression.

It's Pengillstorr. But instead of being old, he's young, vibrant — alive.

He bows his head to me, as if in gratitude for safely delivering his jewel to the Gem Guardian, and then his image fades away and in its place appears emerald-hued lettering, floating above the page.

They hang there for a moment before they snap onto the page, each letter glittering bright green and edged in gold. Helmar needs no urging and begins to read,

Green its scales were set to be

Green to match both leaf and tree
Created to wander forest and dale
Given to roam over hill and vale
Born it was to live life free
And to stand on unbent knee
Three as sentinel both day and night
They to watch with clearest sight
Ever to watch for the one to come
Three to guard the cutter's son
And for him tis the hilted stone
Emerald of power to hand and bone
And from this jewel, the gift to grow
Life itself it may control
Voxtyrmen to give with final breath
Voxtyrmen to bestow upon his death
And for this, I gladly do my part
A willing spirit, ready to depart
Always together, never apart
To remember ever, the sacrifice of the heart.

Phigby leans back and strokes his beard slowly before saying, "Well, I guess that indeed settles it."

"Settles what?" Helmar questions.

Phigby points to the page. "That the guardian must be a cutter's son."

Helmar starts as if surprised. "My father," he says slowly, "was a tanner." He returns Phigby's stare. "He cut leather."

He lets out a long breath. "I am indeed a cutter's son."

"And the jewel is to go to a cutter's son," Amil mutters. "It appears that would be you, Helmar."

Cara squeezes Helmar's arm. "The Gem Guardian," she murmurs, holding him with her eyes before she turns and asks, "Phigby, what does it mean, 'Voxtyrmen to give with final breath, Voxtyrmen to bestow upon his death'?"

"Every dragon tear jewel," Phigby explains, "has a unique name and special powers. In the Old Tongue, Gaelic or Gaelian as some call it, Voxtyrmen roughly translates as the Jewel of Growth. If I understand the ode correctly, its power is over the greenery of Erdron, plants, trees, grass and the like."

"An emerald gem with power over the greenery," Cara murmurs. She turns to Phigby, her face scrunched together as if she's thinking hard. "So — does that mean that there are other dragon jewels, with different powers?"

Phigby nods and slowly replies, "I believe that would be a good assumption."

Cara glances sharply at me before saying, "And does that mean that a tear jewel only comes from a dragon who is about to die?"

Phigby strokes his beard several times as if pondering her question before taking a deep breath. "I can only assume from the way Hooper was given this jewel and from how the ode speaks of a sacrifice of the heart that that may well be the case."

No one speaks for several moments before Amil places his big hand on Helmar's shoulder. "Well, what now, Gem Guardian?"

As if answer, another gust of wind whips the book, and another page appears. This time, the lettering doesn't hover above the page, it seems to float up through the page before it firms itself in lime-colored lettering outlined in black. Helmar swallows and reads,

While many will choose the life of slavery
Others will elect to fight back bravely
From Erdron's four corners an army will march
Hearing the sounds of freedom, they will hark
But just a few at first to join the light
But many will come to stand at the last great fight
But until that time, until that day
When might and right shall battle against Vay
One deed alone must be done
One act to ensure that victory is won
For in that time when the gate is riven
Unto you, a golden is given

And unto you, she shall be
The one who holds victory's key
For if she falls into Vay's vile hands
Then evil and death shall sweep the lands
To hide the golden from Vay's many eyes
A journey to take from mountains to isles
There is no trail, no easy way
The burdens that come most heavily weigh
But before you lies the first path to take
To the giants you now must make
And remind them there with humblest bow
Of Escher's promise and Queenly vow.

With that, the book snaps shut.

"Well," Phigby mutters, "that's certainly clear enough."

"What do you mean, Phigby?" I ask.

"Weren't you listening, Hooper?" Amil answers. He turns and points off to the west. "We're very close to the Golian Domain, the land of the giants." He motions to the book. "If we can believe that, then that's where we're supposed to go."

"Only, we've already been there once," Helmar points out. "Is this saying, we're to go back?"

To Amil's puzzled expression, Phigby recounts the battle between the Wilders and the Golians. Amil sucks in a breath. "You've been to the Colosseun Barrier and lived to tell about it?"

"Yes, my friend," Phigby answers, "indeed, we have."

Amil glances at us and mutters, "You must have had more than just luck on your side."

"Why?" I ask.

Amil's voice is a low, grim rumble. "Because, the Golians' Iron Maidens or Amazos, as they're called are as skilled and brave as any Dragon Knight of the realm. In all of my travels, I've never met or heard of anyone who's ventured into the domain and lived to tell about their experience."

He swings his arm around at the surrounding forest. "It's said that their bows are made from the heart of dragon wood trees that are as old as Erdron itself. Their arrow shafts are thicker than a man's arm and can shatter a boulder into a hundred pieces.

"They can shoot an arrow so high that it almost reaches the stars. In fact, it is said that they use the moons for target practice, and the dark spots on Osa's face are where their arrows struck."

He leans toward me and makes a slashing motion in the air with his knife. "The swords they carry can fell a stout oaken tree with one swing. They can run for three sunrises and sunsets without stopping for food or drink.

"They're so strong that they don't march around mountains — they merely push them aside so that they can pass through. They guard their lands with a fierceness that few can match, and they never miss with bow, lance, or sword."

His eyes take on a wild look, and his voice lowers to a fierce whisper. "And did I forget to mention that when they can get their hands on it, they relish the flesh of roasted Drach and dragon."

He starts to go on, but Phigby reaches out to stop him with one side of his mouth turned up in an amused smile. "And did I fail to mention that our new friend is not only known as Amil the Traveler but also Amil the Embellisher?"

"I was just trying to explain," Amil grumbles, "what we would face in going to that cursed land."

"And a good explanation it was too," I murmur with wide eyes.

"Only," Cara begins, "the Golians did miss us with their arrows, remember? And we skyed right over them and their barrier. That speaks well of our chances with them."

"Yes," Phigby muses slowly, as he strokes his beard and eyes the golden. "That seemed to be the case, didn't it?"

His eyes narrow and he murmurs, "Once before we were directed toward the west, and now," he taps on the book, "a second time."

Helmar slowly says, "It would appear that we're being guided in that direction for a reason."

"Yes," Phigby nods as he pulls at his beard. "So it would seem."

"No matter the reason," Amil replies firmly, "the giants will not welcome us with open arms, but with drawn bows, instead."

"Oh, bosh," Cara answers. "What's a few giants? Once they see we have a golden dragon and more importantly," she lays her hand possessively on Helmar's forearm, "that we journey with the Gem Guardian, I think we'll have no trouble from them."

It's obvious that whatever thoughts that Cara had for Helmar before have only been strengthened. Now, she has a Gem Guardian as a suitor.

Helmar hands Phigby the book, which he promptly deposits in his satchel. Helmar holds the gem for a moment before tucking it securely inside his tunic.

Phigby straightens and says, "Cara, when it comes to the Golians, I believe that they will take notice of the golden, but as far as Helmar is concerned, I wouldn't — "

He abruptly stops when Cara jumps to her feet and rushes over to me. And a good thing too, for suddenly, the ground under me is trying to slide away, and I'm swaying from side to side.

"Hooper," she says as she grabs one arm to steady me, "are you all right?"

Phigby is quick to my other side, holding me up before I fall flat on my face. "Yes, I think so," I answer. I blink a few times at Cara. "In fact, I must be really dizzy, or my eyes aren't working right. I could swear that tree over there just moved. Like it was walking."

She smiles lightly. "I think you must be still feeling the effects of Phigby's medicine. Trees don't walk."

The words are barely out of her mouth when the dragons jump to all fours, their heads up, and with low growls coming from their throats. Scamper huddles against me, pawing at my legs.

At a creaking, groaning sound, Helmar is on his feet, his sword in hand. Amil steps over the log, his ax up and ready.

"Wha — " Cara begins when a sinewy branch flies through the air and strikes her in the head.

She slumps to the ground, lifeless.

23

"Cara!" I shout and drop to one knee next to her. All around us, I hear a ripping, popping noise. The giant trees' roots snap out of the ground, sending clods of dirt and grass spraying skyward. They writhe and thump as if the very ground were on fire and they were trying to escape the heat.

Phigby whirls around and from somewhere inside his robe, he suddenly has a gleaming, silver sword in hand.

With my good arm, I try to lift Cara up by her shoulders. "Cara!" I cry again, but her eyes are tightly closed, and she doesn't answer. Her head, with its magnificent mane of beautiful, auburn hair, slumps back.

More thrashing roots snake across the ground, and it seems the little meadow is suddenly filled with squirming vines as if we'd walked into a nest of slithering vipers.

The dragons stomp their feet and roar at the thumping stems. They hunch their backs and rip at the dirt, their sharp talons tearing up enormous clumps of grass that they send flying every which way.

I hear a deep rumbling as a ring of trees glides across the ground toward us. "The trees are moving!" I yelp.

I gently lay Cara back down, push myself to my feet and whirl around. The trees have us ringed completely and are slowly, but surely closing together like a vise that's going to crush the life from all of us.

An icy gust of wind blows through the trees, sending the treetops swaying. From high overhead, a faint, sinister laugh echoes through the swishing branches. *You cannot flee, you are mine,* whispers a foul voice. A shadow floats through the forest gloom, coming ever closer.

"Vay," I stammer.

The giant trees are closing, tightening their ring. Scamper is chittering madly, the dragons are roaring, and the sprogs screech, clawing at snaking limbs that slide around them.

I stand over Cara and draw my knife — it's all I can do to protect her.

A long, thin branch whips through the air and like Sorg's fist, slams into my chest, sending me sprawling to one side. I suck in a breath from the blow and roll to my feet to gape at what I see.

The branch hovers over Cara, like a snake that raises its head and weaves over its prey before it strikes. I start to dash to her side, but I'm too late. The snaking limb darts downward and wraps itself around Cara. With a snap, it pulls taut and begins to drag her over the ground.

"No!" I cry. I turn to the others for help, but they're in a battle for their own lives. Branches clutch at arms, legs, necks, trying to pull them down to the ground and choke them to death.

I spin to the dragons, but more limbs come flying from all directions, whipping themselves over and around the dragons. A flurry of leafy tendrils shoots out of the air and before I can move, snatch Scamper and carry him away.

I hear a terrified screeping and turn to find the four sprogs are bound by several thick limbs that hover just over the golden. Golden Wind is tearing at the branches, trying to rip them away before a cascade of leafy arms, like a green waterfall, wrap themselves tight around her and pull her to the ground.

The other dragons are caught in the deadly lattice, their heads, bodies, even their tails ensnared and pinned to the ground. Some-how, I get to Golden Wind and plead, "We need help!"

A thin branch wraps itself around her mouth and with my knife, I slash through the supple vine. "The jewel!" she exclaims, before another brown tentacle whips around her muzzle. She swings her head violently to one side, snapping the branch. "Use the jewel!"

"How?" I shout back.

A branch slithers toward me and before I can move, wraps itself around my ankle, and yanks me to the ground. I clutch at the grass, digging my fingers deep into their roots. The golden clamps her fang-lined mouth around the limb and rips it two.

She whips her head over me. "The Gaelian Fae, remember the Ga —" A massive tendril, thicker than Amil's arm wraps around her jaws, squeezing her muzzle completely shut.

Just then, I hear a thunderous cracking and splitting of wood and whirl around. A giant tree trunk, almost as thick as a dragon, has been torn asunder. In the hollow's black interior, I see a glowing face. It's Vay. She leers at me and curls her fingers inward to beckon the branch that has Cara in its grasp. It slithers toward her, bringing Cara closer to the wicked, cruel fairy and death.

"No!" I scream.

I whip around to Helmar to shout for him to use the jewel, but his wrists are held tight by thick vines, and his arms are being stretched out as if the branches would tear him apart.

Another plant is around his neck and two more squeeze his legs. He's struggling with all his might to free himself but the he's held fast.

I spin to Amil and Phigby to seek help, but they are both encased in leafy cocoons and struggling not to be crushed by the smothering limbs.

Two branches shoot through the air, right at me, but at the last instant, I dive and roll aside. I give Cara one last anguished look before I jump over to Helmar.

I try to cut through the limbs, but they're too thick for my little knife to cut through in time. My eyes meet Helmar's. His are full of anger — and fear.

I can think of only one thing to do. I stuff my hand into his tunic and jerk the emerald out. It glows bright in the tiny glen, its emerald hue driving back the darkness. I hear Vay screech in fury, but I ignore her and slam the crystal into Helmar's open palm.

"Use the jewel!" I yell at him.

He struggles to shake his head from side to side, and I suddenly realize he's saying he doesn't know what to do. I stare at the gem in Helmar's hand. He's got it tightly gripped, and its bright glow calls to me like an emerald beacon, but I'm unsure of what to do next.

I jerk my head toward the tree where Vay appeared. Cara's head, arms, and shoulders are protruding from the bark hollow. The tree has swallowed the rest of her. Her upper body sags and I can see the gap slowly closing around her, squeezing the life from her.

I see a dozen rootlike tendrils slinking across the glen, coming for me. Sheer, utter terror fills my mind and heart. I have to do something, I have to help, but what?

I jerk my head around at the golden. She's lying on her side, her eyes on me.

I seem to hear her words again; *The Gaelian Fae, remember the Gaelian Fae.* A vine wraps around one ankle and then another around my other ankle so tight that I think it's going to crush my bones.

A sudden, cooling calm surrounds me and in my mind's eye I can see and hear Osa, Nadia, and Eskar saying, *Vald Hitta Sasi Ein, Power Comes to this One* . . .

"That's it!" I shout. I glance up at Helmar's hand. The vine has squeezed his arm and wrist so tight that he's barely holding the crystal. I slam my hand against his, pressing the jewel into his palm.

"Helmar," I cry out, "say, *Vald Hitta Sasi Ein! Power Comes to this One!*"

He doesn't answer so I yell again, *Vald Hitta Sasi Ein! Power Comes to this One!*

I've barely finished, when, under the vine that's slipped across his mouth, I hear a muffled repeat of my words.

There is a crackling in the air, the ground shakes and a waist-high wave of grass and leaves erupt outward. The surge of greenery crashes against the trees, almost toppling them and splits the writhing roots in half.

Then, a jade-colored pillar of sheer radiance shoots skyward from the jewel. It blasts a hole through the overhanging branches, letting in silver moonbeams that light up the glade. From the moonlight, the crystal seems to gather streams of light until a shimmering jade sphere grows outward.

The luminance begins to whirl, sucking in grass, twigs, and green leafy branches until there's a vortex of foliage that seems to spin faster and faster. Where it touches, the trees' branches pull back as if they can't stand the sparkling sheen's touch.

The ensnaring limbs that bind Helmar, Amil, Phigby and the dragons in a leafy cocoon unravel in a blur of speed and slither off.

The sparkling sphere's luster grows in strength, pushing farther and farther outward. Outside the glowing globe, a darkness grows. It seems to gather in force and then there is an explosion of sinewy branches that writhe against the barrier as if they would pummel it to nothingness.

The emerald sheen touches the tree trunks, and the giant dragon heart trees shudder and shake as if a battle wages over them. The dark mist seems to gather itself one last time while the giant trees bend over the green sphere as if they would crush it.

When the ensnaring branches fall off Helmar, his strength wanes such that I have to hold his arm up. I don't know why, but I thrust it upward with all the strength I have left.

A burst of emerald light explodes outward, and the trees snap back, away from the barrier. The emerald radiance grows brighter still, blanketing the forest. I hear a wail that rises in pitch until it's a shriek of fury and rage that trails off to nothingness.

The gem's emerald glow, like the light that has spread over the trees, dims until it's gone. Tiny leaves and stems flutter down, like a green snowfall, until the forest is once again quiet and still, with no sign of the apparition or her evil designs.

With a shudder, I drop to one knee, completely spent by the exertion of holding Helmar's hefty arm upright. He drops to both knees, drawing in great gulps of air. We stay that way for a moment before we struggle to our feet.

The dragons rise and as a dog jiggles water from its coat, they shake as if they would rid themselves of the foul touch from the enchanted trees.

As Phigby and Amil push themselves upright, I hear a low moan and turn around. It's Cara, draped over a jagged waist-high split in the giant tree that had trapped her in its death grip. Her head and arms droop lifelessly.

The four of us stumble over to her, and together, gently pull her limp form from the opening and ease her to the ground. I stand anxiously beside Amil as Phigby gently brushes back strands of hair from her face. I notice that Helmar has one of her hands wrapped tightly in both of his. "Cara?" Phigby softly calls.

She stays still for several more heartbeats before he calls again. "Cara, can you hear me?"

She answers with a small moan before her eyes flutter open. We all let out a breath in relief. She glances around before her eyes stop on Helmar. "What happened?" she asks weakly.

"We'll answer that in a moment," Phigby brusquely replies. "Are you hurt?"

She furrows her brow while rubbing at her head. "I don't think so."

With Helmar's and Phigby's help, she stands, and I hear a little puff of breath as her eyes catch sight of the broken and torn trees. "What happened?"

Phigby and Helmar exchange a glance and Phigby mutters, "We'll talk about it later. Helmar, we need to leave this place and swiftly."

Helmar gazes up to the moons. "We have a bit until dawn. If we are to sky, now is the time and not in full daylight."

My shoulder aches badly, again, and I grimace in pain. "Hooper?" Phigby questions, seeing the look of pain that crosses my face.

I wave him off. "Have to find Scamper," I answer. I let out a sigh. "And the sprogs, too."

"I'll help," Cara states. Helmar starts to protest but she cuts him off. "I'm fine, really."

"Make it quick, then," Helmar orders. "The rest of us will check on the sapphires and the golden."

Cara and I hurry across the meadow. I point and say to Cara, "The last I saw, the tree roots were dragging Scamper and the sprogs in this direction."

Once we're out of earshot, Cara puts out a hand on my arm. "Hooper, what happened? I need to know."

"What do you remember?" I ask.

She thinks for a moment and then says, "I — I'm not sure. I remember looking at the trees, and then something hit me in the head."

She shakes her head. "Nothing after that."

"That's all?" I question.

She runs a hand through her thick hair and peers at me. "Yes, should I remember more?"

I shrug. "Phigby will tell you the rest. Let's just say, for now, that you were in the wrong place at the wrong time and got hit on the head by a falling branch."

Not exactly the total truth, but the tree limb was sort of falling. Phigby had his reasons for not explaining all, and besides, we really do need to hurry and leave this place.

"You're not going to tell me, are you?"

"Later," I reply. "We need to find Scamper and the sprogs and get out of here." She wrinkles her nose and glowers at me. I hear a familiar chittering and turn toward a nearby tree.

Scamper is hanging upside down by one leg, a vine twisted around his ankle. He's chattering angrily as he tries to undo himself from the entanglement. I hobble over to him, but just before I reach him, the vine loosens, and he falls with a thump to the ground.

I bend over him, and he stares up at me. His eyes are rolling as if he can't get them set right, and a little *aarrghh* . . . escapes from his mouth. I pick him up and dust him off. "You know, if you had just waited a moment longer, I would've gotten you out of that, and you wouldn't have fallen on your head."

He wiggles his legs and paws to make sure they're working before demanding that I let him down. "All right," I say, "but we're leaving, so you'd best go get on your ride or we'll leave you behind."

He races over to the golden while I turn at a call from Cara. "Hooper, I've got the sprogs, but help me, will you? They're having a little trouble walking."

"Coming," I answer and hurry over to Cara, who's got the sprogs in a little huddle.

They seem cowed by the whole event and won't move. "Let's get them over to Wind Song," Cara says. "They're not hurt, just really scared." She picks up two and I grab the other two.

We deposit them next to Cara's dragon when Cara suddenly sways as if she's lost her balance. I grab her arm and hold tight. "Cara, what's wrong?"

"Whew," she breathes out, "for a moment there, there were two of Wind Song and about eight sprogs."

She sways again, and this time, I not only tighten my grip on her arm, I dare to grab the hand that she's holding out as if to steady herself.

"Cara, are you sure you're all right?"

She takes a deep breath and says, "Yes, Hooper, I'll be fine, it's passed."

Cara glances down at our intertwined fingers, and murmurs, "You can let go of my hand now, Hooper, I'm going to need it to climb up."

"Oh, right," I answer. "Sorry." I quickly let her hand go and step back.

She gives me a little smile. "Thanks, Hooper, I appreciate your thoughtfulness, I really do."

She climbs up, and we swiftly get the sprogs loaded. The four little dragons seem unhurt, but they scrunch down in the saddlebags and barely peek over the bag's lip with big and wide eyes. For some reason, I'm glad to see that they came out of the fray unharmed.

I hobble over to the golden. She's lowered her head and is peering at me with an expression of gratitude? Relief? I'm not sure, so I mutter, "What are you staring at?"

"Thank you, Hooper," she says. "You saved us all, you know."

"What I know," I mumble, "is that we need to get away from here before that demon comes back. Besides, it wasn't me, it was Helmar. All I did was hold his arm up."

I take a deep breath. "My last act as caretaker. From now on, Helmar will have to fight Vay on his own. I'm done. No more arrows for me. They hurt too much."

The golden raises her head, peers at the trees and whispers, "I don't think she'll be coming back anytime soon."

"Well, anytime soon," I grumble, "is way too soon for me."

I slip around her and as I do my eyes catch a dark green, perfect circle in the soil. It's the exact spot where Helmar stood when he used the emerald. My eyes grow wide in astonishment.

In the circle's center, green grass is sprouting upward even as I watch. In moments, covering the entire dark oval is new, lush green grass. "Amazing," I breathe to myself.

I hear footsteps and turn at Helmar's voice. "Hooper," he says, "quit staring at the ground, we need to go." He stares doubtfully at the golden for a moment before asking, "Are you sure you can sky on her? Maybe you should ride behind one of us."

I hesitate before saying, "If I were able to hold onto her with an arrow stuck in me, I should be able to hang on, even with one arm."

He shrugs and motions for Amil to help him. Between the two of them, and with the golden holding her head down low, I manage to seat myself. "You're sure?" Helmar asks one last time.

"I'm sure," I answer.

Helmar gives me a curt nod, and the two quickly trot away. It doesn't take long before we're out in the open. One by one, the sapphires bound into the air. Golden Wind asks, "Ready, Hooper?"

I hold onto one of her horns firmly, settle myself a little lower and answer, "I'm ready."

She spreads her wings, catches the wind and springs upward. She makes a gentle turn to the left, beats her wings hard for a bit to catch up with others, before settling into a slow, smooth beat.

I glance at the moons and say, "Helmar is leading us farther southward, I thought we'd head west, more toward the domain. After all, that's where the book said for us to go."

"Yes," Golden Wind answers, "but Amil knows there's only a few places where even a dragon can cross the mighty Denalian Mountains. He's taking us toward the closest."

"I see," I reply. "And after that?"

She slowly answers, "And after that, we'll need to find some Golian giants or they find us."

"Oh," is all I answer.

24

W e sky through the remainder of the night, always heading southward, keeping the King and Queen stars off our right shoulders, as they, like the moons are setting. Night is ending and it couldn't come too soon for me. Vay seems to prefer night's darkness and I want no more of her. That task now belongs to Helmar, the Gem Guardian.

Dawn's first early pink light has Helmar searching for a place for us to hole up for the day as he does not want our little band to be skying in the light. It would be much too easy for someone on the ground to spot a big, golden dragon sailing overhead in broad daylight than in the dead of night.

The forest we sky over is exceptionally thick with birchen and spruce trees, and the few openings we find are way too small to land even one dragon. Helmar motions for us to sky low while he takes Wind Glory higher, trying to get a better view of the countryside and more importantly, a place for us to land.

While we wing just above the treetops, Wind Glory sails above us with Helmar still searching. Even though he's higher than we, I can see the worry lines in his face grow by the moment. The sun has just about fully risen when he abruptly has Wind Glory turn sharply to one side and gestures for us to follow.

Moments later, we cross over a small glade that's just large enough for one dragon to squeeze into and Helmar motions for me to set the golden down first.

As soon as her talons grip the ground I have her sidle off to one side and into the trees to make room for Wind Song, who's followed us down. Soon, we've managed to squeeze all four dragons into a space that's barely big enough for just one.

Once we have the dragons deep under the trees, we do a thorough search for dragon's curse but finding none, we let them graze on whatever they want. They don't feed all that long before they promptly curl up and close their eyes in sleep.

Cara and Helmar get the sprogs out of the saddlebags, place the youngsters practically under the golden's nose and within a few moments, the sprogs are asleep, too.

Seeing that the dragons are settled, Helmar has us gather together and asks of Amil, "Any idea of where we are?"

Amil nods and says, "I believe so. Those three white cliffs we passed over just a while ago? They're what's left of the old chalk mines that belong to House Stord. We're on Stord land, and I'm pretty sure that this is the Grayfar Forest."

"The House of Stord," Phigby muses but Amil is quick to say, "Don't even think about it, Phigby — they weren't exactly known as being trustworthy before, I doubt if circumstances have changed."

Phigby shrugs. "No harm in thinking about what-if's, you know."

"Any villages nearby?" Helmar asks.

Amil screws up his face as if he's thinking deeply before he turns and points southward. "Maybe. Before the chalk pits played out there was a village — I think it was called Sabaville, less than a league or so from the bluffs, where the miners and their families lived."

"That far away from the mines?" Cara asked.

Amil is quick to explain. "The hills past the chalk mines are full of Wood Trolls. The village, if I recall right, was set with the Stord river on three sides with a high stockade on the fourth side."

"Added protection from the trolls," Phigby pronounces.

"Exactly," Amil affirms.

"But if the mines are no longer worked," Helmar asks, "do you know if the village is still there?"

"That I can't answer," Amil replies. "The mines were the main livelihood for most of the villagers and after the chalk ran out, I don't know if anyone stayed in the village."

He reaches down and picks up a handful of dirt. "The chalk was used by the farmers hereabouts to improve the land, without it, the soil's too poor to grow a good crop."

Amil lets the dirt dribble through his fingers as he stares at Helmar. "You're thinking of going into the township," he states.

Helmar nods slowly. "Normally, I wouldn't consider it, but maybe we can buy some food and more importantly — "

"We can get news of what's occurring in the kingdom," Phigby finishes for him. "Which may well aid our cause."

"Helmar," Cara protests, "we'd be taking a huge risk. Don't forget that King's Warrant hanging over our heads. We may be on the fringes of the kingdom, but there's still a chance that the news of our circumstances have reached even here."

"I haven't forgotten," Helmar declares, "not for an instant. But it's partially why we need news. For all we know, the king has rescinded the warrant. If so, we still might be able to get help from His Majesty."

We pass uneasy glances among ourselves, but no one has an answer to his idea before Amil lets out a long sigh and says, "If you're determined to go then I suggest we make it just the two of us and not the whole company.

"I'm not wanted nor named on the warrant, and if I identify myself as a Traveler and you as my companion, then we might be able to accomplish both of your goals without us ending up in the prisoner stocks, or worse."

He wags a finger practically under Helmar's nose. "But you let me do the talking. Understood?"

Helmar claps the big man on the shoulder. "I wouldn't have it any other way. It's a great idea, and that's the way we'll play it."

He then says to Phigby, Cara, and me, "You three stay here, rest and take care of the dragons. Everyone remains in the woodlands under cover."

He smiles at Cara. "However, if you manage to bring down a rabbit, save some for us, we might come back hungry, you know."

"If I bag a rabbit," Cara answers dryly, "I'll let you gnaw on the hide."

Amil nudges Helmar with an elbow. "I don't think she approves of your idea."

"Whatever gave you that impression?" Helmar replies under his breath. He and Amil take a moment to check their armaments, grab a water flask apiece, and then with a wave, march off into the forest.

Cara stands watching them go, her arms folded, her eyes narrowed in obvious annoyance. "Helmar's idea is sound," Phigby mutters to her. "Besides," he goes on, trying to reassure her. "They'll be all right, they know what they're doing."

"He'd better come back in one piece," Cara huffs, "or I'll kill him when he gets back."

Since I've had my share of sleep in the last night or so, I volunteer to keep watch while Cara and Phigby get some much-needed rest. Cara and Phigby find a convenient, large spruce that's conelike in shape, gather some leafy boughs and soft pine needles and stretch out under its spreading limbs. Like the dragons, it doesn't take them long before they're deep in slumber.

I carry Cara's bow, though I still have serious doubts as to my ability to use it, even if I face some nemesis that forces me to try and be a marksman. Amil's mention of Wood Trolls makes me extra edgy, but trolls and dragons usually don't stay in the same neighborhood.

Usually.

But I haven't forgotten that Night Goblin that thought I might make for a tasty snack, and there were four dragons close by even then. I spend most of the morning making a circuit between the sleeping dragons and the slumbering Phigby and Cara.

Scamper shows up every so often, does his own check of the

camp to make sure I'm at the ready and doing my job and then disappears back in the forest, in search of food, no doubt.

Around high sun, Cara wakes and retrieves her bow from me. "Any sign of rabbits or squirrels?" she asks.

I shake my head in answer. "I wish. If there were, I'd have woken you up so that we might have some meat in the pot."

"Wait," she dimples, "aren't you the fellow who told me you always carried around a good rock just in case a rabbit or squirrel showed up?"

I return her smile and shrug. "At the time, it was the best fib I could come up with."

She smiles again before turning serious as she surveys the forest. "I'm going to go a little farther out and try my luck. The scent of dragons might be keeping any rabbits close by holed up, but maybe those farther out will be grazing on the grass patches."

She glances around again. "Water?"

I point off to one side past the sleeping dragons. "I'm not sure but I think there's a stream at the bottom of that hill, but I didn't go that far to see."

"In that case, while I hunt for some meat, you hunt for water. But neither one of us can go very far as Phigby is still asleep."

I nod, turn and head in the direction where I think the stream lies while Cara heads in the opposite direction. I get to the spot where I thought I'd find water only to find that I was wrong.

The channel at the base of the small hill might have running water after a good rain, but right now it's a dry course of rocks overgrown with high grass. I turn back toward our little makeshift campsite and have just reached the still sleeping dragons when I hear a distant peal of thunder.

I stop for an instant as I see movement in the forest and then relax as Cara comes into view. She trots up but to my stomach's disappointment, she's come back empty-handed. "Did you hear the thunder?" she asks.

"Yes, and I was wrong, there wasn't a stream at the bottom of the hill."

"Well," she mutters in answer, "if that's a storm brewing up, it doesn't matter. We won't have to search for water, the water will come to us."

I turn my head at another thunder boom, which is rapidly followed by a second and a third that roll across us before trailing off into the distance, like a wagon crossing a wooden bridge. "Have Helmar and Amil returned?"

A worried expression crosses Cara's face. "No, but they should be back soon. Unless something's gone wrong."

Another rumble crosses the sky. "By the sound of that, I think we're in for a soaking."

She glances up at the sky. "As will Helmar and Amil, I'm afraid."

I shake my head in worry. I know Helmar and Amil meant well, going into the village to find food for us, still, Helmar's carrying Pengillstorr's gem now, and he has to be careful. Very careful.

In the distance comes a crackling high in the air, followed by another growl of thunder. A sudden, strong breeze shakes the trees, sending them swaying.

Another gust whips up a small whirlwind that sends a spray of gritty dirt into our faces and eyes before we can turn away in time.

The sunlight dims and gloom settles over the glen. In the near distance, lightning sears the air, leaving behind a sizzling sound that seems to rip through the sky from horizon to horizon.

The wind is beginning to swish the trees limbs in all directions. Through the breaks in the trees, I can see ominous dark clouds that appear like a row of blackened barrels turned on end, rolling and tumbling through the sky.

Murky clouds suddenly swirl overhead, and lightning splits the sky. Thunder rolls across the sky as if a hundred dragons growled in the darkening gloom. Our dragons have sprung to their feet, their muzzles up and testing the wind.

"This looks really bad," Cara declares, her eyes up, peering intently at the darkening sky. "Without any sort of shelter, we're going to be caught out in the open, too."

I hear heavy footsteps and turn to find Phigby striding toward us.

Another flash of scarlet lightning streaks through the sky, followed by a second bolt. The storm is still some little ways off, but if this is any indication, it is going to be a ferocious tempest. And like Cara said, we have no suitable shelter to ride out the storm.

Phigby stands facing the stiff wind, which flattens his robe against his body. His long, gray hair is whipped about his face as he lifts his nose up just as Scamper does when he's sniffing the air.

He comes to stand beside us, his head turned skyward. After a moment, he relaxes his body and mutters, "It is but a spring storm, the same that we normally get around this time. Nevertheless, we may well find ourselves drenched shortly."

He points to the thick spruces that he slept under. "That will give us some protection," he offers. He eyes me and asks, "Your arm?"

I lift it up and down with a twinge. "A little sore, but I'll manage."

"Good," he says curtly. "You and Cara round up the dragons and get them close to those trees. They'll give us a little added break from the wind and rain.

"Get the sprogs under the golden, she's the biggest and will afford the most protection. It is not uncommon for storms like this to produce hail, and their little bodies would take a beating."

As the storm rumbles closer, Cara and I do as Phigby ordered, and it's not long before we have the dragons in a rough semicircle close to the spruce thicket. I whistle for Scamper, and he immediately shoots out from the brush and scoots under the tree, empty-handed this time.

The three of us have barely ducked under the protecting thick branches when the first raging winds hit. They bring a sudden chill as if they'd brought the north winds of winter back and were pushing spring away.

More scarlet streaks break the gloom, searing the air. A bolt crashes down, splitting a nearby tree, smoke rising from the rent trunk. The lightning strike is so close and the thunder boom so ear-splitting that Scamper jumps into my arms with a loud wail.

A few splatters of rain ripple across the glade, but I can smell more, and heavier, coming on the wind. I have no doubt that when it arrives, even the thickness of the limbs above will not keep out the deluge. It's going to be a wet night for all of us, I'm afraid.

The sapphires, who had been lying on their stomachs, even with the lightning flashing around them, abruptly jump to their feet, their muzzles pointed out toward the glade. Though they're not growling, nevertheless, Cara brings her bow up to bear, and Phigby slides his sword out.

The dragons suddenly part and silhouetted in the meadow's gloom by lightning flashes, stand two figures. Scamper utters a low growl as I reach for my knife even though I know its puny blade will be no match for our intruders.

The lightning comes again, illuminating the two individuals and Cara calls out, "Helmar!"

I let out a breath of relief when I realize it is indeed Amil and Helmar. They quickly push their way past the dragons and face us. Helmar's face is as dark as the raging storm. Amil holds his ax in one hand while he keeps glancing over his shoulder at the wind-whipped woodlands.

In a tone that is as deep and angry as the rolling, rumbling thunder, Helmar says above the rushing wind, "We've been discovered, we must leave, now."

"What!" Phigby exclaims, "Who — "

Helmar's savage chop at the air with one hand stops Phigby from going on. "Villagers, fifty or more, making for this meadow and somehow they know who we are."

He points to the dragons. "We leave now, or we are all dead."

25

Lightning slashes across the sky, jagged bolts that light up the sky as if the clouds were sending down roots of fire into the ground. Between the howling wind and the rolling thunder, practically all other sounds are drummed out, and we have to shout to make ourselves heard. "We can't sky in this!" Cara declares to Helmar. "The sky bolts will knock us out of the air."

Helmar hesitates only for an instant before ordering, "Then we'll have to make a run for it, there's too many for us to make a stand here. Get on your dragons!" he orders.

With his bag slung over his shoulder, Phigby dashes to Wind Rover with Amil right behind him. Cara makes short work getting up on Wind Song. Before I can make it to Golden Wind, from the meadow's far side, I hear wild yelling and screaming.

A horde of barrel-chested men waving long-handled axes, lances and bows appear at the far tree line. Their faces are hard, their intent clear. We can either become their live or dead captives. I can see in their wild eyes that it doesn't matter which.

Cara swivels on Wind Song and unleashes an arrow. The shriek of a dying man answers her shot.

Phigby spins Wind Rover to face the frenzied mob, and a moment later, the glen is lighted up, not by the brilliant flash of lightning, but a harsh stream of dragon fire. The crazed villagers scatter into the woods in all directions. A moment later, Helmar is up on Wind Glory and yells at me, "Hooper, move!"

Actually, I am moving, just not as fast as the others. I whistle for Scamper, and he dashes from under the pine tree and up the golden's leg like a squirrel racing up an oaken tree with a prized acorn. Just as I reach the golden, Cara screams, "Hooper! The sprogs!"

In our hectic rush to escape the frenzied villagers, we'd forgotten the little dragons.

I spin around and helped by the white light of a lightning flash, spot them cowering under the overhanging branches. I'm the closest, so I hobble back as fast as I can. Somehow, I manage to scoop up the squirming heap of screeping, chubbing sprogs in one armload, and whirl around to hurry back to Golden Wind.

The golden is waiting for me with head lowered. I plow against the wind, reach the golden and practically throw the sprogs up on her carapace. In between lightning strokes, I hear the twang of Helmar's and Cara's longbows, but for the moment, the villagers aren't shooting back.

I scramble up on the golden's neck, and I'm no sooner settled than she spins and lumbers for the meadow's center. "No — " I begin, thinking that we need to be running in the opposite direction, but then my next words freeze in my throat.

In the lightning's sharp glare, I can see we're surrounded on all sides. Angry, fierce villagers step out from the tree line, with weapons raised high. A dozen or more of their archers have their arrows pointed straight at us.

The golden pulls up beside Wind Song. Cara has an arrow notched, and her bow hand quivers next to her cheek. She gives me a quick sideways glance and murmurs, "Thank you, Hooper, for rescuing the little ones."

"You're welcome," I whisper, "not that it's going to make much difference from what I see."

A tall, muscular looking man, his dark tunic tight across his chest and waist steps out from the line of villagers. His voice is loud, commanding. "Your dragon fire may kill a few of us, but once we unleash our arrows — you're all dead."

I see Helmar exchange quick glances with Phigby and Amil, and I know just what they're thinking. The man is right. By the time we unleashed fire, their arrows would be well on their way to their mark. Some of them would die, but all of us certainly would.

"What do you want?" Helmar demands.

"A fair trade," the tall man answers. "We want you, the girl, and the golden dragon." He pauses as the man next to him whispers before turning back. "Oh, and the puny, scarred one as well. The others can go free; we have no use for them."

Lightning crackles through the clouds, so many bolts it's as if two of the gods are tossing lightning spears back and forth just for fun.

We all look to Helmar with anxious faces. It's never been said, but it's clear that he's the leader of our company, and now our fate rests in his hands. He hesitates but then calls out, "Give us a moment, we need to talk among ourselves."

He then points Wind Glory's head straight at the tall fellow. "And by the way, if you do unleash your arrows, you'll be the first to fry to death."

The villager hesitates, his eyes on Wind Glory. Helmar's voice was firm, convincing. I have no doubt he means what he says. The man starts to answer when his whispering companion says something in his ear.

The tall man listens, nods, and then responds, "I have a man here who can count to fifty. When he tells me it's time, if you haven't surrendered by then, I shall take that as your answer."

He leans forward and points to Helmar. "And you shall be the first to die."

Helmar doesn't reply but leans over and mutters, "Quick — any ideas?" He looks especially at Phigby, who's fumbling in his bag, but doesn't answer. Amil shakes his head and Helmar swings back to Cara and me.

Cara grimaces, the fury on her face evident but she has no reply, either. I start to say no, when off in the distance, I hear a familiar sound.

My eyes flick to our adversaries for an instant, then back to Helmar. My whisper is almost a growl, "When I say, 'now' we sky."

Helmar emphatically shakes his head. "In this storm? We have more chance against their arrows."

The sound is noticeably closer. "Helmar, think about it," I stress. "Once they have us three and the golden, they'll kill Amil and Phigby. Dead men tell no tales. We need to sky out of here, just not right now."

I can see the doubt etched in Helmar's eyes and I know what he's thinking. If he can't reason our way out of this trap and if Phigby doesn't have any ideas, how can a Hooper?

"I'm with Hooper," Cara abruptly says and gazes at me. "I'd rather die skying on Wind Song than perish from a villager's arrow. Just give the word, Hooper."

"We need a little more time," I urge Helmar, "stall him. Neither the golden nor your jewel must fall into their hands."

Helmar licks his lips before he whirls in his saddle. "My comrades and I want to make an agreement," he yells.

The villager's laugh is as loud and sharp as the lightning overhead. "Can you offer us twice your weight in gold? If you can, then we'll listen. Otherwise, my man says your time is up."

Helmar doesn't have an answer but sits there mute. Longbows creak as they're pulled tighter, the arrow points leveled right at us. "Wait!" I shout. "We have something worth more than our weight in gold, at least double, maybe even triple our weight."

I can hear Cara gurgle over the wind, "Hooper, what are you doing?"

"Buying us just a few more moments," I gurgle back.

"I don't believe you," the man replies. "You're stalling."

"Helmar," I frantically whisper, "take out the gemstone, now."

He hesitates, his eyes glowering at me. He starts to shake his head no, but I plead, "Please."

He glances at the bowmen, and he sees what I see, their bows are as taut as they can reach and only a heartbeat away from flying through the air.

With lips pressed tight, he reaches into his tunic and slides the emerald out. He holds it high, and the emerald's gentle radiance has every villager in awe. "Say the words, Helmar," I mutter, "make the gem glow as bright as the sun."

Just at that moment, a lightning bolt crashes into the center of the glade. I can feel the golden buckle, but she remains upright while I feel as if I've a thousand buzzing bees inside my head. I can barely hold onto Golden Wind, and my whole body feels as if I'm wrapped so tight in a cocoon that I can't move.

I lean over and whisper, "Golden Wind, are you all right?"

She's slow to answer, "I've been better, but it will pass soon."

I manage to raise my head and take stock of my companions. Like me, they're stunned and just barely managing to stay atop their dragons. Helmar seems the worst. He's draped over Glory's neck, though I can see he's trying to right himself though his arms and legs jerk as if he can't control them. I can see in his hand that he's still gripping the gemstone tightly.

I glance around at our adversaries. A good many of them have been knocked off their feet, but most are rousing themselves enough that I know we have but a few moments before they come charging at us, and we're in no shape to fight back.

Through lips that I can barely feel I say to the golden, "Get me next to Helmar."

She stumbles over to Wind Glory. I reach over and pull Helmar upright. "Helmar, use the gem!"

He sways back and forth, mumbling. "Helmar, snap out of it, say the power words, now!"

He raises the gemstone and sort of stares with his eyes rapidly blinking as though he knows he's holding the jewel but doesn't know what to do with it. He starts to waver again, almost falling off Wind Glory if I hadn't caught him in time.

"Helmar," I plead, "listen to me. Say the words after me."

He turns, shuts his eyes for an instant before he reopens them and nods. Slowly, one by one, I repeat the power words with Helmar mumbling each word after me. Finally, I declare, "Now all the words together! *Vald Hatta Sasi Ein, Power Comes to this One!*"

He manages to mumble right after me, *Vald Hatta Sasi Ein! Power Comes to this One!* though I can barely hear him.

An emerald burst of light shoots from the jewel. It sweeps across the glen, illuminating everything in a green glow. Some of the villagers throw up their hands in fright at the emerald brilliance.

The trees, once rocking back and forth, swaying from the rushing wind, straighten, and start to bend toward the dale's center, against the wind, as if to reach the gemstone that shines emerald bright against the darkening gloom.

I swivel on the golden's neck as what I'd been waiting for is now upon us. I glance around; all of us, including Helmar, now seem to have our wits about us again so I shout, "Now! Everyone, sky!"

Without hesitating, the golden springs into the air, unfurling her wings on the way up. Just as she does, we're hit with a roaring gale of wind and rain. The storm has finally unleashed its full fury, and it's like someone suddenly blew out the lone candle in a dark room.

The golden and I are thrust into murk and gloom, buffeted by icy winds and raindrops that feel like we're being pelted by fist-sized stones.

That's what I'd heard in the distance, what I'd waited for to hide our escape, the pounding rain, the rush of the oncoming gale, the darkness that would hide us from the villagers' demented eyes.

Raindrops pound at my face, and I'm all but blinded. However, I know that if I can't see, neither can the archers on the ground. Ferocious gusts stagger the golden in the air, I reach down and push Scamper and the sprogs tightly together under the protection of the golden's carapace.

The golden doesn't fight the roaring wind. Instead, she flies with it, but we're so close to the trees that she actually shreds a few tree-tops. Then, as if a storm titan had belted her with his mighty fists, we're violently jolted up and then down.

It's too much for me, and I sail off. At the last moment, I grab onto her neck scales and hold on with all the strength I have.

My legs and feet strike at branches and leaves as the golden is tossed to one side by a powerful blast of wind. One of the golden's wings goes up, the other down and she's practically on her side.

Suddenly, there's mud and grass just below me, and before we can be tossed back up into the air, I lose my grip.

I'm slipping and sliding through slick grass, eating mud while I try to halt my spinning, rolling ride. I finally stop, staring up into the angry sky, spitting out grass stems and a mouthful of muck.

I roll over to cough up the rest of the glop and to catch my breath. I raise my head and open my mouth. The hammering rain doesn't take but a moment to fill up my mouth and I spit out the mixture of soupy mud and grass.

I do that twice more before I push myself to my feet. The wind is dying down a bit as is the lightning, but it's as if the skies had opened up and a whole ocean of water is streaming down from the heavens. I have no idea where I'm at or where the others are.

For that matter, I have no idea if they even escaped out of the meadow.

I think they did.

Or rather, I hope they did.

I stagger around for quite a while, trying to get my bearings, but it's no use. I'm lost and in the darkness, I can't see a thing to help guide me.

Not that I know where I'd go anyway, but it's comforting to have something firm to aim toward. But between the rain and the wisps of rolling clouds with the occasional lightning bolt, there's little to see or use as a marker of sorts.

I'm not sure how long I stumble around in the rain and wind before I find myself in a small meadow and stop to catch my breath. The rain has lessened, a mere downpour compared to the over-whelming torrent of before and the wind is a series of sharp gusts that's practically nothing compared to the punishing gale that whipped us through the sky.

I take a few steps forward and stop. A single stroke of lightning crackles through the air and in the flash of light I see a ring of hard, angry faces.

Somehow, some of the villagers have found me, and now they're closing their circle of death. They raise their axes across their chests, slowly hefting them up and down. Their eyes are like stone, menacing. They step closer, and I have no doubt that any one of them can slay me with one vicious blow.

From the pack steps the villagers' leader, the same man who threatened us with death by arrow if we didn't surrender. He holds an arm out to stop the advancing bloodthirsty mob.

With a hard glare, he holds up his ax and demands over a gust of wind, "Where is the golden one? Tell me and you live. Keep your lips sealed and I promise you that you'll die slowly, painfully . . . "

His voice trails off, but his meaning is clear. If I offer up Golden Wind, I live for another day. Otherwise, they will slowly hack me to death, ignoring my screams as they slowly slice me into pieces — tiny pieces.

I, of course, have no idea where the golden is, but I quickly think up an answer and open my mouth to speak. Abruptly there is a change in the wind, and to my ears comes a sound that forevermore I will recognize.

I snap my head up, and my eyes widen for just an instant before I throw one arm up into the air.

Talons dip down and wrap themselves around my arm, and with a hard jerk, I'm pulled skyward. I glance back and through the rain, I see the pack leader dash forward and with a roar of rage and frustration, heave his ax at me, but it falls far short of its target.

I'm swinging below the golden, with the wind and the rain blasting at my body. She doesn't fight the wind. Instead, she sails along with the rush. Still, the rainfall is so heavy that I feel like I'm soaring through a roaring waterfall. I can barely breathe as my nose and mouth are constantly filled with water.

I know we have to get as far away from the crazed villagers as we can and so I let Golden Wind slide along with the wind but there comes a point where I finally gurgle, "Put me down, I'm drowning!"

The golden keeps going for just a bit before she swoops down. Somehow, in the thickness of rain and cloud, she finds an open spot in the trees where she hovers for a moment before letting me drop the short distance to the ground.

I hit with a muffled, "oomph," and lie gasping for air.

The golden lands next to me and spreads one wing wide to shield me from the rainfall. A soaked and bedraggled Scamper splashes through the mud and tiny water pools to jump on my chest.

He pushes his little face into mine. *Hrrrrrttt?* he asks.

I take some deep breaths and answer, "No, I'm all right, but believe it or not, I almost drowned up there." I half-laugh. "Drowning in midair. I bet no one's ever died that way before."

I feel a warm breath and glance up to find the golden's muzzle close. "Thank you," I mutter. "I don't know how you found me, but I'm glad you did."

I push Scamper to one side and sit up. "Any idea where the others are?" I ask.

Her eyes take on a worried appearance, and she murmurs, "I believe they were captured."

I roll to my feet. "Captured! They didn't sky out of there when the storm hit?"

She solemnly shakes her head. "I don't think so."

"Captured," I mutter, disbelieving. "How?"

"Just as I spread my wings," she answers, "I heard what sounded like a whirring in the air."

"A whirring? From what?"

"I don't know. But what I do know is neither Wind Glory, Rover, nor Song took to their air. I never heard their wings."

A whirring, I think to myself. Then, a thought comes to me, something I'd seen in one of Phigby's books. "Golden Wind, Amil said that the village lay next to a river. Could it be that what you heard were thick fishing nets flying through the air?

"Nets that we didn't see. They must have thrown them at the same moment that you skyed, and no doubt pulled Cara and the others off their dragons and to the ground. That's why you didn't hear the other dragons sky out of there."

"That may well be what happened, Hooper," she sadly replies. "All I know is that the only dragon wings I heard were my own."

The rain and wind have noticeably lessened, and the lightning has moved off into the distance. I look around. We've landed in a tiny, oblong-looking glade. Tall, thin sprucelike trees hem the glade and form a natural windbreak.

I motion towards the woods. "Let's get closer to the trees, they'll keep out some of the weather, and I need to think."

Once we're settled, I ask anxiously, "Could you tell if any of the others were hurt?"

"No," she murmurs. "The wind was too strong, and it took us before I could hear or see more."

I run a hand through sopping wet, mud-filled hair. I twist around to face the golden and hold out my hands as if I were Scamper pleading for food. "If they've been captured, I — I don't know what to do, Golden Wind. I'm not a warrior or a Dragon Knight."

I pull my knife and hold it up for her to see. "All I have is this. No bow, no sword, not that I could wield either if I had one." I hang my head and slowly plop down into the mud.

My voice trembles as I murmur, "How am I supposed to help them when all I'm good for is to fetch wood and water, or shovel manure?"

I raise my eyes to her. "What do we do? How am I supposed to get into the village and try to rescue them?"

She doesn't immediately answer, and when she does, her response is like a lightning bolt that comes close to knocking me off my feet. "We're not going to the village," she states bluntly. "They won't be there, but elsewhere."

My mouth sags for a moment. "Wha — " I begin, but the golden doesn't let me finish.

She swings her head close. "Hooper, do you want to help your friends?"

"Friends?" I choke. "I don't have — "

"Nonsense! Of course, you do. Scamper is your friend — the sprogs are your friends."

She leans closer. "I am your friend as are the others. You just don't know it or don't want to believe it."

Her eyes are intense, questioning. "Now, do you want to help them?"

"Of course," I snap, "but I can't. If I were a Dragon Knight — "

"But you aren't," Golden Wind cuts in, "so stop wishing for what cannot be, and start imagining what can be."

"Oh?" I demand. "And just what am I supposed to imagine?"

"That you and I together can rescue our friends," she answers.

She stares unblinking at me, and I return her gaze with my own hard stare. We stay that way for several heartbeats until I feel a pawing at my knee and look down. Scamper chitters angrily and I listen for a moment before I say, "All right, all right. Yes, I know she's right, I just hate to admit it, that's all."

I let out a deep breath and mutter, "So, do you know where they've taken them?"

"I believe so," she answers and glances up. The rain and wind are slowly slackening, and the lightning flashes have moved off; the storm is abating somewhat, but it would still be a formidable task to try and sky through.

"There is only one place that they would take them that is nearby and suitable," she goes on to say.

"And where is that?"

"Dunadain," she states.

"Dunadain?"

"Yes," she replies. "The royal keep that guards the river pass at Angbar's Meld on the River Lorell, just below where the Stord River enters the Lorell. But we must wait until the storm clears before skying. Darkness will cover our flight, and then we must wing swiftly."

Wing swiftly. I've had enough of skying rapidly through the air.

"Do we have to sky swiftly?" I ask with a little groan. "I don't do well with swift."

She looks at me as if I just made a silly statement. "Of course you do. You held on with an arrow in your shoulder when I flew so fast that the sapphires were hard put to keep up.

"We cannot be slow about this, Hooper. You can be certain that those who have captured our friends will move very swiftly to collect their reward. They will march through the night and the promised reward will be more than enough for them to ignore the storm and its dangers."

"All right, I understand that, but why," I sigh, "can't we go slow about this? Especially the skying part."

"Because," she answers, "most likely, Dunadain is lightly guarded and will present our best opportunity to effect a rescue. However," she goes on to say with a grim look, "if we wait too long, it would indeed take a whole company of Dragon Knights, perhaps more, to breach the fortress."

She pauses and then says, her voice ominous and dark, "And worse, if we tarry in our rescue, we face not only more archers and men-at-arms, but *she* will come."

She lowers her head until we are eye to eye. "And Hooper, we do not want to face *her* alone, not yet, anyway."

Thoughts of Golden Wind

Hooper doubts his own courage. But haven't we all at one time or another? As we wait for the storm to move off, I ponder, just what is bravery?

Hooper placed his body between a death arrow and Helmar and paid a high price. Physical agony, yes, but worse — he had to endure the wretched presence of the Evil One.

Is bravery the act of dying for someone else? Or is it the willingness to die for another? Must one do one or the other to be considered truly valiant?

Is it the soldier who makes the ultimate sacrifice for his comrades, or who makes a heroic charge against an overwhelming foe, survives and lives to fight another day? Is that bravery?

Yet, what about the mother-to-be who is willing to go to the brink of death itself to bring her little one into the world? Is she not being as courageous as that soldier?

What about the father who may not have to face death arrows, yet gets up every morning and toils all day under a merciless sun to feed his family? Is that not heroic?

Consider the individual who is faced with an overwhelming temptation that is tinged with evil. They sorely, sorely want to give into the enticement but instead shun the desire and choose the right, instead?

Or the person who is surrounded by friends or family, or both, who live immoral lives and expect him or her to do the same? Only, the person chooses a different path, one based in light and goodness. Is that not being intrepid and fearless as well?

It would seem that courage comes in many forms. Perhaps the only true way to recognize it is by how it makes you feel inside, a testimony of the spirit, and that certain sense that what you have done was the right thing.

26

By late evening, the skies clear. Golden Wind, Scamper, the sprogs and I have nestled close to the windbreak. Except for the golden's protective outstretched wing that flutters in the wind, none of us make a sound or move. We're too fearful that a search party will hear us, or stumble across us before we can make our escape once the storm passes.

Normally, Scamper would be off and about, searching for a tasty morsel, but this time, he must sense our precarious situation and stays put, curled up in sleep along with the sprogs.

I huddle close to the golden, shivering in my soaked clothes, trying to draw what warmth from her that I can. There's no dry wood to be found for a fire. Besides, bright flames in the forest would be a dead giveaway and lead our adversaries straight to us.

I admit it, I'm not good at waiting. Especially when every little sound causes you to jerk upright, afraid that the band of wild axmen will come storming into the thicket and take you prisoner — or worse.

Finally, the storm moves off. Golden Wind murmurs, "It's time, Hooper."

I rapidly place the sprogs and Scamper in back of Golden Wind's skull sheath and clamber aboard. The sprogs promptly go back to sleep, hardly rousing even when I shoved them under the golden's carapace.

Baby dragons sleep a lot.

Scamper makes a little nervous circle before he snuggles against the sprogs and closes his eyes. Cautiously, stopping to look and listen with every step, we ease out into the thin glade's middle to a point where it's wide enough for Golden Wind to spread her wings.

"Ready?" she asks.

"Ready, I guess," I reply and tighten my legs around her neck.

She bolts skyward. I wasn't as ready as I thought I was. Even holding onto two of her curved spikes, she bounds so forcefully upward that my head is snapped back, and I see new stars in the heavens for a moment.

She skims just above the treetops, skying so fast that we send the trees swaying in our wake. The wind rushes against my face, but after a bit, I feel comfortable enough to lean over and ask, "I assume that you know the way to Dunadain?"

"No," she calls back. "I thought you knew."

"Me?" I yelp. "How would I know the way?"

I can hear her chuckling over the wind and realize that she's teasing me. That's another thing I never knew about dragons, they have a sense of humor. "Don't worry, Hooper," she answers, "I know where we're going." She dips her wings slightly to the left and then levels out.

With the storm's passage, the night air is clear, crisp, and most importantly, calm. We fly low over the dark countryside. I find that if I snug myself down behind the golden's skull plate that the wind's force is not so great, and I don't have to grip her horns quite so tight.

The moons rise early tonight, sending a gentle light over the landscape. We haven't skyed all that long when we soar over some high hills and dip into a broad valley. In the near distance is a sparkling silver-tinted carpet that runs the wide vale's length.

The golden calls out, "The Lorell River."

She brings us into a tight curve to the right, downriver, and puts herself squarely in the river's center. Less chance of being seen from the riverbank, I guess. As we sail close to the glistening, smooth water, I mutter to myself, "Hooper, as Phigby would say, m' boy, for someone who's never traveled farther than Draconton, you're a long way from home."

At this point in its course, the river takes several grand sweeping bends before straightening and then narrowing. An odd-looking paleness in the distance catches my eye, and I peer keenly ahead.

On each side of the river rise two gigantic mounds of a gray-white rock that appear to glow with a ghostly pallor under the moons. Split in half, the rock forms tall domed pillars between which the river flows through and onward to the sea.

As if she knows what I gaze at, the golden says, "They're called Angbar's Meld. Look to the giant rock on the right hand and to its base, you'll see Dunadain Keep."

I lean forward just a bit and find, just below one of the bastions of granite, a fortress that seems to be cut out of the rock. A high battlement runs between three low turrets and connects to a high tower which forms the fourth corner. Apparently it's the main keep, several stories high and snugged close to the rock wall.

Though Dunadain has no moat, it has a drawbridge that opens into the inner ward but with nightfall it's now drawn tight against the walls, sealing off the castle. There are only a few torches on the battlements, and the only other light I can see is high in the keep itself.

Abruptly, the golden dips her wings to the right, and we rush over a series of squat, wooded hills before angling down to a shadowy meadow. Golden Wind sets her talons down, and we land. She quickly lumbers into a nearby grove and Scamper and I dismount.

At just that moment, the sprogs wake, letting out loud screeps, as if they want to get down too, but I quickly order with a finger in their faces, "Hush! Don't move and stay put!"

They meekly scurry back under the golden's skull sheath and huddle together.

"What's next?" I ask Golden Wind.

"Were you able to see into the courtyard?" she asks.

"No, why?"

"Because that's where they have Glory, Song, and Rover chained. We'll have to get closer to see if we can tell where the others are held. I suspect that they may be confined in the keep's topmost chamber."

"Great," I murmur. "So just exactly how are we going to get all of them out? You did say that the fortress had guards."

She turns away and says over her shoulder as she plods through the thicket, "Let's go see what we can and then perhaps the answer to that will show itself."

We quietly and quickly make our way through a thin birchen stand until we come up to a small knoll that keeps us from actually sighting the keep below. The golden scrunches herself as low as she can, and crawls like a dog on all fours while Scamper and I do our best to stay with her. We peer over the small hilltop to study the small fortress.

The keep lies in darkness except for a few torches on the walls, and a tiny light high in the landside tower. It's so small that I can't help but think that the glow is made from a solitary candle and a meager one at that.

"Hooper," the golden whispers, "do you see the lone light up high?"

"Yes."

"From there, follow the tower wall down to the ground, what do you see?"

I let my eyes follow the line from the tower's high point to its dark base before I shrug. "Other than being a little blacker than the rest of the walls, I don't see anything."

"But you do," she says firmly. "Why is that particular wall darker than the others?"

"I don't know," I answer in an exasperated tone. "Can't you just tell me?"

"I can," she replies, "but that teaches you nothing. Think, Hooper, what would make that wall so much darker all the way up the tower?"

I let out a sigh, squint my eyes and really peer at the tower.

Suddenly, I see tiny flutterings up and down the wall. Leaves, whipping back and forth in the breeze.

"Vines," I state. "There's a vine lattice growing up the tower wall."

"And strong enough for you to climb," she acknowledges. "You have your answer, Hooper. I have no doubt that our friends are held captive in that topmost room, and now you know how to reach them."

"Wait," I protest. "You're expecting me to climb up that? It's one thing to sky on a dragon, it's another to try and climb up a tower that's over a hundred hands high on little, no, make that tiny vine branches."

"The vines are intertwined and quite sturdy," she encourages. "They'll more than hold your weight. Besides, if it were you in that tower, any one of your friends would gladly climb that wall to save you."

I can tell I'm losing this argument. I lean forward a little, desperately looking for another, lower, route into the keep. "Can't we just sky in there," I suggest in a weak voice, "you hit the guards with a blast of dragon fire, and while they're scurrying out of the way, I'll hop off and climb up the stairs to set everyone free."

I like the sound of my plan except that I need to add one thing. "And, oh, while I'm hurrying up the stairs, you keep the guards distracted."

I turn and give her a hopeful smile. "A much better idea than me scaling a castle wall, sturdy vines or not, don't you think?"

She cocks her head to one side as if she's considering my proposal before she says, "I could do that, but let me ask you this. In a heavily guarded fortress like Dunadain, just how far up those stairs do you actually think you'd get before you joined our friends in that upper room as just another captive?"

I start to reply but she shoves her muzzle so close that I'm staring up into her glistening nostrils. *Please don't sneeze,* I think. Dragon snot is particularly icky and smells like burnt garlic. "Not far is the answer," she growls.

I can see I've lost the argument. "All right, all right," I grouse. "You win. I climb. But once I get up there, then what?"

"I'm sure you'll figure that out once you're there."

"Uh, huh," I answer. "That's a big help. And while I'm playing fly on the wall, what will you be doing?"

"Watching," she answers. "What else?"

"Watching? That's all?"

She nods and then says, "One more thing, Hooper. Truly, there is more danger here than just archers and men-at-arms, so be on your guard at all times."

"What do mean by that?" I sputter. "What kind of danger?"

"Just be on your guard," she rumbles and pushes at me with her muzzle. "Now, go."

Scamper starts to go with me, but I reach down and hold him back. "No Scamp," I say and shake my head at him. "You can't climb those vines with me. It's too high and too dangerous, you'll have to stay here."

"Hooper," the golden says firmly, "Scamper is as much a friend to Cara and the others as you are. He wants to help. Take him, you just might find he comes in handy."

Scamper has a pleading expression on his face. "Suit yourself," I tell him. "But remember, I warned you." With that, the golden turns and plods away into the forest gloom.

Watching her go, I mutter under my breath to Scamper, "She's the one with wings, big talons, fangs, and dragon fire and she's the one staying behind to do what? Watch?"

I let out another long sigh, nudge Scamper, and together, we pick our way downhill through the trees until we come to a shoulder in the hillside. I stop to again peer at the river and the fortress.

From my vantage point, I see several guards, their lances at the ready, pacing along the battlement's top. Every so often, one of them stops to gaze between the parapets at the ground below. I don't see any guards outside the walls, just those on the high walkway.

Using the dense underbrush to conceal our movement, Scamper and I move almost parallel to the bastion. We reach a spot where I can easily see the vine-covered tower wall.

Once, Lord Lorell visited Draconstead and instead of dragon

skying as he normally did, he arrived riding a beautiful palomino horse. Beautifully sleek, the horse pranced as it made its way up the lane that led from Draconton. I remember gathering with the other workers to admire the steed.

For some reason, what I remember most, was how the horse's flanks quivered in anticipation as if it couldn't wait for Lord Lorell to release it on a wild, free run through the meadows.

My body trembles and shakes, just like that horse. Not from waiting for a wild dash down to the tower walls, but from the sheer terror of what I am about to attempt.

I put a hand on Scamper's head. "Ready, Scamp?"

He's quivering too, only his is from the anticipation of a wild run through the grass and brush to the tower base.

"Hooper," I say to myself, trying to build up my courage, "the golden hasn't been wrong before, you've got to trust her on this."

I peer again at the fortress. I slowly survey the stonework and the vine web, trying to decide the best place to hide. I lean forward a little to get a better look, and as I do, I notice an irregular darker spot almost in the vine's center.

"Must be a little thicker there," I murmur to myself. "And thicker means a good place to hide from that guard up there."

Just then, Scamper decides to take matters in his own paws and bounds away, headed straight for the tower. "No!" I hiss as I reach out to stop him, but I'm too late.

Muttering under my breath, I tuck myself low and hunched over, scuttle from tree to tree, hoping that none of the guards on the ramparts will spot me and sound the alarm. If that happens, I will have no choice but to turn tail and scurry back to the meadow.

I stop at the last of the larger trees that can shield me from view and peek around the trunk. I can't see Scamper anywhere, but there's one guard at the wall's junction, his lance pointed upward to the stars.

He scans the nearby grounds and then turns to walk toward the other wall corner. A few clouds slide in front of the moon, casting everything in darkness.

This is my chance.

I take a deep breath, gather myself and rush out. Keeping my eyes on the guard, I stumble along, feeling as if I'm making so much noise that I might as well be riding on a lumbering dragon, thumping talons and all. The walls seem like they're ten leagues away, and I'll never get there.

Almost out of breath from both exertion and fear, I stagger the last few steps and brace my back against the stone blocks. They're rough and coarse, and I can hear a slight raspy sound as my tunic scrapes against the chiseled granite.

I turn my head upward to gauge if the guard spotted me. I hold my breath, waiting for the alarm to sound, but all remains dark and silent.

I edge along the mortared wall, placing each step as quietly as I possibly can. I keep my eyes turned upward while I let my left hand slide along the wall. I haven't gone far when my hand and arm disappear into thick foliage. I let out a breath, I've found my hiding spot until the guard turns for the far tower.

A slight touch on my ankle almost causes me to yelp in fright before I look down.

Two mischievous coal-black eyes stare up at me. I swear he has a grin on his face from scaring me like that.

I glare at Scamper for an instant before I swing my gaze upward. I can see a sliver of light, streaming from the window far above. And in the scant glow, I can just barely make out that the vines go up and around the window. Which is a good thing, I think to myself, I'm certainly not going to sky through that window.

I slide into the thicker growth and just to make sure, tug on the vines to test their strength. They seem stout enough, but just then, I hear brisk footsteps on the wall walkway above me.

I quickly glance up. The guard's pace is faster than before, and he has his head tilted slightly as if he hears something, but uncertain as to what.

Uh, oh. The watchmen's hurrying steps tell me that he's grown suspicious, perhaps over the scraping of my tunic against the stonework. I quietly push myself deeper into the vine lattice until I'm flat against the stones, hoping that the leaves will cover me, shielding me from the guard's view.

I hold perfectly still, but with my head turned toward the walkway above. A head appears over the wall. The guard pushes himself a bit farther out to peer at the vines. He doesn't move, just stares at the foliage.

He steps back to bring his lance up, hefting it in his hand. His eyes are focused on my flimsy, leafy barrier, and he cocks his arm as he readies the spear for flight. The lance's cruel honed point glints in the moonlight; targeted straight at me.

It's aimed right at my olive-covered shell which will become my death chamber if his aim is true. The guard's arm slides farther back as if he wants to put as much force behind his throw as he possibly can.

My heart is thumping, and it takes every bit of willpower that I have not to scream out for him to stop. I want to break free and flee for my life, but before I make my move, a strong breeze springs up, rattling and shaking the leaves.

The guard stops and leans forward again, his stare intent on the rustling foliage. His eyes are still hard and locked, but then the breeze blows up against him, causing his jerkin to flap in the wind.

He slowly lowers his lance and straightens. With a last look at the fluttering leaves and the nearby countryside, he lowers his lance, turns and retraces his route back to the wall's far corner.

I let out a long breath in relief and lean my head against the coarse stone. I wait a bit before I step back, and peer intently at the walkway. The guard has disappeared, and I hear the last of his footsteps as he walks his post toward the other watch tower.

"That was close, Scamp," I whisper to Scamper, who through all of this, has held perfectly still. Something I didn't think he was capable of doing.

Scamper answers me by standing on his two back paws and clawing at the air. His meaning is clear; it's time we started our climb. I scratch at my head. The golden said that Scamper might come in useful. I don't know how, but she must have had her reasons.

With a little sigh, I pick him up and set him into my tunic hood. He settles his little rump in the pocket and grabs my head with his front paws. With the extra weight on my back, I mutter, "Now I know how the golden feels."

I again check the wall to make sure it's clear of any guards and start to climb. The limbs bear my weight, but they sway and sag as if I'm walking on a creaky rope bridge. Pushing upward on my bad leg is painful and makes for slow going. It's not long before my leg is trembling and weak each time I pull myself up and brace my foot on a thick tendril.

I'm not sure how far I've come when I glance down. Even with the moonlight, at this height, it's hard to distinguish small features on the ground below. The vine I'm standing on sags and quivers under my weight, and I whisper to myself through lips that glisten with sweat, "And I thought skying on a dragon was bad."

I reach up to grasp the next vine when the limb I'm standing on splits, leaving me dangling and holding on with just two hands. I hear a sound like cloth ripping and look up.

The vine I'm holding onto is pulling away from the wall. Before I can get my feet on the closest nearby stem, the plantlike rope rips from the wall, and I'm suddenly sailing through the air.

To my credit, I manage to stifle my yell. I swing off to one side. Leaves and branches scratch at my face as I scrape against the wall. I grab at anything within reach. Twice I come up with a handful of leaves before I finally manage to snag a thick vine and halt my wild ride.

I manage to plant both feet on a branch and hold tight to my saving bough. If anyone was watching from below, they'd think I was hugging the wall, and they'd be right. I try to catch my breath, panting like a dog in the middle of a hot summer. Scamper makes tiny mewing sounds as if he's regretting his choice to come along with me.

I don't blame him one bit. I glance toward the battlement walkway and wait, but no head appears over the edge to investigate the noise from my wild ride.

"Must be napping," I murmur. "If so, I hope it's a long one."

I don't want to move, but I can't stay here. I reach up, grab the next higher thick stem, and push on, one hand up, one leg up, then the other hand and the other leg.

I decide to keep my face to the wall as looking downward only makes me realize that if I make it to the top, it only means that I may still have to climb down.

I lose track of time. For me, the only thing that matters is grasping the next branch and the one after that, and the one after that. My eyes pick out the next vine, and I reach for it when my hand stops in mid-air.

Voices!

Muted voices, as if someone is speaking in low, hushed tones and so soft that I can neither make out their words nor be sure who is doing the talking.

I glance upward, and a wan smile lifts my cheeks. I'm less than a body length from the window edge. Slower than even before, as I don't want to make any noise, I climb the last few branches.

I reach the window and slowly edge up to peek around one corner of the windowsill. A big grin cracks my face. Cara and Helmar!

Their wrists and ankles are bound, and they're sitting close to each other on three-legged stools. I edge up a little higher and see off in one corner Phigby, and Amil. Otherwise, the room is empty. It was they whom I heard speaking.

Just as I start to scoot up higher, I hear the door creak open and duck back down. I can't see, but I hear firm footsteps and then Cara's sharp, "Daron!"

And then I hear stumbling footsteps and Cara cries out, "Father!"

A gasp almost escapes my lips and for a moment, I almost slip off the vine I'm standing on in complete surprise.

Dragon Master Boren Dracon is alive, as is his son.

Cara is softly sobbing, and then I hear the rustling of clothing and then, "There, there, Cara," in Master Boren's deep bass voice.

"Father," Cara sobs, "I thought you were dead. You and Daron."

Boren's voice holds a terrible sadness as he replies, "At least one of us is, daughter."

"What?" Cara questions. "What do you mean, father?"

Even from outside the window, I can hear Master Boren's deep, mournful sigh. "When your son goes against all that is right, all that is good; when he kidnaps his own father, holds him captive in a cold, hard dungeon. How can he be anything but dead to me?"

"Father, what are you talking about?"

There is a rustling of clothing and Master Boren says, "Shall I tell her, Daron, or is there still a shred of manhood in you that will acknowledge just what you've been doing?"

There's a sharp laugh from Daron and then, "Oh, don't be so self-righteous, father. It's not like you've been perfect all your life. You and I know both know of some of the shady dealings you and Lorell cooked up after the golden was born."

It's not just Master Boren's remarks that hold me fast, there's something in Daron's voice that keeps me from rising up and revealing myself. Master Boren was firm but there was a very real note of apprehension in his voice.

Daron is neither anxious nor uneasy. His tone is hard, cold, confident. "And if you had cooperated you wouldn't have spent one moment in the dungeon, but no, you had to be stubborn and self-righteous so you really brought it upon yourself, you know."

"Daron," Cara chokes out, "I have absolutely no idea of what you're talking about but you need to help us. Untie us so that we can get away from here."

Daron doesn't answer right away. Instead, I hear footsteps in the room, his apparently, and it sounds as if he's pacing back and forth. "No," Daron mutters. "No, I'm afraid I can't do that."

"What do you mean, you can't?" Helmar rasps.

"Because," Daron snaps in reply, "we only have half of what we need." His tone has a tinge of anger, but something else, desperation perhaps.

"Daron," Cara pleads, "what's wrong with you? Cut these bindings and help us out of here."

"Nothing is wrong with me, Cara," he retorts sharply. "In fact, I'm on the right side, it's you and your merry little band here that are on the wrong side.

"But let me explain it to you in simple terms. We have one half of what we need and want in father. Now, we need the other half. Cara, for your own welfare, and father's, I need to know where Golden Wind is, and I need to know now. Where is she?"

Cara doesn't answer. Instead, Helmar says slowly, "A better question is, why are you doing this? I have the feeling it's not to protect the golden or your father."

"Why am I doing this?" Daron replies with a sharp laugh. "That's easy to answer, Master Novice. Unlike you, I want nothing to do with Draconstench. The golden is my way out from doing nothing more with my life than tending to dumb beasts.

"I wasn't born to be a mere dragon herder, worrying if they have enough to eat or if dragon bane has made its way into the meadows. Oh no, you and my father may want that life, but not me, not now, not ever. I want more, much more than that."

My mouth sags open just a bit. I never realized that there was someone else in the world that hated dragons as much as me. But to be like Daron? I shudder at the thought.

For an instant, I hang my head and think, I'm not really like him, am I?

Daron's voice comes again, shrill and terse. "And I'm going to get what I deserve and want, which is a life away from the smallness and boring life I had back there. Mark my words, it will be mine."

Gone are the sobs of happiness in Cara's voice. Instead, she pleads, "Daron, please, please tell me that you didn't have anything to do with the attack on Draconton or Draconstead."

Daron's silence is his answer. Cara's piteous moan tells me that she realizes that her brother knew beforehand that the vicious attack was coming and how destructive it would be. Her brother is a murderer of innocent people, all in the name of ill-gained lucre.

Then I hear Master Boren. "How bad was it, Cara?"

"Completely destroyed," she answers in a hollow voice. "From what I know, everyone is . . . " she can't go on, and I can hear her softly crying.

I can hear clothing rustling again, and I have the impression that Master Boren now faces his son. "You were not only part of the subterfuge that got me to the Manor House and my capture by the Wilders, but you let them destroy and kill — "

"Oh, enough," Daron snaps. "So a few villagers, and a few peasants got killed, and a bunch of old buildings burned to the ground. What do I care about that? Absolutely nothing."

"That's why," Helmar growls, "you didn't want me to leave the Manor House. You intended for the Wilders to capture both your father and me."

"Of course," Daron pronounces snidely. "But just so you'll know, I made certain that neither of you were to be harmed. If the fools had done the job right, we'd have father, you and the golden in hand by now, instead of playing these silly games of scouring the countryside. Now it appears that that rabble of idiots let the golden escape."

He lets a breath out. "But I have the feeling you know where we can find her. So let's make it easy on everyone and just tell me where she's gone."

"You're in league with the Wilders," Cara says in a voice that is so full of disbelief that it comes out as the barest of whispers.

Then, Cara's loud gasp is accompanied by clothing swishing and the squeak of a stool leg that makes me think that Daron has grabbed his sister.

His voice rises in ferocity so that it's almost a snarl. "Don't look at me that way! I didn't kill anyone, the Wilders did all that. Now listen, I made sure that you and father and Helmar were not to be hurt in the raid and you weren't. However, my ability to keep all of you safe now depends on one thing and one thing only — that I can deliver the golden."

"Daron!" Helmar demands. "Let go of her, you're hurting her."

Only heavy breathing breaks the silence but then I hear a grunt and the scrape of a stool as if Daron had roughly pushed Cara away.

"Daron," calls Phigby, who until now had been silent. "I understand why they want the golden, but why your father and Helmar?"

Daron laughs in reply. "That's because you and everyone else have underestimated the Wilders. You think that the Drachen War reduced them to just a small clan that raids along the hinterland every so often.

"But you and everyone else are wrong. Stupidly wrong. The Wilders are so much more than a small band of dragon riders. Their lands extend far beyond what the maps show."

The tone of his voice takes on a tinge of awe. "And their dragon herds? Lorell's puny holdings would be but a few sprogs compared to theirs. Vast lands and all covered with dragons."

I can hear him draw in a breath before saying, "I know, I saw."

"You saw!?" Cara sputters. "You mean you've been to their lairs?"

Daron laughs again. "Lairs! They don't live in burrows like animals, Cara. That's just what they want everyone to believe, to make it seem that they're some sort of ignorant savages."

"All right," Helmar says, "let's assume that we believe you, for now. That still doesn't answer the question, why Master Boren and myself?"

"Yes, Daron," Cara demands. "What do the Wilders want with father and Helmar?"

I hear a few more footfalls as if Daron is pacing again. "Breeding," he finally answers.

"Breeding!" Boren exclaims. "You don't need a Dragon Master for breeding. Dragons are quite capable of doing that all on their own."

"That's true," Daron answers, "if all you were after is the usual varieties of dragons, but not if you wanted very unique, very special dragons. That takes the experience and knowledge of a Dragon Master.

"And I have to admit, there's none better than you, father. Everyone knows that Dragon Master Boren Dracon is the best in all the land."

He pauses and then says, "And a good Dragon Master needs a

good apprentice to help him. After all, father, you are getting a bit old."

"Daron," Phigby asks quietly, "these 'unique dragons' of which you speak, what kind of — "

"I've said enough," Daron responds curtly. "Now listen to me, all of you. If you tell me where the golden is, I may be able to save you."

"Save us?" Cara answers. "Save us from what?"

Daron's voice is a mere whisper, but I can feel its threat even from a distance. "Not from what, Cara."

He takes in a raspy breath. "From *her*."

27

The instant Daron utters *"her,"* the image of Vay rushes into my mind like the frosty breath of a cold north wind. The evil hag leers at me, and I feel a chill sweep over my body as if I had thrown myself again into the spring creek back at Draconstead. Now I understand the golden's warning; Vay is here or is coming, and soon.

I don't know how I know that, but I do.

Is Daron conspiring with Vay? I can't help but wonder, how is that possible? How could anyone follow her wickedness? Then I remember Phigby's lesson with the stones. Daron has chosen to follow Vay, and she not only holds power, she wields life and death in her hands as well.

The thought that anyone would be in league with such a repugnant creature causes me to shudder, which makes the vine I'm standing on shake as well. Before the rustling becomes too loud, and I give myself away, I manage to stop my quaking.

From inside the room, I hear Cara say, "Her? Brother, what are you talking about?"

"Just this," Daron replies in a hard tone, "unless one of you tells me where the golden is, I can't save you. They'll give you to her and believe me, that's not what you want to happen."

I hear fierce anger in Cara's reply. "Daron, why are you doing this to me, to father? We're your family."

Before Daron can reply, I hear firm footsteps and a new voice. "That's easy to answer, my dear. Simply put, your family cannot give Daron Dracon what he desires, above all else."

I don't recognize the new voice but after a few moments of silence, I hear, "And what is that, Prince Aster?" Helmar says almost with a sneer. "Wealth? A royal title, perhaps?"

Aster's answering laugh is derisive. "Oh, nothing so banal, Helmar. Daron will have that and more once we get what really matters."

"Which is?" Helmar asks.

"Power, of course," Aster answers in a no-nonsense tone. "Absolute, unfettered power."

Cara's voice is like a knife slicing through the air. "It *was* you that I saw in Draconstead at the birthing barn. You were the tall Wilder that led the attack. You had the Wilders kill all those innocent people."

I can't see, but somehow I can feel Prince Aster's indifferent shrug. "Yes, unfortunately, sometimes those things just happen. But just so you'll know, you actually helped plan the attack, you know."

Cara's voice is like a frozen river, ice cold, hard and harsh. "I did no such thing, and I would never help — "

"Ah, but you did," Aster is quick to interrupt. "The Winter Carola at the castle, remember? I admit you were a warm, pleasant armful to dance with but more so, you were so eager to answer my questions about Draconstead. The information I gleaned from you was invaluable in planning our attack."

He pauses and laughs loudly. "Oh, but I wish you could see the look on your face. Did you think that we invited you, your father, and Helmar, three commoners for any other reason?"

His laugh is sharp, almost shrill. "Oh, wait, you thought that I, as the second born, without obligation to marry royalty to keep the bloodline pure, was interested in you as a possible bride? That I was wooing you and that's why you were at the ball?"

Aster laughs loudly again. "I am so sorry, Cara, but that thought never crossed my mind. Once I have the golden, I can have any woman, or women, for that matter, that I want. Perhaps then I may consider you as a royal consort, but not now. Not until we have the golden and all that goes with her."

You beast! Cara's voice is little more than a growl, but something in her tone makes me think that the prince's comments hit close to the mark regarding the ball. Poor Cara, I think to myself, she thought the invitation came from a possible royal suitor, only it turns out it came from a royal traitor.

The room becomes quiet, and all I can hear is a low muttering. Then comes the sound of footsteps fading away as if someone has hurried from the chamber.

Prince Aster's voice grows hard. "Enough of the idle chit-chat. Since Daron has failed to convince you to be reasonable, my approach will be a little different. It's very straightforward. Where is the golden? Speak and you live. Remain silent and one of you will die while the others watch."

"You wouldn't dare!" Master Boren protests, "None but King Leo himself has the right to execute us."

In a voice dripping with sarcasm, the prince says, "Then we won't bother with the formality of petitioning His Majesty. He is getting on in age and does so need his rest these days."

He waits, but no one answers. Then, with a snide air, he says, "Very well, since you choose to defy me — Daron, I will let you decide. Who dies?"

I hear the sounds of a struggle and then, "Get your hands off me!" Helmar furiously demands.

Cara yells, "No!"

Daron shoves Helmar's head out the window. He struggles ferociously against Daron. Helmar has his head twisted toward the room and doesn't see me just below the window sill.

"If you don't want your beau to learn to fly without wings, sister," Daron returns in a hard tone, "tell us where the golden is."

"Don't tell them!" Helmar chokes out.

Daron yanks Helmar back inside the room. "Last chance," he says, "tell us, or so help me, I'll throw him from this tower. Make no mistake, Cara, I would like nothing better since he's so special to you. And to you too, right, father?"

Boren mutters in a voice that sounds as if he's aged a hundred seasons, "Son, please, don't do this. Don't betray our family, don't dishonor our name."

I've heard enough, I can't wait any longer. Cara and the others are in the hands of crazed maniacs and even if they knew where the golden was and could tell the prince, I have no doubt that he's going to kill all of them.

I have no idea what I'm going to do, but right now, doing something is better than doing nothing. I rise up and squeak, "Wait! Stop. They can't tell you where the golden is, only I can."

Daron yanks Helmar around and backs away from the window, his eyes wide in astonishment. I scramble up onto the window sill and hop down to the floor. "They can't tell you because she's not where they left her."

Prince Aster takes one look at me, his hand goes to his bandaged arm that's in a sling, and he bawls, "You!"

"Uh, hi there, Prince Aster," I stutter. "Yes, it's me all right. As they say, it appears we meet again." I edge away from the window and stand close to the nearest wall. As I do, I can feel Scamper edge out of my tunic hood and down my back. His sharp claws bite through the goat's hair and I try not to wince as they prick my skin.

I point toward Aster's injured arm. "Sorry about that arm, but you really have to be careful around dragons. They can be a bit temperamental at times and you just never know when they're going to act up.

"Especially when they get a bit riled about what's going on, you know, like when someone is trying to steal them in the middle of the night which means their sleep gets interrupted, which makes them really grumpy and — ”

“Shut up!” Aster shrieks as he draws his sword.

The sight of the sword makes me shut up — for the moment.

“Hooper,” Helmar growls, “what are you doing here?”

“Well,” I answer, my eyes never leaving Aster’s sword, “it appears that I’m here to rescue you, yon fair damsel, and everyone else, too. Especially Phigby, I like to read his books you know, not to mention he makes the best fireworks in the whole kingdom.”

I’m babbling again, stalling for time as I try to think of a way out of this. “Of course, I’ll rescue Amil, too, just — ”

“Stop!” Prince Aster’s command stops me in mid-word. He takes several deep breaths as if to calm himself. His snicker is sharp, loud, and for some reason, reminds me of Hakon and Arnie’s sniggers. He wipes at his eye as if his laughter had brought a tear.

“You?” he sneers. “You are going to rescue your friends, all by yourself, I presume? By chance, you didn’t bring a Dragon Knight army along, just in case your audacious plan didn’t work out?”

“No,” I mutter, “it’s just me against you and Daron the Master Bully so I think that’s about all we’ll need.”

Scamper has reached the floor. I have no idea what the little tub is up to, but he moves so quietly, staying in the shadows, that it appears that neither the prince nor Daron has seen him.

“But I don’t need an army, because I have what you need, meaning Golden Wind. And I’m not going to tell you where she is until you let my comrades go and I know they’re safe and far away from the likes of you two.”

“Hooper, no,” Cara says. “Do you know what it means if they get their hands on the golden?”

I turn to her, scrunch my face together and answer, “Uh, from what I heard, more baby goldens?”

Her eyes and mine meet and she swings her eyes toward the corner where Amil and Phigby sit tied up. I get it. Scamper has managed to stay hidden and is now behind those two.

Suddenly, Helmar cries out angrily and lunges toward me,

fighting against Daron's restraint. "Hooper! Don't you dare tell them where Golden Wind's hidden. Don't be a fool! Once they have their hands on her, nothing can stop them."

He fights so ferociously that for a moment, I think that Daron can't hold him and that Helmar is really going to attack me.

The two tussle in the middle of the room and then I see Prince Aster whip around his blade as if he would run Helmar through. Before he can, though, Amil suddenly flies over Cara and broadsides the prince, sending both of them to the floor in a heap.

Daron slams Helmar into the wall with a loud thud and springs away. Before Amil can stop him, he's through the door and pounding down the stairs.

I reach over and pull Helmar to his feet. I pull out my knife blade and with a quick sawing motion, cut through the knotted bands. "Free the others," he grinds out and rushes out the door in pursuit of Daron.

I jump over to Cara, who wears an expression of sheer shock at seeing me followed by anger at Prince Aster and her brother. While I'm sawing at Cara's bindings, I hear Amil grunting behind me and turn.

He's propped an unconscious Prince Aster up against the wall and huffs, "I guess I hit him too hard, knocked him out cold."

He straightens and runs a hand over his bald head. "I suppose if the king hears about this it'll be the chopping block for me. Attacking royalty, even corrupt ones, is a capital offense, you know."

Cara's bindings drop to the floor just as her father appears at her side. She stands and they embrace, both have tears in their eyes. A moment later, Helmar rushes back into the room. "I lost Daron," he says, "but there's a good chance that there are guards on their way."

Phigby comes to stand beside Boren, rubbing at his wrist where the rope bindings had chafed. "Are we cut off?" he asks Helmar.

Helmar gives a quick nod to Phigby before he turns to me. "Well done, Hooper. You and Scamper played your parts extremely well."

"As did you," I reply. "For a moment there, if Daron hadn't held you back, I thought you were going to beat me to a pulp."

A corner of Helmar's mouth turns up in a faint smile. "I was afraid that the prince would see right through that."

"Royal arrogance," I reply. "We're the little people, we couldn't possibly outsmart him."

"Speaking of," Phigby says as he gazes at the prone Aster. "What are we to do with him?"

"Barter," Amil quickly says. "Our lives for his."

"That may not work," I reply. "He's not the one in charge here."

"What do you mean, Hooper?" Helmar asks. "Is King Leo here?"

"Didn't you hear Daron?" I answer. "Even if His Majesty were here, I'm not sure it would work."

I turn to Phigby. "You heard Daron, didn't you Phigby? He said that he was trying to save you from *her*. He could only be talking about Vay."

"Vay?" Amil sputters. "She's here?"

Phigby holds up a quick hand. "Or on her way. For the moment, let's assume Hooper is right and we can't use Aster as a bartering chip." He turns to me and quickly asks, "How in the world did you get up here, Hooper, and can we escape the same way?"

"Well, I didn't fly," I answer and lead him over to the window and point down.

Helmar and Phigby crane their heads out the opening. "You climbed up that?" Helmar asks in an amazed voice.

"Like I said," I reply, "I didn't fly."

They turn back to the open door and the spiral stairs. "We have one sword and a knife," Phigby states. "That's certainly not going to be much help against men-at-arms with bows and lances." He lets out a forlorn sigh. "And they took my bag."

"So we climb," Helmar says.

He points at the door. "We need to find a way to block that, slow the guards up, even if it's just a bit."

I point to a small table in the corner. "Will that work?"

"Yes," Helmar answers, and bounds over to the table. He hands the lone candle to Phigby, grabs the table, and turns it on one end. After Amil slams the thick wooden door shut, Helmar jams one edge of the table against the door and the other end into a jagged stone edging on the floor.

He pushes it down firmly so that it forms a wedge between flooring and the sturdy entryway. "That won't last long," he announces. "But it's the best we can do."

Amil gestures at Prince Aster's limp body on the floor. "What about him?"

"My first inclination is to throw him out the window headfirst," Helmar grunts. "That's what he deserves, but unlike him, I'm no murderer."

He turns to me. "Are those vines strong enough to hold the two of us if we carry him down?"

I firmly shake my head at him. "I wouldn't if I were you, they're not that stout."

I can see the contortion in Helmar's expression and understand his competing emotions. One part of him doesn't want to leave the prince to be rescued by his conspiring comrades, but at the same time, he can't bring himself to kill the man outright.

Phigby lays a hand on Helmar's arm. "No choice, we're not cold-blooded murderers, so we must leave him."

Helmar turns to Cara and her father. "All right, down the vines, it is, then. Master Boren, you and Cara, first, then Phigby and Hooper. Amil and I will stay behind and try to give you additional time if the guards break the door down before you're on the ground."

"No," I reply. "All of you have to go first."

"Hooper," Helmar responds through clenched teeth, "this is no time to argue."

"No, Helmar," I answer. "You don't understand. This *is* the time to argue. I almost fell climbing up here because of my bad leg. Those vines aren't that secure against the walls, if my leg gives out going down, there's just the chance I'm going to rip through the shoots and bring down all of us."

My eyes are firm, my mind made up. I am not going to endanger any of them, especially Cara.

"Helmar," Phigby says sternly, "like you said, now's not the time to argue. He has a valid point."

With a sharp glance at me, Helmar turns and first helps Master Boren and then Cara through the window. Once they're out, Phigby bundles his robe about him and slides through the opening followed by Amil.

Helmar sticks his head out the window and peers below for a moment before he turns to me. "We'll give them some time to get farther down."

He gazes at me, and I can see in his eyes that he's mulling over something in his mind. He slowly reaches out and places his hand on my shoulder. "Hooper, you are a surprising fellow, and I admit, braver than I gave you credit for. Even if this doesn't work, you have my thanks."

He touches his breast pocket where the gem had been. "For many things."

My mouth sags for a moment. "You mean you still have it? I thought for sure that they would have taken it away from you."

"No," Helmar answers with a puzzled expression. "When the villagers captured us, they took our weapons, but made me put the emerald back into my tunic before they bound my hands. They acted as if they were afraid of the stone."

"And when you arrived here?"

He shrugs. "We've been kept up here the whole time. There's been a guard outside the door who checked on us every once in a while, but no one tried to take the jewel away."

That causes me to raise my eyebrows. Aster and his henchmen wanted the golden, but not the emerald? Surely the villagers told His Highness, the Royal Rat what Helmar carried.

I start to ask Helmar why he thought they hadn't taken gemstone from him when he turns and peers out the window. "Master Boren is having a hard time of it. His stay in the dungeon must have weakened him."

I poke my head out the window and look down. Cara is side by side with her father, helping him slowly down the lattice. He appears to be weak, uncertain of himself as he tries to find the next handhold or foothold. There's nothing we can do but wait, hoping that they don't take too long to reach the ground.

Fortunately, it appears that the guards on the keep walls haven't noticed that their prisoners are escaping using the vine lattice. I turn and pick up Scamper, who after his rope-gnawing trick has been nosing around the room in search of food.

"Time to tuck you in," I murmur as I pick him up. "By the way, that was a great job untying everyone like you did."

Arrrrhhh, he answers as I tuck him into my tunic's hood.

Helmar and I peer out once again. Cara and her father are almost to the halfway point and should be on the ground soon. "Ready?" Helmar asks. I take several deep breaths and swing my arms around to get myself ready for the climb down. "Ready," I answer. "You first and I'll be right behind you."

A sudden chill sweeps over me, and we both turn at the whisper of a sound. I glance down at Aster, but he lies still and silent. The noise comes again, and my skin crawls.

Helmar takes a step toward the door, sword in hand. "What is that?" he whispers over his shoulder. "That's not the sound that boots would make on stone stairs."

I swallow but don't answer. He's right, that's not the sound of men-at-arms hurrying up the stairwell. It's a snake. An enormous serpent that slithers up the stairs. The rasp of its rough skin against the granite steps becomes louder and louder.

In my mind's eye, I can see the huge snake sliding across the stonework. Its beady red eyes centered on the door, its tongue flicking in and out, as it searches for its prey.

Which could only be me and Helmar.

I hurry to the window and peer down. Cara and her father still haven't reached the ground and for some reason, Phigby, and Amil have stopped climbing down. I spin around to Helmar. He's close to the door, his sword point leveled and at the ready.

"Helmar," I plead, "we've got to go — now!"

A blast rips the door off its hinges, slamming into Helmar and knocking him to the floor. Splinters fly across the room, showering me with wooden pellets that prick at face and hands. Helmar lies groaning on the stone flooring, trying to push the door off him and rise to his feet.

I peer over my arm that I'd thrown up to cover my face. Vay is gliding up the stairwell, her robes swish across the cold stone, and I hear the slithering, evil sound again as if she rides on the back of vipers. Even though a torch burns behind her, there's no light about her body, just an ebony aura.

Scamper is chittering madly in my ear and pawing furiously at my tunic. I'm afraid that he's going to do something stupid like attack the evil fairy, or jump headfirst out the window to escape the witch. For the moment, I have no choice but to ignore him.

Somehow, I find the courage to move. I bend over Helmar and lift the door off him. "Helmar!" I shout. "Get up, we've got to get out of here!"

He groans, and staggers to his feet. In stumbling steps, I pull him toward the window. He sways as if he would fall and I have to hold onto him for fear that he will topple through the open window.

I whirl around, Vay is almost to the top of the stairs. We're trapped, there's no way out except through the window, but how do I get Helmar down the vines with his senses askew. I can't carry him and at the moment, he can't climb.

For an instant, I think of shouting for Amil to come back, but neither he nor Phigby could climb fast enough to reach us in time.

I whirl back to Vay and suck in a breath. She's standing just outside the doorway, her cold, red eyes staring as if she thirsts for our blood. From deep within her shadowy hood, I hear, *I will have what is mine.*

She stretches out a hand toward Helmar. I know what she reaches for — Pengillstorr's jewel.

An image forms in my mind, Vay's claws at my throat, slowly squeezing the life out of me while her sinister laugh comes again, and again. Helmar starts as if he's suddenly come awake. He takes one look at Vay and lunges for his sword which lies on the ground.

He points the blade at the evil fairy, standing tall and firm against pure evil. "Take another step," he growls, "and I will run you through."

Vay laughs again. *Think that your puny blade can harm me, Helmar?* she taunts.

At the mention of his name, Helmar jerks as if Vay had slapped him across the face. Seeing his startled expression, Vay hisses, *Yes, Helmar, I know your name. I know all your names.*

I stand frozen, quivering, a puny mouse cornered by a voracious Dread Wolf. Abruptly another image swiftly forms in my mind. "Helmar, the gem!"

This time, he doesn't hesitate but rips the jewel out of his pocket. As soon as he does, Vay abruptly stops. She sucks in a breath as if to draw all the air out of the room. I try to pull Helmar closer to the window, to the vines, but he won't budge.

He stands there, sword and gem outstretched as if the two will ward off Vay's malicious evil. As fast as a snake strike, Vay swings her arm around as if it were a bludgeon of sorts. Helmar is flung against the wall so hard that he slides to the floor, his eyes completely closed.

It's just me and Vay standing but a few body lengths apart. She throws back her head, cackles loudly and throws her arms wide. *What? No emerald dragon to save you, this time, Hooper? No Voxtyrmen wielded by the Gem Guardian? I admit, I made a mistake in trying to kill you the first time as I thought you were Pengillstorr's choice.*

But you turned out to be nothing, after all. So, I will take what is mine, but I am still going to kill you as I don't need you to find the golden.

She starts to reach toward Helmar and the gemstone he holds but just as she does, there is a light, brighter than the sun that pours through the window. Vay shrieks, *No!*

I can feel the presence, just for an instant, of Osa, Nadia, and Eskar.

Behind me, the whole vine begins to shake and shudder before a wall of leaves and boughs explodes through the window. I duck out of the way and go to Helmar. He starts to rouse, and though I struggle with his hefty body, I manage to get him to his feet.

The leafy vines flood the room, rushing around and over, but, amazingly not against us. We're like a rock cleft that splits a sea of green. It's as if the vine knows we couldn't stand against the onslaught. In moments, there's a thick, impenetrable green barrier between Vay and the two of us.

I mutter, "Nice to have help, even when you don't ask for it."

Helmar is a bit wobbly, and I hold onto him for a few moments while he gets his head straightened back on. He pockets the gemstone and mutters, "I think we need to get out of here while we still can."

I nod in quick agreement. "Can you get down the vines? You're still a little shaky on your feet."

"I'd rather take a chance on the vines than stay here with that thing," he declares.

"That makes three of us," I reply as I push aside the vines that cover the window and help him over the windowsill.

He blinks his eyes at me and questions, "Three?" Just then, Scamper pops his head up and chitters at him. Helmar smiles wanly. "Oh, right—three of us."

He takes a firm grip on a stout vine, swings out and begins climbing rapidly down. I watch him for a few moments before I search the vine lattice for the rest of our company.

"Wha — " I begin as I scrutinize every bit of the vinework. All but Helmar have somehow disappeared. I don't see anyone still climbing down the latticework. I slide back and forth, trying to spot Cara or her father, but they're nowhere to be seen. Neither is Phigby nor Amil. I peer intensely at the tower's base, fearful that I'm going to see four dead bodies, but thankfully, they're not there either.

An eerie, wailing sound coming through the emerald wall whips me around. I hear a muttering that's so muted that I can't make out the words. It rises in volume and force until a thunderclap booms with such power that it throws me backward. For a moment, the room shakes as if the thunderbolt's power is going to collapse the fortress walls.

There's a crackling noise coming from the other side of the chamber. I pick myself up off the floor and suck in a breath. I smell smoke, but it's bitter and pungent as if someone has set stinkweed afire.

Scamper is chattering madly, his little paws scratching at my head and throat. Black, wispy tendrils snake through the branches wrapping themselves around the vine runners. Where they touch, the smoke like tentacles begin to pull and crush the greenery.

Vay's dark magic is tearing down the bramble barrier.

The snapping and shredding of leaves and woody branches grows louder, faster. I can't stay here, or Vay's foul tentacles will wrap themselves around my body, holding me for her wrath. I would rather fall to a clean death than have her evil claws rip the life out of me.

I all but throw myself to the windowsill. I swing myself out and frantically kick my feet until I feel firmness beneath my boot soles, and a vine branch takes my weight. I push myself to descend as fast as I can, to escape Vay and her writhing smoke monster.

I hear crackling, snapping and I look up. The topmost part of the vine lattice is now in the grip of the wispy tentacles.

I can't move fast enough; the uppermost vines are beginning to rip away from the walls. I peer downward and know it's hopeless. It's too far. Above me, the greenery is crumbling, vanishing before my eyes. What's left won't hold me much longer.

The branch I'm holding onto peels away from the keep's stonework. I frantically look around for another branch to grab, but I'm too late.

I hear loud snapping, first from above, then to each side; the sound of the vine branches splitting apart. Then the whole mass of greenery — leaves, stems and branches peel away from the stonework as if a giant hand had reached out to strip it away.

I'm falling, the only sounds are the rush of wind and Scamper's plaintiff wails.

They will be the last sounds I ever hear.

28

I'm tumbling like some windblown leaf. Only this time there's no pond of water underneath me, only rock-hard ground. The world is spinning, and I can't — make — it — stop. I want to shriek, shout, scream, at the top of my lungs for help, but all that comes are little gurgles that barely get past my lips.

I'm about to die, and there is absolutely nothing that I can do to stop Fate's hand from grasping me tightly and carrying me to death's bosom.

Scamper is squalling, his little paws grip me so fiercely that they puncture my tunic and bite deep into my skin. I try to grab and pull him to me to cushion his fall, but my arms flail around as if they haven't any life to them.

The wind whistles past my ears, then there is a roaring gust of air and talons close about my body, squeezing me so tight that I can barely breathe. I'm jerked upward so hard that my head feels like it will snap right off my shoulders.

After a moment, I manage to twist around and see the golden's wings and body as she soars higher into the air. Without thinking of what I'm actually saying, I bellow at the top of my lungs, "Let me go!"

Thankfully, she ignores me. She races almost straight up like a golden arrow with wings. I try to see what's happened to the others, but I can't see anything but a dragon underbelly and wings.

We climb still higher into the sky.

And then she lets me go.

"No!" I bawl. "Not now!" I continue to rise in a long arc, my arms, hands, flailing as if I'm trying to grab onto a cloud and hang on by my fingertips. As I'm about to plunge back down again, the golden appears just below me.

Somehow, someway, I land on her back, but I'm sprawled out facing the wrong way. I'm sliding across her smooth hide, my hands scrape and grab against dragon scales trying desperately to find a handhold.

Scamper chitters so loudly that my ears ring. Then, the golden stops to hover in midair, allowing me to twist around so that I can slide forward until I can sit my rump in her neck cradle, but I still don't have a grip on anything.

I'm not positive, but I think that at that moment, the golden must have sensed that I was in a precarious position and in grave danger of falling off. She pushes up her neck muscles, which press me against her skull sheath.

I bury my face into her tough hide. I clamp my legs about her neck in a death grip. I reach out, grab two of her horns and hold on for dear life.

Scamper launches himself out of my tunic hood and dives under the golden's carapace. He's trembling and shaking, apparently not liking our dragonless skying one bit.

Well, neither did I.

The golden ducks her head and the next thing I know, we're speeding straight down, right at Dunadain Keep and the bowmen that are charging across the walkway. "No!" I yelp. "Not that way, you're headed right for them!"

The archers bring their bows up, but instead of aiming at us, they swing around to point at the walkway leading to the tower. My eyes catch movement. It's Helmar.

Somehow, he was able to escape from the vines before they came tumbling down to the paving. The archers have a dead bead on him. He stumbles and then catches himself and sprints down the walkway toward a turret.

I only have to take one look to know that he won't reach safety in time. A dozen or more arrows will impale him before he can lunge through the doorway and into the tower.

Then I realize the golden's plan. "Yes!" I shout eagerly. "Go!"

I feel as if I'm riding a golden comet through the air. The golden has her wings half-folded, her head pointed straight at the keep walls. I lean forward into the rushing wind. The bowmen have their eyes set on Helmar and are so intent on their running target that they don't look up until the last instant.

By then, it's too late.

The golden booms across the fortress walls, the force from her wake blasts a dozen or more archers off the parapet. Their thrashing arms and legs send bows and arrows spraying upward, a fountain of bow shafts and arrow points.

I glance behind and see that those few bowmen who escaped their fellow archers' fate are now in total disarray and running for cover.

They've completely forgotten about Helmar.

I can't help myself and laugh out loud while thumping on the golden's skull. "That was fantastic! Too bad Prince Aster and Daron weren't on that wall."

"Yes," Golden Wind answers, "but we're not done yet."

"We're not?" I mutter.

"No," she states. "We need to set Rover, Glory, and Song free."

We flash toward the battlements, and I see movement on the far wall. I point and yelp, "Golden Wind, more archers!"

The golden dips her wings, we drop below the parapets, out of the bowmen's sight, only to zoom up on the other side and surprise them before they can turn and unleash their arrows.

This time, Golden Wind doesn't use a blast of wind to scatter our foe, she releases a stream of dragon fire.

Shrieks of pain and terror erupt from the battlement. I see several archers, their clothes afire, scream and stumble along the parapet, while those not caught in the hellfire make a wild dash for cover in the nearest turret house.

We sky up and over the walls, and I peer down into the courtyard where the three sapphires are chained by the leg and their muzzles bound by thick rope. They raise their heads expectantly as we flash past and tug at the chains, but they can't break free.

Then, from the shadows, lope several drogs; something I didn't expect to see. They shove their spears, as sharp as Proga lances at the sapphires, making the dragons stop pulling at their chains.

I don't have any idea if those drogs came from Draconstead, or not, all I know is that to free the sapphires, we're going to have to deal with the brutes and their dragon spears.

Suddenly, from the farthermost tower door, Phigby, Amil, and Helmar burst into view, followed by Cara and Master Boren. Phigby is clutching his bag, Amil has his ax while Helmar and Cara each have their bows in hand and quivers slung over their shoulders.

I let out a whoosh of relief. I was afraid that they had been captured again. Instead, they managed to find their weapons. They rush along the stone paving, searching for a way to get off the keep's walls and down to their dragons.

The golden hovers and I shout out, "Helmar! Cara!" They spin around at my yell. I point down into the square. "Drogs, they're holding the sapphires."

They take one look over the wall, notch an arrow, and let fly. I jerk my head around at a drog's shriek. One beast lies crumpled on the courtyard with an arrow sticking out of its head, while another bulbous body totters for a moment, an arrow through and through the neck before it topples face forward onto the paving.

Stunned, the other brutes stare at their comrades and then flee before another of set of arrows finds their mark.

"Get me down there," I shout at the golden. "Cara and the others can't get to the dragons; we need to get the dragons to them."

She swoops down and lands next to Wind Song. Scamper starts to follow me. "Not this time," I order. "You stay there and keep under cover." I push him back onto the golden's skull plate, slide off the golden's neck and hurry over to Wind Song.

I feel a gust of wind as the golden lifts off the paving, but I'm too busy trying to get the pin out of the clamp that holds the chain around Wind Song's leg to wonder why she's leaving me behind.

I work at the thick metal peg with my fingers, before I give up, jerk my knife out and get the blade's point under the pin's flat cap. I push, and prod and slowly the spike starts to slip out from the clamp joint.

A shriek causes me to whirl around with my knife pointed outward.

A dozen drogs are lumbering at me with their spears lowered, only, the first one has paid the price for being in the lead. He's thrashing on the ground with an arrow through his neck. Another arrow slices through the air, and another brute tumbles headfirst to skid along the pavement.

I start to yell for Wind Song to unleash her dragon fire when abruptly I remember that she and the other dragons have their muzzles clamped shut by stout ropes.

Suddenly there's a blast of wind, and I glance up to see the golden carrying Amil by one arm. She swings down and drops him in the midst of the drogs.

Being rather slow and stupid, the drogs don't react fast enough, and before they can whip their spears around, Amil is among them, whirling and slashing at the monsters with his sharp blade.

As Amil wades into the mob, the golden reaches out with her back talons and grabs several of the swine. She beats upward for several moments, higher than the towers before she drops the beasts. They land squarely on two drogs that are furiously charging at Amil.

I can hear the snap and crack as their bones and necks break from the fall. The two that were running in full-throated rage at Amil now struggle under the load of lifeless bodies before Amil dispatches them with two vicious swings of his ax.

Amil is a blur, never staying in one spot for more than an instant.

If Amil were roaring floodwaters, the drogs would be a standing pool of water.

Before one of the brutish thugs can swing his spear around in time, Amil's double-bladed weapon buries itself in his chest. Before the beast has even begun to drop to the ground, Amil yanks his ax out of the thing's chest.

Another drog charges at Amil, but the big man viciously swings his ax up, slicing the monster's spear point off its shaft. He grabs the spear and yanks it toward him. The drog hangs on, stumbles toward Amil, and doesn't realize until Amil buries his ax in his head, how stupid he was not to let go.

Two drogs come at Amil from opposite sides before he's had time to rip his blade out from the dead drog's skull. I jerk my knife out, but I know how foolish it would be to brandish my little knife in front of a brute that's carrying a spear twice as long as I am high. So I do the only thing I can think of and have never done before.

I throw it.

And somehow the blade plants itself deep in the drog's eye. His scream bounces off the keep's wall, but that doesn't stop his comrade from charging straight at Amil, ready to bury his spear point in Amil's chest.

He only takes one more step before the golden's tail whips around, and her two tail spikes rip through his stomach. He stands there for a moment, a blank expression on his face, staring at his guts as they spill out onto the stone paving before his eyes go dull, and he falls over to lie motionless.

The drogs try to get at Amil with their gaffs, but even with their long spears, they're afraid to get too close; afraid that his flashing blade will slice their lances in two.

I hear a meaty thunk! And another drog spins with a screech, pulling at the arrow buried deep in his chest.

Amil charges at the pack, a whirling dervish with an ax that never seems to stop slashing and slicing at thick, gray drog bodies. The remaining brutes have had enough, they turn and bolt away. Amil holds his bloody ax up to me in salute, and I pump my fist in acknowledgment.

I hurry over to the drog that I killed and, though my stomach churns, do what I have to and yank my knife out of its sightless eye. I wipe it on his loin cloth just as Amil yells at me, "Hooper, get the pins out!"

I hobble back to Wind Song's leg chain and using my knife point, manage to wiggle out the metal pin that's holding the clamp. As it drops to the paving with a clink, I turn to glance back at the turret walkway and mutter, "Uh-oh."

Daron and Prince Aster have reappeared, and Helmar is in a desperate sword battle with the two. Their swords flash in the torchlight, and I can hear the repeated clangs as their blades meet.

How Helmar is holding the two off is beyond me. Even with the prince fighting with his left arm instead of his right, it's obvious that he's a master swordsman with either arm.

From the other direction, I see a whole phalanx of men-at-arms, lances at the ready charging down the paved way. Cara and Phigby are racing to head them off, but it will be a dozen armed and angry soldiers against just the two. I've lost sight of Master Boren and don't know where he's gone.

Amil has Wind Glory's leg free and spurts over to Rover to furiously work at the leg clamp. I reach up and grab Song's rope, pull her head down and start sawing through the bindings. I cut through the last strand, and she's free.

I dash over to Wind Glory and start slicing through her ropes. Almost finished, I turn my head and glance at the desperate battle on the walkway.

Helmar is somehow still holding his own, but he's having to give ground to his two assailants. Cara holds her bowstring taut, arrow notched but is holding back from loosing her arrow for some reason.

Phigby is furiously digging into his haversack, for what I don't know. Just as I slash through the last of Wind Glory's ties, I hear Phigby call out loudly with words I don't understand and from his bag he pulls forth a sparkling orb.

The thing looks like it's giving off a shower of sparks. He holds it aloft, still muttering, and then, of all things, lowers it and sends it rolling toward the charging guards, just as if he were bowling for ninepins on the Common back in Draconton.

The ball of light whirls, spins, and hops as it rolls, faster and faster toward the men-at-arms. The front line of guards spots the thing coming toward them and slide to a halt. They bring their lances down as if they would skewer the sputtering sphere.

They scowl at the crackling orb, but there's a hint of fear in their eyes, too. After all, they're used to fighting other men armed like they are, and not being attacked by a ball that spits out tiny flames and sparkles like sunlight off water.

The ball rolls up, stops, and for a moment, just sits there, fizzing. The guards take a step forward, their lance points lowered at the sphere. Suddenly, the globe explodes, sending tiny flashing streaks of light everywhere.

The little blazes swarm upward in a sparkling cloud and then dive toward the guards. My eyes bulge at the sight. The little sparkles are dragons, miniature versions of Golden Wind! They flash in and around the soldiers who swat at them as if a cloud of mosquitoes had descended.

Only these "mosquitoes" squirt flame and fire.

The miniature dragons spew little flames of fire on exposed faces, hands, arms, and posteriors. They flit in and out so fast that it's all the guards can do to dance around trying to swat at them with a hand or swing a lance to try and knock one out of the air.

All to no avail.

The little things are streaks of light, buzzing through the air almost too fast for the eye to see. It's as though dozens of children with sparklers were waving them furiously in the air all at once.

My eyes flash back to Helmar. It's not good. Aster and Daron have him pinned against a parapet. Their slicing, stabbing thrusts are too much. I can see the desperation in his face. He can't hold out much longer.

Then, from out of a tower turret, Master Boren appears. In his hand is a broadsword, and he marches purposefully toward his son and Prince Aster. Now I understand where he disappeared to, he went in search of a weapon.

I catch movement coming from the far tower's door, it's several swordsmen, and they dash toward the parapet battle.

Master Boren and the sword-wielding soldiers arrive practically at the same time. Master Boren takes his place alongside Helmar, while the guards close ranks next to Prince Aster.

It's quickly evident that Master Boren may be a master at one-on-one swordplay, but against that many adversaries, he's outclassed.

With a last vicious yank of my knife, I cut through Glory's rope. The dragons are growling, roaring, stomping their feet, but the pin in Rover's clamp seems to be melded into the chain.

Amil snaps, "Your knife!" I toss it to him and turn back to the battle on the wall.

Both Helmar and Master Boren are in desperate straits while Cara and Phigby are still holding at bay the other lancers. Those guards are still swatting at the buzzing tiny dragons but the moment Phigby's dragons fizz out, they'll be back in the fight.

I've got to go help Master Boren and Helmar, neither can last much longer. "Golden Wind!" I yell out. "Helmar, Master Boren — they need help!" She quickly sets down, and I rush over to clamber up to her neck.

"On the wall!" I shout to Amil. "They're in trouble, I'm going up there." He doesn't answer but redoubles his efforts to get the pesky pin out of Rover's leg chain.

"Sky!" I command and the golden bolts upward, heels over, and we speed right at Aster and Daron. Maybe something in Helmar's or Boren's eyes warned them, as at the last instant, they lunge down and to the side. Not so for the guards. Golden Wind's appearance scatters them every which way.

We wheel around to try again for Aster and Daron but just then, I spot a company of archers running across the far walkway. Their eyes are on Amil and they have a clear shot at the big man.

Phigby's dragon swarm is petering out, but not before they've backed the men-at-arms down the pavement and into the turret. "Phigby! Cara!" I shout, pointing. "Master Boren and Helmar!"

They both spin but while Phigby charges down the crosswalk, Cara lets her arrow fly. It flashes across the courtyard and buries itself in the back of one of Boren's opponents. The man jerks, staggers, drops his sword and crumples to the ground.

Phigby bolts through the corner turret and reappears. It's as if he'd pulled a sword out of thin air, waving it wildly over his head. He rushes down the walkway, his bag bouncing over his shoulder, his foil held high.

"The archers!" I shout to the golden. "Get them before they skewer Amil."

She beats her wings furiously, and we rush through the air. She catches the archers from behind, her back talons knocking archers left and right off the wall. Their screams fill the air as they plummet to their death.

The few that do escape dart away in disarray making for the closest turret tower and safety. I glance down into the quad just in time to see Amil pull Rover's leg pin out and throw it away. The three sapphires are free.

I turn the golden back toward Helmar, Boren, and Phigby. Master Boren has finished his man off and for a moment, father and son face each other, sword point to sword point. Boren stands staring at his son, expressionless, but then he lowers his sword.

He cannot — he will not kill his son.

But Daron has no such qualms toward his father. His bellow is pure rage, and he charges at Master Boren. At the last instant, Phigby leaps between the two, his sword slashing downward, driving Daron's point into the paving blocks.

Helmar and Aster are in a battle royal. Their ringing blows resound in the courtyard. They lunge and slash, back and forth, sparks flying off the edges of their swords as if a blacksmith hammered at their blades in a forge. I'm caught by their furious fight until I catch movement out of the corner of my eye. I groan, "No."

A dozen swordsmen rush from the tower to join with Aster and

Daron. Their blades flash in the moonlight, slowly, but surely driving Phigby, Helmar and Boren back.

"Do you have any fire left?" I call.

"Yes," the golden answers. "But Master Boren and the others are too close, my fire would catch them, too."

"Not if we can get them to move out of range," I answer.

Still, I think, even if the three can't get out of the way, the appearance of four dragons might ward off Aster and his thugs. I glance down into the courtyard to see Amil scrambling up on Wind Rover. I cup my mouth and shout, "Amil, up here!"

He jerks his head up, sees me, and waves. A moment later, the sapphires are in the air. I point at the dueling swordsmen and Amil nods in understanding. The golden rises over the battlement, and I yell, "Master Boren, Helmar, Phigby! Look out!"

In answer, they give a quick glance upward, see the sapphires and turn to run. Aster and his swordsmen stand upright for an instant, startled, but then they too see the oncoming dragons. In complete disarray, they sprint down the walkway, toward the safety of the keep tower.

Abruptly, they stop and are tossed aside by an ebony wedge, darker than night blackness.

Vay floats through the darkness and across the walkway. As she glides over the paving, I hear a scraping noise as if someone is dragging chains. She's slithering toward Boren, Helmar, and Phigby, her eyes glowing an angry red inside her hood.

She sweeps across the stone pavement. Even from a distance, just like her smoke tendrils in the keep tower, her evil reaches out, touches me, and I recoil in disgust at the touch.

But her eyes do not flash toward me. Instead, they're centered on Helmar — she thirsts for the Gem Guardian.

Phigby turns and steps in front of Helmar as if to protect him. He straightens to his full height and faces Vay. The fairy glides up to him and her voice is like the hiss of a giant snake. *I see you,* she rasps. *Why do you fight? You know that you and your weak ones cannot stand against me.*

"We shall not only fight you," Phigby grinds out, "the right shall win the day, and you and all your wickedness shall be once and for all time, cast out."

Her laugh is both a cackle and a shriek. *It shall be you that is cast out. You've chosen wrongly, and the price will be that you shall never return.*

She raises her arms high as she would unleash her powers and threatens, *Now move aside, that one is mine, him and what he carries.*

Neither Phigby, nor Boren, nor Helmar run but stand firm against the evil hag. When they don't stand aside, she brings her hands together with the clap of thunder. A black wave explodes outward, blasting the three backward.

They tumble and roll on the hard paving, slamming against the parapet wall. Helmar and Boren don't move, but Phigby struggles to rise to face Vay again.

The golden sets down on the walkway, placing her body between Vay and the barely standing Phigby as well as Helmar and Master Boren.

As I clamber off Golden Wind's neck, the golden roars defiantly at Vay. Vay laughs and points at her. *You are mine, too, and you shall ever be mine to command and to rule over a whole world.*

I hurry to Phigby, who's wheezing for breath and goes to one knee. He waves me on to Helmar, choking, "The jewel, Hooper, get the jewel."

"It won't do any good," I cry. "Helmar's out cold, he can't utter the power words."

Phigby reaches up, pulls me down so that we're eye to eye. "Hooper," he huffs between breaths and reaches up to place his hand on my tunic where my heart beats loud. "Listen to this, what does it tell you? Think! Each time the gem was used, was it really Helmar wielding the gemstone?"

He tugs at my tunic pulling me a bit closer. "Who really is the Gem Guardian?"

I stare at him, my eyes wide, and my heart thumping in my chest. Could it be true? No, I was only the caretaker, nothing more.

"What are you saying?" I croak, shaking my head, unwilling to acknowledge what my heart, my soul is telling me.

"Only what you know," Phigby answers and presses on my chest, "and what this is telling you."

I jerk back in surprise, my eyes wide. Phigby pulls me around and points at Helmar. "Go, before she claims an innocent one."

The golden's roars fill the night as if she would shake the fortress walls until they tumble down around us. I turn to Phigby, uncertain, frightened by his words.

"I can't be the Gem Guardian," I plead. "No, it has to be Helmar, he's strong, I'm not, I'm only a — "

In the midst of the golden's mighty roars, I hear her voice, soft and calm.

You're as strong as you want to be, Hooper Menvoran, Gem Guardian. Now is your time, take up that which only you can wield and save your friends.

I swallow, slowly turn and stumble over to Helmar. He's breathing, but his eyes are tightly closed. I don't know how long I stand there, hesitant, unsure, unwilling to do what is being asked of me, and yes, terrified that if I take up the jewel, Vay will surely turn her anger and fury upon me.

I'm only Hooper, how can I stand up against Vay with all her dark power and evil magic?

Slowly, I force my trembling hand down to pull the emerald from Helmar's tunic. It glows bright in my hand, warm and alive as if it were a part of me.

I glance at the frond inside. It's completely unfurled and glowing with a radiant emerald hue.

I take a deep breath and stand upright. Vay is slowly, but surely pushing the golden back. It will be but moments before the evil one reaches Phigby and in his weakened condition, he will be no match for her.

An idea forms in my head and I whirl around looking for something living, something from the greenery, but the walkway is completely bare.

As if from far away, I hear the Gaelian Fae's soft whisper,

> *Bring forth the blight, show it the light,*
> *That which you hid, it shall do thy bid.*

In sudden understanding, I reach inside my tunic and pull out the dragon bane that I had placed there in what now seems so long ago. Amazingly, the petals are still alive, still blood-red.

Blood-red, I think, suitable for Vay.

I grasp both the petals and the gem firmly in my hand and march resolutely to stand beside the golden. Vay's eyes flick toward me and the gemstone I hold.

She holds out her skeletal claws. *Give that to me, child and begone or die where you stand.*

I take a deep breath and raise myself to my full height. "No."

At first, my voice is hardly more than a whisper, then the golden roars again and I say in a strong, confident voice, "The Gem Guardian does not answer to the likes of you."

Vay stands frozen in place, her eyes widen in sudden understanding before she hisses, *You!*

"Yes," I answer with my face and eyes locked hard. "It was just Hooper all along."

A gust of wind beats at me as the golden takes to the air. I hear other wings and without turning know that the three sapphires have joined Golden Wind.

I thrust Pengillstorr's jewel high, throw the petals in the air, and shout, *Vald Hitta Sasi Ein! Power Comes to this One!*

The dragons unleash their fire on Vay.

The emerald's glow reaches out, focuses the dragon fire so that Vay is caught in a maelstrom of fire and fury, a caldron of scalding, sizzling flames that matches the color of the dragon bane. The blaze surrounds her, a fiery whirlwind with her in the center.

The petals spin around Vay, faster and faster until they burst into a raging blood-red pillar that roars upward into the night like a crimson whirlwind. The blaze lights up the keep as if a dozen dragons stood on the parapet walls and unleashed their fire into the evening sky.

For an instant, Vay stretches out her arms as if she would attack the firestorm and her shriek seems to shake the bastion walls. *I will have what is mine!*

For an instant, she holds back the firestorm, then an aura of light surrounds me and the dragons. I feel the presence of the three, their strength added to mine. Vay's scream of *No!* is so loud, so desperate and angry that I fear that the paving will crack under us, and we will be crushed by an avalanche of stones.

Then there is an explosion of flame and black smoke, and when it clears, Vay is gone as are her three sisters.

The dragons cease their fire, and I slump over, for the moment drained by the confrontation with Vay. The dragons settle to the walkway, and I hear hurrying footsteps.

Amil puts an arm around my waist to hold me up. "Are you all right, Hooper?" he asks.

I nod and murmur, "Yes, I think so."

"Well," he answers as he scrutinizes my limp body, "to tell you the truth, you may say you're all right, but right now you look like an old limp sock that someone has wrung dry after washing."

I give him a faint smile. "And that's just about how I feel, too."

I straighten and turn. Standing together, looking at me, are Phigby and Helmar while Cara helps her dazed father sit up on the blackened paving stones. Cara peers at me, with an expression as if she doesn't recognize me, or perhaps, doesn't want to recognize and acknowledge me after what just happened.

Phigby wears a satisfied look, whereas Helmar has an expression that's part anger, hurt, bitter disappointment, and a large part that's surprise.

The surprise part I understand well.

Phigby strides up to me and with the golden looking on, says, "Well done, Hooper Menvoran."

"Hooper Menvoran?" I stammer, "What — "

"It's Gaelian, Hooper," he answers. "It means 'the one who guards the gems.'"

"How did you know?" I sputter, "I truly thought that — "

He holds up a quick hand. "Now is not the time, we've bought ourselves a few moments of freedom, I suggest we put it to good use."

Without another word, Helmar helps Cara get Master Boren up on Wind Song, and the others scramble for their dragons. I tuck the gem away, and as I do, I feel a warmth and a faint pulse against my skin.

I let out a breath. The gem is back where it should be, and I feel the weighty mantle of guardianship descend.

I have no doubt now who the Gem Guardian is, but will I be strong enough to bear the burden, to wield its power as Pengillstorr would have me, in honor of his sacrifice of the heart?

Only time will tell.

Thoughts of Golden Wind

Treachery. Evilness. Tainted and lost lives. Disappointment and anger.

Victory coupled with the wretched sorrow that only a loving and caring parent can know.

The true Gem Guardian finally revealed.

A tiny seed planted but will it sprout? Do we not all start small in mind and spirit? The question is whether or not we stay that way our whole lives. Only we can answer that query.

How then, to help this seed grow? To reach for the light when it is so much easier to stay in the shadows and accept the darkness as the right and real world?

How can I help Hooper see what he must do, to carry this burden? Its weight will be heavy, perhaps even more than that which he already carries.

A vibrant seed needs fertile soil, adequate water, and plentiful sunshine to grow. Otherwise, it shrivels and dies. As it is with seeds, so it is with souls whether they be dragon or Drach.

My eyes see that Hooper's journey will find him planted deep in the soil of adversity, tragedy, heartbreak, rage and ruin but also enduring comradeship, friendship, love.

There will be times that he will be showered in temptation, weakness, cowardice and only faith, strength, and courage will protect him from drowning and losing his fight.

May the abundant sunshine of truth and light forever break the dark clouds of wickedness that begin to sweep across the world and may Hooper's inner light guide and protect him from partaking of the Evil One's guile and temptations.

Otherwise, he too will become a lost seed that shrivels and dies.

For all of us, pray that that does not happen.

29

A s we sky toward the woodlands, I glance back to see Prince Aster with his sword held high and in one final fit of rage, heaves it at us. Daron, on the other hand, stands beating his blade on the bastion wall, sending sparks shooting into the night.

I take a certain sense of satisfaction in seeing the two like that, but as I bring my glance back to my companions, I see tears in Cara's eyes that slide down her face in long streaks that she makes no effort to wipe away.

Tears of joy at finding her father alive. Soul-wrenching anguish at seeing her father's torment over Daron. Tears of love for her brother and tears of hatred for what he has become.

My face slackens as I realize that my sense of satisfaction is hollow, compared to the depth of Cara's loss. And my own loss will be not seeing Cara smile for a long, long time.

The golden takes us quickly to a small meadow, and I point down. "The sprogs!" I call to Cara and Helmar. The three sapphires glide to the glade while the golden circles overhead. Cara and Helmar quickly get the sprogs into Wind Song's saddlebags and then we're ready to go.

Moments later, with Master Boren back on his beloved Wind

Rover and Amil riding behind, Helmar and Phigby on Wind Glory, and Cara on Wind Song we're skyborne. Once they're aloft, Golden Wind again takes the lead, and we sky away from Dunadain Keep.

"Where are we going?" I call out.

"Where we are supposed to go, Hooper," she answers back.

"Where's that?"

"You'll see," is all she says.

She turns us away from the river valley and toward a line of small hills to the west. We follow the rolling peaks for a long while before she slows and heels to the left in a long arc. When she straightens, my eyes widen at what I see in the moon's glow.

"Mountains," I state.

"Yes, Hooper, those are the Denalian Mountains. The boundary that marks the Golian Domain."

"Oh," is all I say. In the moonlight, their snowcapped peaks have a glistening silver sheen. They're so tall I wonder how their tops don't scrape against the stars.

"Is that where we're going? To the mountains?"

"There and beyond," is her answer.

We sky through the night until there is a brightening to the east. The golden swings gently to the left, gliding just above the trees, whose green and orange leaves flutter in the light breeze. We sail over a river, its turquoise tint noticeable even in the early morning light.

She glides down to a soft landing in a small meadow. In the distance, the mountains stand sharp and tall, the peaks catching the first of the dawn's pale pink light.

It's Dragon Glow, only I don't see blood anymore, just the light's beauty against the mountains.

I prod Golden Wind off to one side under some low hanging trees, away from the others for the moment. Scamper is quick to bound from the golden and head off on a hunting foray.

I slide off the golden, stroke her neck for a moment and murmur, "Thank you for saving me back there. If you hadn't, Scamper would have one less friend."

She swings her head around to me. "As would I."

Friends? I take a deep breath. If you save someone's life, does that mean that they're your friend? I'm not sure. I haven't forgotten that it was dragons that murdered my family. And that memory will forever be deep and tender.

But still, can I judge Golden Wind by those dragons?

Is that right? Is it fair?

I turn and see Cara and Helmar helping Master Boren toward some fallen logs where he can sit. Pain, deep, enduring hurt is etched on his and Cara's face, and it's not from weariness, the long sky ride, or a physical wound. Their agony goes deeper, straight to the soul.

I let out a breath. "Cara and Master Boren grieve."

"Two good people," she murmurs, "wounded deeply."

"By Daron," I mutter in disgust.

"Yes," she murmurs, "what little hope that Boren had left for his son has been crushed under Daron's choices. Daron has broken his heart, left him angry, particularly at himself. He blames himself for his child's waywardness and terrible decisions."

She lets out a long sigh. "In his mind, his hopes that Daron would be a formidable soldier for good, for right, have been crushed, cast aside in a cascade of decisions that have left Daron nothing more than one puny member in the pack of evil ones."

I gaze at the two, my heart crying for Cara's sake. "And Cara," I respond, "is not even trying to hold back the tears, which isn't like her. She must hurt so very badly."

I peer at the golden. "Is there anything I can do to help? To ease the pain? Will she ever smile again, be happy?"

"For now Hooper," she answers, "this is a time for she and her father. Hopefully, at some point when the pain subsides, she will smile again, feel happiness in her heart."

She sighs, "But all in its own time Hooper, all in its own time."

I step around to face her and for some reason, I reach up and scratch her between the eyes. Her eyes get a blissful look, and I swear, she practically purrs. I give her a good, long scratch, and when I'm done, I step back.

She opens her eyes, gazes at me for a moment before murmuring, "What was that for?"

I shrug. "Oh, I don't know. You just seemed to need it, that's all."

Have you ever seen a dragon grin? It's not pretty, full of fangs and smelling a bit of sulfur, and certainly not like one of Cara's stunning smiles, but still, I sort of liked it.

I glance toward the mountains. For some reason, I'm pulled to them, and I wander over to a small knoll to stare up at the mighty granite ramparts. The Dragon Glow has given way so that each peak shines as if it has a bright beacon lit on the very top.

I hear plodding footsteps and know the golden has followed. Moments later, I hear lighter footsteps. The rest of the company has joined me in gazing at the mountains.

Phigby rubs shoulders with me, and without looking at him, I say, "Phigby, I am so confused."

I touch my tunic where the emerald lies, "How is it that I'm — "

"That you are the guardian and not Helmar?" He peers at Helmar, who is listening intently, his own questions showing clearly on his face as well as a certain stony hardness. "Helmar is a good man, big, strong, and keen of eye and mind.

"However, it's not the physical stature of a man or woman that makes them who they are, but rather the fullness of their heart. You needed to empty yours first of bitterness and hatred, and fill it instead with purpose and humility."

"But, I'm not a cutter's son," I protest.

"Ah, but you are," Phigby firmly replies and lays a hand on my shoulder. "Your father was a woodcutter."

I suck in a breath as the image of my childhood home fills my mind. "The—the logs of our cabin — "

"Hewn from the forest by your father and brother," Phigby answers.

"But, Phigby," Cara objects, "you said that Helmar — "

"Was and is a cutter's son too," Phigby replies, "but I never stated that *he* was the Gem Guardian. I only repeated what the ode said, that the Gem Guardian would be a cutter's son."

"But you implied that I was," Helmar says bitterly. "Why was I led to believe that I was the guardian?" His tone is not only harsh, it's demanding.

Helmar is not taking it well that he's not to carry the gemstones. He thought he'd found his way to climb up that ladder of his only to have the ladder jerked out from under him.

Now, instead of standing on the mountaintop's grandeur, for all to see, he's been shoved back down the mountain slope, and worse, by someone like me.

By a Hooper, someone who is nowhere close to being a Helmar.

Phigby takes in a deep breath and in an apologetic tone answers, "I am sorry, Helmar, that was my doing. You see, I suspected that Hooper was the guardian all along."

He pauses and then says, "It is possible that a dragon gem might be passed to a caretaker for certain reasons, but under the circumstances of how Hooper came to acquire the jewel, I highly doubted that that was the case.

"Pengillstorr came into Draconstead willingly, just to find Hooper, also knowing that he would have to give up his life in doing so. I do not believe that he would have carried out such an act if he was merely giving his heart stone to a caretaker."

He shrugged his shoulders. "I was fairly confident that Hooper was the guardian and not you, and only he would be able to wield its powers."

"You used Helmar," Cara states in an ice-cold voice. It is more of an accusation than a simple statement.

She too is having a hard time accepting that Helmar, with all his abilities, is not the chosen one. She flicks her eyes toward me. I can see confusion, disappointment, the building anger, and I can see how easily it would be for her to hate me.

Even more so, now that it's evident that Daron is siding with Vay and the Wilders, her frustration, her embarrassment and loss runs deep, and she's not ready to accept that Helmar, her love, has been pushed aside for the likes of me.

"Yes," Phigby freely admits. "But for a good reason. Until Hooper was truly ready to accept the mantle, we needed to keep Vay distracted, have her attention diverted elsewhere until he would be able to stand and face her."

"You could have gotten Helmar killed," Cara protests in a raised, harsh voice. "Vay thought he was the guardian and focused all her evilness toward him. Did you even think about that or were you so intent on protecting Hooper that you were willing to sacrifice the strongest of our company just for Hooper, the weakest among us?"

I bite down hard on my lip, but I don't speak up. After all, she's right. If Helmar were a mighty dragon heart tree, I would be the tiniest sprig in the forest. That's why I'm still in shock over where I now stand and wondering if it's not a mistake, that Phigby is wrong, and I really should be handing the Voxtyrmen back to Helmar.

Phigby's eyebrows furrow in profound sadness, and he places a hand on Helmar's broad shoulder. "Yes, I knew the chance that we were taking with Helmar's life, and if Vay had succeeded in her evil plans, it would have been as if she had thrust a Proga lance deep, deep into my heart."

His eyes meet Helmar's. "It was a bitter, bitter thought to contemplate and I would have been miserable for the remainder of my life."

He pauses before straightening to say, "However, though I fully admit that that may well have happened, we must remember and accept the fact that we are in a war with Vay. A war that will extend beyond the Northern Kingdom's boundaries and determine the fate of our world."

He takes a deep breath and gravely murmurs, "And, we must all accept the fact that each of us may be called upon to offer up the ultimate sacrifice."

He touches my tunic where the gemstone lies. "Just as a very special emerald dragon did," he says of Pengillstorr, "so that we now have his gemstone with which to face Vay and her minions."

I glance up at the golden. Her ears are forward, listening, but her expression is impassive, stoic. I give her a little glare, and she returns my look with a dignified, unapologetic gaze. I can't help but wonder if she too, knew all along.

I turn back to Phigby and shake my head. "I still don't understand, Phigby. Of all the people on Erdron, why me? I'm the least — "

"Hooper!" his bellow is like one of the distant mountains, towering, massive. "Even the least among us has worth and dignity, and that includes you!"

He takes a breath. "And never, ever forget that."

I hear thudding footsteps and turn to see the sapphires gathering behind us in a semi-circle. The golden joins them, and they lift their heads to let out a giant roar that rolls across the meadow and the forest beyond.

The little sprogs join in and do their best to mimic the dragon's thundering roar, but it's not much more than a loud squeal.

As the dragon's roar fades away, Scamper comes bounding up to nuzzle against my legs, and Amil takes a step forward to study my face before he speaks. "In all honesty, Hooper," he rumbles low, "with something as precious as a dragon jewel, I would prefer someone who can wield a sword or ax, and can string his own bow."

Such as Helmar, I think to myself.

He takes in a deep breath. "However, in all my travels I've learned that it's not always the reach of your sword arm that determines how far one's heart can stretch."

He holds his great ax up. "My blade is yours."

Slowly, with obvious reluctance, Helmar puts a hand on his sword hilt. "To protect the golden and the gem, you can count on my sword and my bow."

"And I pledge my bag," Phigby quickly states.

That brings a lighthearted moment, but I can see that Master Boren has a frown on his face as he glances first from me, and then to the golden. The expression on his face tells me all that I need to know.

He cannot accept that his former dragon dung shoveler now rides the mightiest dragon in the world.

For an instant, I see a pang of jealousy cross his face. I nod to myself in understanding. If anyone should be riding Golden Wind, it should be the greatest Dragon Master, and not Hooper, the mightiest manure mover.

After all, the stench of dung still scents my clothes, my body is still scarred and weak. In their eyes, I'm only a few days removed from being the guardian of the slurry pile. And instead of wielding a dragon gem, I should be brandishing a rake and shovel.

It's obvious that Master Boren and Cara are holding back, neither acknowledging me as the Gem Guardian. Cara's eyebrows are furrowed together, and her face is a bit darker than normal.

Her mouth is skewed to one side, and her eyes don't have their usual sparkle. Then, slowly, as if she did so reluctantly she takes her father's arm and both turn away from me and the others. Helmar quickly follows the two.

To Phigby, Amil, Scamper and the dragons, I may be called to carry Pengillstorr's gift, but to Cara, her father, and Helmar, I am still only a Hooper.

Having Cara reject me is sharper than any Proga lance that's ever been thrust into my body, and I'm tempted to rip the gem from my tunic and toss it away as it seems to be the object that's come between us.

What does it matter if we won the battle of Dunadain Keep if I've lost Cara even if only but for a friend? In the eyes of the others it may have been a victory but to me, I feel as if Aster had plunged his sword clean through my heart.

If this supposed honor that I am to carry, this "Gem Guardian" title is to cause heartache between us, then do I really want what it represents? Am I willing to bear this price, this searing of my own soul as I see her walk away with her back turned, perhaps forever to me?

I start to go after her, but Phigby is quick to lay a restraining hand on my shoulder. "She and her father," he murmurs, "need time to think, and that is exactly what we shall give them."

I hesitate, my eyes still on Cara but with an aching heart at her obvious resentment. I slowly turn my gaze from her and meet the golden's stare. She gives me the barest of nods. "Well Gem Guardian," Phigby mutters, "what now? Where would you have us go?"

I hesitate before I raise my hand to point at the daunting mountain barrier that rises before us. "There," I murmur, "and beyond."

I stare long and hard at the peaks, trying to still my churning emotions, and the near overwhelming weight that's descended on body and mind. No one speaks for a long time, each locked in their own thoughts. I look to Phigby. "I have so many questions now."

I touch my tunic where the gemstone lies. "What does this do? What does it mean?"

I peer intently at him. "I once asked you, 'who are you?'"

I take a deep breath. "Now I'm wondering who am I?" I give him a half-hearted shrug. "How do I find the answers?"

He studies my face for a bit before saying, "The same way any of us find answers, Hooper. We take life's journey and along the way, if we're lucky, we find the answers we seek."

"A journey," I mutter.

Phigby lifts a hand toward the towering granite peaks that rise before us. "Yes lad, and yours, and ours, I think, has just begun."

A new journey, I think to myself, one that will obviously be dangerous but even as I dwell on the dangers we may face a sudden thought comes to mind.

I give Cara a swift glance. A journey where yes, I might find the answers to my life's questions, but more so, perhaps I can somehow prove myself to Cara and regain her friendship.

If so, that alone would make any journey, no matter how hazardous worth the effort.

I straighten, tighten the belt around my tunic, and lift my head to gaze at the mountains that seem to march like granite walls from horizon to horizon.

"Then," I murmur to Phigby, "that's good enough for me."

THE END

The story continues in Book Two
The Queen's Vow

OTHER BOOKS BY GARY J. DARBY

Fantasy:

The Legend of Hooper's Dragons

Book One: *If a Dragon Cries*

Book Two: *The Queen's Vow*

Book Three: *On Wings of Thunder*

Book Four: *The Roar of Wings.*

Book Five: *A Dragon Storm Rises*

Book Six: *On Moonlit Wings*

Book Seven: *Wings of Fire*

Book Eight: *Sacrifice of the Heart*

Science Fiction:

The Star Scout Saga

Book One: *Star Rising*

Book Two: *Fallen Stars: Darkest Days*

Book Three: *Star's Honor*

Book Four: *When Stars Fall*

Book Five: *How Far the Stars*

FROM THE AUTHOR

Thank you so much for reading *If A Dragon Cries*, book one in my *Legend of Hooper's Dragons* series and no, the story doesn't end there. The story continues in book two, *The Queen's Vow* which is now available on Amazon.

Thanks to all who've mentored me in this grand journey of being a literary storyteller, it's been a great ride.

If you'd like to share your thoughts about this novel, or the upcoming books in the series, feel free to email me at garyj.darby@gmail.com. I'm also on Facebook. I'd love to hear from you either way.

And if you can find it in your heart to do so, a review on Amazon or Goodreads, or a shout out on your social media platforms would be most appreciative. Free advertising is a blessing to starving writers, you know.

Like to know what's upcoming in my writing? Visit my website: GaryDarbysBooks.com Again, thanks so much for reading my novel and I truly hope that whatever you read will bring you wonder, awe, and uplifting thoughts.

ACKNOWLEDGMENTS

Professional copy editing services provided by Marthy Johnson of Copy Editing Services (CES). You may contact her at 907.720.2032 or e-mail: mjces@gci.net if you're an established or a budding author who needs a little help, well, maybe a lot of help with those clunky commas, or pesky pronouns, or strangled sentences.

She's also the author of *Write or Wrong*, a nifty reference manual that all authors should have in their personal library as well as *Breakpoint Down*, an excellent mystery novel.

You might want to check out her newsletter, *Word for Word,* just for writers that will help you avoid the pitfalls and potholes of writing in this convoluted language we call English, or as I sometimes refer to it, Anguish. You can subscribe to her newsletter by contacting her via email.

Dedicated to the girl of my dreams and fantasies, my eternal sweetheart, Pamela and to our children and grandchildren who fill our days with wonder and awe.

Printed in Great Britain
by Amazon